W9-DBG-102

GLORIOUS SURRENDER

"You're a beautiful, desirable, passionate woman, and you were meant to be mine! And, my sweet wife, you'll not remain cold to me for long!" Alex pulled Marianna to him and kissed her with an impassioned vengeance. His arms tightened about her like bands of steel and Marianna grew faint as her traitorous body soon responded.

She moaned softly as he lifted her in his arms and carried her slowly to the bed. She was perilously close to being beyond all rational thought as she became aware only of Alex, of his sensuous masculinity, his strong arms tenderly lowering her to the softness of the down quilt.

"No! Please, no!" Marianna whispered as his lips now began roaming almost feverishly across her face, caressing her slender neck, then gently brushing the vulnerable spot where her pulse was beating so rapidly. As his lips moved downward to tease her pale, smooth flesh she gasped, her head moving restlessly from side to side, her mass of dark curls fanning out across the pillow in splendid disarray.

Suddenly she felt languid and weak, and almost dizzy with pleasure. She was trapped once more by the devilish rogue who was now her husband—and by the force of her own desires!

MORE CAPTIVATING HISTORICAL ROMANCES!

SURRENDER TO DESIRE (1503, $3.75)
by Catherine Creel
Raven-haired Marianna came to the Alaskan frontier expecting
adventure and fortune and was outraged to learn she was to marry
a stranger. But once handsome Donovan clasped her to his hard
frame and she felt his enticing kisses, she found herself saying
things she didn't mean, making promises she couldn't keep.

TEXAS FLAME (1530, $3.50)
by Catherine Creel
Amanda's journey west through an uncivilized haven of outlaws
and Indians leads her to handsome Luke Cameron, as wild and
untamed as the land itself, whose burning passion would consume
her own!

TEXAS BRIDE (1050, $3.50)
by Catherine Creel
Ravishing Sarah, alone in Wildcat City and unsafe without a
man's protection, has no choice but to wed Adam MacShane—in
name only. Then Adam, who gave his word of honor not to touch
his Yankee wife, swears an oath of passion to claim his TEXAS
BRIDE.

SAVAGE ABANDON (1505, $3.95)
by Rochelle Wayne
Chestnut-haired Shelaine, saved by the handsome savage from
certain death in the raging river, knew but one way to show her
thanks. Though she'd never before known the embrace of a man,
one glance at the Indian's rippling muscles made her shiver with a
primitive longing, with wild SAVAGE ABANDON.

SURRENDER TO ECSTASY (1307, $3.95)
by Rochelle Wayne
From the moment the soft-voiced stranger entered Amelia's bed
all she could think about was the ecstasy of his ardent kisses and
the tenderness of his caress. Longing to see his face and learn his
name, she had no idea that he hid his identity because the truth
could destroy their love!

*Available wherever paperbacks are sold, or order direct from the
Publisher. Send cover price plus 50¢ per copy for mailing and han-
dling to Zebra Books, 475 Park Avenue South, New York, N.Y.
10016. DO NOT SEND CASH.*

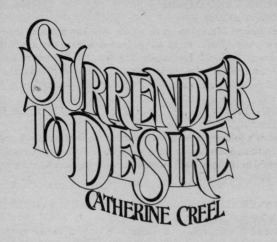

SURRENDER TO DESIRE

CATHERINE CREEL

ZEBRA BOOKS
KENSINGTON PUBLISHING CORP.

ZEBRA BOOKS

are published by

Kensington Publishing Corp.
475 Park Avenue South
New York, N.Y. 10016

Copyright © 1985 by Catherine Creel

All rights reserved. No part of this book may be reproduced in any form or by any means without the prior written consent of the Publisher, excepting brief quotes used in reviews.

First printing: January 1985

Printed in the United States of America

To those "Echo Ladies"—Frances, Norma, Judy, and Vonda—for advice, encouragement, babywatching, locksmiths, etc.

And to Craig and Caleb, for their love and tolerance.

One

"Marianna? Marianna Markova?" the young man's immature voice could be heard above the mixture of sounds being generated by the ship's crew unloading the heavy wooden crates of fruit and other such cargo beneath the cloudless blue sky.

The young woman standing so regally upon the gray, weathered planks at the far end of the dock turned her head in the young man's direction as he briskly made his way toward her, causing the astonished fellow to suddenly draw up short before her as she fixed him with a puzzled look from her startlingly clear blue-green eyes. The young man was obviously taken aback by the overwhelming loveliness of the raven-haired beauty, his widening brown eyes unable to refrain from hastily sweeping up and down her slender yet well-endowed form as she stood waiting patiently near the ship's lowered gangplank.

The height of 1898 Paris fashion, her traveling costume was quite elaborate and undeniably fetching. The gown which molded her slim, corseted curves to perfection was of a deep blue moiré, expertly trimmed in a soft, natural sable which formed a high collar to frame her unmistakably well-bred features. Her dark, luxuriant curls were swept upward in the back and allowed to cascade freely downward against the slender column of her neck, topped off by a round sable hat. There was certainly no outward evidence to indicate that she had recently endured the strenuous journey from Russia to Alaska, no apparent sign of the weariness or considerable trepidation she was experiencing as she waited in growing confusion for the young man to speak again.

"You are Marianna Markova, aren't you?" he inquired after noisily clearing his throat. He couldn't help noticing the way the appreciative eyes of the crew kept straying in the woman's direction.

Marianna, who had by this time begun to feel more than a trifle anxious when it appeared no one was coming to meet her, frowned slightly before replying in a soft, pleasant voice.

"Yes, I am. But who are you? And where are my aunt and uncle?" Her words were clear and enunciated in the most proper English, tinged only faintly with traces of her Russian heritage.

"I'm your cousin Andrei," he answered with a quick boyish grin. "Mother and Father are waiting for us in the carriage," he explained, nodding to indicate where a man and woman were seated in the open conveyance at the opposite end of the long, narrow dock. "Sorry we were a bit late in coming to meet you. Are these all your bags?" he asked, glancing down toward the two overstuffed valises at Marianna's feet.

"No," she murmured in a preoccupied manner, though she managed to return Andrei's grin with a faint smile of her own. "The captain was kind enough to have my trunks taken over to the shipping office." Her father had never once mentioned anything about a cousin, she mused as she gazed at Andrei, who was lifting the bags now, one in each hand. She noticed that he was not much taller than herself, and very near the same age, though perhaps a year or two younger. His dark, wavy hair and small brown eyes and his thoroughly aristocratic features served to remind her of her father. But then, she thought as Andrei began leading the way along the dock, her father had certainly never been given to grinning at her as her young cousin had just done.

She raised an elegant hand to shade her eyes against the bright rays of golden sunshine, straining to make out the faces of her aunt and uncle who were awaiting her in the carriage. She vaguely wondered why Andrei was carrying her bags, why her uncle's servant was not doing the task usually reserved for those of that particular class. It occurred to her then that she had never bothered to find out if her uncle was as wealthy as her father, since she had naturally assumed that any member of the noble family of Markova would be of the wealthy aristocracy.

A sudden gust of wind threatened to snatch the pert little hat from her head, and Andrei smiled companionably as he remarked, "I expect you're quite worn out. We didn't know exactly what day your ship would be arriving. We don't get near as many ships through here since the gold rush started. But, you probably know all about that, since you were in Seattle yourself a few days ago. I suppose you were really quite fortunate to get here at all, what with anything that can float going on up to Skagway." He paused a moment and glanced across at his cousin's lovely, inscrutable features. "Mother has been so impatient to get a look at you! It isn't every day we get to meet someone new from our own family. I hope you're going to like it here with us in Sitka. I'm sure it isn't anything like the mother country, but I'm not really a fair judge of that since I've lived here all my life." He continued chatting amiably until they finally reached the carriage.

The man who had been sitting inside immediately stood and climbed down to help Andrei with the bags, leaving Marianna to raise her eyes to her aunt's face as the older woman rose slowly to her feet and quietly announced, "Marianna, we are so happy to have you here with us at last. I trust your journey was a pleasant one. I am your Aunt Sonja, and this is your Uncle Frederick." She smiled politely in welcome, but Marianna's perceptive gaze glimpsed no accompanying warmth in the woman's dark green eyes. She appeared very austere, dressed in a somber dress of brown velvet, an ugly bonnet sitting atop the graying brown hair which was drawn severely and unbecomingly away from her rather pinched face. Marianna once again silently cursed the fact that her father had forced her to come, but she merely nodded in her aunt's direction and murmured a cordial response before being suddenly caught up in an affectionate embrace by her uncle.

"Marianna! My own brother's little daughter! How I have looked forward to seeing you again. Why, you are a beauty, just like your dear mother! I know you will not remember," he said with a laugh, his voice deep and rumbling, "but I last saw you when you were but still in your cradle, not too many days before your poor mother . . ." he began, breaking off abruptly as his eyes caught a stern, silencing glance from his wife. He was large and a bit rotund, his round face partially hidden by a thick expanse of black beard. Again, Marianna was reminded of her father, and yet her uncle was so very different from his older brother. He was smiling at her with such genuine warmth that she briefly returned his embrace before allowing him to assist her up into the carriage. She took a seat upon the upholstered cushion beside her aunt, arranging her full skirts about her, then watched as her uncle and cousin seated themselves across from her.

"I received a letter from your father only last week," her aunt told her as the driver cracked his whip and the horses began pulling the carriage away from the dock. Marianna's gaze was drawn back toward the ship for a brief instant as her aunt continued. "He wrote me that you would be traveling with an older cousin of yours, a woman by the name of Maria Veronovitch. And yet I see that she is not with you," she pointed out with a severe frown.

"No, I'm afraid poor Maria was still rather ill and could not continue with the last part of our journey,"

Marianna quietly explained, returning her level gaze to her aunt's disapproving countenance. "She was forced to stay behind in Seattle, where I left her in the care of some people who know her family. She intends to join me here once she is recovered." How displeased poor Maria had been at her young cousin's insistence upon journeying onward to Sitka alone, Marianna silently recalled.

"We are very glad to have you with us, my dear," Uncle Frederick spoke as he and his son both smiled at her again. "I have a great many questions to ask you, but I promise that I will be patient and wait until after you have rested and have had your dinner!"

Marianna flashed him a smile of gratitude, for she was indeed not feeling up to a barrage of questions at the moment. When neither her aunt or uncle or cousin said anything else, the expression on her lovely young face grew pensive. She turned her head to gaze upon the city of Sitka as the carriage rolled past on its way to her uncle's house near the outskirts of the town.

The city was not very large, she mused, smiling to herself now as she saw that the main street was lined with charming little wooden buildings that were very similar to those one would find in a small settlement back in Russia. There was a beautiful, quaint old church in the center of the town, and she was pleased to note the colorful flowers that appeared to be blooming everywhere. People who were strolling along the streets were dressed in much the same fashion as those back in Russia, she also noticed, and she now recalled what she had read of Sitka once she had finally resigned herself

12

to the disagreeable fact that she was going to be forced to spend her entire summer there.

Sitka was situated on Baranof Island, which in turn rested on the shores of the Pacific Ocean. Originally established as an important trade center for the Russians, it now served as the capital of Alaska, since Alaska itself had been purchased from the Russians several years earlier. It was a unique place where native and Russian cultures blended, for the Indians were still very much in evidence, a fishing and lumber town that was conveniently situated only a few days' sailing time from Seattle. The entire island was covered with huge trees and inhabited by several species of birds and wild animals, particularly bald eagles and fierce brown bears. Marianna vaguely wondered if she would perhaps have an opportunity to see more of the island during her visit.

Her interested gaze was now drawn to the sparkling blue waters of the harbor ahead as the carriage made its way out of the center of the city. The harbor itself was dominated by the towering, snowcapped Mount Edgecumbe, and the island's spectacular mountainous surroundings made it seem like a wild northern paradise. Marianna reflected that she should feel at least some measure of gratitude toward her father for sending her to such a beautiful place, but, she then reminded herself with a deep frown, he still should not have forced her to come!

It had all started with the occasion of her twentieth birthday only a few short weeks before, she recalled, the corners of her beautiful mouth curving down into another frown of remembrance. There had been that summons from her father, the father she had seen infrequently throughout her years abroad. She had been living with Maria, her spinster cousin, in London at the time, where she had been for the past two years since completing her education at Europe's finest boarding schools.

She remembered all too well the anxiety she had felt upon meeting with her father again after so long a separation. He had always seemed to blame her in some way for her mother's death, but he had at least seen to it that she had been very well provided for, paying for her schooling and then generously allowing her to live in London with only Maria as her chaperone. On the rare occasions that she had been summoned home to the family estate in Russia, her father would invariably chastise her for what he perceived to be her stubborn, willful independence, for the latest escapades in which she had been involved.

It wasn't precisely that she was a troublemaker of any sort, but rather that she sometimes felt the overpowering urge to rebel against the strict, stifling rules of genteel behavior that were imposed upon her at school. The past two years in London, when she had been the toast of both social seasons, she had somehow managed to drive away even the most eligible of suitors who had so ardently courted her. Maria was always direly predicting that her young charge would live to regret her heartless ways, that she was ruining every chance for future happiness with her headstrong manner. But, Marianna now thought, heaving a tiny sigh as the carriage began slowing down, there had certainly been no chance for happiness with any of the boring young fops who had paid court to her! And now, now to be sent to Sitka for the entire summer, as if she were nothing more than a naughty child . . .

"Here we are, Marianna," Andrei announced as the driver pulled the horses to a halt. Marianna raised her eyes to the two-storied house which overlooked the harbor, surprised to see that it was a perfectly lovely structure that reminded her of an oversized dollhouse. It was painted a sparkling white and trimmed in pale yellow, the upper balcony edged by a small picket fence. There were flowers growing all about the grounds, and the huge, towering trees which surrounded the house only made it seem even more like a place out of some childhood fantasy.

But, she told herself as her uncle assisted her down from the carriage, as charming as her uncle's house appeared to be, it could certainly never compare to the grand estate owned by her father. Again, she wondered why there was such a vast difference between the two brothers, but she had no time to ponder the situation as her aunt began leading the way inside the house.

"I'm sure you would like to rest and have your bath before the evening meal," Aunt Sonja remarked. "I'll have Andrei bring your things up right away. We have arranged with the driver to bring your trunks round in the morning." She gathered her brown skirts in one hand and began climbing the stairs as Marianna silently followed, gazing curiously about at the house's interior, which she saw was furnished in simple but elegant taste. "This will be your room," the older woman announced as she swung open the door at the far end of the landing. Marianna stepped inside and turned back to face her aunt with a polite smile.

"Thank you very much, Aunt Sonja. The room is quite lovely. I shall be down for dinner in an hour, if that meets with your approval."

"Of course. I'll have the housemaid sent up to draw your bath right away." She didn't speak again before leaving Marianna alone in the room and closing the door softly behind her.

Marianna strolled thoughtfully across the carpeted floor to pause before the gilded mirror which hung above the ornately carved chest. She reached up and removed her hat, then suddenly made an expressive grimace at her reflection.

Aunt Sonja was very much like the headmistress of a school she had attended several years ago, she mused with a defiant toss of her raven curls. She whirled about and plopped down onto the white, embroidered coverlet upon the large four-poster bed, oblivious to the fact that she was creasing her exquisite traveling gown.

The room was really quite cheerful, she decided as she peered critically about. There were white lace curtains at the windows, and the pastel tones of yellow and blue used throughout the upholstery and wallpaper combined to give a very feminine effect. She was surprised that such a charming house belonged to her dour aunt, and she smiled mischievously to herself as she lay back and languidly crossed her arms beneath her head, deep in thought once more.

Her aunt and uncle had closeted themselves in the parlor downstairs, sending Andrei away on an errand. Sonja made certain that Marianna was occupied in enjoying her bath and turned to her husband with a customary frown on her face.

"I tell you, Frederick, the girl is not at all what her father led me to expect! Why, from what that brother of yours wrote, I was expecting a girl who behaved little better than a spoiled brat, a girl with a penchant for causing trouble and defying authority at every turn. I must admit that it is a considerable relief to find her so subdued and well-mannered. I don't believe we're going to encounter any difficulty with her after all," she finished with a rather smug expression, a triumphant gleam lurking in her usually dull eyes.

"I suppose not," Frederick muttered as he lowered his portly frame into a velvet-covered chair near the window and proceeded to pour himself some cognac from a crystal decanter on the small oak table beside him. "After all, she is dear Vera's daughter, isn't she? Though, come to think of it," he thoughtfully added, "I must say that Vera was a good deal more spirited than her daughter seems to be. But, she was still the sweetest, most warmhearted . . ."

"I've heard more than enough about the saintly Vera for these past twenty years!" Sonja irritably snapped, snatching off her ugly bonnet and jabbing the hatpin back into the unresisting fabric with a vengeance. She settled herself on the carved settee opposite her husband, her features flushed with a pale color.

17

"Whatever the girl is, I wish your brother hadn't put upon us the task of telling her about the marriage. How like him to behave so cowardly!"

"Perhaps he doesn't wish to make her go through with it after all," Frederick hopefully offered. "Maybe he has changed his mind, Sonja. You know, I for one have never really liked the disagreeable business of arranging marriages for one's children," he decisively remarked, lifting the glass to his lips once more.

"He has not changed his mind!" his wife emphatically retorted as she turned an icy glare upon him. "His last letter only reconfirmed his plans for his daughter. And it doesn't matter how you personally view the matter, everything has been arranged for nearly twenty years and must be done. There is the family honor at stake, Frederick Markova, and don't you forget it!"

"But, what if Marianna refuses? What if she isn't as agreeable about this as we hope her to be?"

"Agreeable or not," Sonja replied, rising to her feet now and moving sedately to take a pose near the large front window, "she must fulfill the obligation. And something else, Frederick," she said, turning back to him. "I have come to the conclusion that she should be told right away."

"But I thought we agreed to wait for a few days, to allow Marianna some time to rest and get to know us better!" her husband argued, a look of concern on his bearded face as he set the glass back down upon the table.

"Well, I have decided that now is the best time to tell

18

her. After all, Alexander's ship will be arriving in only a few days' time! No, Frederick," his wife pronounced, making it all too evident that she had made her decision and would brook no interference from him, "we shall tell her tonight after dinner. If she is anything at all like the well-behaved young lady she appears to be, things should go smoothly enough. It will give her the time to accustom herself to the idea before Alexander arrives home," she pointed out as she crossed the room to the doorway. She paused a moment and turned back to Frederick as she remarked with a faint smile, "After all, what young woman wouldn't be pleased to learn that she is to marry such a man as Alexander, the grandson of a countess?" With that, she left the room and climbed the stairs to dress for dinner, leaving an unusually somber Frederick in her wake.

When Marianna appeared downstairs for the evening meal, she was feeling much refreshed. She had bathed and donned a fashionable gown of soft blue silk, her thick hair brushed to a gleaming radiance and secured at her neck with a blue ribbon, a simple style that was nevertheless quite elegant. Dinner passed pleasantly enough, with Andrei entertaining his cousin with bits of information and gossip about Sitka and its colorful past. Her uncle also took great pains to ensure that her spirits were lifted with his delightful witticisms and anecdotes, and only Aunt Sonja spoke little, though Marianna was aware of the way the woman seemed to be staring at her several times during the meal. She, in turn, answered her uncle's many questions concerning her father and her homeland, as

19

well as telling him a little of her life in London.

Afterwards, Andrei announced that he had some urgent business to attend to, and proceeded to take himself off after apologizing to his cousin for having to leave her on her first night there. In truth, he was none too pleased that his parents had ordered him to absent himself from the house for an hour or so, and he was curious as to their reason for doing so. But he left Marianna alone with her aunt and uncle as the three of them strolled from the dining room into the parlor.

"Here, Marianna, come and sit beside me," her aunt unexpectedly suggested as she took a seat upon the settee and gently patted the cushion beside her. Marianna did as she was bid, watching as her uncle sank down into his favorite chair nearby.

"I hope you enjoyed your first evening with us," he said as he withdrew a cigar from his coat pocket and bestowed another of his broad smiles upon Marianna. He liked his niece, liked her very much, and he very much regretted his wife's decision to tell her about the marriage that evening.

"Very much, thank you, Uncle Frederick," Marianna responded with a brief smile of her own. Still determined to be on her best behavior, she had come to the conclusion that she would probably be allowed much more freedom to do as she wished during her stay with her aunt and uncle if she behaved as a polite young lady who knew her place. Her place! she thought with an inward laugh, hiding the smile that played about her lips.

"Well, now that we have become a bit better acquainted," Aunt Sonja began, then paused a moment to gently clear her throat. "Your uncle and I have something very important to discuss with you." The woman was not entirely devoid of maternal feelings, and she was tempted to postpone the announcement when Marianna crossed her hands in her lap and gazed expectantly at her aunt, her beautiful eyes deceptively innocent and open.

"Yes, Aunt Sonja?"

"Your father meant to tell you of this himself before sending you to us, but he failed to do so. He has therefore instructed us to be the ones to tell you, and he has also assured us that we shall have your full cooperation in this matter," the older woman spoke with a sharp, meaningful glance at Marianna.

Marianna was none too pleased with the sound of her aunt's ominous statement, and was unable to suppress a deepening frown as she quietly demanded, "May I ask what you are talking about?"

"It was something that was arranged many years ago, Marianna," her uncle broke in at that point, silenced again by a sharp look from his wife.

"Yes," her aunt began once more, forcing a smile to her own lips as she turned back to her niece. "Yes, it was something that was arranged not long after your birth, my dear. It was your mother's fondest desire, you see. She and your father both agreed that it was for the best if you were to marry the son of her cherished friend. That's why they arranged the marriage so many

21

years ago."

"Marriage?" Marianna repeated in surprise and bewilderment.

"Actually," Sonja continued as if the younger woman beside her had not spoken, "Alexander is a few years older than you, but your mother and his were as sisters to one another . . ."

"Surely you are not serious!" Marianna declared with a short, humorless laugh as she looked at her aunt, then her uncle, then back to her aunt again.

"I'm afraid we're quite serious," Uncle Frederick spoke softly from his chair. "Arranged marriages used to be quite the custom, you know."

"I don't care if they were the custom or not!" Marianna countered with spirit, her eyes flashing. She was still in a state of shock at what she had just heard. This must be some sort of cruel jest of my father's! she told herself.

"Marianna," her aunt now spoke in a soothing tone of voice as if she was speaking to a child, "it was agreed upon that the marriage would take place before your twenty-first birthday. Your father thought that now would be the best time to fulfill the obligation."

"Obligation? I suppose that is all I am to my dear father now, the means with which to fulfill an obsolete obligation?" Marianna angrily cried. Her aunt and uncle were quite startled at their niece's emotional outburst, and they exchanged slightly helpless looks as Marianna suddenly jumped to her feet and flounced toward the doorway, her blue skirts swaying softly about her.

"I assure you that you can do no better than Alexander, for his grandmother is a countess, and he is a considerably wealthy young man!" her aunt desperately exclaimed. "It is your father's command that you marry this man!"

"I refuse to be a pawn in my father's autocratic little game!" Marianna vehemently retorted, whirling about to face them again. "I will never, never consent to such a farce!"

"But that was the very reason your father sent you here . . ." her uncle attempted to explain, quite distressed at the way his niece was taking the news. He told himself that he should have stood firm with his wife, that they should have given the poor girl more time to adjust. . . .

"I am well aware of the reason I was sent here!" stormed his beautiful young niece, her face flushed and very angry, a terrible pain deep in her heart at what she perceived to be her father's cruel betrayal. It had been bad enough to believe he was displeased with her and was banishing her to Sitka for the summer, but now, now to discover that it had only been a ploy to marry her off to a total stranger, and all because it had been arranged when she was still a babe . . . well, she simply would not do it!

How could he have done such a thing to his only child? she silently raged as she stood framed in the doorway, her aunt and uncle staring speechlessly at her. No matter what her parents had decreed so many years ago, she could never even think of entering into an arranged marriage! As she stared furiously back at

23

the older man and woman, she vowed to herself that she would think of some way to extricate herself from this latest difficulty, even if it meant running away!

Sonja Markova and her husband watched as the young woman fled from the room. They turned to one another in stunned silence. It seemed that their niece wasn't at all the biddable young woman they had foolishly believed her to be. No, she was instead precisely what her father had written, a willful, headstrong, fiercely independent girl who needed a strong hand to control her! And that, they both were thinking as they resumed their seats, was something Marianna's future husband would be well able to provide!

Two

Marianna's first night in Alaska was spent restlessly tossing and turning in her bed, her thoughts in an unending tumult. She still found it difficult to believe that her own father had betrayed her in such a manner, that he had lacked the necessary courage to tell her of his scheme. As she lay upon the soft mattress on the large bed, she stared, unseeing, toward the pale, silvery moonlight filtering through the lace curtains at the windows, and she suddenly sat bolt upright in the bed, her thick, dark tresses swirling in glorious disarray about her shoulders.

"Oh, how could he!" she fumed aloud, hot tears gathering in her stormy eyes. No matter that her relationship with her father had never been close and loving, she had certainly never believed him capable of such emotional cruelty. To try to force her into marriage with a man she had never even seen! And how could her dear, sweet mother have agreed to such an arrangement? From what she had always heard of her mother, such an act of betrayal would have been entirely foreign to her nature. What had her parents been thinking all those years ago to agree to such a loathsome plan?

Her aunt and uncle were going to be of no help, either, she angrily thought as she tossed her head in defiance, her bright curls bouncing once again. Her aunt was much too staid and proper and unbending, her uncle obviously too weak and too frightened of his domineering wife. No, she decided as she heaved a weary sigh and lay uncomfortably back upon the bed again, they would attempt to force her to do her father's will, and would certainly offer no sympathy in her defiance.

But what about her cousin Andrei? she suddenly mused, sitting up in the bed again and tossing the pillow aside, a thoughtful frown appearing on her lovely face as she leaned forward to rest her chin upon her knees. She was still uncertain about what sort of assistance Andrei might be persuaded to offer, but intended to find out right away. Perhaps she could convince him to aid her in escaping from the island. Then the frown on her face deepened, as her thoughts took another turn.

What about the stranger who was playing such an integral part in the ruination of her life? she silently raged. What sort of man was he to agree to an arranged marriage with an unknown woman? Surely this Alexander must be some sort of weak, spineless creature—to allow his own wife to be chosen for him in such a manner! She already hated the man, hated him without knowing anything at all about him, save for the fact that his first name was Alexander and his grandmother was a countess. What did she care for titles? she asked herself with an exasperated sigh. She herself was possessed of several noble titles, and wasn't her father rich and powerful?

Whoever this Alexander was, she vowed with fierce determination, her eyes flashing blue-green fire, she would never, never agree to become his wife! She turned and retrieved the pillow, punching its unresisting softness with a vengeance as she lay back down, drawing the covers up over her shivering form. She was clad in nothing but a thin muslin nightgown, unaccustomed to the cool nights Sitka had to offer. The force of her anger allowed her little rest as she finally closed her eyes.

Throughout the next three days, however, Marianna's determined efforts to find some solution to her disturbing predicament were continually thwarted, either purposely or not, by everyone around her. She was not exactly kept a prisoner in her uncle's home, but she was allowed very little freedom, and Andrei was always at her side whenever she ventured from the house. Although Aunt Sonja persistently attempted to tell her niece more about her intended husband, the younger woman obstinately and quite forcefully refused to hear anything more on that particular subject.

She tried to enlist Andrei's help, but to no avail. She attempted to make him understand how desperate her plight truly was, but he was fearful of the retribution he would suffer at his mother's hand if he dared to cross her. He was a sympathetic listener, however, and

Marianna was grateful for his companionship. Also, because of Andrei, she was afforded the opportunity to discover several things she wished to know.

She persuaded him to escort her down to the docks one day after receiving permission from her aunt for an afternoon of shopping in the town. There, she was able to ascertain the fact that the next ship was scheduled to arrive within a few days' time, and she began secretly plotting her escape, intent upon returning to Seattle and seeking refuge with the ailing Maria there.

She planned to steal away from her uncle's house the night following the ship's arrival, taking only what she could carry in one small bag. She would then bribe the captain of the ship into maintaining his silence about her identity as a passenger. Sitka was not a very large city, and Marianna was well aware that word could possibly reach her aunt's ears before she was able to make good her escape if she did not practice extreme caution. In the end, she knew she had only to bide her time.

Whenever she took her meals with her aunt and uncle, she would speak very little, which they naturally attributed to her rather moody disposition brought on by her obvious displeasure with the arranged marriage and their own determination to ensure her obedience to her father's command. They could not know the vast amount of scheming which was taking place in Marianna's head, and were unaware that she was impatiently counting the days until she would run away.

Marianna was also forced to endure several social

calls with her aunt, though she did try to be friendly and to politely answer all the questions concerning her life in London and her wealthy father in Russia. But whenever the subject of her future husband was mentioned, she would hastily excuse herself and retreat to the opposite corner of the room, or was sometimes able to flee outside into the cool summer air. She was staunchly determined not to discuss her so-called future husband with anyone! It stung her fierce pride that her aunt had apparently informed everyone on the island about the unusual aspects surrounding her niece's arranged marriage, and Marianna was driven to exhibit the rebellious spirit that had always caused her such trouble during her years as a schoolgirl. The good ladies of the town found it strange that she reacted in such a manner, but her aunt would merely make the excuse that her niece was a high-strung girl who was feeling a bit under the weather and was naturally as nervous as any bride-to-be would feel, especially given the unusual circumstances.

Finally, the fateful day arrived when Aunt Sonja came bursting into the parlor in the middle of the sunny day, her eyes sparkling with uncharacteristic excitement. Marianna and her uncle were engaged in a very competitive game of chess, and the two of them looked up in mild surprise when Sonja flung open the doors to exclaim, "Alexander's ship has arrived at long last!"

"What's that you say, my dear?" her husband casually inquired, his attention wandering back to the game. He had been pleased to discover that his beautiful young niece was such a formidable opponent at the game.

"I said that Alexander's ship has arrived! Oh, Marianna, we must go upstairs and get ready at once! We are to go and greet your future husband right away!" her aunt declared.

"I have absolutely no intention of meeting the man," Marianna quietly but firmly insisted, returning her own gaze to the chessboard on the table before her. Her pulse, however, quickened at the news. The ship had arrived! She thought no more about the man she was supposed to marry, intent only upon making her plans to leave when the ship made its return voyage to Seattle. She was so preoccupied with thoughts of escape that she gapsed in astonishment as her uncle suddenly pulled her gently to her feet beside him.

"We must do the right thing, my dear. We must go and meet Alex. I promised his grandmother that we would do so." He looked unusually stern, and Marianna angrily realized that she was going to be given very little choice in the matter. But, it doesn't matter, she triumphantly thought as she pulled abruptly away from her uncle and swept from the room. She would soon be gone, and then would hear no more of having her entire future arranged for her by others!

She was still too preoccupied to fully appreciate the sunlit scenery of the mountainous landscape as she rode in the carriage beside her aunt on their way to the waterfront. Her aunt had insisted that Marianna change her dress, and now Marianna admitted to herself that she was pleased she would at least be looking her best when she met the hated stranger.

Her curvaceous form was encased in a pretty gown of light blue, a shade which served to accentuate the unusual color of her eyes. The bodice was cut in a heart-shaped design across her swelling bosom, and the full, gathered skirts were trimmed in creamy Brussels lace. The style was most becoming to her, for fashion dictated that a woman wear a tightly laced corset at all times, in order to achieve the popular hourglass effect. Marianna, however, had never really needed the aid of such a contraption, but she wore it nonetheless, which only made her slender waist appear even smaller. She had also donned a hat made of straw and adorned with a single blue feather, and it perched upon her thick, curling hair which had been arranged stylishly upon her head. She had never looked more ravishing, though she told herself that she had never cared less. She viewed the meeting with the man called Alexander as an inconsequential, tedious event, for she had persuaded herself that she was not in the least bit curious to know what he looked like.

She suddenly began to wish that she hadn't gone to such trouble to make herself so presentable, though her pride would be salvaged when the despicable man saw for himself that she was not some ugly old maid being forced upon him! She was drawn out of her silent reverie by her aunt's words.

"If only you had let me tell you a bit more about Alexander," Aunt Sonja irritably remarked as the carriage rolled along in haste. "He will naturally expect you to know something about him!"

"I don't care to know anything about him. I tell you again, I shall never consent to marry him!" Marianna retorted, then lapsed into silence again. Her aunt and uncle merely shook their heads at one another, and it wasn't long before the driver pulled the carriage to a halt in much the same spot where it had been waiting for Marianna several days earlier. As she allowed her uncle to help her down, she gazed curiously about, taking note of the large crowd that had gathered along the docks.

"It hasn't been long since the ship dropped anchor," Uncle Frederick observed as he viewed the passengers still disembarking. "Alexander is probably still on board." As he strained to see among the many men, women, and children milling about the area, he turned to his wife and said, "You and Marianna wait here. I'll go and see if I can find Alex." He replaced his hat atop his head and strode away through the crowd. Sonja, meanwhile, drew her niece along with her to a cluster of animatedly chattering women several yards away, women Marianna had met only the previous day at a tea given by one of her aunt's friends.

"How exciting this must be for you, my dear!" one of her aunt's associates remarked with a trill of laughter. She was a short, pudgy matron who affected the disagreeable habit of nodding her head a good deal too often, and Marianna found her all-knowing attitude exasperating, although she treated the woman with outward respect. The women soon began talking of fashion, leaving Marianna free to turn and gaze pensively toward the moderately sized steamship that had docked less than half an hour earlier.

It wasn't long before she was afforded the opportunity she had been so impatiently awaiting. Her aunt became so engrossed in her gossip with the other ladies that she didn't notice her niece slowly edging away as Marianna scurried through the crowd toward the ship.

I must find the captain at once! Marianna told herself, taking special care to remain hidden within the crowd as she made her way toward the end of the dock and the ship's lowered gangplank. She caught her breath in sudden alarm as she glanced up to see her uncle striding in her direction, and she was fortunate enough to be able to avoid being seen by him as she veered off to the far edge of the narrow wooden dock. She raised her head again, satisfied that no one had appeared to notice her, and she began walking carefully toward the gangplank again, finding it rather difficult as she was traveling against the tide of the passengers who were still leaving the ship. Finally, she was forced to abandon her efforts to go on board at the moment, and she stepped cautiously toward the end of the dock again, stifling a shriek as she suddenly collided forcefully with another person who had been standing behind her for several seconds without her knowledge.

"Oh!" she gasped aloud, terrified for a brief instant that she was going to be knocked into the swirling waters beneath the dock. She felt two strong arms encircling her from behind, and she gasped again as she was abruptly spun about to face her rescuer.

"It's a good thing one of us was paying attention," the tall, laughing stranger spoke in a deep, resonant voice, his arms still clasping a shocked Marianna against his broad chest. She raised her widened eyes to his face, too stunned for the moment to speak. He was quite handsome, she thought, his rugged good looks a far cry from the pale, aristocratic dandies she had known in London. Beneath his seaman's cap she could see his thick, sun-streaked auburn hair, and she suddenly became aware that his eyes, which could easily be likened to burnished gold, were still silently laughing at her. She noticed then that he was dressed in a dark blue coat with gleaming brass buttons, and she realized that she must be standing within the embrace of the ship's captain himself.

"Are—are you the captain of this vessel?" she breathlessly inquired, drawing abruptly away now from the handsome young stranger and straightening her dress rather primly. She could feel her cheeks flaming when the man's golden eyes moved slowly and quite boldly up and down her body, and she raised her chin proudly as her beautiful eyes flashed at his insolence.

"I guess you could say that. I happen to own and command her," the man lazily replied, crossing his muscular arms against his chest, still staring down at Marianna with eyes full of mingled appreciation and amusement. He was very curious about the proud beauty before him, for he was certain that he had never seen her in Sitka before. He smiled quizzically down at her as she unexpectedly grasped hold of his arm and

34

began tugging him firmly along with her to the rear of the shipping office several yards away. He allowed himself to be led along, watching with a great deal of interest as she paused to peer cautiously back around the side of the small building, apparently satisfied when she saw that they had been unobserved.

"I have something of the utmost importance to discuss with you," Marianna announced in a hushed tone, glancing up into the man's amused eyes once more. "And I wish for our conversation to be kept private," she sternly cautioned him, unaware of the fetching sight she made as he stared down at her with rapidly increasing curiosity. He decided to play along with her little game, schooling his handsome face to remain impassive as he gruffly replied, "All right. What is it you want with me?"

"I wish to return to Seattle when your ship leaves here. I am prepared to pay you well for my passage."

"Why would I demand anything more from you than the other passengers?" he sardonically asked, his interest more and more aroused.

"Because I wish for my presence on board to remain a secret. If you'll only consent to do that, I'll see to it that you are well rewarded."

"But what if the ship isn't bound for Seattle?" he then queried, a smile tugging at the corners of his mouth. He was clean-shaven, his skin bronzed by many hours in the sun, and Marianna was once again unable to resist comparing him to the pale young men who had courted her.

"I shall be happy to pay you extra for whatever it

35

takes to make Seattle your destination," she haughtily responded, her bright eyes narrowing ever so slightly as she gazed up at him. The man was going to be more difficult than she had imagined! she told herself with an inward frown. He certainly didn't behave like the captain of a ship, nor did he look entirely like one. For one thing, she mused, he was rather young, not more than thirty, and he was also a bit too handsome, at least when compared to the ships' captains she had encountered thus far. But, whether he looked or acted like the captain, she was determined to make him agree to take her to Seattle!

"Are you by any chance running away from someone?" he suddenly probed, the expression on his face growing a bit stern. What was there about the young woman that made him feel so protective toward her? he asked himself in bemusement. What business was it of his if she was running away? And just why the devil was he allowing her to believe him to be nothing more than the captain?

"I fail to see why that should be any of your concern," Marianna stiffly countered, her raven locks blowing softly in the faint breeze that swept behind the shipping office. She told herself that she had best hurry and complete her business with the exasperating man, for surely her aunt and uncle would begin searching for her soon. "Well, will you agree to take me to Seattle or not?" she impatiently demanded, reaching inside her small embroidered bag to withdraw a sum of money.

"Is it your husband you're so bound and determined to get away from?" the man asked with a devilish grin on his handsome face, his golden eyes glinting with humor. "If so, I can well understand why you'd want to keep our little discussion a secret. If you were my wife, I'd not be willing to let you go, either!" he added with a deep chuckle, causing Marianna's cheeks to brighten again at his further insolence.

"I have no hus—" she started to deny, then broke off abruptly. "I have told you that it is no concern of yours why I wish to leave, only that I do indeed wish to do so!" she angrily snapped, her eyes flashing once more as she faced the man defiantly. "Now, I haven't the time to stand here and argue with you about the matter. Will you agree to take me to Seattle or will you not?" she demanded again, her voice rising a bit in her growing annoyance.

"Even if I agreed, the ship won't be seaworthy again for several days. We encountered some pretty bad storms and she sustained some damage. So, you see, my dear young lady," he told her with another disarming grin as he suddenly began moving closer, his eyes staring deep into hers, "I could not take you away with me on this ship even if I wanted to." Marianna felt unaccountably breathless as she met his gaze, and she took an involuntary step backward, causing her to stumble upon an uneven plank of wood. She would have lost her balance again if not for the man's powerful arms about her waist, and she raised her eyes to his face, not at all certain what there was about him that seemed to affect her so strangely as she struggled to free herself from his grasp.

Before she quite knew what was happening, the bold

captain had lowered his head, his warm lips capturing hers in a searing kiss which lasted several long seconds. Finally, Marianna tore away from him and stood facing him with her eyes narrowed in fury, her full breasts rising and falling rapidly beneath her bodice.

"How—how dare you!" she seethed, shaking with the force of her outraged dignity.

"Perhaps now you'll go on home where you belong and forget all this nonsense about going to Seattle," the handsome stranger remarked with a broad smile, his even white teeth flashing in the sunlight. He watched in deep amusement as Marianna paused long enough to throw him a murderous glance, before spinning about on her heel and flouncing away, the soles of her high-top leather boots connecting noisily with the wooden planks. She was even further infuriated when she detected the distinct sound of deep, rumbling laughter behind her, and she quickened her steps as she furiously made her way back down the dock and into the crowd to find her aunt and uncle.

"There you are, my dear!" Aunt Sonja spoke at Marianna's elbow a few moments later. "Your uncle and I have been looking everywhere for you." It was obvious from the scowl on her face that she was quite displeased with her niece.

"I was merely taking a walk," Marianna murmured in response, still not having fully regained her composure after the disturbing incident which had occurred. She was so angry she could barely speak, and she was paying little attention when her uncle joined them a few seconds later.

"I can't seem to find Alexander anywhere," Uncle Frederick declared with a look of puzzlement, shaking his head as he took his wife's arm and started propelling her back toward their carriage as Marianna followed in silence. "Marianna, I don't understand what could have happened to him, but you'll have an opportunity to meet him tonight."

"Tonight?" his niece repeated in surprise, finally heeding her uncle's words.

"Yes, we've been invited to the home of the Countess for a very grand affair which she is giving to celebrate Alexander's homecoming," Aunt Sonja explained. "And, of course, the party is also to celebrate his upcoming nuptials," she added. She had known about the planned event for several days now, but had been unwilling to listen to a barrage of Marianna's angry, defiant remarks about it.

"Everyone we know will be there," her uncle commented as he helped the two women up into the carriage. "I'm sorry, though, my dear, that you didn't get the chance to meet your future husband before having to face him publicly tonight," he remarked with a heavy sigh.

"I will not be going!" Marianna insisted in a low, even tone of voice, the majority of her turbulent thoughts still elsewhere. She unconsciously raised a gloved hand to her lips, still able to recall the pressure of the handsome young captain's mouth upon hers.

"Nonsense!" her aunt uttered severely. "You will do nothing, absolutely nothing to disgrace our family name! Alexander is a perfect gentleman, and you, my dear, will be expected to behave yourself in a proper fashion! We'll have none of your defiant little antics this evening!" she concluded, glaring a warning in Marianna's direction.

Marianna opened her mouth to reply in less than polite terms, but firmly clasped it shut once more. What did it matter? she asked herself. After all, she would be gone within the space of a few days, wouldn't she? She would escape from the island soon, and would never again have to bother with the dilemma of her arranged marriage.

Thinking of her escape again, she was reminded of the arrogant man who had kissed her so passionately a few short minutes ago. He was undoubtedly the most insufferable, insolent, egotistical man she had ever encountered! she fumed as she stared outward now upon the blue waters of the harbor. How dare such a man force himself upon her that way! If she hadn't wished for their discussion to remain a secret, she most assuredly would have told her uncle and then allowed him to deal with the scoundrel! And, what was even worse, she furiously reflected, was that she had been unable to get him to agree to take her to Seattle!

I'll find a way yet! she silently vowed as the carriage rolled homeward in the warming afternoon sunlight, the breeze bringing a rosy color to her cheeks. I'll find a way to make him take me to Seattle when that ship leaves, even if I have to stow away to do so!

Three

"What you are saying, my dear Countess, is that you actually sent for me under false pretenses!" the tall man spoke with a slight edge to his deep voice, making it all too evident to the silver-haired woman reclining gracefully upon the upholstered chaise that he was quite displeased with her.

"Not entirely," the woman responded, an irrepressible twinkle in her lively brown eyes. "I must admit that my message to you was a bit exaggerated, but I believed it to be the only way I could possibly persuade you to return to Sitka at this time."

"Very well," Alexander Nicholai Michael Patrick Donovan remarked with a mocking smile on his handsome face as he sauntered forward to stand before his grandmother's fondly smiling countenance. "I take it that you think you have a very good reason for employing such 'unusual' methods. After all, that blasted letter of yours made it sound as if you were very nearly on your deathbed!" he said with another frown of annoyance. "Now, just exactly why was it so

41

important to you that I return home at this time?" he demanded, crossing his muscular arms against his broad chest as he cast a stern look upon the woman.

"You've no idea how very much you resemble your dear grandfather when you glare at me in that odious manner!" the old lady retorted with a slight shake of her head as she met his gaze without flinching, the corners of her mouth curving upward into another tolerant smile. She mused to herself that this devilishly attractive grandson of hers was almost an exact double for her beloved Nicholai, particularly, she reflected with an inner sigh, when attired as he was now. Nicholai had also loved the sea, and had told her many times how much he reveled in the sense of absolute freedom he experienced whenever standing upon the deck of one of his ships.

"Grandmother," Alex's tone deepened, his features growing even more severe in warning.

"I'm truly sorry I had to call you away. But, you know very well how I feel about your being up there in that Godforsaken place when you certainly have more than enough to occupy your time and talents here at home!" Countess Borofsky declared with an expressive wave of her hand as she rose steadily to her feet in order to confront her grandson on a more equal level. She was quite tall, though still several inches shorter than the striking young man before her. However, her regal bearing and aristocratic demeanor made her presence seem even more imposing. She had been the pampered daughter of a wealthy nobleman in Russia, traveling to Sitka with her new husband nearly fifty years earlier, when Alaska had still been the property of her home country. Though her parents had pleaded with her not to go and had direly predicted ruin and misfortune, she had never once regretted her impulsive decision. She and Nicholai had made a good life for themselves in Alaska and built a prosperous business together, raised a family of three beautiful daughters, and remained very much in love throughout their many years together.

"I don't want to get started on that again just now!" Alex firmly insisted as he turned abruptly away and moved to take a stance near the huge stone fireplace on the opposite wall. The exquisitely decorated room was bathed in the golden afternoon sunlight, but a blazing fire burned beneath the carved mantel. "You already know my reasons for what I do. But I certainly don't want to talk about that. What I want to know is why you went to all this trouble to get me here!" he spoke with another deep frown as he stared toward the dancing flames below. He had believed his grandmother to be dying and so had abandoned the work that was so important to him, only to arrive home and discover that the Countess was not in the least bit ailing. It wasn't like her to be so deceitful, he reflected as he inclined his head in her direction once more. But, his temper was already beginning to cool, for he was never able to remain angry with her for long. However, he was still very much determined to find out what had prompted her to behave in such an uncharacteristic manner.

"I'm afraid you will not like what I have to tell you,"

the Countess finally admitted with a faint sigh, sinking slowly back down onto the chaise and meticulously arranging her lavender silk skirts about her. She was still very attractive, her figure only slightly fuller than when she had married the young, penniless Count Borofsky so long ago. "Alex, my dear, why don't you sit down and allow me to try to explain everything to you as best I can?" she suggested with a conciliatory smile as she gestured toward the overstuffed wing chair beside the chaise. She was satisfied when he did as she bid, although she didn't fail to notice the warning gleam in his golden eyes. She knew he was extremely annoyed with her because of what she had done, and yet she told herself that she had only done what she deemed necessary under the circumstances. "Again, I am sorry that I was forced to employ such extreme tactics, but it's only that I knew you would refuse to come if I told you the truth of the matter. But first, I should like to have your promise that you will hear all I have to say before flying off the handle at me!"

"I can only give you my word that I'll do my best," Alex muttered wryly, unbuttoning his seaman's coat now and making himself more comfortable in the chair. He was naturally very curious to hear what his grandmother had to say, but, as he glanced away for a brief instant, he caught sight of the hat he had carelessly tossed aside several minutes earlier. He was suddenly reminded of the young woman down at the ship that afternoon, of their amusing encounter. He could still see the girl's beautiful, stormy face after he had kissed her, and he again wondered what had prompted him to take such action. It had been an impulsive act, he decided as the ghost of a smile appeared on his face. He had only thought to teach her a lesson, and yet he could still vividly remember the feel of her soft, rounded curves beneath his hands, could still feel her warm, inviting lips beneath his own . . .

"Alex, will you please pay attention to me!" the Countess sharply demanded, breaking in on his thoughts. "I do wish that you would forget all about that wretched place for a brief time! As I was saying, I have arranged for us to host a special celebration of sorts here this evening. I have invited most of the people we know on the island, but there will be one person in particular whom I wish you to meet."

"And who might that be?" Alex inquired with no apparent interest.

Here, the Countess hesitated, for she was suddenly not at all certain that she was proceeding with things correctly. She knew all too well what an independent, headstrong, impetuous man Alex had turned out to be! She also knew that he was going to be even more incensed with her, and yet, she staunchly decided, the whole thing was a matter of family honor, wasn't it? So, she took a deep breath of determination and finally answered, "Your future bride."

"My *what*?" Alex repeated in disbelief, his eyes widening and the mocking grin returning to his handsome face.

"I might as well tell you straightaway. Your parents arranged a marriage for you when you were still a boy. The girl is the daughter of your mother's dearest friend.

She arrived in Sitka only a few days ago. She and her family will be present at tonight's affair."

"Surely you are not serious!" Alex responded with a short laugh as he leaned back in the chair once more.

"I'm afraid I am quite serious," replied his grandmother with a curt nod. "The arrangement was made so long ago, you see, and I did not know if the girl's father would actually wish to go through with it when the time came . . . but, he has apparently decided to do just that. We therefore have no choice but to honor the agreement made by your parents."

"The devil!" countered Alex with a dangerous look in his golden eyes as he leapt to his feet and confronted her grimly.

"Alex, we have no choice!"

"This doesn't even bear discussing!"

"Why else do you think I had to employ such desperate methods to get you here? The girl's father insists that the marriage take place at once. Your parents gave their word. There is the family honor to consider—"

"Family honor be damned!" he interrupted with a fierce scowl. "I can't believe you're actually trying to convince me to go through with this preposterous scheme! Surely you know me better than to think that I'd ever even consider entering into an arranged marriage! Family honor or not, you should know better than to try and trick me into something like this!"

"Arranged marriages have long been a tradition with the finest families in Russia—" the Countess attempted to explain, only to be cut off once more.

"We are in Alaska, Grandmother, not Russia!" Alex pointed out with another dark look as he heaved a sigh of exasperation. He didn't know which made him angrier—that his grandmother had called him away without good cause, or the fact that she was now expecting him to care about some outdated tradition his parents had for some unfathomable reason chosen to follow.

"Your mother was Russian," the old lady proudly replied.

"And my father was an Irishman! But what difference does any of that make?"

"Alex," his grandmother calmly sought to reason with him, "you must listen to me. Your mother and father strongly believed that the two families should be allied through this marriage. It was especially what my daughter wanted for you, to marry Vera's daughter. The girl is several years younger than you, and only just arrived from Russia. I am told that she is quite a fetching little thing, and you are already well-acquainted with her family here in Sitka."

"I don't give a damn if she's the most ravishing creature on the face of the earth!" he replied through clenched teeth, striving to regain control of his fierce temper. A few seconds passed before he spoke again, this time with more composure. "You could have saved us both a great deal of inconvenience if you had only told me about this before now. It's a pity the girl had to come all this way for nothing. I hope that you will make my apologies to her, as well as to her family."

"But surely you will at least be here to meet them this evening?"

"Why? There's no reason for me to do so. Besides, I intend to be sailing back to Skagway within a few days."

"Alex, please," the Countess entreated as her grandson turned to leave. He paused at the sound of her voice, and she softened her voice even further as she asked, "Please, my dear, be at my side tonight. No matter what your personal feelings in this matter, there will be many guests to entertain, people who will be expecting you to be here. And, it can do no harm to meet the poor girl, can it?" She suddenly sounded rather forlorn, and Alex's heart softened in spite of his anger as he glanced back at her.

"All right. I'll be at your side this evening, but I don't want to hear another word about arranged marriages, is that understood?" he firmly commanded. When his grandmother nodded once in silence, he swung open the heavy, panelled door and strode from the room.

Countess Borofsky heaved a long sigh of relief as she rose to her feet and moved slowly toward the doorway. She was drained from the little scene with Alex, though she mused now that things hadn't gone as badly as she had dreaded they might. After all, she thought with a faint smile on her lips as she swept from the room and up the wide, curving staircase in the center of the grand old house, Alex would at least be there tonight. And that was the first step.

*　　*　　*

Alex Donovan was indeed at his grandmother's side as they greeted their guests later that evening. The house was nearly overflowing with the noble families of Sitka, the men in their starched white collars and dark suits, the women in their silks, satins, velvets, and colorful plumes. The majority of those in attendance already knew Alex, for he had been born in Sitka. He was liked and respected by his peers, and most especially by the young ladies of the town. Many a determined young lass had cast her eyes in his direction, hoping for a permanent attachment to the handsome, wealthy grandson of the Countess, but to no avail. It was generally acknowledged that Alex Donovan heartily appreciated feminine charms, but did not take them too seriously. By now, however, nearly everyone on the island appeared to have heard the news of the marriage that had long ago been arranged between Alex and Frederick Markova's beautiful young niece, although Alex was blissfully unaware of that fact when he descended the staircase to take his place beside his grandmother.

He was looking considerably different from the seaman he had earlier appeared to be, for he was now attired in an impeccably tailored black coat and spotless white linen shirt, his black trousers molding his lithe, muscular legs to perfection. His ruggedly handsome features appeared even more tanned above the snowy whiteness of his collar, the golden streaks in his auburn hair catching the bright glow of the crystal chandelier which hung from the high ceiling of the large entrance hall. The house itself was quite old, having been constructed nearly a hundred years earlier, although it had been greatly altered by the Countess and her late husband. It had grown and changed as had their fortune and family, and it was now the finest house on the island. Thus, it was no surprise that everyone who entered its elegant doorways still gazed about with something akin to awe to find such splendour. Alex behaved every bit the perfect gentleman as he welcomed the arriving guests beside his equally elegant grandmother.

"I see that you were apparently quite serious when you mentioned you had invited nearly every living soul on the island!" he remarked in an amused undertone to the Countess, who cautioned him to smile and speak politely as he greeted what he believed must surely be the hundredth couple of the evening. A string quartet was playing softly in the background, and Alex noticed that several of the younger guests were now beginning to dance in the brightly illuminated ballroom. He was vastly relieved when he spotted an old friend he had not seen for quite some time, and he hastily excused himself to speak with the young man, but his grandmother sternly cautioned him to return within two minutes.

"Don't forget, Alex," she told him as he merely smiled and took himself off, "we still have guests who have not yet arrived!" She herself was increasingly curious to meet the young woman she had heard so much about, and she certainly wanted Alex to be present when the Markovas arrived.

However, it was during Alex's absence from his

grandmother's side that Marianna arrived with her aunt, uncle, and cousin. She was not at all impressed with the elegance of Countess Borofsky's house, for she had not wanted to come. But she forced a cool smile to her lips as her aunt presented her to the tall older woman who stood alone to welcome them.

"Countess, I should like for you to meet our niece, Marianna Markova. Marianna, this is the Countess Borofsky, a very dear friend of the family's for many years," Sonja announced rather loftily. Her hair was swept upward in a comically elaborate style, her dress of dark coral satin cut in a more frivolous fashion than she usually affected. The Countess found herself thinking once again that the woman seemed to go out of her way to make herself unattractive. But she turned her attention to Marianna, and she was both pleased and surprised at what her eyes beheld.

"Marianna, my dear, how pleased I am to make your acquaintance. I'm afraid my grandson is detained at the moment, but he should be back shortly. I am so happy to welcome you to my home." The Countess spoke warmly, her brown eyes lighting with mingled approval and interest. The girl was indeed quite beautiful, she mused, smiling to herself and wondering how Alex would react when he met her. Marianna's raven curls were drawn up and away from her face, fastened high upon the back of her head, and a mass of the dark tresses cascaded down her back. Her gown was stunning, for it showed her slender yet rounded figure to the best advantage. It was fashioned of pale yellow satin, the rounded neckline cut low across her full young bosom. She was wearing a single strand of pearls around her slender neck, her lips curved into a polite smile as she extended her hand gracefully.

"Thank you, Countess," she murmured, telling herself that it didn't matter to her in the least whether the woman's grandson was there to welcome them or not. She had absolutely no desire to meet the man, and she was very much aware of the way the Countess seemed to be silently appraising her, as if she were some brood mare to be considered for the family's prize-winning stud! Her blue-green eyes flashed with a sudden fire, and the Countess caught a glimpse of that fire before Marianna moved away to allow her uncle and cousin to be greeted by their hostess as well.

"Come along, Marianna. There are still so many people who are anxious to meet you," Aunt Sonja insisted as she and the others moved toward the ballroom.

"It's rather odd that Alex wasn't there to meet us," Uncle Frederick remarked with a brief frown as he escorted his niece into the crowded room. "But then, he always was a bit out of the ordinary," he added with a chuckle as he patted Marianna's hand, which lay upon his arm.

"It doesn't matter, Uncle," Marianna assured him. She was forced to endure several introductions throughout the next half hour, before finally persuading her cousin to assist her in reaching the long, gleaming table where a most impressive feast had been arranged for the guests. She saw that there was fresh salmon, fruit, pastries, and other assorted foods, as well as champagne, fruit punch, and other beverages to quench the thirst of the many people who were now dancing in the center of the ornate room. She eyed the table a bit wistfully, for she suddenly remembered that she had not eaten anything since much earlier in the day. But just as she was about to take up one of the dainty china plates and help herself to some sustenance, her aunt found her again and pulled her over to a group of ladies clustered several yards away from the table.

"Marianna, I told you, there are many people who wish to meet you! I would greatly appreciate it if you would endeavor to look a bit more interested!" her aunt whispered in her ear as they reached the waiting group.

Interested! Marianna silently fumed as she nonetheless cordially smiled and spoke briefly during the endless introductions. Why on earth should she be feeling the least bit interested in tonight's affair? After all, she had no desire to be here, and she was sick and tired of hearing everyone's gushing comments concerning Alexander. Not that anyone had mentioned anything at all about the arranged marriage that was now such public knowledge. Oh no, they were much too discreet for that! she told herself in growing vexation. It was simply that several people, particularly the women her aunt's age, had meaningfully asked her what she thought of Alex. It had given her a small amount of pleasure to reply that she had never met the man and then to watch their astonished expressions!

Perhaps he was just as unwilling as she, she suddenly mused as she pretended to listen to a freckle-faced young man who had been staring at her for quite some time. The idea had never occurred to her before now, and her eyes narrowed almost imperceptibly as she gave it further thought. Her thoughts, however, were soon interrupted as she found herself surrounded by a growing circle of admirers, many of whom began pleading with her for the next dance. Marianna wanted nothing more than to escape outside into the cool night air, and she was finally able to accomplish just that when she sweetly asked one of the young men she had just been dancing with to fetch her a glass of the fruit punch. When he was gone, she managed to slip unnoticed out the multipaned glass doors that opened onto the terrace, which in turn overlooked a fragrant, flower-filled garden.

Marianna took a deep breath, inhaling the fresh aromas that drifted on the gentle wind, and she peered upward toward the three-quarter moon which shone from behind a thin veiling of clouds. She was glad that she had remembered to take up her lace shawl on her way out, and she now flung it about her shoulders, drawing it close about her body as the night air threatened to chill her.

She gazed out upon the lamp-lit garden, then farther toward the dark waters of the harbor in the near distance. She stepped closer to the carved wooden railing which surrounded the terrace, moving away from the revealing light of the crowded ballroom.

"Well, well, it seems there is another adventurous

soul in attendance this evening!" a man's voice spoke behind her, startling her as she whirled about to face a man who had only a moment earlier stepped out from the ballroom. Marianna was at first afraid that he was someone sent by her aunt to fetch her, but as the man moved closer and she saw his smiling face more clearly, she gasped aloud in stunned surprise.

"You!" she breathed, a fiery blush rising to her cheeks as her eyes widened and then narrowed.

"The little runaway!" exclaimed the man with a mocking grin as his golden eyes twinkled mischievously. "You're certainly the last person I expected to find out here!" He stepped closer, but Marianna began backing away as he slowly advanced, until she felt the terrace railing at her back. The two of them were well within the shadows now, hidden from view from those inside the music-filled ballroom.

"What are you doing here?" Marianna imperiously demanded, her chin lifting proudly, her blue-green eyes flashing with renewed indignation. He was outlined against the bright glow which emanated from the house, making him appear even larger as he smiled mockingly down at her. The moon cast a silvery light upon the two of them as they faced one another on the terrace, the night wind gently rustling the leaves on the garden plants.

"I might ask the same of you," the tall, handsome stranger replied with one sardonically raised eyebrow. He looked vastly different from when she had seen him earlier that day, and she thought briefly of pushing past him to seek refuge inside the ballroom, but she did not want him to think her cowardly simply because of that one meaningless kiss he had forced upon her!

"I certainly wouldn't have thought someone like you, a mere ship's captain, would be the sort of guest the Countess would invite!" she haughtily remarked, annoyed to discover that his presence disturbed her so much. "Indeed, I wonder that you were ever allowed admittance at all, especially since you are definitely no gentleman!" she scathingly finished. She could feel her cheeks flaming again as his golden eyes moved boldly to the creamy flesh of her breasts rising and falling above her rounded bodice.

"Ah, but then I wasn't pretending to be a gentleman when we encountered one another this afternoon," he answered with a low chuckle, his amused gaze moving upward to her angry, beautiful face again. He was surprised to discover that he was very glad to see her again, and he couldn't refrain from asking, "Just why were you trying to run away like that?"

"I've already told you that it's none of your business!" Marianna furiously retorted, finding it difficult to breathe with the maddening fellow standing so close, when his eyes seemed to be trying to peer into her very thoughts. She told herself that she should leave, that she should have nothing more to do with him, and yet she found she could not but stay. Her expression grew both puzzled and wary when the man softly stated, "Perhaps I can be of some assistance to you if you'll only tell me what it is that troubles you."

"The only assistance I need from you is to agree to take me to Seattle!" Marianna replied rather crossly, drawing the lace shawl unconsciously across her bosom.

He stared down at her in silence for a few moments, finding himself increasingly affected by his close proximity to the beautiful young spitfire. She was unlike any woman he had ever before encountered. She was definitely intriguing.

Marianna, on the other hand, was torn between the impulse to escape from those searching golden eyes and the determination to make him agree to help her escape from the island when his ship was once again seaworthy. She suddenly wondered if he remembered the kiss he had forced upon her as vividly as she did, and she blushed as he proceeded to smile a slow, lazy smile before speaking again.

"What if I told you that I might, just might, mind you, agree to help you get to Seattle if you'll tell me your true reason for wanting to leave?"

"I fail to see how my reason for wanting to leave should matter to you at all!"

"Nevertheless, I refuse even to consider the matter unless you agree to tell me the truth," he spoke with a disarming grin as he glanced away for a brief instant. Marianna was infuriated by what she thought to be his superior manner, and she was once more tempted to flare up at him and then flounce away, but that would still leave her in the unfortunate position of having to find some way to escape before her aunt and uncle attempted to force her into marriage with the hated Alexander.

"Very well," she finally capitulated with an ill grace,

moving stiffly away from him and turning her gaze upon the harbor once more. "I need to get away as soon as possible, for my family is attempting to force me into an unwanted marriage."

"And just who is this unlucky fellow who appears to have earned your scorn?" he mockingly asked as he stared down at her dark hair, which shone almost blueblack in the moonlight.

"I don't know him. That is, I know him only by his name. You see, his parents arranged the marriage when I was still but a babe," she admitted, the pain of it still making itself known deep in her heart. She was surprised when the man did not make any sort of reply, for she had expected him to say something, and she turned back around to face him with a defiantly questioning look on her lovely young face. "Well, I have told you. Will you agree to help me now?"

Alex's initial, stunned surprise quickly turned into outright amusement at her words. He was certain that there could only be one arranged marriage causing so much trouble in Sitka at the moment, and Marianna was astonished as he suddenly threw back his head and laughed aloud in pure enjoyment of the absurdity of the situation.

"I fail to see the humor in what I have just told you!" she furiously seethed, convinced that the man must be totally daft. She nearly stamped her foot in mingled rage and frustration when he merely continued to laugh, and she now wrathfully pushed past him, intent upon flying back into the crowded confines of the ballroom.

She gasped in surprise as Alex's hand closed firmly about her wrist, as he forcefully detained her, and Marianna angrily demanded, "Let go of me!" She attempted to free herself from his iron grasp by twisting her arm, but her efforts were entirely futile against his superior strength as he held her quite easily.

"Wait," he commanded, controlling his mirth now, though his eyes continued to sparkle. "You don't understand. It seems we—" he started to explain, only to be cut off by Marianna's infuriated voice.

"If you don't unhand me this very instant, you—you degenerate sailor, I'll scream!" She was taken aback when he merely proceeded to laugh at her words, and before she thought about what she was doing, she brought her hand up and struck him across his tanned cheek, shocking both herself and him. She was unprepared when the smile on his face was abruptly replaced by a fierce look, and she gasped again as he roughly pulled her back to him, his powerful arms locking about her before she could escape. She fought against him with all her strength, her mouth opening to cry out for help, when his arms tightened about her like bands of steel and his mouth descended upon hers with bruising intensity.

Marianna continued to struggle vigorously for several more seconds before suddenly being overwhelmed by very disturbing sensations that were before this moment entirely foreign to her. She was so shocked by what she was experiencing that she ceased to fight against him any longer, and she began to feel faint as his lips moved demandingly, passionately upon her own. She trembled involuntarily as his arms held her tightly against him, as his mouth possessed hers with a masterful skill. One of his hands moved to the softness of her rounded hips, pressing her shockingly, intimately against his masculine hardness. His lips enticingly trailed a blazing path from her lips to the slender column of her neck, then lower to the full curve of her breasts above the low-cut bodice of her gown. She gasped at his boldness, as well as at her own helplessness to resist him. Nothing like this had ever happened to her before!

When he finally lifted his head, his golden eyes staring deep into the blue-green depths of her own, she pushed against him with all her might, hot tears gathering in her flashing eyes as she swept past him, her skirts swirling about her ankles as she flew across the surface of the moonlit terrace. She thought she heard him calling to her to come back, but she was unable to think of anything but getting away from him. She could feel her face burning with embarrassment, and her breath caught on a gasp as she reached the glass doors, nearly colliding with her uncle who was stepping out from the ballroom.

"There you are, my dear!" Frederick spoke with a broad smile, before his eyes traveled past her to light upon the tall man standing just within the shadows at the far end of the terrace. "Well, I guess you two somehow managed to find one another after all," he grinned down at his niece.

"You—you know that man?" Marianna asked in disbelief, glancing briefly in Alex's direction.

"Of course!" her uncle replied with a laugh and a look of bemusement on his bearded face. "Alex, I'm sorry we haven't had a chance to speak before now, but . . ." he began as he turned back to the man who was now walking toward them.

"Alex?" Marianna repeated in shocked amazement. She turned slowly toward the man who now stood towering above her, her eyes wide as saucers as she met his amused gaze.

"Alexander Nicholai Michael Patrick Donovan, to be exact," the tall, handsome man spoke with a charmingly crooked grin. "The very man, I'm afraid, you wished to avoid."

Four

Marianna stared speechlessly up at Alex for several long seconds, her beautiful features registering mingled astonishment and a rapidly increasing fury. Alex, on the other hand, was smiling quite unconcernedly down at the outraged young lady before him, an unholy light of amusement in his golden eyes as he waited patiently for her to speak once more. He was fully prepared for the torrent of angry words which issued forth from what he perceived to be her thoroughly adorable mouth.

"You—you knew all the time!" she cried accusingly, her eyes flashing blue-green fire. "How dare you! How dare you seek to humiliate me like this, to amuse yourself at my expense! You've known from the very first, haven't you?" she furiously demanded, the delectable curve of her full breasts rising and falling above the low-cut bodice of her exquisite gown.

"Actually, no. Not until a few moments ago," Alex replied with a maddening grin, a grin which Marianna interpreted as being more like a triumphant smirk. His handsome face became a blur as hot tears began swimming in her blazing eyes, and she could feel the bright, telltale color flooding her face as he continued to stare calmly down at her.

"Alex! Marianna! What's all this—" a very confused Uncle Frederick attempted to inquire, only to be abruptly cut off by his niece, who seemed totally oblivious to his presence now. He was shocked by her temperamental outburst, and he glanced worriedly toward Alex.

"You lie!" seethed Marianna, striving unsuccessfully to control her dangerously rising temper. "You knew, Mr. Donovan! How could you not have known, when everyone on this entire island has been talking about the two of us, gossiping about our arranged marriage? How very enjoyable all this must have been for you!"

"It wasn't until a very short time ago that I was apprised of the disagreeable fact that our little 'predicament' was so public, Miss Markova," Alex responded rather mockingly, his fascinated gaze never leaving Marianna's flushed face. "I can assure you that I did not set out to humiliate you." Although this last was spoken quite earnestly, the devil of merriment never left his golden eyes.

"You're nothing more than a deceitful, lying—" Marianna irrationally raged, breaking off when she could suddenly no longer find adequate words with which to vent her intense displeasure. Her anger was fueled by the memory of the burning kiss he had forced upon her lips only a few minutes earlier, as well as by the hateful recollection of her own traitorous response.

"Marianna!" Uncle Frederick ventured to scold, but his niece paid him no heed. Instead, she raised her head proudly and glared back up at the tall, handsome scoundrel who had already served to cause her so much trouble and embarrassment.

"You are a cad, Mr. Donovan, and I despise you even more than I was prepared to!" she flung at him, before spinning about on her small, slippered heel and storming back into the gaiety of the ballroom.

"Alex, I . . . I'm terribly sorry," Frederick remarked in apology for Marianna's rude behavior. "I don't know what could have gotten into the girl. Would you mind telling me what the devil has been going on between the two of you out here?" He was extremely discomfited by the volatile little scene he had just witnessed, and he was curious as to what had prompted his niece to display such a shocking want of manners.

"The bride and groom are merely becoming better acquainted with one another," Alex sardonically murmured in response, his thoughts still centered on Marianna. He watched quite intently as she made her way swiftly through the crowd, then disappeared through another doorway at the opposite end of the room. Alex's expression grew even more pensive, though a faint smile still lurked about his lips as he heard Frederick say, "I'm afraid the girl is a bit high-strung, my boy."

"I gathered that," Alex quipped, his smile deepening as he turned to face his friend.

"I hope—well, I hope you won't think too harshly of her."

"Quite the contrary," Alex assured him, glancing back toward the ballroom again.

"I suppose she gets it from her father, my older brother, you know," Frederick admitted with a nervous laugh. He hesitated for a moment, noticing the way the younger man seemed to still be staring after Marianna. "Alex, there is something I'd like to say."

"Yes, Frederick, what is it?" He glanced at the other man for a brief instant, before his gaze returned to the ballroom.

"Well, I want you to know how proud I am to welcome you into our family. After all, my boy, I've known you nearly all your life! I'm glad that you've agreed to this arrangement between the families. Things would have been damned awkward otherwise, wouldn't they?" he finished with another short laugh. The Countess herself had reassured him that the marriage would indeed take place as planned, that she had managed to convince her strong-willed grandson to agree to the marriage. But, the confrontation he had just witnessed between the betrothed couple served to cause him renewed anxiety, and he was even more perplexed when Alex suddenly excused himself and sauntered away into the ballroom.

It took Alex several interminably long minutes to make his way across the large room, for he was greeted by nearly everyone he sought to pass. He finally emerged into the front entrance foyer, intent upon finding Marianna, though he himself was still uncertain as to his motives for doing so. As he approached the library on a sudden instinct, he was rewarded by the sound of Marianna's voice within, and he placed a hand upon the ornate brass handle, turning it ever so slightly and opening the door just enough to allow him to make out what was being said. It wasn't at all like him to be so willing to eavesdrop, but he was suddenly possessed of an overpowering curiosity to hear what Marianna was saying to the other occupant of the room.

"Andrei, you simply must agree to help me! You're my only hope!"

"You still haven't told me why you're so upset!" Andrei countered in obvious exasperation, marching away from his cousin and taking a stand before the fireplace.

"Yes I have!" she angrily disagreed. "I've told you that it's because of that odious man!"

"And I'm telling you that I don't understand why you're acting like this!" When he had glimpsed his beautiful cousin fleeing from the ballroom a few minutes ago, he had naturally rushed after her, anxious to discover the source of her obvious distress. And then, to find out that it was none other than his very good friend Alex Donovan who had caused her to behave so strangely. Alex! Andrei felt something akin to hero-worship for his friend, for Alex had been like an older brother to him for a number of years. He knew that Alex could charm any lady he chose, so why was Marianna standing here insisting that his friend was nothing more than an arrogant, hateful rogue?

"Things are even worse than I ever imagined they would be!" Marianna declared in a voice charged with tumultuous emotion. "I detest him, Andrei!"

"But you've only just met him! Surely if you give this a little more time . . ."

"No! I will never, never marry that man!"

"Just what in heaven's name happened to make you hate him when you've only just made his acquaintance?"

Marianna opened her mouth to reply, but hastily clamped it shut once more. There was certainly no way she could explain to Andrei about the impassioned, demanding embraces his friend had forced upon her! She knew no way to explain the almost violent reaction she felt when Alex Donovan took her in his arms. She had only encountered the man twice in her entire life, and yet he already possessed the power to infuriate her far beyond reason, something no other man had ever been able to do!

To think of marrying such a man was thoroughly impossible! she silently fumed, whirling away from Andrei and angrily sweeping across the floor to the opposite corner of the dimly lit room. If he had been the spineless creature she had so often envisioned, if he had been ugly or deformed as she had thought he might possibly be . . . but no! He was the most handsome scoundrel she had ever seen, as well as the most insufferable and high-handed! She could never marry such a man, and she turned back to her young cousin with her eyes flashing fire once again.

"I must get away, Andrei! Now. This very night. And you must help me!" she dramatically pronounced, flying to his side and clutching at his arm with both of her hands, her eyes very large and luminous in her beautiful face.

"How on earth am I supposed to do that?" he impatiently exclaimed, resenting the uncomfortable position in which she was placing him. He felt honor-bound to help her in some way, and yet he felt that to do so would betray his friendship with Alex. And, there was still the not-so-inconsequential matter of his parents and what they would do to him if he helped Marianna escape.

"There must be someplace where I can hide until he leaves Sitka! He told me himself that he's planning to leave here again in a matter of days. Surely you can think of someplace where I can remain until I can manage to escape from this island!" Marianna insisted, pressing a hand to her forehead as she began pacing back and forth across the marbled tile floor of the well-stocked library. Her skirts swirled angrily about her trim ankles as she clenched her hands into fists at her sides, desperate to find some means of escape from what she perceived, from what she had convinced herself to be, a fate worse than death.

If she had been totally honest with herself, however, she would have realized that it was not the matter of the arranged marriage that was serving to make her so angry at the moment, but rather Alex Donovan himself. Before he had arrived upon the scene, he had been a faceless object of contempt to her. But now, now he was revealed to be a handsome, virile, totally masculine fellow who made her feel a disturbing lack of self-confidence. She, who had always been so sure of herself with any man, was now supposed to place herself at the mercy of such a domineering rake? Never! she vowed to herself once more.

"I think I know of a place," Andrei finally answered after appearing to give the matter considerable thought.

"Where?" Marianna anxiously demanded, returning quickly to his side.

"A fisherman's cottage on the far side of the island. The old man and his wife live there all alone. You'll be safe with them. They'll take good care of you until we can find a way to get you away from Sitka. I've known the old man since I was knee high. He'll do whatever I ask."

"Oh, Andrei, thank you!" Marianna cried in profound relief, embracing her boyish young cousin with exuberance, thereby causing him to flush uncomfortably. "I shall owe you a debt of immense gratitude for the rest of my life if you'll only help me to get away!"

"Let's see now . . ." Andrei murmured, moving away and stroking his whiskerless chin as he grew thoughtful again. His face suddenly came alight with enthusiasm as he said, "I'll arrange for a carriage to be waiting for you at midnight! You can climb out of your window and down the trellis on the side wall. We'll be off before anyone suspects anything at all!" Gone was the previous reluctance as he contemplated the adventure of it all. "I'll get two of our fastest horses in case they do try to follow us. But, Mother and Father are both sound sleepers. I seriously doubt if they'll even hear a thing."

"That sounds perfect!" Marianna happily declared. She and Andrei discussed a few other details before agreeing that they had best return to the party before their absence became too conspicuous. Neither of them noticed that the door was slightly ajar as they walked arm in arm from the library, nor did they happen to glimpse the tall man who watched the two of them from his vantage point near the foot of the spiral staircase.

"Marianna! Andrei! What are the two of you doing out here?" Aunt Sonja demanded sharply. She was perturbed because she had been unable to locate either her son or her niece for several minutes, and she was extremely anxious for Marianna to be properly introduced to her betrothed. If they could find Alex, she reminded herself with a frown. She hadn't been able to find him, either, and she was in a particularly foul temper as she hurried forward to grasp each of the two young people by the arm. She began propelling them back toward the ballroom, but a deep voice at their backs arrested their steps.

"Good evening, Sonja. I trust you are enjoying my grandmother's little get-together?" Alex inquired quite pleasantly. He suppressed a smile of pure amusement when he noted the way that both Marianna and Andrei started guiltily at the sound of his voice. He faced Sonja Markova with a very sober expression on his handsome face as he bowed slightly in her direction.

"Alex!" Sonja exclaimed with pleasure, presenting her hand to him. "Where have you been hiding all evening, you naughty boy?" she chastised him with what she believed to be a dazzling smile.

"I'm terribly sorry, but I have been unavoidably occupied elsewhere. Hello, Andrei. Good to see you again," Alex spoke with a friendly grin as he turned to the younger man.

Andrei stammered uncomfortably for a moment beneath Alex's golden stare, managing to murmur, "Hello, Alex. I'm glad to see you back."

"Alex, my dear boy, have you been introduced to my niece yet?" Sonja asked, drawing a stubbornly silent Marianna forward.

"We have 'encountered' one another this evening, but have never been formally introduced," replied Alex with a mocking gleam in his eye. He stared down at Marianna, a polite smile on his face.

"Marianna, may I present Alexander Donovan, Countess Borofsky's grandson. Alex, this is my niece, Miss Marianna Markova," Sonja made the introductions, quite pleased with herself.

"Miss Markova," Alex said, bowing courteously in her direction. "It is a pleasure to welcome you here tonight."

"Thank you, Mr. Donovan," Marianna answered frostily with a brisk nod at him, refusing to meet his taunting gaze as she kept her eyes fastened on a spot somewhere beyond his head.

"May I have the honor of this next dance, Miss Markova?" he unexpectedly asked, causing Marianna to gaze up at him in surprise. Just as she was opening her mouth to rudely deny his request, her aunt practically shoved her into Alex's arm, saying, "Go ahead, my dear! You two enjoy yourselves." Sonja smiled to

71

herself in supreme satisfaction as she watched her niece being led away by the dashing young man. Andrei gazed anxiously after the couple, then was forced to endure a severe scolding from his mother for absenting both himself and his cousin from the evening's festivities.

"Let go of me!" Marianna hissed as soon as they were away from her aunt. Alex, however, maintained a firm grip on her upper arm and ignored her command, leading her into the very middle of the crowded ballroom and then taking her into his arms for the dance. At that moment, the musicians struck up a waltz, and Marianna held herself stiffly erect as Alex began to whirl her round and round in the movements of the dance. She told herself that she would have to endure his hateful presence for only a short time longer, that she would be free of him within a few hours' time.

"What's the matter, my dear fiancée?" Alex inquired with a mocking smile as his amused gaze made contact with her fiery one.

"I am not your fiancée!" she fervently denied, feeling unaccountably breathless as his steely arm tightened about her. She was all too aware of his closeness, of his large hand tightly clasping hers, of the faint aroma of brandy which hung about him.

"But I have been given to understand that everything has long been arranged," he cheerfully replied, enjoying their little battle. He realized how very much he liked having her in his arms as they danced. In truth, he found her to be highly desirable, thoroughly entrancing, and certainly more intriguing than any other young lady he had ever known. After all, he mused, no other woman had ever resisted his devastating charm when he chose to exert it, none had ever professed to despise him simply because of a few stolen kisses. Marianna Markova, he told himself with an inward smile, was indeed quite intriguing, not at all what he had expected when his grandmother had told him about the preposterous scheme that afternoon.

"I don't care what our families arranged! You know that such a thing is absolutely impossible! I cannot believe that you would ever agree to marry a woman who is nothing more than a stranger to you, a woman who happens to find the idea of marriage to you to be totally repugnant!"

"I didn't agree," he calmly replied.

"You—you didn't?" Marianna gasped in disbelief and astonishment, staring up at him now with widened eyes, forgetting for one brief moment her extreme dislike of the man.

"But then, that was before I met you!" Alex added with a roguish grin as his golden eyes sparkled mischievously. "You see, I had no idea what sort of beautiful little wildcat awaited me!"

"Oh! You are insufferable!" Marianna snapped in renewed annoyance, striving vainly to free herself from his grasp once more. He held fast, however, and she was forced to dance the remainder of the seemingly endless waltz with him, though she refused to allow him to bait her further. She was all too conscious of the attention they were attracting as they moved about the dance floor together, and she overheard several admiring comments regarding the betrothed couple and what an attractive, fortunate pair they were. It was almost more than she could bear. When the music finally ended, she broke away from Alex and flounced toward the doorway, finding her Uncle Frederick in a matter of seconds.

"Uncle Frederick, please take me home!" she pleaded, pressing her fingertips to her temples as if in pain.

"What is it, my dear? Are you ill?" he asked with genuine concern, placing a supportive arm about her trembling shoulders.

"I have a dreadful headache. And I'm afraid that I shall be terribly ill all over the Countess's elegant floor if you do not take me out of here at once!" she cried, grasping her uncle's arm, her color much heightened. Her aunt and cousin joined them at that moment, and although Aunt Sonja protested, the Markova family proceeded to take their leave of their hostess right away. Their hostess's grandson, however, was once again nowhere to be found, though Countess Borofsky graciously conveyed his regrets at having missed bidding them goodnight.

"The Countess was undoubtedly disappointed, and more than a little disapproving, at our early departure!" Aunt Sonja irritably commented as they rode homeward. "And Alex—why, I can't imagine what he will think of you, Marianna! After all, it was very important that you make a good impression on him." She directed a severe frown at her niece before continuing. "Though, I must say, Alex was behaving rather oddly himself this evening. It isn't like him to make himself so scarce during one of his grandmother's parties. And he must have surely known that tonight's affair was a celebration of sorts. Why, everyone there was talking about the two of you! And you behaved so rudely!" she finished, fixing Marianna with another narrow look.

"Can't you see that the poor girl is unwell?" Frederick unexpectedly rushed to Marianna's defense as he kept his arm about her, patting her arm consolingly.

Marianna moaned softly for effect, keeping her face hidden from her aunt's sharp gaze so that the older woman wouldn't see the way her lips were curving into a triumphant smile. She would be free this very night! Free of her sour, restrictive aunt, free of the loathsome threat of marriage to that despicable scoundrel known as Alexander Donovan!

He would soon discover that she was no weak little miss who would gladly jump to do his bidding! No, she mused in satisfaction, no, Mr. Donovan, you will never again be afforded the opportunity to insult me, to manhandle me!

But no matter how valiantly she tried, she could still not forget the encounter with him upon the terrace earlier that evening, could not erase the memory of his disturbing kiss. No man had ever kissed her that way before. No man had ever dared! But it didn't matter now. Nothing mattered but getting away from him before it was too late!

Five

When the ancient grandfather clock in the downstairs hallway melodiously chimed the fateful hour of midnight, Marianna was impatiently seated upon her bed, attired in a most becoming dark amber traveling suit, an overstuffed carpetbag clutched in one hand. She heaved a sigh and crossed to the window for what seemed to be at least the hundredth time within a quarter of an hour. Peering below into the moonlit semidarkness, she frowned, then glanced farther out toward the glistening waters of the picturesque harbor in the distance. She was preparing a return to her seat on the bed when she finally spied a carriage quietly being drawn to a halt a short distance from her window.

"At last!" she breathed aloud in relief, scurrying back to snatch up her carpetbag. She tossed it out of the window to the man who stepped down from the closed fourwheeled vehicle and stood waiting. She didn't bother to spare her cousin so much as a glance, so intent was she upon making good her escape, though she did pause to wonder vaguely why Andrei had seen fit to bring along a driver.

Marianna experienced a brief moment of trepidation as she gathered up her full skirts and proceeded to hoist herself upon the windowsill. It occurred to her that what she was about to do would be considered quite shocking and decidedly unladylike, but she did not care. She had already judged the large trellis fastened to the outside wall to be strong enough to support her weight, but she nonetheless hesitated a few seconds before swinging out of the window and then carefully finding her footing upon the wooden slats, her gloved hands grasping the windowsill for support. Thick green vines clung to the trellis and threatened to impede her descent, but she took a deep breath of determination, flung her long skirts over one arm, and began climbing cautiously downward, her hightop black leather boots steady upon the trellis. Nevertheless, she was grateful for the support of Andrei's hands about her slender waist as she neared the ground.

"Andrei, do you really think—" she started to question in a whisper, only to gasp as she turned to behold the face beneath the widebrimmed hat. Her brilliantly blue-green eyes grew round as saucers and before she could utter another sound the man had clamped an iron hand across her open mouth and was lifting her bodily, carrying her easily to the waiting carriage and then thrusting her unceremoniously inside, following closely after her as he swung the door closed behind them. His large hand returned to silence Marianna before she could catch her breath, and the driver perched upon the open seat above lost no time in cracking his whip above the heads of the well-matched team of horses. The carriage lurched abruptly forward, causing Marianna to be thrown headlong into the arms of Alex Donovan.

"What do you think you're doing? Let me out of here at once!" she indignantly commanded, her eyes blazing as she frantically pushed against him. "Take your hands off me! Where is Andrei? What have you done with him, you fiend?" she raged, experiencing a rising sense of panic as he merely gripped her arms with his strong hands and held her back against the velvet cushions of the seat as the carriage sped forward into the night.

"There's no need to become hysterical, my dear Miss Markova," Alex remarked with a sardonic little smile. "And, if you'll only agree to end this wrestling match between us, I'll allow you to sit calmly and without restraint," he added with a deep chuckle, his tanned, handsome face mere inches from her own.

"I am not hysterical!" she angrily retorted, continuing to struggle. She gasped as he suddenly pinned both her arms behind her back, bringing her even closer against the muscular hardness of his body.

"I take it then that you're not going to consent to come along quietly?" he asked with a mocking grin, his golden eyes gleaming with an unfathomable light.

"If you do not release me at once, I shall scream!" Marianna courageously threatened, squirming and twisting in a futile effort to free herself.

"Go ahead. There's no one else to hear you, save the

driver. And he happens to be a very loyal and faithful servant," Alex smoothly replied. "Now, if you'll just calm down a bit, I'll release your arms. Otherwise, I'll be forced to continue holding you captive like this. Although that isn't at all a disagreeable prospect," he remarked, his appreciative gaze moving boldly from her flushed and angry face to the soft curves which were pressing so intimately against him.

"Let go of me, I say!" she imperiously commanded once more, startled when Alex suddenly complied. She immediately began rubbing at her arms where his steely grip had faintly bruised her flesh, and she glared militantly across at him as she edged backward upon the seat, pressing herself as far as possible into the corner. "Why are you doing this?" she demanded. "And where is my cousin?"

"Andrei is perfectly safe. I merely persuaded him that his part in your foolhardy little scheme would prove very disadvantageous to him, so, in the end, he was forced to see reason. As for my substituting myself in his place," he told her with another faintly mocking smile, crossing his arms nonchalantly against his broad chest, "I couldn't allow you to proceed with your disastrous plans."

"What right have you to interfere?" Marianna furiously countered.

"Every right, my dearest fiancée," Alex answered with a sharp, meaningful glance in her direction. "After all," he added with a disarming grin, "we're going to be married."

"What?" she exclaimed in disbelief, experiencing no

small degree of shock and alarm at his words. "You—
you cannot possibly be serious!"

"Oh, but I am. Quite serious. You see, I've given the
matter quite a bit of consideration since encountering
you again this evening. I've decided to go through with
the arrangement after all."

"You cannot mean that!" she passionately declared,
beginning suddenly to feel as if she were trapped in
some sort of nightmare. "You must be insane even to
consider such a thing, and madder still to believe that
I would ever consent to be your wife!"

"You'll consent," he replied with supreme self-
confidence, causing Marianna to experience an overwhelming urge to slap his arrogantly handsome face.
Instead, she suddenly reached for the door on her side
of the carriage, desperately attempting to wrench it
open and fling herself outward, apparently oblivious to
the fact that the vehicle was moving along at an
alarming speed. She cried out as Alex moved swiftly to
intercept her, pulling her roughly backward.

"What are you trying to do, break your neck, you
fool?" he gruffly demanded as he administered a brisk
shake to her arm.

"Let go of me!" Marianna wrathfully snapped,
jerking her arm from his grasp, her eyes flashing. Their
gazes locked in silent combat for a few long seconds,
until Marianna abruptly queried, "Where are you
taking me?"

"Nowhere in particular at the moment. In fact, we
may very well drive around all night."

"Why? What are you planning to do with me?" she

haughtily inquired, her beautiful head lifting proudly as she favored him with a disdainful, wary look. She told herself that she really need have no fear of him, for, after all, he wouldn't dare attempt to dishonor or harm her in any way. Or would he? a tiny voice at the back of her mind persisted in asking, causing her to experience a certain alarm once more, though she vowed that Alex Donovan would never see any evidence of it.

"I am merely going to make you see reason. That is," he patiently explained, as if to a child, "you are going to consent to marry me before this night is through." There was no longer any amusement lurking in his eyes, nor upon his perfectly serious features. He suddenly appeared very dangerous.

"Then you must surely be a lunatic, Mr. Donovan, for I shall never consent to marry the likes of you!" she bravely declared with a defiant toss of her raven curls.

"You will consent to it," Alex merely repeated.

"But can't you see that I have no wish to marry you? Can't you understand that such a marriage would never work?" she exclaimed, her voice rising.

"Oh, but I believe we'll deal quite admirably together," Alex disagreed with a quick smile. "Really, you ought to feel flattered, at least a little, for I've never wanted to marry any woman before now. When my grandmother first informed me of that ridiculous arrangement between our families, I was just as much set against it as you are. But, after making your acquaintance, my dearest Marianna, I changed my mind," he informed her with a certain light in his golden eyes as he began slowly edging toward her.

Indeed, he reflected, he had undergone a complete change in attitude! It certainly wasn't characteristic of him to go about abducting beautiful young ladies in the middle of the night and telling them he was going to marry them! Nevertheless, he mused as he stared across at the defiant young woman who seemed so determined to deny him what he suddenly wanted most in the world, he knew he must have her as his bride, a fact that was more startling to himself than it could ever be to anyone else!

"But I have definitely not changed *my* mind, Mr. Donovan!" Marianna vehemently responded, abruptly moving away and settling herself upon the opposite seat. Her eyes widened as Alex merely took a seat beside her again, and she desperately said to him, "You cannot make me agree! No one can force me to marry a man I do not wish to marry!"

"I don't believe force will be necessary. If you'll only stop being so damned obstinate, you'll see that a marriage between us is the best solution for everyone. It will satisfy our families' sense of honor by fulfilling that agreement made by our mothers so long ago. And I don't think it will prove to be so intolerable for you. After all, I have been told upon more than one occasion that I'm not exactly a loathsome specimen of a man," Alex remarked with an unabashed grin as he began moving closer to her again. Before she could escape this time, his hands closed about her wrists, forcing her to remain and face him.

"Marianna," he now spoke in a soft, resonant tone that caused her to glance up at him in confusion, "why don't you just admit that our marriage is inevitable?"

"Never!" she answered in a voice charged with emotion, squirming frantically within his grasp.

"I usually get what I want, you know," he stated in a low voice as he pulled her relentlessly toward him.

"Then you had better prepare yourself for defeat in this particular matter!" she defiantly asserted, finding herself perilously close to tears now, though she did not know why. The man was making her feel so strange, so frightened, and yet so very confused. "I do not love you! You do not love me! Surely you are not the sort of man who would be willing to ruin the rest of his life merely to fulfill an outdated family agreement!"

"But I'm not willing to marry you because of the arrangement," he told her, his golden gaze holding her own bewildered one. "You see, I believe I may already be falling in love with you."

"That—that's impossible! And, even if it were the truth, it wouldn't matter, for I most assuredly do not feel the same about you!"

"No?" he questioned softly, pulling her tight against him now. "Oh, not that you realize it yet. But you cannot deny that there is something very powerful between us, something that even you cannot resist. Why don't you just admit it?" he murmured as his head lowered, his face disturbingly close to hers. Marianna began fighting against him with all her strength, gasping as she read the fierce intent in his unwavering gaze, as his lips finally descended and triumphantly captured hers.

Alex proceeded to kiss her thoroughly, his lips

growing hard and demanding as Marianna attempted to pull away. She was aghast when she felt herself beginning to melt beneath his tender assault, her mind a turbulent whirl. She pushed against him one last time before one of his hands captured both of her wrists and he yanked her so closely against him that she felt seared by the heat emanating from his lithe, masculine body. She moaned softly as his lips sought a response from her, as she became overwhelmed by the strange sensations assailing her. His arm tightened about her so that she could scarcely breathe, and she was hardly aware of the moment when his other hand released her wrists and slowly moved to the pearl buttons of her highnecked bodice.

Alex kissed her again and again, his lips alternately tender and passionate, while his fingers began deftly undoing the delicate buttons. Marianna told herself that she should fight him, that she should not allow him to treat her so shamelessly, but she seemed powerless to stop him. She felt herself growing faint as his warm mouth trailed a fiery path downward from her lips to the slender column of her neck, then lower still to the rounded curve of her full breasts now revealed above her camisole and corset.

"No!" she cried breathlessly as his hand moved to gently clasp her breast, as his lips gently teased the exposed flesh. She became terribly frightened by what he was making her feel, and she abruptly renewed her struggles. "No!" she demanded in a louder voice, striking out at him now with clenched fists. She was surprised when he unexpectedly acquiesced and released her, the expression on his handsome face inscrutable as she flung herself to the opposite corner of the carriage. Her cheeks were flaming, her breathing quite uneven as she clutched at her bodice, snatching it closed as Alex merely stared across at her. A heavy, intense silence hung between them for several long moments as Marianna sought to regain her composure.

"How dare you!" she finally gasped, shocked at what he had done, at what she had allowed him to do. She silently berated herself again and again, though Alex was forced to bear the brunt of her anger.

"I dare for the simple reason that you are mine, because you belong to me now," Alex spoke with a solemn look on his face, though the corners of his mouth turned up almost imperceptibly. "I'll tell the driver to turn the carriage around now," he calmly announced.

"You're taking me home?" Marianna hopefully asked.

"No. I'm taking you to my grandmother's house. You'll remain there until our wedding. I certainly don't intend to let you out of my sight until we're safely wed!"

"I will not—" she began to protest hotly.

"You will!" Alex masterfully commanded in a deep voice that made it evident he would brook no further resistance. "You have absolutely no choice in the matter. You are going to marry me whether you agree to or not. And there'll be no more of these foolish attempts to escape! The wedding has already been arranged. Your father is your legal guardian, my dear, and he has decreed that I shall become your husband, that you shall be my wife. You have no choice!" he repeated, one hand moving upward to rap loudly upon the roof of the carriage. The driver apparently heard the signal and slowed the vehicle to a halt, then expertly reined the horses about and headed back toward town.

"Doesn't it make any difference to you that I happen to utterly despise you?" Marianna stormed, casting him what she hoped to be a particularly withering look.

"None," he replied with another mocking grin. "But I don't really believe that you despise me at all. Especially after the way you responded to me only a few short moments ago," he remarked, his eyes brimming with fond amusement, and something else that Marianna chose not to notice.

"Why, you . . . you . . ." she prepared to offer him a scathing retort, so angry she could not speak. She felt humiliated, and she once more contemplated throwing herself from the carriage, but bitterly realized that she could never hope to win against the man's superior strength.

"What's the matter, my dear? Don't tell me you've run out of insults to hurl at me?" Alex sardonically quipped, chuckling to himself.

Marianna glared murderously across at him and remained mulishly silent. It infuriated her that she felt so helpless against him, that her own father had placed her in such an abominable position. She was to be forced to become the wife of a man she thoroughly detested—sacrificed for the sake of family honor!

But, she reflected as a sudden thought occurred to her, all was not necessarily lost! If she did agree to go through with the wedding, not only would she be saving her family from disgrace, she would also be saving herself from the continuing rule of her autocratic, uncaring parent. No longer would she have to answer to her father, to do as he commanded. She would be free of him once and for all, free to live the life she chose.

Of course, she reminded herself as she returned her attention to the arrogant rogue across from her, who at the moment appeared deep in thought, she would have to manage to escape immediately after the ceremony. But no one would expect her to run away once the wedding had taken place! she thought triumphantly. Her family's honor would be saved, her father's last command would be obeyed, and she would be free!

How was she going to get away, though? she asked herself as she began plotting her escape. Andrei would probably be of no help after what had occurred this night. No, she would have to rely upon herself. She would have to find someone who would consider the handsome sum she was willing to pay to be well worth the risks.

As the carriage rolled past the docks, Marianna glanced outside, her eyes widening as she spied an unfamiliar ship anchored there. Another ship had arrived! she told herself in growing excitement, her mind spinning. Now she would be able to leave the island, return to Seattle, collect Maria, then return home to London!

I shall do it! she decided, feeling her entire body coming alive with renewed spirit and determination. She would marry Alex Donovan, but she would never be his wife!

Thinking of what had occurred between them in the carriage, she could feel herself hotly blushing again. But she would not think about that! She would not think about the way he made her feel. No, instead she would concentrate on the way he would react when he discovered his bride gone so soon after their wedding. She was now convinced that she would emerge the victor from the challenge Alex Donovan had offered her.

Six

Although Marianna's aunt and uncle, and also Alex's grandmother, considered it a bit unusual when Alex informed them that Marianna would be staying at the Countess's house until the wedding, none of them dared question Alex. They were only too pleased that the marriage was going to take place. Aunt Sonja and Uncle Frederick didn't even bother to inquire as to the reason Alex had come to fetch his future bride in the middle of the night, and Marianna was so furious with them that she would barely speak to them when they called upon her later that same day.

The wedding was arranged rather hastily. It was to take place a mere two days later. Marianna was at least grateful for the fact that she was allowed to spend much of the intervening time alone in her room, a lovely and spacious bedchamber which the Countess informed Marianna had once been used by her own daughter, Alex's mother.

By the time the wedding day arrived, Marianna was actually impatient for the ceremony to take place, for she had been fortunate enough to successfully bribe one of Countess Borofsky's servants into securing some vital information for her, information regarding the ship she had glimpsed from inside Alex's carriage. She was elated to discover that the ship was planning to sail the very afternoon after the wedding ceremony was scheduled, and she was more than ever determined that, with enough money, she would be able to persuade the captain to take her along.

Now, as she allowed one of the maids to assist her in preparing herself for the wedding, she was dismayed to feel certain nagging doubts. What if she failed to get away after the wedding? What if Alex managed to find her before she could leave Sitka? How could she bear the thought of Alex Donovan as her husband?

Her hands trembled slightly as she raised them to adjust the veil over her luxuriant raven tresses and sternly ordered herself to relinquish any thought of failure. She turned to face her image in the large, gilded mirror after the maid finally left her alone, and she gasped softly at her startling reflection.

The bridal gown she was wearing was exquisite! she thought, turning to view it from every angle. It was a highwaisted dress fashioned of gleaming white satin and delicate, spidery lace, the low, rounded bodice trimmed with tiny seed pearls, the full sleeves made of matching lace. It was indeed a beautiful gown, and Marianna admitted to herself that she looked splendid in it. However, the Countess had informed her that the dress had also belonged to Alex's mother, and Marianna suddenly frowned, experiencing a sharp twinge of guilt. The dress had been worn by a woman in love, a bride eager to be joined in matrimony with her husband. What right did she, Marianna, have to wear it, when she felt nothing but extreme dislike for her future husband?

Nothing? that insistent voice in the back of her mind asked, causing her to whirl angrily away from the mirror and her gleaming reflection. It was true that Alex Donovan disturbed her, that he was able to make her angrier than anyone else had ever been able to do, that he was both arrogant and handsome, as well as hatefully domineering! She frowned again as she recalled the scene in the carriage the night before last. Perhaps some women found such a man irresistibly attractive, but she most certainly could not be counted among their number! She heaved an angry sigh and turned back to the mirror, her color a becomingly rosy hue.

If she could endure the next few hours, she would no longer have to so much as think of Alex Donovan, save for the time that she demanded an annulment, which would be as soon as possible upon her return to London. She possessed several friends in high office there, and she was confident that one of them would be able to extricate her from this unwanted marriage when she apprised him of the true facts. She would never again have to be reminded of the scoundrel who had served to make her life miserable for these few days!

He hadn't even bothered to speak with her beyond the merest of civilities since bringing her to his grandmother's house. He had behaved as if she were nothing more than mere chattel for him to treat as he pleased! Since he had barely glanced in her direction, he had been unable to see the contemptuous glares she shot him. But, she consoled herself once more, the man would soon be served his due!

Marianna spoke very little as she rode along in the carriage as it made its way toward the church in the center of the town, a small, beautiful building with stained glass windows and surprisingly impressive architectural touches. It seemed as if everyone on the island who was acquainted with Countess Borofsky and her handsome grandson was in attendance, and there was much whispering among the guests regarding the obvious haste of the wedding. It was generally acknowledged, however, that the young couple must have been so taken with one another that they were naturally impatient to be wed.

The next hour passed with excruciating slowness for Marianna. She felt as if she were still trapped in some strange dream as her uncle led her down the long, narrow aisle to the accompaniment of the traditional wedding march. She glanced at the people who were standing and staring at her as she passed them, then looked ahead to where Alex Donovan stood awaiting her beside the altar.

He was smiling at her, appearing every bit as self-confident and arrogantly sure of himself as she knew him to be! He was undeniably handsome in his dark suit and spotless white shirt, his features tanned and golden above his collar, his sun-streaked auburn hair catching the lights inside the church. As his golden gaze captured hers, she was startled to see a certain glow come into those eyes, an unfamiliar light which perplexed her, confused her, and very nearly caused her to stumble before her uncle presented her trembling hand to the man who would become her husband within a few short minutes.

I cannot go through with this! Marianna frantically thought as she felt Alex clasp her hand in one of his large ones, pulling her insistently forward as the two of them faced the minister in his starched white robes. She peered sideways at Alex through the folds of her whispery veil, willing herself to remain calm as she felt her heart racing.

Before she quite knew what was happening, the minister was quietly asking if she would agree to take Alex Donovan as her husband, to love him, honor him, to obey him. She visibly hesitated then, for she was suddenly seized with the powerful impulse to turn and flee, to run as if her life depended upon it. How could she possibly repeat such vows when she fully intended to break them as soon as possible? she asked herself in increasing panic.

"She does," Alex answered for her in a low, steady tone, causing her to swiftly raise her eyes to his handsome face in anger. She opened her mouth to vigorously deny it, but the look which passed between them in that moment told her that she must go through with it, that there was no turning back.

"I—I do," she finally murmured as the minister stared expectantly at her.

After a brief prayer and a few more words, Alexander Nicholai Michael Patrick Donovan and Marianna Natasha Vorina Markova were declared to be husband and wife. Marianna felt numb as Alex reached out for her, and she did not come to life until his strong arms slipped about her and his lips claimed hers in the traditional kiss. She attempted to push away from him, but he held her fast, forcing her to endure a very long and decidedly passionate kiss. When he finally released her, her cheeks were brightly flaming, her beautiful eyes blazing, and the appreciative assembly laughed and softly cheered their approval.

"Now you must smile and behave as if you are the happiest woman alive," Alex mischievously whispered into her ear as he grasped her elbow and began leading her back down the aisle, a broad smile on his own face.

"I could not accomplish that even if I were the most talented actress in all the world!" Marianna seethed in response, relieved when they finally reached the back of the church. She immediately jerked her arm away, turning her back upon her new husband as she disdainfully lifted her head and began marching outside into the cool summer day. She could hear Alex's low rumble of laughter behind her, and she gasped as he caught up with her and lifted her up into the carriage for the short ride back to his grandmother's. A celebration had been planned and insisted upon by Countess Borofsky.

"Aren't you the least bit curious as to what I have planned for our honeymoon?" Alex questioned with a slight grin as he sat across from her in the carriage.

"No!" Marianna snapped, her nerves stretched nearly to the limit.

"Just the same, I can assure you that you will enjoy it. In every way," he added with another devilish twinkle in his golden eyes. He laughed softly once more, quite pleased with the way things were going. Now that he had succeeded in getting the beautiful little spitfire to the altar, he would waste no time in making her love him as he was now certain he loved her. Though he realized he wouldn't be afforded much time in which to woo his new bride, he knew that he could do it. He would win her heart and make her admit that they were indeed meant for one another.

Marianna merely narrowed her eyes at him, her mouth compressing into a thin line of displeasure. She was almost sick with impatience, anxious to put her plan into action. She dared not think about what would become of her if she were unable to escape. Just the thought of Alex Donovan touching her again, kissing her again as if he owned her, was enough to make her more determined than ever to get away!

When they arrived back at the house, Alex led his unusually quiet new wife into the ballroom. Several people had already arrived, and it was not long before the grand house was filled with the sounds of music and laughter. Alex and Marianna were toasted again and again by the throng of well-wishers, and the members of the two families united by the marriage beamed in happy approval, except for Andrei, who secretly wondered what in the world his headstrong cousin was planning now.

Marianna found herself unable to stray very far from the watchful eye of her new husband. But when he became involved in conversation with several of his old friends, she finally managed to slip away and hasten up the winding staircase to her room. She didn't know exactly how long it would be before Alex or someone else noticed her absence, so she hurried to remove her wedding gown and don her traveling suit. She once more stuffed a few of her belongings into her carpetbag and clutched it in one hand as she hurried from her room, then crept down the hallway to the servants' stairway.

Satisfied that she had remained unobserved, she scurried across the drive to the rows of carriages, careful to remain unseen by any of the drivers who were talking and partaking of the wedding punch generously provided for them. Finding a carriage left unattended, she climbed unobtrusively up into the driver's seat and took a firm grip upon the reins, snapping them lightly and causing the horses to set off at a swift pace. She maneuvered the carriage easily through the streets to the dock where the ship was preparing to weigh anchor. Quickly leaving the carriage in charge of a young man she paid handsomely to return it to the Countess's house, she hurried across the wooden planks of the dock and swiftly marched up the gangplank and aboard the moderately sized steamship.

"Here now, miss!" she heard a man's voice rumble behind her. She whirled to face a tall, burly fellow who appeared to be the very man she wished to find, judging from his captain's coat and cap. "What are you doing on board? Can't you see that we're fixing to cast off?" He was much older than Marianna and appeared kind enough, though he was frowning at her in obvious annoyance.

"You're the captain of this ship, are you not?" she breathlessly asked.

"That I am, but you'll have to leave now," he insisted, taking hold of her arm and propelling her back toward the gangplank.

"One moment, please!" Marianna exclaimed, hanging back. "I wish to become one of your passengers!"

"We're not carrying any passengers this trip. This is a cargo ship now, miss. And we're not equipped to take on any females!" he answered with another frown and a curt shake of his head.

"But I'm willing to pay you very well for your troubles! I need desperately to get away from Sitka!" she pleaded, gazing up at him with tears effectively gathering in her beautiful eyes. "I can't explain it all to you now, but I simply must leave this island, and without further delay!" she added, withdrawing a silk handkerchief from her skirt pocket and raising it gracefully to her eye, hoping that the man would be moved by her tears. She was satisfied when he appeared to hesitate for a moment, and she hurried to suggest, "If we could just go below, I'll try and explain my predicament to you. I . . . I just don't know what I'm going to do if I don't get back to Seattle soon," she said, her voice breaking upon the last word as she began weeping dramatically into the handkerchief, watching from the corner of her eye as the man shifted uncomfortably before her.

"Well, all right. I don't suppose it will hurt to hear what you have to say," he finally capitulated, escorting her below. It didn't take Marianna long to convince him to grant her passage on his ship, especially when she presented him with quite a large sum of money, with the promise of more to come if he would see her safely to Seattle.

As she watched Sitka growing smaller and smaller in the distance from her vantage point in the tiny, airless cabin the captain had assigned her, Marianna smiled to herself. If only she could see Alex Donovan's face when he discovered that she had outwitted him! However, she was surprised to feel a certain sadness tempering her sense of triumph, a sadness she didn't understand. Perhaps it was simply because she had actually grown quite fond of Sitka itself, had come to appreciate the island's peaceful beauty and tranquil atmosphere.

But, she reflected as she staunchly turned away from the porthole, she would soon be in London again, back where she belonged. She was resolved to put these past several days behind her and get on with her life as if none of that had ever happened, as if Alex Donovan had never entered her life. Why then was she feeling what seemed to be disappointment at the thought of resuming her rather uneventful life?

Less than a quarter of an hour later, Marianna was surprised to hear the ship's engines quieting, even more startled to hear shouting above. Curious as to what could possibly be happening, she quickly left the confines of her cabin and proceeded to the steps that led up to the deck, unmindful of the captain's stern admonition that she remain below and out of sight of the crew. She now paused upon the top step as she perceived voices raised in anger.

"And I'm telling you that I will have a look at your passenger!" Marianna heard a familiar voice demanding.

"Alex!" she gasped aloud, her eyes widening in profound shock. How had he found her? How on earth had he been able to come on board the ship once they had cast off? She stepped forward, remaining concealed behind the small door as she peered around it, experiencing another wave of fearful dismay as her eyes fastened on the handsome, angry countenance of her new husband.

"And I say that you've no right to make any demands on board my ship!" the captain growled, scowling fiercely at the younger man who towered above him despite his own considerable height. "Just what the hell do you mean by chasing after us in that blasted schooner of yours, anyway?"

"I was told that a woman came on board your ship shortly before you sailed. I have reason to believe that the woman in question is my wife!" Alex spoke with a grim expression on his face.

"Your wife?" the captain repeated, obviously surprised. "She didn't say anything about a husband," he mumbled, half to himself.

"Nevertheless, I believe the woman on board is indeed my wife. And I wonder if you're aware of the fact that I could have you charged with kidnapping?" Alex threatened.

"Kidnapping! Now wait just a minute!" the captain blustered. "She told me she was running away from a cruel stepfather. Said she had been beaten and was desperate to get to Seattle to her cousin there. She sure as hell didn't say anything about being a runaway wife!"

"I'm willing to forget your part in the matter if you'll just forget you ever saw her. Now, where is she?" Alex demanded.

The captain hesitated for a fraction of a second, cursing inwardly as he realized that he'd never be able to collect the rest of the money the young woman had promised him. There was still the chance that the man before him was lying, but he certainly didn't look like any stepfather!

"All right," the older man responded with a deep frown, sorry that he'd ever let the girl on board, "she's below."

Marianna gasped in alarm as Alex began striding purposefully across the deck toward the steps where she was hidden. She turned and desperately flew toward her cabin once more, closing the door and bolting it behind her, not realizing that it was a futile gesture. For within the space of a few short moments, she watched wide-eyed as Alex easily kicked the door open, the flimsy bolt splintering the doorframe as it gave way.

"So it is you after all," Alex calmly stated as he ducked his head and entered the cabin, his steady gaze resting upon Marianna's pale face. "I will not go back with you!" she breathlessly exclaimed, her voice not entirely steady as she glared across at him. This was a very different Alex Donovan from the one she had seen thus far. Gone was the laughing, cocky rogue who continually mocked her with his disarming smiles. In his place stood a flinty-eyed stranger who suddenly seemed extremely dangerous, though he still behaved quite calmly. In his golden eyes, however, she could see barely concealed fury, and she grew frightened.

Alex moved with a swiftness that amazed her, his hands grasping her firmly about the waist before she could move. He picked her up and tossed her over one shoulder as if she were nothing more than a sack of meal, his muscular arms closing about her legs to hold her as he turned about and stalked from the cabin.

"Put me down! I will not go back with you! I will not be your wife, Alex Donovan! I hate you! Do you hear me? I hate you!" she shrieked, pummelling his broad back with her clenched fists. He ignored her completely, however, climbing the steps with his unwilling burden and marching back across the deck toward where his own ship was waiting. Marianna could feel her face burning as she heard the laughter from the crew, and she glanced toward the captain to plead with him for help, further infuriated to see that even he was now smiling as Alex carried her to the side and proceeded to toss her unceremoniously overboard into the brawny arms of one of his own crew.

"Sorry to have troubled you, Captain," Alex politely remarked as he turned back to the man for a brief moment. "But, it never pays to become involved in these domestic matters, does it?" He chuckled softly, then climbed back down the rope ladder which had been flung over the side. He had had a devil of a time getting the man to allow him to board the larger ship in the first place, only succeeding when he mentioned something about a mistake in the man's cargo. Alex's crew, consisting of three trusted men, expertly guided the smaller vessel to a safe distance as the steamship's engines roared again and it continued on its way, now minus its one passenger.

"That was a very foolish thing to do, my dear wife," Alex remarked to Marianna as he began moving toward her, his handsome face unsmiling as he paused to tower above her. The warm sunlight beat down upon them as the masted schooner sliced through the blue-green water, the color almost a perfect match for Marianna's flashing eyes.

"I told you that I will not go back with you!" she announced once more in a tremulous voice, still unable to believe that he had found her, that she had failed to escape him.

"We're not going back to Sitka," he told her, his voice very low as he stared down at her.

"What do you mean?" she asked in bewilderment. "Where are you taking me?"

"Welcome aboard for our honeymoon cruise, my dearest little bride. We're heading for Juneau. And I can assure you that we're going to take as long as possible to get there!" Alex replied with a decidedly meaningful gleam in his eyes as his arm snaked out to catch her about the waist, pulling her across the deck with him.

Seven

Alex thrust Marianna roughly inside the cabin that had been prepared for them, a surprisingly spacious room that was furnished quite tastefully. There was a three-quarter bed near one corner, a table and two chairs, and a carved oak chest. It was a decidedly masculine room, with its warm, rich tones of gleaming wood and brass, and it was softly illuminated by the late afternoon sunlight filtering in through the sheer curtains at the half-dozen portholes. Marianna, however, was in no mood to admire her husband's taste in décor, however, and she whirled to face him squarely as he slammed the door resoundingly behind them.

"I have never been treated so shamefully in all my life! You are little better than a barbarian, Alex Donovan! How dare you humiliate me in front of all those men that way! Did it never occur to you to treat me with at least a small degree of respect and common courtesy, instead of constantly manhandling me and dragging me about as you seem so prone to do?" she stormed, her color becomingly high and her bosom heaving with indignation.

"You deserved far worse than that for deserting your husband, Mrs. Donovan, and so shockingly soon after the wedding, at that!" Alex countered with biting sarcasm, no evidence of his customary good humor in his piercing gaze as he remained near the doorway, facing her across the room. It was quite obvious that he was just as incensed as his wife, but Marianna was determined not to allow herself to be intimidated by him.

"I have tolerated all I can from you! You have done nothing but degrade me and insult me from the first moment we met! I insist that you allow me to proceed to Seattle, to return home to London where I belong. I demand my freedom from you without further delay!"

"You belong nowhere but with your husband," he curtly answered, striving to keep his own damnable temper in check. He had never been quite so angry in his entire life as that moment when he discovered that his new bride had fled. Nor so absolutely determined. "You are my wife now, Marianna. It's time you started accepting that unalterable fact!"

"I refuse to be your wife!" she cried, bristling beneath his golden stare. She abruptly presented her back to him, her stance proud and rigid as she stared out unseeingly toward the passing landscape and sparkling waters.

"Whatever possessed you to run away like that?" Alex unexpectedly demanded, crossing the few feet that separated them in two long strides. "What the hell made you think that I'd ever let you go?"

"I agreed to marry you, but not to be your wife, not to live with you!" Marianna snapped with a defiant shake of her head, her raven curls streaming willfully out of their pins and cascading riotously about her face and shoulders. What was she to do now? she frantically wondered, her mind racing about for an answer to her dilemma. How was she going to make him see that they did not belong together, that their marriage was nothing more than a farce? It suddenly occurred to her that perhaps the wisest course of action at this particular time would be to attempt to calmly reason with him. She therefore sought to regain her composure and conceal her inner wrath as she turned slowly to face him again, outwardly cool and poised.

"Mr. Donovan," she began, her voice steady, "I agreed to marry you for the sake of my family's honor, and for no other reason. As you yourself once reminded me, I had no choice in the matter. I was compelled to go through with today's ceremony in order to fulfill that ridiculous arrangement between our two families. Therefore, you must see that we cannot possibly remain together as if truly husband and wife. Why, we are still virtual strangers to one another!" she pointed out.

"On the contrary," Alex disagreed, a faint smile playing about his lips now, his eyes never leaving her face as he edged a trifle closer, towering above her and making her feel extremely uncomfortable, "I think we know each other very well. There are certainly many fascinating details about my life you have yet to learn, and there is a great deal I wish to learn about your own," he remarked with a brief grin, his anger apparently forgotten. "But, understand me, my dear bride," he spoke with a grim look on his handsome face, his eyes gleaming dully, "you are mine now. And I have every intention of holding what belongs to me!"

"I do *not* belong to you!" Marianna vehemently denied, her temper flaring once more in spite of her resolve to remain calm. "I want no part of you! I shall return to London, where I shall seek an annulment of this so-called marriage with all haste. I shall never belong to any man, and most especially not to you!" She pushed past him with all her might, flying to the door and wrenching it open, only to shriek loudly in frustrated dismay as Alex caught her and yanked her back inside, lifting her off her feet with one powerful arm about her slender waist as he kicked the door closed once more.

Marianna fought him like a tigress then, so desperate by this point that she was hardly aware of what she was doing. She kicked and flailed against him in a frenzy, her back pressed against his muscular body as he held her suspended in air. Her struggles were momentarily stilled as he laughed softly in her ear and lovingly murmured, "What a little firebrand you are, my love! It will give me great pleasure to tame you. But, never fear, I'll not attempt to break that admirable spirit of yours!"

"I am not your love!" she hotly retorted, twisting within his grasp as she finally succeeded in placing a well-aimed kick to his right shin. She gasped in astonishment as she was released and stumbled forward until she managed to regain her balance, then spun about to continue the battle. Her freedom, however, was short lived, for in the next instant Alex seized her again and pulled her hard against his unyielding body, his lips crushing hers with startling swiftness.

Marianna could feel hot tears stinging her eyelids as Alex kissed her, his lips warm and fiercely demanding upon hers, his powerful arms allowing her no possible escape. She wasn't certain if it was her new husband she feared so desperately or herself, but she staunchly refused to surrender to him, willing herself to fight him with the very last of her strength. Her firm resolve did not last long, however, for she felt a disturbing lightheadedness assailing her as his lips became more tender and seductively persuasive, his hands more gentle as they caressed her soft curves. It was then that she decided to try a new tactic, and she suddenly became cold and impassive within his embrace. Alex raised his head to glare down at her, his countenance appearing almost savage in the soft light of the cabin.

"No, Marianna," he murmured in a voice barely above a whisper. "No, my love, you'll not remain cold to me! I'm going to make you want me as much as I want you. I'm going to make you care for me as I care for you!"

"You don't care for me at all!" she cried, meeting his gaze with bitter disbelief. "You could not possibly care for me and treat me this way!"

"You're wrong," he quietly stated as she remained still within his embrace for one brief moment. "It's because I do care that I want you to be my wife in every way, that I want you to share my life. I care more than I ever believed possible. I went through absolute hell when I discovered you gone today!"

"Only because you view me as your possession, because you regard me as some sort of prize that you won and is now to be guarded!" Marianna flung at him, renewing her frantic struggles.

"You're much more to me than a mere possession, my love. You're a beautiful, desirable, passionate woman, and I'm going to make you realize that you were meant to be mine, that you were indeed fashioned to be my mate! Oh no, sweet wife, you'll not remain cold to me for long!" Alex vowed commandingly, before his lips swooped down upon hers and he began kissing her with an impassioned vengeance. His arms tightened about her like bands of steel, and Marianna began to grow faint as her traitorous body began to respond. But her mind still told her that she should never surrender, never give in to the strange weakness she was feeling, the deep, unfamiliar yearning that was building like a flame inside of her as his lips moved upon hers.

She moaned softly as he lifted her in his arms and carried her slowly toward the bed. She was perilously close to feeling beyond all rational thought now, as she became aware only of Alex, of his sensuous masculinity, his strong arms tenderly lowering her to the softness of the down quilt. As soon as she felt the bed beneath her, however, a semblance of reason returned to her and she scrambled quickly away, crying out in alarm as she felt her full skirts caught by Alex's hand, leaving her helplessly poised for flight upon the edge of the bed.

"No!" she spat at him, attempting to jerk her skirts from his firm grasp. "I will not be raped by you!"

"Raped?" Alex loudly repeated, momentarily taken aback by her declaration. He startled her by throwing back his head and laughing in pure, unbridled amusement, causing Marianna to tug at her captured skirts with an even more furious determination.

"I refuse to surrender myself meekly to you like some sort of trollop!" she raged, then gasped in utter dismay as the buttons which fastened her velvet skirts gave way beneath the increasing pressure which now strained them beyond their limit.

"I can promise you that rape was not at all what I had in mind!" Alex sardonically quipped, one eyebrow raised mockingly as he masterfully yanked the skirts swiftly off and away from Marianna, leaving her clad in her fitted jacket and petticoat. She would have tumbled to the floor if not for his arm snaking out to catch hold of her ruffled petticoat, and she began slapping viciously at his hand as she cried, "How dare you! Let go of me!" She tugged with all her might, finally managing to slide from the bed, but the unmistakable sound of her petticoat tearing caused her to draw up short. She could scarcely believe it when her eyes lowered and she viewed herself clad in nothing more now than her velvet jacket and undergarments. Her long, shapely legs in their black stockings were revealed beneath her fine silk, lace-edged bloomers, which reached only to just above her knees. She glanced toward Alex, her cheeks flaming, only to discover that he was staring at her in open admiration, visually caressing the enticing form presented to him. She turned and ran as he leapt from the bed to give chase.

"You can't escape me this time, Marianna. What's going to happen between us is inevitable!" Alex declared as Marianna positioned herself behind the questionable security of the table and chairs. As Alex lunged to one side, his arm reaching out for her, she picked up one of the small wooden chairs and cast it in his path, causing him to curse as he stumbled over it.

"If you dare to lay a hand on me again, Alex Donovan, I shall jump overboard!" Marianna dramatically vowed, dodging him again by fleeing to the other side of the table.

"I wouldn't make such rash statements if I were you!" he retorted with an unconcerned grin. Apparently tiring of this latest contest between them, he lifted the table and sent it crashing across the cabin, then swiftly moved forward to catch an open-mouthed, wide-eyed Marianna. As she screamed and fought him, he tossed her unceremoniously back upon the bed, then placed his hands upon her shoulders and one of his legs across both of hers to keep her a prisoner beside him.

"I think we've had enough of these little games for now, Mrs. Donovan. There's no need for you to be afraid of me. I give you my word that I'm going to do my best to see to it that you enjoy our honeymoon," he told her, smiling boldly down at her, his face mere inches from her own. Before she could open her mouth to offer a bitter reply, his lips silenced her with a searing kiss. Within seconds, his hand had unfastened the buttons of her jacket to reveal the fullness of her breasts above her corset and lace-trimmed camisole.

"No! Please, no!" Marianna whispered in desperation as his lips began roaming almost feverishly across her face, caressing her slender neck, then gently brushing the vulnerable spot where her pulse was beating so rapidly. As his lips moved downward to tease the pale flesh of her rounded breasts, she caught her breath, her head moving restlessly from side to side, her mass of dark curls fanning out across the pillow in splendid disarray.

The touch of Alex's warm mouth on the tops of her breasts caused her to squirm uncomfortably, and she was perplexed and confused by the sensations she was experiencing. Her legs felt suddenly languid and weak, and she was shocked when her hands moved with a will of their own, her fingers entwining themselves in Alex's thick auburn hair as he relentlessly continued with his passionate assault.

Marianna did not understand what was happening to her, could not comprehend why she was reacting as she was—only that she was rendered powerless to stop Alex as his hand now crept inside the waistband of her bloomers. His other hand soon followed as his lips returned to claim hers, his large hands clasping her firmly rounded buttocks as he slowly moved to position himself above her, bringing her softness upward against the evidence of his increasing desire. She gasped again as she felt him impatiently tugging the undergarment from her lower body, the cool air upon her feverish skin. She trembled violently as his long fingertips caressed her between her pale thighs. He kissed her until her mouth felt swollen and bruised, wreaking havoc upon her senses. Then, he was gone. He stood beside the bed, hastily divesting himself of his own clothing.

Marianna suddenly realized that she was lying half-naked upon Alex's bed, that she had lost control for the past several minutes. She panicked then and attempted to escape him one last time, drawing the quilt about her as she bounced off the bed and headed for the doorway, not knowing what she was going to do, only that she was terribly frightened of what would happen if she did not flee. She got no farther than the foot of the bed this time, before Alex caught her and jerked the quilt from her body, then turned her to face him as they stood together beside the bed.

She gasped in shocked amazement when she saw that her husband was now entirely naked, and her eyes tightly closed as her face burned. But, he allowed her no time for further thought, lifting her high in his arms and placing her back upon the bed, then lowering his body atop hers. He impatiently ripped away the upper half of her camisole, exposing even more of her full bosom to his gaze. His lips returned to hers, his hand once again moving to the sensitive juncture of her thighs. Within a short time Marianna once more became aware only of the strange, overwhelming feelings Alex was creating in her with his skilled, tempestuous lovemaking.

"Marianna, my beautiful love," he whispered in her ear, before parting her thighs with his knee and carefully easing himself into her inviting warmth. She cried out softly at the sharp pain, but it was swiftly followed by a rapturous yearning that threatened to consume her. Her hands instinctively grasped Alex's shoulders for support as he moved faster and faster, before skillfully bringing them both to a bursting fulfillment as they crested the waves of passion.

Marianna was left quite pale and breathless at what had just passed between them. Alex lay beside her now, cradling her in his strong arms, neither of them speaking a single word. Finally, Alex raised his head to peer downward at his wife's face, gently moving aside the curtain of dark curls that concealed her expression from him.

"Marianna?" he quietly said.

She lay perfectly still, her eyes tightly closed against the onslaught of fresh tears. She refused to look at him, to answer him, and he wisely decided that it was best not to force the issue for the present. Later, he told himself with an overwhelming feeling of contentment, there would be time for talk between them. He sighed and lay back down, drawing his wife's curved form up tight against him, his own eyes closing peacefully.

Marianna bit at her lip to prevent the sobs that were welling up inside of her from escaping into the quiet stillness of the cabin. She silently berated herself again and again, until she was finally overcome with both emotional and physical exhaustion and at last drifted off into troubled sleep beside her husband.

Eight

Marianna awoke with a start, her eyelids fluttering open in alarm as she felt herself being turned gently upon her side. She immediately attempted to sit upright in the bed, only to be firmly pushed back against the pillow.

"What are you doing?" she breathlessly demanded.

"Sorry to wake you," Alex replied amiably, his hands busily working at the laces of her corset. "I thought it was about time I got you out of this torturous contraption. There!" he pronounced in triumph as he finally loosened the last string.

"I didn't ask for your assistance!" snapped Marianna with a frown, gasping as Alex proceeded to yank the corset away from her. He surprised her further by sending it flying across the cabin to land on the floor near the doorway.

"I don't want you wearing the blasted thing from now on," he commanded, his gaze returning to his wife's indignant countenance, then moving boldly and quite leisurely downward.

Marianna realized then that she was now totally exposed to his burning gaze, for he had already somehow managed to remove her shoes and stockings without disturbing her slumber. She hastily grabbed the sheet which lay bunched up at the foot of the bed and drew it up over her naked form to protect herself from that golden stare. Alex merely laughed softly at her defensive action and quipped, "It's entirely too late for such maidenly modesty, Mrs. Donovan!" He noticed the sudden apprehension in her lovely eyes and reluctantly turned away, climbing from the bed with an easy, animal grace as Marianna kept her eyes downcast in embarrassment, though she did catch a glimpse of his muscular thighs and buttocks when he turned to draw on his trousers. "I don't know about you, dear wife, but I happen to be famished! I'll have something brought down right away," he cheerfully declared, smiling down at her again as she stiffened beneath the covers. She slowly raised her eyes to his face, blushing as her gaze encountered the broad expanse of his bare chest.

"I'm not hungry!" she quietly retorted.

"Nevertheless, I'm going to see to it that we're provided with our traditional wedding night feast," Alex answered, flashing her another disarming grin. As he left the cabin, Marianna glared resentfully after him.

She vaguely wondered what time it was, for the cabin was still softly bathed in pale golden light. Glancing up at the clock which hung on the opposite wall, she noted with mild surprise that it was half past eight in the evening. Already familiar with the unusually long hours of daylight in summertime Alaska, she realized that it wouldn't even begin to approach twilight for another hour or two. The fact that the sun had not even set made what had earlier occurred all the more shameful, she bitterly reflected as she turned upon her stomach in the bed.

"Why? Why did I allow it to happen?" she berated herself aloud, heaving a sigh as she closed her eyes and buried her face in the pillow. Why was Alex Donovan able to make her lose control of herself whenever he kissed her, whenever he touched her as he had done? What power did the man possess to make her forget everything so easily?

It was still so painfully humiliating, she thought, recalling the manner in which she had clung to him, had behaved as a wanton in his arms! It was as if someone else had taken possession of her body and forced her to behave so unlike herself. And yet, she told herself with another long sigh, it had been none other than Marianna Markova who had allowed herself to be swept away by passion, passion for a man she supposedly detested. Only, she realized with dismay, she was no longer Marianna Markova. She was now, in every sense of the word, Alex Donovan's wife. Marianna Donovan.

What am I to do now? she asked herself in desperation, rolling back upon her side as she pulled the covers up to her chin and stared unseeingly up at the ceiling. She, who had always appeared so proud and aloof, who had always been pleased with her ability to mask her true feelings, now felt utterly defeated and confused. How could she respond so passionately to Alex Donovan? And what was to become of her now?

"I'd advise you to get out of that bed and put something on in order to spare yourself considerable embarrassment," Alex remarked as he entered the cabin, interrupting her miserable, silent reverie. "Though I must confess that I find your present state of undress to be fetching, I don't think I'd care for my man Ivan to see you that way when he brings us our meal." His golden eyes were brimming with fond amusement, and Marianna could feel her face coloring. She hadn't even thought about the fact that she was still lying naked in the bed.

"Will you kindly turn your back so that I may get up?" she frostily asked as he continued to stare expectantly down at her.

"As I told you earlier, there's nothing to hide from me. I'm your husband now, remember?" he reminded her with a decidedly humorous gleam in his eyes.

"I will not get up with you standing there staring at me!"

"All right then," he startled her with his easy capitulation, "just this once. After all, it certainly wouldn't do for a new husband to deny his bride such a simple request, would it?" He slowly turned about to face the door once again.

Marianna hesitated a moment before easing herself from beneath the covers and out of the bed, though she quickly snatched the quilt off the floor and draped it around her naked body as she stood up. It was then that she saw her clothing strewn all about the cabin, and she blushed furiously once more as she recalled the manner in which her clothes had been torn from her body. Now she was faced with a decidedly uncomfortable dilemma, for she hadn't the vaguest idea of what she was to wear.

"You'd best hurry, Mrs. Donovan. Our supper will be arriving soon," Alex cautioned, folding his arms across his chest.

"I don't have anything to wear," Marianna finally admitted, feeling both angry and helpless.

"I forgot to tell you," Alex said, nodding his head to indicate the carved chest a few feet away, "I had some of your things brought on board before the wedding. I believe you'll find everything you need in there."

Marianna narrowed her eyes at his broad back, reflecting that the arrogant man appeared to have thought of everything in preparation for their little cruise. But she quickly pattered across the floor in her bare feet and opened the chest, drawing out several articles of clothing and dressing as quickly as she could. When a knock sounded at the door a short time later, she was attired in a simple frock of soft blue wool that molded her well-formed, albeit corsetless, curves to perfection. She was in the process of gathering up her thick raven tresses and coiling them into some semblance of order when Alex opened the door to admit a man very near his own age. The other man was smaller and thinner, his features dark and not unattractive, and he smiled broadly at Marianna as he carried the large silver tray of food into the cabin.

"Marianna, this is Ivan. He's been with my family since we were boys. Ivan, this is my new wife," Alex announced, moving to set the table and chairs to rights so that Ivan could place the tray upon the table.

"Very glad to have you aboard, Mrs. Donovan," Ivan politely remarked, nodding his head briskly in her direction.

"Thank you, Ivan," Marianna responded with a faint smile, flushing a bit beneath his admiring scrutiny. She wondered what the man must think of her, for he and the other crew members had been witnesses to the disgraceful manner in which Alex had dragged her off the other ship and then below to this cabin. In fact, she suddenly recalled, Ivan had been the one to catch her when Alex had tossed her down to the schooner! Her cheeks flamed even brighter as she hastily averted her face.

"That will be all for now, Ivan," Alex stated a bit gruffly, noting the way the other man couldn't seem to take his eyes off Marianna.

"Yes, Alex," Ivan mumbled, backing out of the cabin and nearly losing his balance as he stumbled upon the threshold. Alex closed the door after him, then began removing the covers from the plates upon the tray.

"Come, dear wife. I'm sure we could both do with a bit of sustenance. It's been a very long and—interesting day," he commented, causing Marianna to whirl about and look at him with a flash of anger in her eyes. She chose not to answer him, however, and merely seated herself at the table, discovering that she was suddenly quite hungry in spite of herself. She was grateful that the food proved to be quite delicious, and also that Alex did not attempt to engage her in conversation while the two of them ate their fill of the fresh poached salmon, creamed potatoes, fruit, and cheese. Afterwards, Alex announced that he was going to leave her alone for a time while he went back up on deck.

"I should like to have a bath," Marianna ventured to say before he left, hating to ask him for anything, yet setting aside her pride for the moment. She felt the overpowering need to soak her tired body in a tub of hot, soothing water.

"All the modern conveniences right at your fingertips," Alex replied as he sauntered across the cabin to open a narrow door that Marianna had not previously noticed. Inside was a water closet and a decorated hip bath. "Is there anything else you'd like, Mrs. Donovan?" he asked with a broad grin, his eyes dancing with obvious devilment.

"I would appreciate it if you would cease calling me that!"

"Why? It's your legal name now."

"Not by choice!"

"Then I'll have to think of something else to call you. A husband must have a pet name for his wife, you see," he said with a mocking smile, appearing deep in thought for a few seconds. "I know," he declared, smiling again as he moved toward the doorway, "I'll call you 'Annie.'"

"Don't you dare!" she cried indignantly, fuming as he opened the door and left her alone in the cabin.

It wasn't long before Ivan returned with two large

121

buckets of steaming hot water which he poured into the bathtub. He brought two buckets of cooler water a few minutes later, then left Marianna to her bath.

She swiftly undressed and eased herself down into the tub, filled nearly to the brim with water. She luxuriated in the comfort of the water's warmth for a while before taking up a cake of soap and scrubbing vigorously at her skin until it was pink and glowing. She stood and wrapped herself in the large, thick towel which hung beside the tub, then strolled back into the cabin, uncoiling her shining mass of hair and brushing it thoroughly. That done, she was intent upon retrieving the clothing she had left on the bed.

Alex, however, returned at that moment and he paused to stare at his beautiful young wife as she stood before him clad only in a towel, leaving very little indeed to his rather active imagination.

"I thought you would at least have the decency to knock before entering!" she angrily remarked, instinctively clutching at the towel to hold it secure. She noticed that Alex's own hair appeared damp, as if he too had taken a bath. She saw that he was now attired in a clean shirt and trousers as well, and that he carried his seaman's jacket in one hand.

"And I thought I had given you more than enough time," he responded with only the hint of a smile playing about his lips as he tossed his jacket negligently across one of the chairs. When he raised his eyes to her stormy face once more, there was a certain gleam in his golden gaze, an unfathomable expression on his handsome features as he continued to stare down at his wife in the darkening cabin. There was very little daylight left by now, but Marianna had left a single lamp burning in the small room where she had just bathed. Its light cast long shadows upon the opposite wall of the cabin as it played across their faces.

"Will you please allow me to dress?" Marianna firmly demanded. She felt a shiver travel the length of her spine, though she attributed it to the fact that she must be getting chilled from standing there in nothing more than a towel.

"That won't be necessary," Alex replied in a low, husky voice, reaching upward to begin unbuttoning his shirt as his eyes still held hers.

"What are you doing?" Her brilliant blue-green eyes grew very round as she watched him remove his shirt. He then took a seat in the chair and eased off both his boots, then stood once more to draw off the rest of his clothing while Marianna could only stand and watch helplessly and with inexplicable fascination. When she finally realized that she was staring at him, actually watching him undress, she whirled about to present her back to him.

"What's the matter, Annie?" Alex asked in a voice full of loving mischief.

"Don't call me that!" Marianna snapped, knowing full well that he had to be totally naked by then. She knew it was useless to try to run from him. And yet she told herself, she would not meekly surrender to him! She would not allow him to believe he had conquered her and become her master! No, she decided, her eyes bright with determination, she would continue to fight him. And eventually she would manage to escape him forever!

"You have no idea how very desirable you look in that towel, dear wife," he spoke behind her, "but, I'd like it a great deal more if we dispensed with such barriers between us!" he stated, his hands closing upon her shoulders now as he spun her swiftly about to face him.

"This will not be like the last time!" she bravely declared, her eyes flashing defiantly up at him as he towered above her.

"That's true. It won't. It will be quite different," Alex agreed, his voice deep and resonant as his head slowly lowered. He ignored Marianna's frantic struggles as he wrapped his muscular arms about her and drew her close, his lips touching hers with a gentle persuasiveness before growing increasingly passionate and demanding. Despite all of Marianna's firm resolve, she could feel herself melting against him again, and she hated both Alex and herself for it. His arms tightened about her with a fierce possessiveness as his mouth plundered hers, as his masculine hardness was pressed intimately against her trembling softness. She found it difficult to so much as squirm within his embrace as she still desperately told herself she must resist.

"Haven't you done enough harm already?" she tearfully cried as Alex's lips released hers for a brief moment and moved to nibble seductively at her ear.

"I don't seek to harm you, Marianna, only to love you," he murmured in a voice barely above a whisper, his hands gently clasping her buttocks as his lips returned to her mouth. Before she quite knew what was happening, the towel she had wrapped about herself was floating heedlessly to the floor below, and Alex's golden eyes seemed to scorch her skin as he momentarily drew back to feast upon her exposed loveliness.

Her smooth, silken skin still glowed from her bath, and her dark, abundant hair streamed wildly about her shoulders and fell to her slender waist, its gleaming blackness in vivid contrast to the shimmering paleness of her womanly curves. Her full breasts were firm and high, her legs long and graceful, her hips enchantingly rounded. She looked up into her husband's solemn countenance as if in a dream, unable to move or scarcely breathe as he continued to stare down at her. Her own gaze was then irrevocably drawn to his exposed masculinity, and she was awed by the absolute beauty of his well-muscled body. Every inch of his sun-bronzed form appeared lean and hard. She blushed as her eyes involuntarily fastened on the evidence of his growing desire.

"You're so very beautiful, my love," Alex softly murmured as he reached out for her again. Marianna, however, took a step backward, gazing up at him in overwhelming confusion. Once again, she did not seem to be her own self, and she could only utter a weak protest when Alex moved to lift her in his strong arms and carry her toward the bed.

"Please, Alex, please . . . don't," she managed to plead, her voice barely above a whisper.

"Don't fight it, Marianna," he huskily replied,

lovingly placing her upon the bed and lowering himself beside her. "It was meant to be this way between us." He grasped the arm she raised weakly to try to ward him off, placing it about his neck before claiming her lips with his own, his hands expertly caressing her curved hips and thighs. He was concentrating on making her want him as much as he wanted her, and Marianna dizzily realized that she was quite powerless to fight against the rising tide of desire he was so skillfully creating in her, the desire that threatened to consume her whenever he kissed her as he was doing now. His lovemaking held none of the furious swiftness of that first time, for now he was instead proceeding with excruciating slowness, patiently initiating her into the special, rapturous world that only the two of them could share.

Marianna moaned deep in her throat as his warm mouth moved to her breast, his tongue lazily and sensuously circling the nipple before he gently sucked the tantalizing peak. When he moved to do the same to her other quivering breast, his long fingers began enticingly stroking the delicate, secret place between her white thighs, causing her to move her head feverishly from side to side upon the pillow. He continued to arouse her with infinite tenderness, and Marianna was unable to deny the flames of ecstasy building deep within her.

She caught her breath sharply when he made it increasingly obvious that he was intent upon kissing each and every inch of her trembling flesh. She feebly attempted to protest, but his lips trailed a searing path downward, before she was gently turned upon her side in order for his masterful lips to caress the sensitive backs of her thighs, her smoothly rounded buttocks, and the satiny curve of her back.

By the time he took her in his arms once more and rolled so that she was beneath him, she was nearly beyond all thought, for he had purposefully and expertly seduced her into forgetting all about her earlier resolutions and denials. She was ready for him when he finally positioned himself above her and slowly eased within her velvety warmth, and her arms clasped him tightly to her as he increased their passion by moving more and more rapidly, until Marianna cried aloud at the waves of pleasure which shot through her when the two of them soared heavenward.

In the soft afterglow of their tempestuous union, Marianna could find no voice for words. She felt utterly drained, content for the moment to lie peacefully within Alex's warm embrace as they both sought to regain the normal tempo of their breathing. He cradled her against his broad chest, the fluffy mat of auburn hair which covered his skin now damp and curling.

"I told you it would be different this time," he remarked with a sigh of pleasure as he pulled her closer, his fingers brushing at the raven locks beneath his chin. He was startled a few seconds later when she suddenly pushed fiercely against him, rolling swiftly away and jerking the covers up over her nakedness. Her blue-green eyes were turned upon him in renewed anger, and they were brimming with unshed tears as she faced him in the semidarkness of the cabin.

"It should never have happened!" she cried, her thick tresses streaming about her face and shoulders in glorious disarray. "How could you do such a thing to me, when you know I want nothing more than to end this undesirable marriage and try to forget we ever met?"

"What just happened between us should finally prove to you that we were indeed meant to remain together as husband and wife!" Alex firmly insisted, attempting to draw her back down beside him, then frowning deeply as she resisted.

"It proves nothing to me beyond the contemptible fact that you are a pompous, arrogant, notorious seducer of unwilling women!"

"Isn't that somewhat of a contradiction, my dear?" he sardonically quipped, one eyebrow arched mockingly as the corners of his mouth turned up into a faintly amused smile.

"Oh!" seethed Marianna, her face blushing rosily. "How I despise you, Alex Donovan!"

"Really? That certainly isn't the general impression I received from you only a few short minutes ago." When she raised a hand to strike at him, he seized hold of her about her slender waist and pulled her abruptly back into his embrace, effectively holding her captive while she silently fumed. After several moments of struggling vainly against him, she appeared a bit more subdued, so Alex relaxed his hold a trifle as the two of them lay together in the bed.

"You know, you've displayed an amazing lack of

curiosity, Annie, my love," Alex spoke quietly, unperturbed when Marianna maintained a stony silence and stiffened in his arms. "You haven't once asked me why we're on our way to Juneau, nor what we're going to do once we reach our destination. And you've also never bothered to inquire about where the two of us will live once we return from our honeymoon." Again, she made it perfectly clear that she was determined to ignore him completely, prompting him to chuckle softly. "I must say, I've never seen such a lack of curiosity in a woman!"

"Perhaps that's because I do not care to know what you have in mind, because I do not intend to live with you anywhere!" she finally couldn't refrain from retorting. She was suddenly beginning to feel exhausted and sleepy, lying there warm and secure in Alex's arms as the ship rocked gently to and fro in the icy Alaska waters.

"Regardless of your misguided intentions, my dear little bride, I'll tell you what I have in mind. But not until morning. I think the two of us have had enough sparring for one day," he commented with a contented sigh, drawing the covers up over them both and keeping Marianna snugly against him.

She was much too weary to argue with him further. She was also much too weary to spend much time in self-recrimination for the impassioned, shocking manner with which she had responded to him. She closed her eyes and allowed him to hold her within the comfort of his strong arms as she drifted off into welcome unconsciousness.

Nine

Marianna stretched long and lazily in the warmth of the bed as she lay blissfully in that dreamy, hazy world which exists between sleep and wakefulness. Reluctantly easing her eyes open a trifle, she turned her head drowsily upon the pillow. It took several more seconds before she became fully aware of her surroundings and sat abruptly upright, glancing hastily down at the empty space beside her.

The memories of the previous night came flooding back into the front recesses of her mind, causing her to blush and groan inwardly at the recollection. Raising her knees toward her chest, she buried her face in the folds of the covers, her bare arms encircling her bent legs.

What had occurred immediately following her bath the night before had been humiliating enough, she miserably reflected, but she had then proceeded to respond brazenly to Alex yet again when he had awakened her with a tender, provocative kiss just before dawn, his knowing hands already boldly working their sensuous magic upon her soft, supple curves.

She raised her head and gazed at the spot in the bed where her husband had slept beside her, frowning pensively as she noted the slight indentation which still remained from the weight of his body. Heaving a sigh of resignation, she was forced to admit to herself that Alex Donovan's touch set her afire, that he possessed the ability to render her defenseless in that one particular area. The admission was not an easy one, but most definitely an undeniable one, given the ardent manner in which she had behaved upon three separate occasions.

What was happening to her? she asked herself in bewilderment as her eyes focused on a porthole, the morning sunlight already warming the chilled glass. How could she possibly react with such fire and abandon to Alex's lovemaking, when she had done nothing but proclaim both to him and to herself that she despised him? It surely wasn't possible to feel the reckless, dizzy passion she felt in his arms and truly dislike him, was it? she pondered in deep puzzlement, her beautiful features drawn into another slight frown. And had it truly been only yesterday, less than twenty-four hours ago, that she had been bound in marriage to him?

It was all so confusing! She had never reacted so violently to anyone in the course of her young life as she did to the dashing rogue she had married. Why was the man able to affect her so? And how on earth was she to deal with the swift and monumental changes that had been wrought in her life?

Tightly closing her eyes, she moved a hand to her forehead as she frowned yet again. Her mind, she mused as another tiny sigh escaped her lips, had borne so much confusion and turbulent contemplation throughout these past few days! It certainly wasn't at all like her to spend so much time in introspection. She asked herself once more why Alex Donovan had ever come into her life, why she had allowed herself to be wed to such a domineering, conceited, arrogant, irresistibly handsome scoundrel!

Impatiently tossing back the covers, she slid from the bed and padded across the floor into the small room where she had bathed the night before, faintly surprised to discover that her body felt slightly stiff and sore as she performed her morning toilette. She had finished dressing and was in the process of brushing out her mass of tangled locks when the door swung open to reveal Alex, who flashed her a particularly beguiling smile as he sauntered inside the cabin, his eyes moving intimately up and down the length of her body.

"I had thought to find you still abed, my love," he remarked, moving closer as she merely turned her back upon him and continued with her hair. She schooled her face to remain impassive as she glanced at his reflection in the mirror, and she was dismayed to feel her face coloring rosily as he closely watched her.

"And I had thought I might be afforded at least a moment's privacy!" she countered, slightly berating herself for the way her fingers trembled upon her raven curls as she angrily stuck a pin into their thickness. She was wearing a lovely gown of soft lilac, though she had been deeply annoyed to find that it fit her more snugly than usual as a result of her lack of a corset. She had been sorely tempted to lace herself up in the thing just to spite Alex, but had realized that he would in all likelihood merely strip it off her again without warning!

"I've been up for hours now," Alex replied, still staring intently at her. His sun-streaked hair, she noticed, was wind blown, his virile form encased in his dark blue seaman's garb. "I thought I'd let you sleep a while. I believe that to be the usual custom following the wedding night. Nevertheless, I'd say it was rather considerate of me, wouldn't you?" he teasingly queried, his golden gaze softening as she finally whirled about to face him.

"Considerate?" Marianna bristled. "You wouldn't know the meaning of the word!" She attempted to sweep disdainfully past him, but he caught her against him and pressed an unexpected kiss upon her parted lips. She was left feeling oddly disappointed when he just as suddenly released her, a smile on his handsome face once more.

"Why don't you come up on deck with me? I think I may have been a bit remiss in not allowing you some fresh air before now. It's a splendid morning, Annie."

She opened her mouth to retort that she'd not go anywhere with him, but her good sense triumphed over her resentment of him, for she realized that she really did want nothing more than to escape from the stifling confines of the cabin and bask in the warm sunshine and sea air above. She remained obstinately silent as she snatched up her cloak and preceded her husband from the room, climbing the few short steps to reach the polished deck. She was, however, uncomfortably aware of Alex's presence behind her as they stepped out into the glorious morning light.

Marianna was awed by the breathtaking beauty her eyes beheld as they scanned the passing landscape. The deep, rich blue waters were studded with forest-clad islands, islands of all shapes and sizes that were covered in varying shades of green. There were towering mountain summits that appeared to be reaching for the beckoning sky, huge glaciers, blue-tinted gleams of snow and ice among the mountain's pinnacles. The air was fresh and crisp and smelled faintly of the forest aromas and salty waters. The wind whipped playfully at Marianna's hair as she drew the hood of her cloak up over her head, reveling in the sheer splendor of the wonderfully clear day. She temporarily forgot all her perplexing problems and her animosity toward the man beside her.

"Why, it's . . . it's almost beyond description, it's so incredibly beautiful!" she remarked aloud, prompting Alex to smile to himself with pleasure as he led her farther out into the wind and sunshine. The two of them simultaneously grasped the rail for support as the schooner sped through the roughening swells, the salty spray threatening to soak them whenever the vessel encountered a large wave.

"You'll certainly never see anything like this elsewhere!" Alex spoke proudly, noting with satisfaction that Marianna didn't utter a single protest as he slipped a supporting arm about her shoulders. "Look there!" he instructed, pointing now to indicate a pair of bald eagles soaring majestically above the shore of a small island in the near distance. "This is what Alaska is all about, my love. This wild, free beauty you see before you!" He was forced to raise his deep voice to be heard above the roar of the wind, and Marianna glanced up at him in surprise when she detected the obvious love he held for his homeland.

Later, Alex introduced her to the other two crew members, young men much like Ivan who spoke politely and quite reverently to her. Throughout the remainder of the morning, she listened with increasing curiosity and interest as Alex told her about the various sights he pointed out to her. She became almost mesmerized by the country's magnificence and the sound of Alex's resonant voice. She watched as the ship passed several small icebergs floating peacefully by, and as a huge whale breached in the icy blue waters only a few yards away. She had never enjoyed nor appreciated the scenery on a voyage as she did now, and she was a little disappointed when Alex announced that it was time for them to go below for the noon meal.

"We'll be in Juneau within a couple of hours now," he told her as he leaned casually back in his chair and crossed his arms against his muscular chest, having already finished his plate of food. He peered across at his wife, who swiftly raised her eyes to his face as she slowly returned her glass of wine to the surface of the table.

135

"What then?" she asked after a moment's hesitation, dreading the answer. She had absolutely no notion of what to expect from him. The momentary truce the two of them had enjoyed while up on deck was now abruptly shattered as thoughts of the future intruded.

"So, you are indeed at least a bit curious!" commented Alex with a soft chuckle, his loving gaze fastened on her slightly flushed countenance.

"I merely wish to know how soon this so-called honeymoon will end!"

"It has most definitely been an authentic honeymoon, my love," he replied with another mocking grin. "But I take it you aren't enjoying our cruise?"

"How could I possibly enjoy it?" Marianna bitterly retorted, her beautiful face wearing a stormy expression, her brilliant eyes flashing blue-green fire as she abruptly rose to her feet and flounced away from the table. She turned back to face him with the unmistakable light of battle in her gaze once more, determined to have it out with him once and for all. "I was forced to wed you, Alex Donovan, despite the fact that you were little more than a stranger to me, despite the fact that you seemed to take some perverse pleasure in always taunting me and seeking to infuriate me at every turn! However, I did my duty. I did as my father commanded, as had been so rashly decreed by our families so long ago. Since then, I have been subjected to every possible form of humiliation and insult! You forcibly dragged me aboard this ship, keeping me here as a prisoner, only to . . . to—" she broke off, her cheeks glowing brightly as she sought for adequate words, her bosom heaving dramatically beneath the high-necked bodice of her gown.

"To ravish you?" Alex supplied in amusement, rising to his feet now as well and stepping slowly toward her, pausing inches away as she stared up at him in anxious expectation. His handsome face suddenly grew very solemn, his golden eyes faintly gleaming as he quietly said, "Whatever I've done, Marianna, I've done because I love you." He made no move to touch her, merely stood there towering above her as he closely scrutinized her reaction. Her reaction was one of silence and obvious bewilderment, for she had been astonished to feel the way her heart leapt within her breast at the sound of his words.

"You—you do not love me!" she finally murmured, swiftly averting her face as she silently scolded herself for feeling so breathless at his proximity to her. "You only wish to use me, to use my—my body!"

"Quite untrue," he calmly disagreed. "I want all of you, Annie. Each and every part of you, body and soul. I love you," he repeated. Her eyes met his once more as she proudly lifted her chin and defiantly cried, "You cannot possibly know what love is, Alex Donovan!"

"Tell me, dear bride, when did you become such an authority on the subject of love?" he teasingly inquired, his eyes brimming with indulgent humor now. "Can you honestly say that you have ever been in love?"

"No," she hated to admit, her gaze moving downward as he smiled at her. She had experienced little of love in her young life. Her mother, she had been told, had loved her more than anything else in the world. But her father, she sadly recalled, had never shown her much compassion or affection. Only her cousin Maria had loved her, had truly cared about her all these years. She glanced back up at the man before her and stubbornly declared, "But I know perfectly well what love is supposed to be! And you appear to have no insight whatsoever into that particular emotion!"

"That's where you're wrong," he countered, still making no move to reach out for her as he stared down into the depths of her eyes. "For I know now, without a single doubt, that I love you. And, what's more," he added with only the hint of a smile on his face, "you'll soon realize that you love me as well."

"Never!" she cried.

"One should be extremely careful about using that word," Alex lightly remarked, surprising her by moving away and resuming his seat at the table.

"I give you my solemn vow that I shall pay you back in kind for all of this one day!"

"I certainly hope so," he sardonically quipped, his gaze sweeping quickly across her soft curves, leaving her in no doubt as to his meaning. "In fact, I'll look forward to that day!"

"You are insufferable!"

"Before you begin hurling all those insults at my head again, why don't we return to the subject at hand? That is, our arrival in Juneau. I plan for us to remain there for two or three days."

"And then what?" Marianna angrily demanded, refusing to return to the table, instead standing rigidly near the doorway.

"Then you'll return to Sitka. Properly chaperoned, of course."

"What do you mean?" she asked in confusion.

"I mean that I'll arrange for a cousin of mine who lives in Juneau, a woman several years older than yourself, to accompany you back to my grandmother's house. I've already written to her. The return voyage will take only the better part of a day. We've purposely taken much more time than was necessary to reach Juneau on this cruise, but then you're already aware of my particular reasons for that."

"I don't understand," Marianna declared, facing him with an increasing air of puzzlement. "Are you not planning to return to Sitka with me?"

"Nothing would please me more," he informed her with a faint sigh as he raised a glass of wine to his lips. "But I must return to Skagway. I have business there. It may be several weeks before I can return home again. And that, my love, is precisely why I fully intend to make good use of the little time left to us before we must part!" he asserted.

"You cannot be serious!" she furiously responded, facing him with her hands on her hips. "You actually expect me to return to your grandmother's house and sit and wait patiently for your return as if I were nothing more than some spineless little creature? Have you heard nothing I have said? I intend to return to London at once and seek an annulment!"

"An annulment is entirely out of the question now."

"And why is that?"

"Because, my beautiful Annie," he answered, rising

slowly to his full height and frowning down at her, "you are now my wife in every sense of the word. You belong to me. There will be no more talk of your returning to London, nor about putting an end to our marriage!"

"You cannot stop me!" Marianna obstinately insisted, involuntarily taking a hasty step backward as his golden eyes dangerously narrowed.

"I can and will!" he assured her, looking increasingly grim as he sought to maintain a tight control over his rising temper. He loved her, loved her more than life itself, and he certainly wasn't about to allow her to escape him now! He admired her courage and her fierce pride, but he still had far to go in taming the little wildcat he had married! He sought to reason with her, speaking more calmly. "It's too late for an annulment. You might as well accept that fact. And there's something else you should take into consideration whenever you're tempted to follow any of those foolish notions that always seem to be entering your beautiful little head. There's a distinct possibility that you may already be carrying a child."

"A child?" Marianna repeated in astonishment, for the thought had never once crossed her mind.

"You are my wife now, Marianna. Rest assured that you'll remain Mrs. Alex Donovan until death do us part!" he declared in a steel-edged voice. "I can promise you that there would be hell to pay if you ever tried to leave me. And if you ever were to attempt something foolish, I give you my word that I would find you and bring you back!"

"Oh! How I hate you!" she raged, the tears

swimming in her beautiful eyes as she glared militantly up at him. He was no better than her father! she furiously reflected. He did not care about her at all; he had only used her. Alex Donovan had amused himself at her expense. And now, now he actually expected her to meekly sit at home with her embroidery while he went upon his merry way. It was simply too much for her already strained emotions to bear, and her temper violently exploded.

She threw herself upon him with a vengeance, catching him off guard as she began desperately pummeling him with her clenched fists. Her raven curls tumbled riotously out of their pins and swirled about her stormy face as she struck blindly out at him. Alex stood perfectly immobile for a few seconds, allowing her free reign to express the full force of her anger, before his large hands shot out to firmly grasp her wrists.

"Feel better now, firebrand?" he asked with a soft, low chuckle as she continued to struggle.

"I shall escape you yet! I will not return to Sitka as you command, Alex Donovan! I will not be kept a prisoner there!" she vehemently cried, still attempting to inflict at least a small measure of bodily harm upon him.

"You'll do as I say!" Alex masterfully stated, tiring of this latest skirmish between them. He seized her about her slender waist and pulled her relentlessly toward him, capturing both her hands in one of his as he stared down into the fiery depths of her eyes. "I don't want to leave you. I love you, Marianna. I'd like nothing better than to be able to return to Sitka with you, but that happens to be impossible at this time. You'll simply have to trust me, to believe me when I tell you that I must leave you for a while."

"I will not be sent back to your grandmother's house as if I were nothing more than a cumbersome, naughty child!" she adamantly declared, pushing ineffectually against his muscular hardness. "How dare you think you can treat me this way! It's perfectly obvious to me that you consider me to be nothing more than some sort of loose woman who is to be used and then cast aside at your will. I will not surrender to such insult. I shall return to London at the very first opportunity, no matter what you say!"

"Then I give you fair warning that you had best prepare yourself for the humiliation of being forcibly dragged home by your husband!" Alex told her with a severe frown. "I don't want to hear any further talk of London. When you're a bit more rational, you'll realize that returning to Sitka and waiting for me is the wisest course of action. My grandmother will welcome you with open arms. And you'll have the opportunity and the time to decide what sort of house you'd like. After all, I certainly don't intend to live under the same roof with anyone else save you, my love!" he remarked with the merry twinkle returning to his eyes.

"You believe you've won, don't you?" she resentfully answered, her eyes blazing. "Well, you have not won, and you will not!" Her wrists were beginning to ache from her struggles, but Alex continued to hold her fast.

"Why not allow the victory to belong to us both?"

Alex suggested in a low voice as he released her wrists just long enough to wrap his powerful arms about her and hold her captive for his kiss.

Marianna choked back a sob of defeat as his lips claimed hers, as he once again subdued her with his seductive embrace. Somewhere in the back of her mind, she staunchly reminded herself that Alex may very well have won this latest battle between them, but she was still quite determined to win the actual war!

It wasn't much longer, however, until all such thought, indeed all thought, fled her mind as she was swept away by the exquisite torture Alex so skillfully inflicted.

Ten

"You will undoubtedly find Juneau to be quite a bit rougher than Sitka," Alex remarked to Marianna, startling her a bit as she stared toward the magnificently situated city the schooner was now swiftly approaching. Standing alone at the rail for several minutes, Marianna was still so incensed with her husband that she could barely speak, despite the tumultuous, impassioned union the two of them had shared only a short time earlier.

"Will I?" she coolly replied, pretending total disinterest. Her mind was literally spinning with various plans and schemes as the schooner's pace began to slow.

"Yes, but then Sitka had quite a headstart," he good-naturedly informed her as the crew now began scrambling about in their preparations to drop anchor. "Juneau is still young. Already a mining town, it's really boomed since news of the Klondike spread. Most of these ships you see will be sailing on up to Skagway, carrying the gold-seekers and supplies."

Pausing for a moment, he glanced down at her inscrutably. His wife, however, obstinately refused to so much as glance in his direction. Alex smiled again, pleasantly adding, "I think you'll enjoy our stay here, Annie, my love. The hotel happens to be among the finest in all Alaska. There's been a great deal of talk about moving the capital here to Juneau. Perhaps the next time we come, I'll have the honor of escorting you to the governor's ball."

Marianna remained silent, continuing to stare toward the city nestled against a towering backdrop of mountains and massive icefields. A covering of low, gray clouds prevented her from glimpsing the uppermost spire of the one looming mountain which held Juneau so securely at its base. Next time indeed! she indignantly told herself as the schooner was expertly maneuvered through the channel.

She couldn't help noticing that Juneau was a bustling place quite different from Sitka, just as Alex had said. The channel was filled with an odd assortment of seagoing vessels, as well as a smattering of small icebergs which proved to be such a nuisance to the captains. Raising her eyes upward again, she vaguely noted the winding streets, narrow and hilly lanes lined with an array of buildings.

It still amazed her that everything appeared so lush and green. She had always imagined Alaska to be nothing but a frozen wasteland. But then, she mused with a faint smile curving her lips, everyone in London had believed much the same of her Russian homeland. Her gaze returned to the flurry of activity on the wharf, which was just ahead now, the docks overflowing with a noisy crowd.

"At least it isn't raining," said Alex, firmly grasping her arm and prompting her to turn and frown at him. "It's time we went ashore. Ivan will bring our things later."

"You needn't keep manhandling me!" she proclaimed, attempting to free her arm from his grasp. She was dismayed at the tremor of emotion which ran through her at his touch.

"I don't want to take any chances of losing my beloved bride," he replied with a quick smile. He led her across the deck as the schooner finally dropped anchor. Several heads turned to stare at the striking young woman as she and her handsome escort disembarked and began walking up the crowded hill toward the hotel.

Marianna glanced curiously about as she strolled beside Alex, a thoughtful expression on her face. She was thinking that there must be some way for her to slip away from Alex in such a busy port, for there were people everywhere, though it was obvious that men vastly outnumbered women. Still, she reflected, she was certain she could somehow manage to conceal herself from him if only she could get away.

Arriving at the hotel in the center of town, a garish three-storied stone building less than a quarter of a mile from the docks, Alex led Marianna inside and signed the register. The desk clerk rang for a young man to carry their bags up the narrow staircase to their room. Marianna pulled abruptly away from Alex as the door closed after the young man had wished them a pleasant stay. Alex proceeded to lock the door, removing the key and dropping it into his coat pocket. He then turned back to his wife.

"Temper, temper, my love," he lazily admonished, watching in amusement as his wife moved to take a stance at the single large window. She was afforded a clear view of the docks, frowning imperceptibly as she perceived Alex's schooner anchored directly in her line of vision.

"I sincerely hope your latest annoyance with me hasn't spoiled your appetite," Alex remarked as he removed his jacket and tossed it negligently into a velvet-upholstered chair near the door. "I know of a particularly good place to eat a few blocks from here." He strolled across the carpeted floor of the gaily decorated room, swinging open a door to reveal the bedroom, a canopied four-poster therein. Another door led into the bathroom, and he casually moved to place his hands upon his wife's shoulders. "Would you perhaps care for a bath before we venture out to see the town?"

"No, thank you," she frostily answered, her entire body rigidly erect as she remained still, continuing to stare out the window. His solicitous manner would not soften her firm resolve to escape him! She would not allow him to send her back to Sitka as if she were nothing more than a child. She would not!

"Marianna," Alex said, turning her about and placing a finger beneath her chin to lift her stormy face toward his, his tender gaze meeting her flashing one, "can't we at least call a truce for the length of our stay here in Juneau? We have such a short time left to us, my little wildcat. I propose that we make the most of it."

"I am warning you, Alex Donovan, that I will not give in. I will not return to Sitka and wait for you!" she declared once more. When she opened her mouth to offer another scathing pronouncement, however, his lips closed upon hers. Though she struggled angrily, it was several long seconds before he raised his head and released her, smiling unconcernedly down into her flushed face as he said, "I think it best if we drop the subject for the moment, don't you? I, for one, intend to take a much-needed bath before embarking upon a day of sightseeing. Would you care to join me? The tub is sizeable enough to hold the both of us," he suggested with a wolfish grin.

"You are insufferable!" retorted Marianna, whirling back around as Alex merely chuckled softly. She turned her head to glare in his direction as he disappeared inside the bathroom and closed the door.

I must get away from him! she repeated to herself, her gaze flitting about the room now as if she would find something to help her escape. She refused to think about how she felt while in his arms, the way he could make her forget about anything else when the two of them were together in that rapturous embrace she could not resist. She would think only of the way he had ruined her life, of his abominable plans to pack her off to his grandmother in Sitka while he went adventuring!

She began pacing, her gaze returning to the

bathroom door every few seconds as she detected the sounds of Alex taking his bath. She frowned darkly as he began singing an old Irish ballad at the top of his lungs, her fiery gaze narrowing as she contemplated throwing something at the door. As she turned back toward the window, however, Alex's discarded jacket caught her eye from where it still lay upon the chair near the doorway.

She frantically snatched up the jacket, a brief search yielding exactly what she had breathlessly hoped she would find. The key! Alex had carelessly left the key to the room in the inside pocket of his jacket, and Marianna nearly laughed aloud at his uncharacteristic mistake. She wasted no time in gloating, however, as she flew to the bathroom door and fitted the key in the lock, turning it with hands that were not quite steady. She swiftly rattled the doorknob to make certain the door was locked, then nearly jumped when Alex's voice boomed out, "Marianna! What the hell are you doing there?" Marianna stood and waited in breathless anticipation as she heard Alex splashing from the bathtub and then attempting to turn the knob. "Marianna, open this door! Open the blasted thing, damn it, before I break it down!" he angrily threatened, making her grateful for the door which separated them.

"Farewell, Alex Donovan!" she couldn't resist calling, before scurrying across to the door of the room, unlocking it, and fleeing out into the hallway. She could still hear Alex pounding upon the door and shouting, but her quickening steps had soon carried her down the staircase and out of the hotel. She was oblivious to the curious stares she attracted as she hurried along, making her way through the crowded streets until she was several blocks from the hotel. Her one thought was of escape, and she had no idea as to where she would manage to hide from Alex, nor what she would do now that she was alone in the rough boomtown.

She was free at last! It was an exhilarating thought as she gathered up her full skirts and made her way farther and farther away from Alex Donovan, away from the man who had tormented her for what had seemed like an eternity. She told herself, however, that she couldn't be entirely sure of success until managing to sail away from Juneau somehow. She didn't know where she would go after that, since Alex had made it all too clear to her that he would find her if she attempted to return to London. What was she to do now? she wondered, nearly out of breath as she climbed yet another hilly street. Whatever she did, she must not allow Alex Donovan to find her!

Alex, meanwhile, was carrying out his threat to break down the bathroom door. He was in a particularly dangerous mood as he crashed back out into the main room, clad only in a thin towel which barely covered the lower portion of his tall, powerful frame. He started out of the room to give chase to his wife, then abruptly halted as a woman strolling down the hallway screamed in outrage, making him realize that he could hardly go searching for his wife wearing only a towel. He stalked back into the room and hastily pulled on his trousers and boots, his golden eyes narrowed with suppressed fury as he once again hurried from the room.

Damnation! he muttered silently, furious with himself for having forgotten about the key, more furious still with Marianna for daring to run away. Not only was he angry with her, but also concerned about her safety, for Juneau was not the sort of town where a beautiful young woman such as his wife should be gallivanting about without the protection of a man.

He ground out yet another curse as he paused to decide which way to begin his search, his gaze scanning the streets outside the hotel. Thinking that he'd never forgive himself if any harm came to his wife, he nonetheless made a silent vow to tan her hide as soon as he caught up with her. Finally deeming it wisest to return to his schooner and enlist the aid of his crew, he turned his determined steps in the direction of the docks as he began silently praying that he would find Marianna before nightfall.

Marianna was unaware of Alex's concern as she hurried along, nearly colliding with several people as she pressed almost blindly onward. She glimpsed fewer and fewer women and began to grow a bit frightened when she glanced over her shoulder and spied two bearded, coarse-looking fellows who appeared to be following her. Telling herself that surely nothing would happen to her in broad daylight, that she could always scream for help if the need arose, she nevertheless began walking faster.

The two men were still behind her as she noticed that she was entering a fairly deserted part of town, an area where the few buildings were little more than shacks. She became aware that the men were closing the distance she had attempted to put between them and herself, and she became increasingly alarmed.

Dear Lord, she feverishly prayed as she realized she was apparently in very real danger, please help me! Not knowing where to turn, she headed down a sidestreet, hoping to make her way back to the main part of town. She had not traveled more than fifty feet when the two men made their move and started running toward her, prompting her to gasp in horrified terror as she gathered up her skirts and tried frantically to escape, a scream dying in her throat as the men easily overtook her, each of them seizing one of her arms and yanking her to an abrupt halt.

"Let go of me!" Marianna found voice enough to cry, struggling violently in their grasp.

"What say you, Deke? Think we ought to let her go?" one of the foul-smelling creatures sarcastically remarked to his companion, laughing evilly as he grasped a handful of Marianna's dark tresses, his other hand moving to her bosom.

"Hell, no!" replied the man called Deke, also laughing as he appeared to enjoy Marianna's struggles. When she opened her mouth to scream for help, his hand clamped roughly down across her jaw. "Now we ain't gonna have none of that. Me and Sims here only want to have a little fun. Ain't nobody gonna get hurt if you just cooperate."

Marianna nearly fainted as the fellow brought his craggy face closer to hers, his bloodshot eyes boring deep into her wide, horrified ones. Though she continued to twist and squirm and kick, she felt tears of helplessness filling her eyes. She screamed against the dirty hand covering her mouth as the man called Sims suddenly grasped hold of the bodice of her beautifully tailored traveling suit and ripped it downward, his fingers returning to grip the thin fabric of Marianna's camisole which still covered her heaving breasts. Before he could move to bare her breasts completely, the voice of another woman behind them imperilously demanded, "Let her go, you damned, muleheaded bastards!"

"What the . . ." muttered Deke as both he and Sims jerked about with Marianna still held captive between them. Their eyes widened at the tall, attractive young blonde who stood belligerently glaring at them, her gray eyes steady and challenging, her hands on her hips.

"It's that LaRue woman!" exclaimed Sims, as if Deke could not see her and recognize her as well.

"I said to let her go!" repeated the blonde, obviously not in the least little bit afraid of the two men. Marianna stared hopefully in the other woman's direction, still unable to speak as the hand remained across her jaw.

"And just why should we do a fool thing like that?" Deke mockingly retorted, he and Sims glancing at one another and laughing again.

"Because, if you don't, I'll see to it that the both of you can't crow anymore," she coolly threatened, an unmistakable Southern twang to her voice as she added with a faint little smile, "and you know I can do it, too." There was a certain gleam in her lively gray eyes that caused Deke and Sims to believe her. To reinforce her threat, she pulled a small silver derringer from her skirt pocket and levelled it at their chests. Within seconds, Marianna found herself released, then stood watching in numbed shock as the two men scurried away and out of sight.

"Are you all right, honey?" the tall blonde asked, genuine concern mirrored on her face as she hurried forward to place a comforting arm about Marianna's trembling shoulders. "It's a good thing I happened to be traipsing along this road today. I generally don't make it a habit to come down this way," she continued rambling amiably on, smiling down into Marianna's tear-streaked face.

"Th . . . Thank you," Marianna composed herself enough to say, clutching at the torn shreds of her bodice and smoothing the tangled curls from her face. "I . . . I don't know what I would have done if you had not come along!" she remarked with a shudder, still unable to believe all that had just occurred.

"No need to think about it now. Deke and Sims aren't the worst sort I've come across, but they'd just as soon slit a man's throat as look at him. But enough of that kind of talk. What's your name, honey? And what in blue blazes are you doing in this part of town?" She stepped away from Marianna then, fixing her with a curious stare.

Marianna finally noticed the unusual appearance of the woman she knew only as LaRue, from her almost brassy blond locks piled high atop her head to her tight, lowcut red satin dress. She silently wondered if the woman was perhaps one of the sort who consorted with men for money, then was immediately ashamed of her thoughts. Whatever line of work the woman pursued, she had rescued her from a terrible fate, and for that Marianna owed her a debt of gratitude.

"My name is Marianna Markova," she answered, omitting her new surname. "And I am running away from a man who . . . who abducted me from my family in Sitka several days ago!" she finished, raising her head with inward defiance at the lie.

"Is that so?" the other young woman remarked with just the hint of a smile on her painted lips. It was obvious that she didn't know whether to believe Marianna or not, but she appeared to give the matter no further thought as she then said, "Well, Marianna Markova, my name is Kate LaRue. And if you're truly running away from someone," she announced, eyeing Marianna critically, "then I have a proposition which might interest you."

"A proposition?" repeated Marianna warily, her face coloring slightly beneath Kate's knowing gaze.

"I'm a singer, Marianna," Kate informed her with a disarming grin. "I've been entertaining the men here in this hellhole for nearly a month now. That's the reason those two rascals who attacked you recognized me, the reason they knew I've got friends in Juneau who'd make them pay if they dared to so much as lay a finger on me." She paused for an instant, then thoughtfully murmured, "You sure aren't the sort I expected to find.

155

But then, that's exactly the reason I think the two of us would be such a novelty act."

"What do you mean?"

"I'm planning to sail on up to Skagway in the morning," explained Kate, "and I'm looking for a partner."

"You're going to Skagway?" Marianna responded, her thoughts returning to Alex. He was probably looking for her by now! It puzzled her that she suddenly experienced a feeling of warm security at the thought of him, but she had no time to ponder the reason for her puzzlement as Kate continued.

"I've been planning to for some time. As I said, I'm looking for a partner. My other one ran off with a miner a couple of days ago, the ungrateful little—well, just the same, she should have at least told me she was planning to take off. I could make a go of it on my own, you understand," she said, making it apparent that Marianna was supposed to follow her line of reasoning, "but I still think I'd make more money in the long run if I had a partner. And that's where you come in, Marianna Markova."

"You mean you want me to come to Skagway with you?" Marianna asked in bewilderment, a picture of Alex flashing unbidden into her mind once more.

"Unless you're wanting to return to that family of yours in Sitka?" Kate asked with another knowing smile.

"No!" Marianna vigorously replied, then added more calmly, "I have no wish to return there at this time. But, why do you wish to enter into a partnership with me, Miss LaRue? You don't even know me. And precisely what sort of partnership are you talking about?"

"Can you sing?" Kate abruptly demanded, her eyes narrowing a bit.

"Yes, moderately well. I received a great deal of musical instruction as a schoolgirl."

"Musical instruction?" Kate laughed aloud at that. "Hell, honey, I'm not talking about polite little soirées. I'm talking about getting up on a stage in front of hundreds of men, men from all walks of life, and singing your heart out to them, making them think of their womenfolk back home, making them forget all about their troubles for a while. Do you think you'd be able to do that?"

"I don't know," Marianna honestly answered, appearing to give the matter serious consideration. It was all happening so quickly, she mused, pressing a hand to her forehead as she stood there in the cool afternoon air and clutched her torn bodice to her bosom, still feeling shaken from the effects of the attack upon her person.

If she agreed to go along with this Kate LaRue woman, it would at least solve the problem of getting away from Juneau, she reasoned with herself as Kate patiently awaited her answer. And it might be exciting actually to perform upon a public stage, to sing the way Kate had described. But, she thought as her husband's face swam before her eyes once more, Alex Donovan would be in Skagway! How on earth could she hope to remain hidden from him if she journeyed to the same town where he would be?

Then again, a tiny voice from deep within piped up, why should she concern herself with Alex at all? Skagway was even more of a boomtown than Juneau, a place overrunning with people. There was nothing Alex could do to her there. Besides, she reflected, it would afford her considerable satisfaction to confront him there, to flaunt her disobedience to him. She would show him that she had no intention whatsoever of remaining tied to him in any way. She would show him that she, too, longed for adventure and excitement, that she was no longer the same sheltered girl she had once been. Alex Donovan himself had seen to that, hadn't he?

"Well, what do you say?" Kate finally interrupted her thoughts. "With your dark hair and my blond, we'll be a sensation!"

"But, I have no money or valuables with me to pay for my passage to Skagway," Marianna informed the other woman with a slight frown, glancing downward at her torn and dirty garments. "And I have no other clothes with me—"

"No matter. If your other things are anything like the dress you've got on, you couldn't use them anyhow. I know what I'm wearing isn't exactly suited to a proper tea party, but it's more in the line of what those lonely men up in Skagway will be wanting to see. So, will you do it?" she asked again.

"Yes, Miss LaRue. Yes, I'll become your partner," Marianna finally agreed, smiling warmly now. Her smile quickly faded as she said, "But, I've got to keep hidden from the man who abducted me until we leave Juneau!"

"We'll hide you at my place. He'll never think to look for you there," insisted Kate as she linked her arm through Marianna's and began leading her back toward the other part of town. "By the way, there's just one more thing. Marianna's a bit too high sounding for a saloon singer. Not that there aren't several other gals with fancy names up in Skagway already. But, I want us to sound more down home, more like the sort of gals the men can feel like they're on the same level with. 'Kate and Marianna' just doesn't sound right, if you know what I mean."

"Well, I suppose I could call myself 'Annie,'" Marianna suggested, then could have pinched herself. She had always hated Alex's little nickname for her. Now she would be saddled with it!

"That's perfect!" responded Kate, beaming with pleasure. "'Kate and Annie.' Has a nice ring to it, doesn't it? The singing team of Kate and Annie will take Skagway by storm, you just wait and see!" she confidently pronounced. She and Marianna soon arrived at Kate's lodgings, a very small, unpainted boarding house just around the corner from the hotel where Alex had taken Marianna several hours earlier. Marianna glanced anxiously toward the hotel before allowing Kate to lead her inside the building.

Alex, at that moment, was still combing the streets of Juneau. He had missed seeing Marianna with Kate by mere seconds, rounding the corner near the hotel to make yet another search of the main street. He had already sent Ivan and the other two members of the crew out to scour the city for any sign of his wayward bride, but to no avail. He refused to give up hope of finding her, however, as he began peering inside each and every establishment he passed along the street.

Where the devil could she be? he asked himself for the hundredth time, a worried look on his handsome countenance. He loved the little vixen to distraction, and he'd be damned if he'd allow her to slip away from him so easily! But, as the day wore on and his questions and searching turned up nothing, he grew increasingly anxious. Trying not to think of what sort of ill fortune might have befallen Marianna, he desperately enlisted the aid of several friends in Juneau to assist him in finding her. The day turned into evening, then into the short semidarkness of night, with Alex behaving like a man possessed.

The night seemed endless for Alex as he refused to rest, refused to even pause in his efforts to locate his wife. His men became concerned about his frame of mind by daybreak. It wasn't until several hours later that Alex finally chanced to hear of his wife's whereabouts.

It was Ivan who brought him the news that Marianna had been seen leaving the boarding house around the corner of the hotel with a young blond woman everyone knew simply as Kate. Alex listened with a tight-lipped expression on his face, both overjoyed to learn that Marianna was safe and enraged to realize that she had successfully eluded him while causing him such anguish.

"Where is she now?" Alex harshly demanded of Ivan, causing the other young man to experience a moment's pity for the errant Mrs. Donovan.

"The two of them boarded a cargo steamer for Skagway a few hours ago."

"Skagway?" Alex muttered grimly, appearing downright murderous for an instant before his brow cleared and he gave a short laugh. "Then let's set sail for Skagway without further delay."

"But, we still need a few supplies and—"

"Supplies be damned! We won't need any supplies for the swift trip I plan to make!" Alex declared as he and Ivan strode back down to the docks. Alex's thoughts centered on his wife, and he smiled to himself, causing Ivan to glance at his employer in puzzlement.

So, Marianna had first defied him by running away, and then had even gone so far as to sail off to Skagway, knowing full well that her husband would be arriving there himself. He couldn't help but admire her audacious courage, and yet he still experienced an overwhelming urge to wring her beautiful neck! He looked forward to their next confrontation as he and his men raised the schooner's anchor and sailed away from Juneau, following the same course his wife had taken less than four hours earlier. The course would take them past the wild, unspoiled beauty of the countryside alongside the Inside Passage, which neither Marianna nor Alex would appreciate.

Eleven

Marianna awakened early the following morning, her body stiff and tired as a result of an uncomfortable night wedged into a corner of a tiny, airless cabin on the steamer which was only an hour or so out of Skagway. She raised herself up on one elbow, glancing down at the still-slumbering form of Kate beside her. There were numerous other women crammed into the close confines of the room, and Marianna wrinkled her nose in distaste at the unpleasant odors which permeated the small space.

She heaved a faint sigh as she peered down at her wrinkled gown, an old and faded calico of Kate's that she had traded for the torn finery of her previous costume. A sudden giggle welled up inside of her at the thought of how she must look. Gone was the refined and elegant Marianna Markova, and in her place was a bedraggled, common-looking lass named Annie who slept on the bare floor along with the actresses, singers, laundresses, cooks, wives, and various other "ladies" who were traveling to the gold-rush town of Skagway.

What would her father say if he saw her like this? she mused with an inward smile, running her fingers carefully through her lustrous curls in an effort to smooth out at least some of the tangles. What would Alex Donovan think of her? she then thought, frowning as he intruded into her thoughts yet again.

He would know by now that she had successfully escaped him, she reflected with another tiny smile, chuckling to herself as she recalled the way he had so ominously threatened her while pounding ineffectually on the door the day before, the way she had triumphantly left him calling her name. She would have at least some small measure of her revenge upon him when he arrived in Skagway and found her there, living adventurously as a songstress and doing quite well without him!

"Morning, Annie," she heard Kate sleepily whisper beside her. She smiled down at the woman who was only a few years older than herself, but seemingly so much more worldly and mature.

"Good morning," Marianna whispered in response. "Do you suppose we might leave the cabin now? I'm terribly afraid these close quarters are beginning to make me feel a trifle ill!"

"Things are a bit crowded, aren't they?" quipped Kate with a crooked grin as she began rising slowly to her feet. "I could use a bit of stretching myself. Besides, the two of us need to get ready."

"Ready for what?" asked Marianna as she stood and put a hand to her aching hip.

"For our arrival in Skagway, of course! We've got to

look a damn sight better than this," she remarked, glancing at her own disheveled appearance, "if we expect those men to pay good money to hear us sing!" She snatched up her carpetbag and led the way across the cracked wooden floor toward the doorway, stepping carefully so as not to tread on any of the other women. Marianna followed closely behind, grateful for the rush of cool air which met them as they stepped out into the passageway.

She and Kate watched with mingled anticipation and nervousness as they stood along the steamer's railing an hour later, the town of Skagway in the nearing distance. Marianna was awed by the sight which met her eyes, for the town was very different from what she had expected.

The "town" appeared to be little more than a profusion of shacks and tents on the flats between the canal and the towering mountains in the background. There were several other ships docked along the long wharves, and there seemed to be people, animals, crates, barrels, and noise everywhere. Skagway looked ten times more uncivilized than Juneau, she decided in the moments the steamer neared the dock, and she and Kate turned to one another with expressions of growing trepidation as the steamer dropped anchor.

"It's a bit larger than what I thought it would be," remarked Kate, giving a final pat to her curled locks as she perceived the crowd of men assembled on the wharves. "But, what the hell, that just means there'll be even more lonely prospectors who'll stand in line to hear us sing!"

"It appears as if most of them are here to meet the ship!" Marianna ruefully commented, gazing a bit fearfully at the crowd of men who began to cheer as they caught sight of the women at the rail. Marianna glanced anxiously down at her colorful attire, feeling ill at ease. Kate had insisted upon dressing her in a bright yellow satin dress, its full skirts shorter than Marianna normally deemed necessary for the sake of modesty, its heart-shaped bodice cut daringly low across her swelling bosom. Kate's costume was even more outrageous, she mused as she turned to look at her new friend, but the thought didn't provide her with much comfort as she noticed the way the men were so boldly leering at them.

The other women began lining the ship's railing now, the bright morning sunlight beating down upon their heads. The crowd grew increasingly boisterous when the gangplank was lowered and the passengers began disembarking. Though the steamer was commissioned to carry cargo, its captain frequently supplemented his income by agreeing to provide passage for eager gold-seekers and the like. There were few men on board this time, however, making the ship's arrival greatly anticipated by those who had gathered on the docks. While it was true that a sizeable number of women had already journeyed to the town that served as the major gateway to the gold fields of the Klondike, they were still greatly in the minority.

Marianna's expression grew quite apprehensive as Kate grabbed her hand and tugged her along toward the gangplank. She was beginning to wonder if she had acted wisely in deciding to come to Skagway, in believing that she could entertain men such as those who were so unabashedly ogling her. Her new friend leaned close to encouragingly murmur, "Chin up, Annie! You'll get used to the attention in no time. There's no need to look so terrified of them. They aren't going to bite, you know. They just want to have a little fun." Marianna opened her mouth to demand what Kate meant by "fun," but the words were lost as she gasped suddenly, alarmed to find herself seized by an eager admirer who had grown impatient and had stalked up the lowered gangplank, heading straight for the woman of his choice. He tossed her high in his arms as she cried out and pushed frantically against the large, burly fellow, indignantly demanding that he release her at once. He merely laughed and held her as if she weighed nothing more than a mere babe, saying, "You're just about the prettiest little thing I seen yet!" He laughed again, his voice ringing out even above the accompanying hoots of appreciation. Marianna threw a helpless look in Kate's direction, surprised to see her friend joining in the laughter as she, too, was snatched up and carried down the gangplank into the waiting crowd.

"Unhand me at once!" Marianna haughtily commanded, still struggling in the large man's arms. She gasped again as she found herself surrounded by a throng of men on all sides, each and every one of them apparently eager to get closer for a better look, to welcome her personally to Skagway. The men, most of them direly in need of a bath and a shave, were dressed in coarse trousers and shirts, dirty and travel-worn jackets, and boots completing their rugged attire. Marianna was beginning to feel faint as the crowd pushed closer and closer, and she renewed her efforts to force her captor to release her as he began striding toward town with his prize.

"Kate! Kate, what should I do now?" she frantically exclaimed, watching as the blond woman was tossed playfully into the arms of another man several feet away.

"Relax, honey!" Kate laughingly responded, apparently reveling in the rambunctious attention she was receiving.

Marianna, however, did not enjoy it and grew more indignant with each second. By the time the crowd had reached the end of the docks and was stepping into the mud, Marianna reached out and forcefully twisted the ear of her burly captor, prompting him to bellow with pain. She watched breathless and wide-eyed as his scraggly features became suffused with an angry color, and she pushed against him with all her might as she viewed the dangerous light in his narrowed gaze, the surrounding men erupting into gales of raucous laughter.

"It doesn't look to me like the little lady is enjoying your company, Clyde," a smooth voice called lazily from a short distance away. The crowd grew abruptly silent as the man known as Clyde jerked about with Marianna still clasped tightly in his arms.

"What the hell have you got to say about it?" Clyde roared, reminding Marianna of a large black bull she'd once seen back in England. Her own grateful gaze flew to the man who had dared speak in her defense, and she was pleasantly surprised at what she saw. He was standing back upon the edge of the wharf, appearing casually unconcerned as he placed one hand in the pocket of his well-fitting black trousers, his other hand replacing a thin cigar to his lips. He was darkly attractive, tall and obviously full of self-confidence as he unhurriedly pulled a watch from his vest pocket and glanced down at it.

"Isn't it about time you and the others got on with whatever it is you do all day, Clyde? As for the lady there, I'd say she would greatly appreciate it if you'd just set her down gently and be on your way."

The spectators surrounding Marianna remained quiet and still, their interested gazes flitting back and forth between Clyde and the man who dared interfere. Marianna felt nearly faint with relief as she was finally released, her legs threatening to give way, her knees feeling weak as her feet met the muddy ground. She stood watching as Clyde appeared to forget all about her, striding forward with evil intent in his dark eyes.

"This don't concern you, Caine," he grumbled, halting mere inches away from the other man.

"I've decided it does," Caine lazily replied, negligently replacing his watch inside his vest pocket. Marianna noticed that there were several other men now moving to stand in a semicircle behind the man known as Caine, all of them appearing to be ready to defend Caine's self-assured authority. Clyde hesitated only for an instant, a mixture of rage and indecisiveness playing across his coarse features. He ground out a curse, narrowing his black eyes at Caine and at the men behind him before abruptly jerking about and pushing his way furiously through the crowd, fixing Marianna with one last threatening glare as he stalked past her and lumbered away.

Caine sauntered toward her now, the rest of the crowd slowly dispersing and trudging along the muddy path toward town. Marianna was left a bit bewildered by it all, and she smiled hesitantly up into Caine's darkly attractive, cleanshaven features.

"Thank you, Mr. Caine. I am most profoundly grateful for your timely assistance!"

"Most willing to be at your service, Miss—" he answered, his statement trailing off as he waited for her to complete it.

"Markova. Ma—Annie Markova," she hastily amended, remembering Kate's admonition about her name. She smiled gratefully up into his face once more, unaware that she was only serving to captivate him further.

Lyle Caine stared intently down at Marianna, his rather hawkish gaze causing her growing discomfort. A faint, rosy blush appeared upon her beautiful young face and, in that instant, Caine decided he must have her.

Marianna didn't fail to notice the telltale gleam of interest in the man's brown eyes, and his obvious admiration left her feeling a bit unnerved. She nodded curtly in his direction before turning about, noticing that the two of them were completely alone at the end of the wharf. Suddenly remembering Kate, she was dismayed to discover no sign of her friend as her searching gaze swept the immediate area.

"Your fair companion is in all likelihood down at my place by now," Lyle informed her, strolling forward to gaze directly into her upturned face once more.

"Your place?" repeated Marianna in puzzlement.

"My saloon. That's usually where the newest girls end up. I'll be more than happy to take you there myself," he gallantly offered, though there was a certain boldness to his gaze as it swept up and down the length of Marianna's form. She felt her face flushing hotly as his eyes rested briefly on the rounded curve of her breasts, and she resentfully mused that she didn't relish being classified as one of the "girls." She visibly hesitated, prompting him to add, "I wouldn't advise searching for her on your own. There's no way of knowing if Clyde might decide to return." This last he spoke with a disarming smile.

"Very well, Mr. Caine," Marianna reluctantly agreed, his words having the desired effect upon her. Placing her hand gracefully on the arm he offered her, she regally strolled beside him, her polished leather boots already splattered with the brown mud which seemed to be everywhere.

She peered curiously at the buildings as Lyle Caine escorted her down the wide main street of Skagway, the two of them attracting a myriad of curious stares as they went. Marianna was surprised at the number of businesses which were jammed into such small spaces. There were hardware stores, restaurants, hotels, saloons, drugstores, and even a photography studio. She saw that there were many more women than she had expected to find, some of them dragging children behind them as they scurried about the mudcaked boardwalks lining the street on either side.

"You appear somewhat unprepared for what you see," Caine casually remarked, steering her past a crowd of men arguing in front of one of the saloons. The saloons were as varied as the rest of the town, and most of them were already overflowing, despite the fact that it was still before noon.

"It's such an exciting place, isn't it?" Marianna breathlessly pronounced, feeling an unexpected sensation of exhilaration at being in such a town. She watched with a fascinated, wide-eyed gaze as several wagons were pulled down the street by unmatched teams of horses, as dogs ran alongside men on horseback and a group of women, dressed in much the same shocking fashion as herself, laughed and flirted with some young, fresh-faced miners outside one of the gaming halls. Other men were busily laying tracks down the very center of the main street, tracks that would be traveled by the new railroad which would carry the prospectors over the White Pass and on into the Klondike.

"With nearly fifteen thousand people now swelling its ranks, it ought to be," commented Caine with a deep chuckle. Marianna was so absorbed in looking about, she had forgotten all about her earlier anxieties and had even forgotten about Kate once more. She was a bit startled when Caine gently pulled upon her arm, saying, "Here we are. And, unless I'm greatly mistaken, you'll find your friend inside." He swung open the hinged half-doors, ushering Marianna inside the brightly lit, smoke-filled room.

"Annie!" she heard Kate shouting before she had taken more than half a dozen steps. The blond woman was smiling broadly as she made her way swiftly through the throng of her new admirers. "I was beginning to get a bit worried about you," she spoke in a raised voice, striving to be heard above the rumbling talk and loud laughter of the saloon's patrons. There were several boisterous comments made at Marianna's appearance, while Lyle Caine merely stood leaning against one corner of the long, polished bar and watched the two women, a strange half-smile on his face.

"Kate, I don't see how I'm going to be able to—" Marianna began in a low voice that was barely more than a whisper as the two of them quickly moved toward one corner of the large, garishly decorated room in an attempt to keep their conversation private.

"Don't let what happened down on the docks scare you," Kate swiftly interrupted. "They were only showing their appreciation, honey. You'll have to get used to it sooner or later. Now," she said, abruptly changing the subject, "we've got to set about finding a place to work. I noticed that you came in with that fancy-looking character over there," she remarked, nodding her head briefly in Lyle Caine's direction, "and one of the men just told me that he owns this saloon. So it's only natural that we should approach him first. You go on over there and ask him for a job, Annie," Kate easily commanded, taking hold of Marianna's arm and tugging her gently forward.

"I?" Marianna exclaimed with a sharp frown. "I wouldn't know how to begin!"

"Well then, it's time you learned. I sure as hell wouldn't have picked you for my partner if I didn't believe you've got some backbone beneath that ladylike exterior of yours!"

"But we've only just met!" Marianna protested, annoyed when Kate continued to pull her forward. She became aware of the fact that a great many of the men in the saloon were watching the two of them, that Lyle Caine himself was still staring at them with avid interest, a faint smile curving his rather sensual lips. "And I thought we would be entertaining in a different sort of establishment!" she whispered, anxiously eyeing their surroundings. Never having ventured inside a saloon before, she was dismayed to think that Kate actually intended for them to appear in such a place.

"This 'establishment' is exactly the right place for us to sing!" Kate insisted, a note of irritation creeping into her voice. "We damn sure can't start out in some fancy music hall somewhere, leastways not here in Skagway!" She abruptly released Marianna's arm, though her eyes moved pointedly toward the bar. Marianna was left with very little choice, and she took a deep breath of determination, watching as Kate moved

173

away and took her place amongst the appreciative customers once more.

"Mr. Caine," said Marianna, marching rather stiffly to confront him, "it seems that my partner and I are in need of employment—" she began, but his upraised hand interrupted her.

"Say no more, Annie Markova. The two of you have a job here." That charming smile of his flashed once more.

"But you don't even know what we wish to do," she pointed out to him.

"Whatever it is, you're hired," he insisted. "You can start today."

"We are entertainers, Mr. Caine," Marianna coolly announced, feeling increasingly ill at ease with the way he was looking at her, the way he seemed to be so amused at her. "We should like to sing in your—your saloon."

"Fine. I could use a pair of singers right now. And, if you're half as good as you look, then you stand to make quite a bit of money," he declared, emphasizing his words with a quick wink down at her. "How about starting tonight at eight? I'll put the word about that you and your friend there," he added, nodding toward Kate, "were the rage of New York, newly come to Skagway to entertain these poor, lonely souls."

"But I've never even been to New York!"

"Then that will be our little secret, Annie Markova," he told her with another low chuckle. Feeling a sudden chill run the length of her spine, and confused by such a

174

reaction, she politely thanked him and hurriedly collected Kate, promising that the two of them would return to the saloon well before eight o'clock. She was unaware that Lyle Caine sauntered over to the doors of his saloon to stare pensively after her as she and Kate made their way back down the boardwalk toward the hotel Kate insisted they visit next.

They were fortunate to procure two separate rooms at the white, two-storied hotel standing near one end of the unpaved street. The proprietor loftily informed them that the two rooms had been vacated less than an hour earlier. It was highly unusual for them to remain unoccupied for even that long, he added, eyeing the two young women with unabashed curiosity.

The two rooms were furnished pleasantly and were surprisingly clean. Kate declared that she wanted nothing more at the moment than to take a bath, and Marianna announced that she, too, wished to bathe and wash some of the dust from her hair before venturing out again.

Marianna's new partner was waiting for her in her room when she returned from the bathroom located at the opposite end of the carpeted hallway, having been forced to wait patiently for her bath while two other young women took their turns. She was toweling her lustrous raven curls dry as she stepped through the doorway, clad in a simple cotton wrapper she had borrowed from Kate.

"It's time we talked about what we're going to sing tonight," said Kate, laying out Marianna's costume

175

upon the quilt-covered iron bedstead. "You know, it's a good thing you and that other partner of mine are of a size," she thoughtfully murmured as she smoothed the creases from the dress.

"What sort of songs do you usually sing?" questioned Marianna, closing the door behind her and taking a seat on the bed. Streams of golden sunlight filtered in through the faded gingham curtains at the single window, softly illuminating Marianna's shining hair. Kate glanced up at the beautiful, aristocratic young woman, a sudden frown on her own attractive countenance.

"Where do you come from, Annie?" she unexpectedly asked, momentarily forgetting about the matter of the songs. She looked much younger and more vulnerable with her long blond hair swirling about her shoulders, her well-rounded figure encased in a cotton wrapper much like Marianna's. Her face was devoid of powder at the moment, and Marianna was faintly surprised to glimpse light brown freckles sprinkled across the other woman's nose.

"From Russia, originally, though I was educated in England. I have resided in London for the past two years," she answered readily enough, though she grew evasive when Kate then queried, "And what about that family of yours in Sitka? Won't they be worried about you?"

"Perhaps," replied Marianna with a tiny, noncommittal smile. "But I should like to forget about Sitka and my family for the time being. I have every intention of enjoying complete freedom and independence, the first time in my entire life I have been so . . . so unconfined!" she finished with a defiant toss of her thick curls, Alex's handsome face swimming before her eyes. Kate said nothing for the space of several seconds. She stared speculatively down at the young woman she had befriended.

"Annie, I'd like to get something straight between us," she finally spoke quietly, her solemn gaze catching Marianna's and holding it. "I won't pry into your past. I won't even ask you the real reason you were running around Juneau all alone." She paused and held up a hand as Marianna opened her mouth to offer the same explanation she'd given before. "None of that matters now. It's entirely your own business. All I ask in return is that you grant me the same respect, that you don't go probing about in my life as well. I had a feeling about you from the first time I saw you, a feeling that the two of us would turn out to be a great team. We might even get to be close friends. But then again, we might not. All I ask is that you do your damnedest to make me glad I took you on."

"I shall respect your privacy, Kate," Marianna responded, suddenly feeling a real kinship with the surprising young woman, who was so different from all the other women she'd ever known. "And I give you my word that I shall attempt to do my best when we are singing."

"Well then," Kate remarked with a sigh and a quiet little laugh, "let's get down to business! Since I seriously doubt you've ever even heard the kind of songs these men will be expecting us to sing, we've got a lot of work to do before tonight!"

Alex Donovan stood at the railing of his schooner, impatiently watching the scenery fly past in his haste to get to Skagway. Once again, he gained immeasurable satisfaction by picturing all sorts of punishment for his beautiful, headstrong bride, punishment that would usually end with his sweeping her up into his arms and carrying her off to bed. He savored the thought as he briskly commanded his crew, for what to them seemed to be at least the thousandth time, to increase the vessel's speed.

Silently praying that Marianna would be safe until he could find her, he nevertheless felt the rage boiling up inside of him once more at the thought of her willful defiance. At least, he told himself with a scowl, she would not have been in Skagway for more than a few hours before he docked there himself. Surely, in such a short space of time, she could not get into too much trouble, could she?

He comforted himself with that thought as his hands tightly gripped the railing, the force of his hold turning his knuckles white as the sails whipped tautly in the powerful wind, each moment bringing him closer to a highly anticipated reunion with his maddening, desirable love.

Marianna's presence in Skagway had placed him in a most unfortunate position, presenting him with a troublesome dilemma he had not yet determined how to solve. The last thing he wanted was for her to become involved in his dangerous business there, to find her being used as a pawn, a means to hamper his own undercover activities.

He cursed himself again for his mishandling of the entire affair, but his thoughts continually strayed to memories of Marianna's soft, delectable curves pressed against him, her lovely face glowing with the passion she had tried so desperately to deny.

Twelve

"Well, I suppose we're about as ready as we're ever going to be," said Kate, smiling broadly in obvious satisfaction. She faced her reflection in the gilded mirror, frowning suddenly as she critically surveyed her appearance. Her brow cleared just as swiftly, and she bestowed a final pat upon her curled blond locks. "I'd say we make a fine pair!" she concluded with a decisive nod.

"We do look rather striking, don't we?" agreed Marianna, moving to appraise her own reflection once more. She still had difficulty in recognizing herself, so altered was her appearance. The simple lines of the tight-fitting red velvet dress molded her admirable curves to perfection, though she sighed inwardly at its immodesty. A great expanse of her rounded white breasts was displayed above the low neckline, and an equally scandalous portion of her slender legs was revealed in their black stockings below the raised hemline. Kate had assisted her in dressing her lustrous black tresses in a rather simple style atop her aristocratic head, a small, feathered cap completing the desired effect.

Kate looked resplendent in her blue velvet, designed along the same lines as her partner's, her fairness serving as a perfect foil for Marianna's dark-haired beauty. Marianna was quite pleasantly surprised at the picture the two of them made, believing them to exude a certain elegance, in spite of their scandalous costumes.

"Let's get going, honey. I'd hate like hell for us to be late on our first night out!" declared Kate, grabbing Marianna's hand and leading her from the hotel room. She continued to make amiable conversation as they strolled out of the hotel and down the boardwalk, the two of them attracting a great deal of attention once more. Kate smiled engagingly at several of the men they passed, her flirtatious manner causing her partner to glance at her in perplexity. Marianna sighed inwardly, musing that such behavior would never be easy for herself, for she was well aware of the fact that she was quite naive, an innocent in the ways of the world.

But, she then reflected, staying close beside her friend as they made their way down the crowded street, she was no longer entirely innocent—Alex Donovan had seen to that! The unwanted recollection of such memories brought a sudden blush to her lovely face, her blue-green eyes flashing with inner fire.

"Well, here we are. Take a deep breath," suggested Kate, her lips curving into a faint smile as they paused just outside the doorway of the Golden Nugget Saloon.

Marianna felt almost breathless with anticipation as she and Kate stepped inside. The noise and smoke and smell of strong spirits hit her full force as she momentarily hung back. She gazed wide eyed at the unfamiliar sight, noting the half dozen other women dressed in their bright velvets and satins, the tables where the patrons were engaged in various games of chance, the man who sat at the piano in the far corner, his energetic efforts producing gay strains of music which only added to the din.

Marianna's fascinated gaze moved upward to the myriad of lamps which hung from the high, beamed ceiling, and she was unaware that Lyle Caine was approaching her, his hawkish eyes grazing up and down her well-displayed figure. Kate smiled a bit coquettishly up at him as he neared, saying, "Evening, Mr. Caine."

"Good evening, Miss LaRue, Miss Markova," he politely responded, bowing ever so slightly in their direction. He seemed to have eyes only for Marianna, however, and she experienced a twinge of uneasiness at the way his gaze never wavered from her face. He was quite attractive in his black jacket and trousers, his spotless white shirt and red satin vest, but she told herself that there was something indefinable about him which caused her to feel discomfited. She merely nodded at him, her lips curving into a cordial smile.

"I'm happy to report news of your appearance here tonight has already caused quite a sensation," remarked Caine, turning to view the boisterous activity with visible satisfaction. "It's always good for business

182

when word gets around that the Golden Nugget is presenting a new act, particularly one that features such beautiful ladies as yourselves," he finished with another smile at Marianna. She was relieved when Kate took her hand once more and said, "If you don't mind, Mr. Caine, we'd like a few minutes to freshen up before going on. I think the two of us ought to go on backstage." She, too had noticed the intensity of the man's gaze whenever it rested on her partner, and she began to grow wary. She silently chided herself for her motherly instinct to protect the girl, but she consoled herself with the fact that Marianna was so painfully inexperienced when it came to smooth characters such as Lyle Caine.

"Of course. Right through there and up the stairs to your right," he directed, his hand moving casually to point the way. Kate and Marianna murmured their gratitude in unison, before they began making their way across the crowded room and toward the small, brocade-curtained stage. It took them quite some time to travel the relatively short distance, due to the numerous men who insisted upon buying them drinks and enjoying the pleasure of their company as they attempted to move past. Finally, however, they found themselves behind the curtains of the stage.

"Oh Kate, I'm not at all certain I'm going to be able to keep my promise to you!" Marianna spoke in distress, her stomach churning with anxiety, an anxiety that was fast increasing as the fateful hour grew near.

"You'll manage. Just don't think about all those men out there. Pretend you're at home in your own parlor, singing for your family and friends. Once we get started, you'll be surprised at how quickly you'll start to relax."

"I . . . I certainly hope so. But, quite honestly, this isn't precisely what I expected when I so impulsively agreed to sing with you!" she ruefully admitted, smoothing down the velvet of her dress, her hands not quite steady.

"Everything has happened so quickly, my head is spinning!" It occurred to her that she had left Juneau only the morning of the day before and that she had been Alex Donovan's captive bride immediately prior to that. Could it really have been only a few short days ago that she had been forced to participate in that mockery of a wedding? Sitka, her Aunt Sonja and Uncle Frederick and dear Cousin Andrei, seemed so far away. But, she suddenly remembered, Alex Donovan would be arriving in Skagway soon, if he had not already done so. The prospect of facing him again caused her anxiety to return with renewed strength as she and Kate heard the crowd on the opposite side of the curtain quietening.

"Gentlemen," Lyle Caine's cultured voice rang out, "it gives me great pleasure to present to you, direct from a highly lauded engagement in New York, the two most beautiful young women our fair city has yet welcomed. I give you Kate and Annie!" An outburst of loudly enthusiastic response followed, the applause and cheers almost deafening as Kate and Marianna stepped forward through the parted curtains. Marianna gave swift and silent thanks for the fact that she possessed a memory adequate enough to allow her to have learned the songs Kate had taught her earlier that afternoon, but she had no more time in which to think about anything other than her performance as Kate signalled the man at the piano to begin, having earlier paused to hand him a list of their night's repertoire.

The first tune she had chosen was a slow, plaintive ballad by the name of "Aura Lee," a great favorite with the lonely and homesick prospectors. Marianna felt her voice growing stronger with each note, her voice sweet and clear and blending perfectly with Kate's lower, more resonant tones. Her confidence increased as the room was bathed in still silence, and she peered outward at the faces of the men, feeling an undeniable satisfaction, a sense of accomplishment for the way she and Kate were able to affect their audience.

There were tears glistening in the eyes of more than one man before their song drew to a close. They quickly followed it with a spirited rendition of the lively, flirtatious "Kiss Me Quick and Go," then continued on in this same light-hearted vein for the space of several more songs, before finishing with a simple, moving rendition of "After the Ball."

Marianna was overwhelmed by the appreciative response she and Kate received as they stood smiling upon the stage. She was momentarily alarmed when some of the men began tossing small, shiny objects their way, even more startled when she realized that they were throwing coins and small nuggets at the feet of the two women who had entertained them so well.

"Kate! Why, they're—they're throwing money!" she

exclaimed, her voice barely audible above the roar.

"This is what I meant when I said Skagway was the best place for us to sing!" Kate happily remarked. "The two of us can make more here than singing in the fanciest music hall anywhere else!" She smiled broadly at the men who continued to shout and applaud, until finally deeming it time to withdraw. She and Marianna bowed slightly and stepped backward, the curtains falling forward to close with a flourish. Kate was instantly kneeling on the stage floor, gathering up their earnings.

"I had no idea our simple entertainment would prove to be so profitable," Marianna commented in astonishment, following Kate's example and bending downward. "Why, we must have amassed a small fortune in one single evening!"

"No fortune, I'm afraid, but a healthy start," corrected her friend, clutching the folds of her short, full skirt to form a basket for the coins and nuggets. "Of course, you can't expect them to react the same way every time, but at least we do get to keep everything we get. Lyle Caine knew exactly what he was doing by taking us on, Annie. Why, we'll draw the men like honey draws flies! Didn't I tell you the two of us would be a big success?" She spoke with a delighted laugh, her eyes shining. "I knew I was doing the right thing when I took you on!"

Marianna felt a surge of pride at the compliment. She had done it! She had performed on the public stage, in a saloon no less, and had done it well. It perversely occurred to her to wonder once again what her dear, domineering, aristocratic father would think of her right now! She could just imagine the shocked reactions of her London friends, the stern disapproval of her former teachers and governesses! It was an exhilarating sensation, this feeling of high adventure, and she decided that she liked it very much. She could never, never return to being the spoiled, stifled Marianna Markova after this night—from this moment onward, she would seek truly to become "Annie," the young woman with enough talent and courage to sing before an audience of rowdy prospectors, gamblers, and the like!

Lyle Caine appeared backstage soon thereafter, offering his congratulations on their success. Marianna was too absorbed in her own happiness to take offense at the manner in which he took hold of her arm and stared boldly down into her face. Her cheeks were still faintly flushed with excitement, her beautiful eyes sparkling.

"I've arranged for the two of you to have supper up in my room. You'll be singing again in an hour," Caine informed them, his eyes glowing with an unfathomable light as he maintained his grip on Marianna's arm.

"Thank you, Mr. Caine. How very thoughtful of you," she gratefully responded while Kate stood by and watched the way Caine's eyes seemed to devour her young friend.

She and Marianna were pleasantly surprised by the elegant surroundings in which they found themselves a few moments later. The room, located at the top of the carved staircase, was large and roomy, sumptuously decorated with flocked wallpaper and red carpets. The furniture was large and masculine, and the whole effect was one of rather gaudy grandeur.

A table had already been set for them, and they were grateful to find it laden with a variety of dishes. Neither of them had realized how famished they had become, and it wasn't long before they had eaten their fill. They talked and chatted gaily until a knock at the door disturbed them. The door swung open without hesitation, revealing one of Caine's men who had come with the message that it was time for them to sing once more.

"How many times a night do you think he'll expect us to perform?" Marianna whispered as they followed the man back down the staircase.

"Probably not more than a couple. But I'll sing until I'm hoarse, just as long as we keep doing so well!" replied Kate. "This is what I've been dreaming of, Annie. I aim to make as much as I can, as quickly as I can. We won't have to be here long until we've got enough to buy us a place of our own."

"A place of our own? What do you mean?" They moved backstage again, critically checking one another's appearance and adjusting their curls.

"I plan for the two of us to take our earnings and invest it all in a place right here in Skagway."

"What sort of place?" inquired Marianna, an expression of puzzled interest on her lovely face.

"Oh, I was thinking a restaurant might be nice. Not just a restaurant, mind you, but a place where the men could come to get their bellies filled and hear us sing at the same time. I know we could do well, Annie. All we need is enough money to buy us a little place here on the main street," she explained, her blue eyes shining with enthusiasm.

"Do you know anything about operating a restaurant?" Marianna practically questioned, surprised and faintly amused at Kate's enterprising plans.

"A little," was all her friend would say. Any further discussion was set aside as Lyle Caine announced them once again. Marianna appeared more relaxed and self-confident than the first time as they began to sing.

Kate didn't fail to notice the looks of envy she and Marianna received from the saloon girls, but she was shrewd enough to realize that she and Marianna should set themselves apart from the other women no matter what ill feelings such behavior aroused. She told herself that she sure as hell hadn't come all the way to Skagway to be treated like just another floozy—things were going to be different this time.

Marianna was almost sorry when she and Kate reached the end of their performance once more. They were singing "Beautiful Dreamer" when the saloon doors suddenly swung open and a tall, golden-eyed man strode inside, his steps abruptly halting as he caught sight of the two women on the stage across the brightly lit room.

Several conflicting emotions played across his handsome face as he stared unblinkingly toward the dark-haired songstress—first, stunned astonishment and disbelief, followed by a profound relief at having found her, then an irrational anger that she was so obviously well and enjoying herself, and lastly a furious jealousy that she was displaying herself so immodestly before so many appreciative onlookers. A deep scowl marred his tanned features as he ground out a blistering curse and instinctively began stalking forward without pausing to consider his actions. He fortunately, however, regained his composure within seconds, and moved to take a rigid stance at the long, polished bar, schooling his countenance to remain outwardly impassive as he continued watching Marianna with a dangerous gleam in his golden eyes. She had yet to notice him among all the other men at the bar.

"Well, if it isn't my old friend Donovan," Lyle Caine mockingly observed, catching sight of Alex and sauntering in his direction. The music in the background was swelling to a crescendo, the voices of the two young women flowing vibrantly toward the song's completion. "I heard you'd left town." His lips curved into what was more a sneer than a smile as he fixed Alex with a challenging look in his dark eyes.

"What's the matter, Caine? Don't tell me you actually missed me!" Alex sarcastically countered, tearing his gaze away from Marianna. Caine didn't fail to notice where the other man's attention had been drawn, and he smiled again as he said, "Pretty, aren't they? Particularly the dark-haired one." He withdrew a cigar from his coat pocket and lit it with deliberate, unhurried movements, all the while glancing across at Alex.

"Where'd you find the songbirds?" Alex forced his

tone to remain casual, his demeanor to appear only mildly interested. Damn! he swore to himself, his turbulent emotions firing his temper. It was bad enough finding his own wife singing in a saloon, but why did it have to be the very one that belonged to Caine?

"It was easy," boasted Caine. Changing the subject for a moment, he asked, "Staying in town long this time?"

"Why should it matter to you?"

"Oh, just thought you might like to play a few rounds of poker. You still owe me the chance to win back some of my loss from the last time, remember?" Though he said all this with a faint smile, there was no humor in his eyes. Alex opened his mouth to reply, but the song suddenly ended, and his gaze irrevocably returned to the stage. His eyes narrowed imperceptibly as the audience erupted into applause and cheers, several more coins and nuggets tossed Kate and Marianna's way before the two of them disappeared behind the closed curtains.

"I hope it's the blonde who's caught your fancy, Donovan," remarked Caine, removing the thin cigar from his mouth. He glanced at the stage and back at Alex.

"I take that to mean you've already staked a claim on the other one?" He leaned against the rounded edge of the bar, tipping his hat back upon his head and grinning companionably at the other man. Alex was only a trifle taller than Caine, and slightly more muscular. They were close in age but worlds apart in every other aspect, and Alex felt jealous rage boiling up inside of him at the implication of Caine's words.

"Something like that." He saw the way Alex's eyes moved sharply away from him then, and he turned to see Kate and Marianna approaching. They laughed and talked with several of the patrons as they strolled forward, Marianna feeling much more at ease now as she thanked the men for their highly vocal admiration. She moved away from Kate, who was occupied in flirting with a dreamy-eyed young prospector, and smiled as she caught sight of Caine. Her gaze traveled farther, then stopped.

Marianna's steps abruptly halted, and she stood as if transfixed, the smile on her beautiful face fading rapidly. Her heart was pounding in her breast, her pulse racing alarmingly as she stared toward Alex. Though she had tried desperately to obliterate the memory of his handsome face from her mind, she was all too familiar with every contour, every line. He was returning her stare with noticeable intensity, and she silently berated herself for feeling the old weakness descend upon her.

"I'd like to congratulate you, Miss Markova, on yet another outstanding performance," Caine declared with silken charm, stepping forward to draw her arm through his. "It seems you've made yet another conquest," he added, drawing her along with him toward an unsmiling Alex. "The man's name is Donovan, and he happens to be quite adept at cards," Caine mockingly announced, a certain edge to his voice. "The lady's name is Annie Markova," he then

192

told Alex, his own eyes narrowing now, "and, in the event you ever need reminding, she will remain under my protection as long as she works for me."

"Very glad to make your acquaintance, Miss 'Annie' Markova," Alex sardonically responded, slowly removing his hat and bowing ever so slightly in Marianna's direction. His gaze caught hers for only an instant, but the two of them were aware of the currents passing between them. Swiftly glancing away from her and back at Caine, he said, "In fact, I look forward to seeing a great deal more of you and your lovely partner." It was his turn to smile with mocking defiance at the other man. Caine's features became flushed with well-controlled anger as Marianna stood silently by and watched the interchange, not at all certain she understood what was happening.

She did, however, understand that her fateful confrontation with Alex Donovan had finally arrived. But, she told herself in bewilderment, it wasn't a confrontation at all! He behaved as if he'd never set eyes on her before, had apparently not mentioned to Caine that she was actually Mrs. Alex Donovan. Why had he chosen to behave in such a baffling manner? What sort of deceptive game was he playing now?

"Are you new to Skagway, Mr. Donovan?" she coolly inquired, deciding that she would show him she was capable of remaining calm, composed, and detached in his presence. She also wanted to demonstrate that she was not in the least little bit afraid of him. But, she was furious with herself for suddenly experiencing a certain breathlessness. What did he intend to do? she anxiously wondered.

"Not exactly," drawled Alex, his searing gaze returning to her face.

"Well, Mr. Caine, how'd we do?" Kate was heard to happily question, chuckling softly as she now came to stand beside Marianna.

"Remarkably well, Miss LaRue," replied Caine, before unexpectedly grasping her arm and tugging her gently forward. "Kate, I'd like to introduce you to Alex Donovan," he proclaimed.

"It's a pleasure, Mr. Donovan," said Kate, a bit bemused at Caine's behavior, yet nonetheless genuinely pleased to make the acquaintance of the tall, good-looking man with the golden eyes. She smiled winningly up at him, disappointed when he merely nodded in her direction, his gaze moving back to her partner's faintly blushing countenance. She concealed her disappointment, however, as she turned back to their new employer. "Well now, Mr. Caine, if it's all right with you, I think it would be best if Annie and I called it a night. I know it's still a mite early, but I don't want to risk wearing out our welcome on our first night here."

"Of course. I leave it entirely up to you two charming young ladies," Caine gallantly replied, frowning inwardly as he took note of the way Marianna kept stealing glances at the other man.

"Come on, Annie. It's been a long day and I think it's time we turned in," said Kate, ushering the younger woman away and toward the doors. "Evening, Mr. Caine, Mr. Donovan," she called over her shoulder.

Marianna allowed herself to be led along, holding her head high as she swept past Alex and favored him with one last piercing look. She and Kate were soon outside and on their way back to the hotel, marching silently past the open doorways of the other saloons and dance halls, the laughter and music and other noises drifting outward into the dusky twilight.

They reached their destination without incident, and it was not long before they stepped inside Marianna's room, Kate leaning against the door as Marianna sank gratefully down onto the softness of the bed.

"Suppose you tell me what all that was about," suggested Kate, gazing speculatively down at her friend. She began carefully tugging the pins from her bright hair as Marianna did the same.

"What do you mean?" How like Kate LaRue to notice everything!

"You know damn good and well what I mean. What was going on between you and Caine and that man called Donovan?"

"Nothing at all. Mr. Caine was merely introducing me to the man. It seems he, like the others in the saloon, was appreciative of our performance."

"You've never met him before?" probed Kate.

"Of course not," Marianna easily lied, a telltale blush rising to her cheeks. How in heaven's name could she possibly explain Alex Donovan and his role in her life to Kate?

"All right. I promised you I wouldn't pry, so I won't. But just the same," she remarked, opening the door and pausing on the threshold as she glanced back at

Marianna, "if you ever want to tell me, I'll listen. It doesn't matter whether you know him or not, just as long as you don't allow whatever's going on to interfere with our plans. And," she added, genuine concern on her attractive features, "I'd watch out for Caine if I were you."

Marianna smiled warmly at her before she left, then grew pensive after Kate had gone. She did not like having to lie to her new friend, but what else was she to do? She certainly couldn't reveal the fact that she was actually married to Alex Donovan. Not when she wanted nothing more than to forget she'd ever met him.

As for Lyle Caine, she thought as a tiny sigh escaped her lips, she would certainly heed Kate's warning there. The man made her feel uneasy, though she couldn't comprehend exactly why. She would keep him at a distance and do her best not to encourage him in any way. As charmingly attractive as he appeared, there was something about him which served to frighten her a bit. Perhaps it was the coldness of those dark eyes of his, she mused.

Rising from the bed, she suddenly realized how very weary she was feeling, and she set about preparing for bed. After making a trip down the hallway to the bathroom, she closed and locked her bedroom door. Drawing off her red velvet dress, her undergarments, and then her stockings, she donned a clean cotton nightgown, one that had belonged to Kate's former partner. She climbed beneath the covers of the bed, then leaned over to turn down the lamp on the small oak table beside the bed. Softly sighing, she settled down upon the feather pillow and closed her eyes.

Marianna soon drifted off into a troubled sleep, visions of Alex Donovan's mocking, handsome face invading her dreams. She was awakened by a soft, rustling sound less than an hour later, and she was just reaching toward the lamp beside her bed when a large hand closed over her mouth, stifling her gasping scream.

Thirteen

Marianna's eyes widened in terror. She struggled instinctively against the powerful arm that snaked across her slender waist to keep her imprisoned upon the bed, the firm hand remaining across her mouth. A deep, familiar voice abruptly stilled her efforts as it whispered softly against her ear, "Easy, my love. Remain quiet and still or else I'll be forced to employ less gentle means!"

Alex! Her eyes flew to the face mere inches from her own, and she felt nearly faint with relief as she viewed the mocking grin on his handsome countenance. Her relief was instantly replaced by intense fury at the way he had frightened her, and her beautiful eyes flashed murderously up at him in the semidarkness as she began fighting him once more. Alex merely chuckled softly, easily keeping her down on the bed.

"You should know by now how futile your struggles are, dearest Annie. Your delightfully feminine strength, however fiery, is no match for mine." He brought his face even closer, his golden eyes probing deep into Marianna's outraged gaze. "I've a score to settle with you, sweetheart, and I'll not be swayed."

She felt a tremor of fear deep inside at his gently spoken threat, though she told herself she would never allow him to know it. As his hand moved the slightest bit across her mouth, she took advantage of the opportunity to open her mouth wide, her teeth clamping down upon his hand with a vengeance.

Alex ground out a savage curse, but he gave her no time to scream as the hand returned across her lips, the arm across her waist pushing her even deeper into the soft mattress of the bed. Marianna could see the dangerous light gleaming in his narrowed gaze, a grim look on his face, and she grew afraid once more, though she was still determined to conceal her fear.

"Try that again, my beloved little firebrand, and I'll not be held accountable for my actions!" he spoke in a low, resonant voice that was laced with steel. "You may kick and squirm and glare at me all you please, but I mean to take you with me."

Take her with him? Marianna silently repeated the words, her mind spinning in desperation to try to think of some way to prevent it.

"You should never have run away from me. Do you have any idea what absolute hell you put me through? I envisioned all sorts of dangers and perils in which you might have found yourself. Instead," he said, his voice growing harsh with anger, "I discover that you've defiantly taken yourself off to Skagway, that you have apparently lost all reason and are displaying your considerable charms in Lyle Caine's saloon! Damn it, woman, how in blazes did you manage to cause so much trouble in such a short time?" Her only response was to narrow her eyes at him and become rigid beneath his arm. He started to say something else, but apparently thought better of it and clamped his mouth shut, his expression one of well-controlled fury.

Marianna drew in her breath sharply as she watched Alex lean over her, then actually climb upon the bed, his legs straddling her as he swiftly repositioned his arm to grasp her shoulder. He moved his hand to withdraw something from the pocket of his jacket, and she became alarmed when she perceived his intention to gag her. Though she struggled mightily against him, her legs flailing and kicking, her hands doubling into fists to pound helplessly upon his muscular chest, he succeeded in wrapping the piece of cloth about her mouth and behind her head, expertly securing it into a knot.

Marianna was so infuriated at his treatment of her that she forgot all about her earlier fear of him, and she screamed repeatedly against the gag as Alex suddenly seized her and flipped her upon her stomach on the bed, then proceeded to bind her hands behind her back. Tears of helpless rage filled Marianna's eyes as her ankles were bound as well, until she was left feeling drained and defeated face-down upon the bed.

Alex swung off the bed and quickly snatched up a blanket from a chair in the corner, tossing it over the still and silent form of his wife. Within seconds, he had reached downward, seized Marianna, and slung her over his shoulder like a sack of grain. When she shrieked against the gag in protest of such humiliation and attempted to upset his balance, he brought his large hand down to land forcefully against her conveniently placed backside, achieving the desired effect as she stilled and quietened once more. Swiftly moving to the door, he eased it open and stepped cautiously out into the hallway, before making his way toward the back staircase of the hotel, accessible from a door at the far end of the long hallway.

Pleased that he had apparently remained unobserved, Alex carried Marianna down the steps and away from the hotel. Since nearly all the town's inhabitants were either asleep or in the saloons and gaming halls, Alex was able to stride undetected toward the wharves. If anyone had chanced to see him, he mused, it was highly unlikely any alarm would be sounded. Skagway was one of the roughest places on earth at that time, and there were so many crimes and strange goings-on at all hours of the day that his actions would be for the most part ignored.

Arriving at the dock where his schooner was anchored, he carefully transferred his soft burden to another pair of waiting arms, climbed on board himself, and then reclaimed his blanket-wrapped wife. Marianna was feeling faint when she finally felt herself lowered to the bed in Alex's cabin, all the blood having rushed to her head throughout Alex's hurried abduction of her. The stifling folds of the woolen blanket were removed, and she drew in a deep breath as her flashing eyes immediately searched for, and found, her husband.

"Well, here we are again, my love. I've been looking forward to this moment with great anticipation," Alex remarked with a sardonic grin on his handsome face as he towered above her. "You can scream and fight all you like now, for I once again hold you aboard my schooner. It appears the two of us are destined to spend a great deal of time in this cabin, doesn't it?" he tauntingly quipped, ignoring her fiery glare as he began untying her bonds. Within moments, she was rubbing at her wrists and ankles, still speechless despite the fact that the gag had been removed.

"What? Have you no scathing insults to hurl at my head, no threats of dire revenge?" he sarcastically queried, his eyes never leaving her flushed, beautiful face as she sat motionless upon the bed, her wrathful look speaking volumes. Marianna's expression sobered as he said, "I wanted to wring your adorable neck when you ran away from me! I was half out of my mind with worry, though I doubt if hearing that causes you much remorse."

"Remorse?" Marianna finally retorted, bouncing off the bed to confront him squarely, her eyes blazing. "Why should I suffer any remorse for escaping you, the insufferable scoundrel who held me against my will?"

"You are my wife. Your place is with me," he quietly reminded her, no trace of humor evident in his own gaze.

"Very well then, Alex Donovan! If my place is with you, then why were you sending me back to Sitka?" she indignantly countered.

"I've already told you my reasons. You deliberately disobeyed me by coming here!"

"And I will continue to do so! I wanted none of this marriage, remember? I wanted none of you!"

"Then why did you come to Skagway?" he asked with just the ghost of a smile on his features. "If you were so determined never to see me again, why did you come to the very place you knew I would be?" He crossed his muscular arms against his broad chest as he stared down at her.

"I certainly did not come here because of you!" she vehemently retorted. "Skagway simply happened to be the destination of my singing partner, a generous and kindhearted young woman who was good enough to offer me the opportunity!"

"Well, it sure as hell seems to me that if you truly wished never to set eyes on my face again, you'd have fled to a place where the chances of that happening were comfortably remote. And, as for you and your singing partner," he declared with an edge to his voice, "what are you doing singing in a saloon? Have you lost your mind? Don't you realize what all those men are going to assume?"

"They'll merely think that Kate and I wish to entertain them!"

"They'll think *that*, all right, but they won't think your desire to entertain them stops on that damned stage!"

"How dare you insinuate such a thing!"

"I'm not insinuating anything, dear bride. I'm only telling you the way things are. What's more, Caine himself already appears to have formed the opinion that you are his personal property!"

"Lyle Caine has been nothing but a very kind and helpful gentleman!" Marianna fumed, feeling a twinge of guilt at her defense of the man. He hadn't been everything that was proper, but he hadn't actually made improper advances, either.

Alex's golden eyes narrowed, a darkly menacing scowl crossing his sunbronzed countenance as he stared down at her. The surge of jealousy which welled up inside him at the recollection of the way Caine had warned him away from Marianna only served to add fuel to his already flaring temper.

Marianna defiantly faced him, her head proudly erect. She silently berated herself for ever being so foolish as to believe herself safe from him. She had never truly believed he would be able to recapture her once she was in Skagway; she now regrettably saw the error of her assumption. If she did not somehow manage to escape him again, he would send her back to Sitka. And that, she firmly resolved, was something she could not allow.

"You'll never get away with it this time, Alex Donovan!" she boldly stated, undeterred by the dangerous gleam in his eyes. "I have friends now, friends who will be only too happy to assist me in remaining here in town!"

"I wouldn't count on it," he replied with a swift, maddening grin of pure amusement. "You see, it would be very unfortunate for your 'friends' if they attempted to interfere. But that doesn't matter, since I've already reclaimed what is rightfully mine and will have you far away from here, on your way back to Sitka, before they even know you are gone," he finished with supremely confident satisfaction.

"I'll only run away again!" she dramatically uttered. "I will not allow you to exercise any control whatsoever over my life! I've discovered quite a few things about myself in the short time we've been apart, dearest husband, and I am not the same. I am not the same helpless, foolish creature I was when you tricked me into marrying you!" she vowed with admirable spirit.

"Helpless?" Alex repeated, then emitted a short, deep laugh. "Never helpless, my love. As for this great transformation you seem to believe has occurred, I see little evidence of it," he remarked, eyeing her critically, his gaze sweeping up and down her body with bold intimacy. "You appear much the same as I remembered. Of course, I've never seen you wearing anything quite like that nightgown you have on, but I'll soon remedy that!"

"You most certainly will not!" she fiercely disagreed, shaking her head so that her cloud of dark hair swirled about her shoulders. "As I have already told you, Alex Donovan, I will no longer be bullied or ordered about by you! While it is true that we are legally husband and wife, you yourself have hesitated to make that fact known here in Skagway."

"What are you talking about?" he curtly demanded.

"Why did you not tell Lyle Caine that I am your wife?" she triumphantly questioned. "There must be some reason you do not wish people here to know. I suppose it has something to do with your 'business,' but it matters not. All that matters to me is that you no longer have any authority over me!"

"Do you think not?" Alex casually murmured, leisurely uncrossing his powerful arms. "While it's true that I have very good reasons for not wanting Caine or any others in town to connect the two of us, I have no intention of allowing that to prevent me from taking what is mine! By this time tomorrow, it will not matter what anyone in Skagway believes, for you will be on your way back to Sitka!"

"I will not!" Marianna obstinately protested, her color high and her eyes flashing their familiar blue-green fire. She suddenly pushed frantically against him, bolting for the door. She had already wrenched it open and was poised upon the threshold, screaming for assistance at the top of her lungs, when Alex caught her again.

"Stop it, you little fool! Do you want Ivan and the others to think I'm actually carrying out my threat to wring your neck?" he mockingly asked, dragging her back inside and slamming the door with his booted heel.

"Let go of me!" she furiously commanded, gasping as she found her feet leaving the floor. Alex lifted her squirming form and deposited her on the bed, then placed his own muscular litheness atop her outraged softness.

"Haven't we played this little game before?" he spoke in a voice brimming with amusement.

"That's all it is to you, isn't it? A game!" she seethed,

still refusing to surrender to the inevitable.

"No, my love. It's much, much more than that," murmured Alex, a gentle smile on his handsome face as he moved to take her lips with his own. Marianna was shocked at the waves of desire washing over her at the first touch of his seductive mouth. Though she tried desperately to fight against the familiar weakness, it was impossible.

"How I've missed you, Annie," Alex whispered, draining the last of her resistance with his potent kisses. Her arms moved to entwine themselves about his neck, her lips returning his searing kiss with a matching ardor of her own. His tongue tenderly ravished hers, his hands tugging impatiently at her primly highnecked nightgown.

Marianna gasped softly as the nightgown was pulled from her trembling body, as Alex removed his own clothing with remarkable speed. As always, she no longer possessed the power, nor the will, to stop him, and she gave herself up to the almost painful need deep inside of her, a need which increased to a fever pitch with each gentle caress, each passionately demanding kiss.

Alex moaned quietly as Marianna's fingertips trailed with whispering softness across his smoothly muscled back. His warm lips nipped gently at the softness of her ear, before traveling lower to the silken flesh of her breasts. His hands were filled with the full roundness of her breasts, his mouth moving to nuzzle with excruciating slowness at one of them, his skillful tongue wreaking havoc upon her senses as it swirled round and round the sensitive, rosy nipple.

"Oh, Alex! Alex!" Marianna gasped, her fingers curling convulsively in his thick, sun-streaked auburn hair as he moved to inflict his delectable torture upon her other quivering breast. Her head moved restlessly upon the pillow, her eyelashes fluttering closed.

The powerful yearning was building with rapid intensity as his provocative mouth teased lazily at her navel, before moving lower still. Then, she was gently turned upon her stomach, Alex's long fingers smoothing aside her thick mane of hair as he began trailing a fiery path downward with his lips, caressing the pale loveliness of her neck, her trembling shoulders, the alluring curve of her back, the exquisite slope of her hips and buttocks, and the smooth white flesh of her thighs and legs.

Marianna gasped again and again at his gentle seduction, unprepared for the intensity of the sensations he aroused within her. Her eyes flew open in breathless confusion as Alex's hands firmly, yet tenderly, grasped her rounded hips and pulled her up and toward him where he was kneeling on the bed behind her.

There was a question in her mind as he pulled her back into his embrace, a question that was swiftly answered when she felt his manhood probing her velvety warmth. She drew in her breath upon another sharp gasp as he plunged deep within her.

Alex's hands held her at her slender waist, and he began moving, slowly at first, then with increasing fervor and desire. Marianna was momentarily shocked at the position in which she found herself, but she was soon lost to all thought as she moved in the age-old rhythm, straining back against Alex as he sent her own passion spiraling upward. She was certain she would be driven mad as his hands moved tenderly to squeeze her breasts, his lips branding her with searing intensity as the two of them blended in perfect unison, their mutual, shattering fulfillment leaving them stunned and breathless.

In the soft afterglow of their tempestuous love-making, Marianna allowed Alex to gather her close. Her beautiful face was glowing and flushed, her soft curves coated with a fine sheen of perspiration. It was several long moments before Alex spoke, startling her as his voice, rich and vibrant, sounded in the silence of the lamplit cabin.

"Isn't this where you tell me how very much you despise me, dear wife?" His teasing words were accompanied by a soft chuckle, his chest shaking slightly beneath Marianna's head.

"Perhaps," she answered with a tiny smile, still and languid against him. "But, to be honest," she admitted with a sudden frown, "I've no idea exactly how I feel about you, Alex Donovan."

"That's just about the most encouraging thing you've ever said to me, my love!" he declared while administering a teasing shake to her shoulder. "I was all prepared to do verbal, if not physical, battle with you yet again, and here you tell me that you do not despise me after all. It would be much easier, and a good deal more peaceful, if you would but admit that you care for me."

"I'm still so confused," responded Marianna with a deep sigh. "Once again, you have succeeded in upsetting my orderly life!" she accused him with a faint frown on her lovely face.

"Orderly life? What orderly life? I find you right in the middle of one of the most hellish boomtowns ever in existence, singing half naked in a saloon!"

"I was not half naked!" she strongly protested, raising up on one elbow to face him now. "I admit that my attire was a bit, well, a bit immodest, but I was not half naked!" She settled back down beside him, saying, "Besides, I've decided that I like it here. It's exciting and different, a far cry from anyplace I've ever been before."

"That's exactly why I'm sending you back to my grandmother in Sitka!" Alex ruefully stated. "You don't have any idea what Skagway is really all about. It's full of every kind of degenerate low-life, every kind of confidence man and greedy prostitute and crook imaginable. For every honest prospector, there's at least twice that many men seeking to cheat him out of what little gold he manages to find. And, as far as the saloons go," he added with a dark scowl, "they're the center of all the vile activity going on. You damn sure couldn't have picked a worse place to go adventuring than Lyle Caine's saloon in Skagway!"

"I find it difficult to believe that the town is as abominable as all that. Why, Kate and I have had no trouble whatsoever since we've been here. No one has bothered us. The men in the saloon were rowdy, but certainly did us no harm. As a matter of fact, the two of us made quite a bit of money in one single night!" she finished proudly.

"You'll have all the spending money you desire back in Sitka," Alex pointed out firmly, his hand tightening upon her arm.

"I do not intend to return to Sitka and play the part of a bored, obedient little wife! You are fortunate enough to go where you please, to do as you please, to experience all the high adventure you wish, Alex Donovan, and I believe I am entitled to do the same!"

"Fine. You can have all the excitement and adventure you want, but it will have to wait until I return to Sitka and fetch you."

"But, since I'm already here in Skagway—" she began, only to be abruptly cut off.

"I won't be swayed, so it's useless to try. I'm sending you back to Sitka first thing in the morning," he masterfully proclaimed. Following a moment of silence, a moment in which tension filled the air between them, he relented enough to tell her, "Even if I were to keep you here in Skagway with me, there's still the matter of your true position as my wife. You were right when you said that about my wanting to keep it a secret. It's best if no one knows. But, it so happens I must leave Skagway tomorrow. I'll be gone for at least a week. No, my love," he concluded with a sigh as he hugged her close once more, "the safest place for you is in Sitka! I'd not be able to rest if I didn't have the assurance that you were safe."

"Then you will also have the assurance that I will

only run away again!" she threatened, growing angry again. She attempted to pull away from him, but he refused to release her.

"Don't try it, Marianna," he cautioned in a deceptively low and even tone of voice. "I'm warning you. You won't enjoy the consequences if you try anything as foolhardy as running away again!"

"I'm not afraid of you, Alex Donovan!" she haughtily insisted, pushing against him as her eyes began flashing once more. He would never change! she bitterly thought. So arrogant and domineering, so sure of his power over her!

"You had best learn to obey me," Alex tightly replied.

"There is nothing you can do to induce me to obey you when I do not wish to do so!" she rashly countered, a tiny shriek escaping her lips as he suddenly yanked her into his arms, rolling so that she was beneath him.

"Isn't there?" he quipped with one mockingly raised eyebrow, chuckling softly at her struggles to escape.

"There will come a day when you will regret ever having set eyes upon me!"

"Only if you grow fat and ugly and even more shrewish," he retorted, a boyish grin on his handsome face. "But, in truth, I should love you even then." He silenced her scathing reply with his lips, and it wasn't long before she moaned and gently cried aloud, begging him to take her, no longer caring for the moment that he was such an arrogant and domineering scoundrel.

*　　　*　　　*

Marianna awoke to find Alex gone. She hurriedly sat upright in the bed, her expression growing stormy as she viewed the pale, golden light of the summer morning streaming in through the portholes. She knew with a certainty that her husband believed he had already said his farewells to her, that he was probably well on his way by now.

Their night together had been pure magic, she reflected with a heavy sigh. But, magic or not, she still had no intention of sailing back to Sitka! If he believed he could seduce her into being obedient, if he believed he could render her helpless by employing such means, then he was going to be sorely disappointed!

Tossing back the covers with a vengeance, she climbed from the bed and flew across the floor to the large chest, smiling to herself in triumph as she discovered that her clothes had been neatly folded and replaced inside the drawers. Quickly donning an elegant plum velvet gown, as well as slipping on her silken, lacy undergarments, she hurried across to the door and eased it open.

"Good morning, Mrs. Donovan," Ivan cheerfully remarked, smiling warmly down at her from his stance outside the cabin door. "We will be weighing anchor as soon as we finish loading the supplies." Marianna murmured something unintelligible and angrily closed the door.

There must be some way I can get off this ship! she told herself, pacing back and forth, her skirts gently swishing with each step she took. She paused to raise her face toward the warmth of the sunlight at one of the portholes, and it was then that the idea occurred to her.

Of course! she mused in satisfaction, moving to take action. If she could only get the casement of the porthole open, she thought, eyeing it speculatively, she was certain she could squeeze out of it.

Much to her dismay, she discovered the latch was locked, the lock refusing to budge as she wrestled with it. But refusing to admit defeat, she turned about and hastily scanned the room for something she could use to pound upon the lock and thereby loosen it. She smiled to herself when her gaze fell upon the iron doorstop on the floor just outside the bathroom.

Seizing the small, heavy object, she scurried back across to the porthole and carefully aimed it at the lock. She raised the doorstop and brought it down forcefully against the obstinate lock, hitting it three more times until it finally gave way.

Marianna gathered up her full skirts and used a chair to position herself high enough to try to squeeze through the porthole. It was an extremely tight fit, but she pushed herself through, then carefully made her way along the narrow railing toward the bow of the ship. She stopped abruptly, holding her breath when she heard the sound of voices nearby.

"Well, that ought to do us," a man was saying as he placed the last box of supplies upon the schooner's deck. "Guess we may as well get going now."

"Yeah, Alex would have our hides if we delayed long enough to have someone come looking for his wife," another crew member remarked with a quiet rumble of laughter. "I never thought I'd live to see the day Alex Donovan was bested by a woman!"

"He wasn't bested," the other young man quickly argued. "He got her back, didn't he? And if we don't stop wasting time, we're never going to get out of here and back home!"

Marianna heard them laughing companionably as they set about making preparations to sail. Telling herself that it was now or never, she climbed from the railing onto the deck, then hesitated for a moment while her eyes searched for the three men. She saw them at long last, but Ivan and the other two were so preoccupied with their various chores that they did not so much as glance in her direction as she climbed up onto the dock and scurried back down the long wharf, ignoring all the men who spoke and called to her as she flew past.

She had done it again! Her absence would probably go undetected by Alex's crew for several hours. And she was convinced that, with Alex leaving town, they would never attempt to interfere with her. She smiled to herself as she hurried along, back toward the hotel, breathing deeply of the fresh, crisp morning air as she went.

"Annie! Where on earth have you been?" she heard Kate's voice asking as she stepped inside the lobby of the hotel.

"I . . . I decided to take a walk," Marianna answered, obviously breathless from her exertions. Her eyes were sparkling, her cheeks becomingly flushed, though Kate attributed her friend's high color to the walk.

"You had me worried," said Kate with a casual smile.

"I thought we might go have some breakfast and look the town over."

"An excellent idea," agreed an enthusiastic Marianna, prompting her friend to glance at her in momentary puzzlement. But Kate merely shrugged to herself as the two of them set off, and it didn't occur to the usually observant blonde, at least not until much later, to wonder where Marianna had acquired her elegant gown.

All the while Marianna was congratulating herself on having slipped from Alex Donovan's grasp yet again, she was haunted by vivid memories of her rapturous night with him. She began to wonder where he was going when he left Skagway, what sort of business had brought him to Skagway and then away to his mysterious destination. Most of all, she wondered what he would say or do when he returned to Skagway and discovered her still there.

Fourteen

Marianna's enchantment with performing in a saloon ended quite abruptly a few short days later. Even before the unsettling incident occurred, she was beginning to enjoy the boisterous surroundings less and less. Though she and Kate remained immensely popular, which was no easy feat given the number of competitive establishments featuring their own entertainment, Marianna kept remembering Alex's words regarding Lyle Caine's saloon.

She began noticing what was happening whenever she and Kate were not on stage. Men crowded around the gaming tables, triumphantly yelling when they chanced to win, complaining loudly of being cheated when they did not. It puzzled Marianna that so very few of the men seemed to garner much in the way of winnings.

"Those poor men," she murmured with a slight frown, she and Kate leaning against the bannister on the upstairs landing on their fourth night there. "Why do you suppose they keep throwing their money away

217

like that?"

"It's a mystery to me. I guess it gives them something to do," Kate replied with apparent disinterest.

"It just seems as if they seldom win anything," Marianna murmured.

"That's the whole idea, honey," the blond woman dryly retorted. "Didn't those fancy gentleman friends of yours back in London ever gamble?"

"Yes, but it was quite different. It was much more refined, more . . . well, it appeared to be more evenly matched. At least one never heard of a gentleman cheating another! Here, however, there are a number of men who appear to genuinely believe they've received unfair treatment. Whenever there's the slightest hint of a disagreement, Mr. Caine is there to say whatever it is he says to smooth things over." She had noticed the way Lyle Caine would stroll casually about the room, watching all the proceedings with his dark, piercing eyes. He would pause frequently to have a brief word with the men who were in charge of the shell game, the roulette wheel, the cards, and the dice.

"Of course," Kate flippantly remarked, placing one hand on her hip and the other on the carved bannister. "He certainly isn't running this place just for the hell of it, you know. I've seen his type plenty of times before, Annie. There's probably dozens of others in Skagway just like him, though I've heard he seems to run things."

"What do you mean?" The two of them were attracting a great many stares as they stood just outside Caine's private room, passing the time until they would perform again.

"He's an experienced confidence man, a crook, a no-account bastard who doesn't care how many men he cheats, just so long as he gets what he thinks he's got coming to him. You can damn sure bet he knows the outcome of just about every roll of the dice, spin of the wheel, and deal of the cards," Kate grimly declared, her eyes narrowing as she peered down to where Caine was pausing near one of the tables. "And those painted trollops he keeps in here aren't any better when it comes to a square deal, which is exactly why I've wanted to make it plain that the two of us are different."

"Why are we singing here if it's such a dishonest establishment?" Marianna asked in genuine puzzlement.

"Because we don't have enough money to move on just yet. And at the rate we're going, it'll take another three or four weeks," she answered with a heavy sigh. Marianna said nothing, her own gaze drawn downward to Caine. He was now leaning casually against the bar, his hawk's gaze sweeping slowly over the noisy, smoke-filled saloon.

Although he had never truly bothered her, had never declared any intention toward her, she was perceptive enough to realize that he had formed some sort of attachment for her. He was always staring at her, always making it a point to come backstage after a performance and personally congratulate her. Once again, she recalled what Alex had said, and she grew increasingly uneasy.

Alex. No matter how desperately she endeavored to

forget him, he was always there at the back of her mind. Every night after she undressed and climbed beneath the covers of the bed, she vividly recalled their last night together. She would toss and turn restlessly upon the bed, always awakening the next morning with an inexplicable feeling of loss. It perplexed her greatly, and she sternly told herself she would have to try even harder to push him from her thoughts. But, she was forced to admit with a tiny sigh, there was no way she could keep him from her dreams.

"Annie. Annie, did you hear what I said?"

"What?" She turned back to Kate, the other woman's words serving to draw her out of her silent reverie. "Oh, I'm sorry, I was thinking of something else," she faltered, her cheeks faintly blushing. She raised her eyes to Kate's face again, suddenly glimpsing Lyle Caine moving up the staircase toward them.

"It's almost time for you two to go on again," he spoke pleasantly enough, his eyes moving swiftly past Kate to fasten on Marianna.

"I was just telling Annie the same thing," Kate drawled with a rather mocking little smile.

"If you don't mind, Kate, I'd like to have a private word with your partner," he lazily announced, holding his cigar in one hand, the other hand in the pocket of his dark, pinstriped trousers.

"Well, I—" Kate hesitated, unable to miss the silent plea in Marianna's blue-green eyes.

"We'll go into my office," Caine smoothly proclaimed, grasping Marianna by the arm and steering her through the doorway. Marianna threw one last apprehensive look over her shoulder at her friend. Kate herself appeared to be none too pleased at the way Caine had spirited her partner away.

"Sit down and make yourself comfortable." He quietly closed the door behind them, his hand gesturing toward a velvet-covered settee a few steps away.

"I'd rather stand," Marianna stiffly replied. She felt suddenly overwhelmed by the deep red and gold of the room, by the polished, massive furniture. She never felt that way whenever she and Kate took their supper here, which they had each night following their first performance. Now, even the room appeared to have taken on a menacing aura.

"You know," Caine began, flashing her a smile which did not quite reach his eyes, "you and Kate have worked out pretty well here, haven't you?" He sauntered away from her and over to a velvet-draped window near a huge rolltop desk. Marianna watched him silently and warily. "In fact," he continued, "you've worked out so well that my place is doing more business than ever before. Which brings me to the reason I wanted to speak with you." He drew the cigar leisurely away from his mouth, his eyes never wavering from her face. "I have a proposition to make to you, Miss Markova. I'd like for you to stay on here as my partner."

"Your partner?" she breathlessly repeated in amazement.

"That's what I said. I happen to believe the two of us would make quite a successful team."

"But—but what about Kate?"

"She'll have no trouble finding another place," he answered, waving slightly as if to dismiss Kate entirely. "You won't be needing her any longer. You'll have me." He moved toward her, pausing momentarily to toss his cigar into the brass spittoon on the floor beside the desk. "I hadn't really given much thought to taking on a partner till I met you."

"I don't know what to say!" Marianna murmured, shocked at his proposition. "Why would you want me as your partner, Mr. Caine? I know nothing whatsoever about running a saloon! Why, I've only been in Skagway four days, and—"

"I told you to call me 'Lyle,' remember?" he interrupted with a faint smile.

"But I know nothing about your type of business!" she continued ignoring his last remark. Indeed, she told herself, from what she had recently seen and heard, she desired to know nothing more about it, either!

"I'll be more than happy to teach you all you need to know," Caine assured her in a low, suddenly husky tone. He was standing mere inches away from her now, the strong aroma of cigar smoke, mingled with a trace of whiskey, hanging about him.

"Even if I were interested, which I am not, I would never, never consider dissolving my partnership with Kate!" she indignantly protested.

"Kate LaRue can take care of herself. You're the one who needs looking after," he commented with a quiet chuckle, his dark eyes probing into her startled gaze. Before Marianna quite knew what was happening, he had wrapped his arms about her, yanking her close as his lips captured hers in a hungry, bruising kiss. She struggled violently against him, striving to jerk her head away, but to no avail. One of his arms moved to clamp about her squirming body, imprisoning both her arms, while his other hand moved to fasten in her thick curls.

She felt herself growing faint as he pressed his sensuous, practiced mouth upon her unwilling lips, his arm holding her so close she could scarcely breathe. She was left pale and shaken when he unexpectedly released her a moment later, a look of smug triumph on his face.

"How dare you!" Marianna gasped, stumbling backward and grasping the settee for support. "This is no doubt what you intended all along, is it not? All that nonsense about a partnership between us was merely to persuade me to be more 'agreeable,' wasn't it?" she spoke with cold fury, her eyes flashing brilliantly.

"Don't try and deceive me by trying to appear the picture of outraged maidenly modesty," Lyle Caine mocked, amused at her fiery reaction. "I've had my eye on you from the first moment I saw you so angrily defying Clyde down at the wharves. I knew there and then, Annie Markova, that you were a woman with enough spirit, enough fire and passion beneath that lovely, dignified exterior of yours to more than match any man's desire."

"That's the only reason you allowed Kate and me to perform in your saloon, wasn't it? You expected me to display my gratitude by offering myself as a . . . a . . ." she seethed, then broke off as she searched for words.

"A whore?" The insulting term made Marianna wince, while Caine merely chuckled and said, "No, my dear Miss Markova. I'd be blind not to see that you're a different breed from all the others. What I had in mind was an exclusive agreement between the two of us."

"You mean as your mistress?" she angrily demanded. Her color was high, her raven tresses falling in glorious disarray about her trembling shoulders. Lyle Caine stared at her, his eyes narrowing as he mused that her beauty was only heightened by her anger.

"As my partner," he pointed out, sauntering back toward the desk and reaching down to take up a piece of paper. "I've already taken the liberty of having an agreement put in writing. All that's left is for you to sign it."

"I refuse to so much as consider it!"

"You're making a big mistake," he said, replacing the paper on the desk as he began moving toward her again with slow, unhurried steps. "I'm offering you the chance of a lifetime, my dear. You'll regret it if you so foolishly refuse even to think about it."

"No, Mr. Caine," Marianna insisted, her voice vibrating with emotion. "While I appreciate the fact that you have allowed my partner and myself to sing in your saloon, I most assuredly do not appreciate the disgusting proposition you have just put to me!" She gathered up the full skirts of her costume, heading for the doorway. She wanted nothing more than to escape from the room, to escape from the man who apparently believed her to be no better than a common trollop, no matter what he had said to the contrary.

"Wait." His command was simple and brisk, and Marianna hesitated, her hand already grasping the doorknob. She slowly turned back to face him, still feeling numb and upset.

"Yes?" she icily questioned.

"I think you ought to know that I intend to do everything in my power to change your mind." As she opened her mouth to offer him another indignantly wrathful response, he good-naturedly cut her off, saying, "I won't mention it again for the time being. It was not my intention to drive you away, my dear Annie. I hope you'll not allow what just happened to interfere with the arrangement we now have."

"You want Kate and me to continue performing here?" she blurted out in confused surprise.

"Of course. That is, if you think you can remain under the circumstances."

"What circumstances?" she demanded, eyeing him suspiciously.

"Knowing that I intend to win you, fairest Annie, and that I'll stop at nothing to do so! But, you have my word, at least for as long as my patience holds out, that I'll not force my attentions on you." He smiled disarmingly across at her, bowing slightly in her direction, his eyes gleaming with a dull light.

Marianna stared at him, not knowing whether to believe him, not knowing whether to tell Kate what had happened, and not knowing whether she should run from the saloon and never look back. Alex's handsome face swam before her eyes. She had defiantly told him how much she reveled in her adventurous new occupation, her new surroundings. What would he think if she left Caine's saloon? And what about Kate? she asked herself, sighing inwardly. Another month or so, Kate had said. If they could hold out that long, they would be able to buy the place Kate wanted.

"Very well, Mr. Caine," Marianna finally agreed, holding herself stiffly erect. "We shall remain, but only if you are true to your word." She glanced at him one last time, distressed by the flash of desire she saw reflected in his dark eyes.

"Until my patience runs out," he quietly reminded her, watching with a faint smile as she hurriedly left the room. Telling himself that he was a fool, that he should have taken what he wanted as he'd always done before, Lyle Caine wandered back to the desk and stared unseeingly down at the paper he had placed there.

No, he thought, his expression one of fierce determination and cold calculation, this way was better. For some inexplicable reason, he wanted things to be different with this fiery, headstrong little beauty named Annie Markova. That she had received a refined and cultured upbringing was quite obvious; that alone made her vastly superior to the other women he had known. And he would have her, he vowed to himself, a chilling smile on his suavely attractive countenance.

Marianna, meanwhile, nearly collided with Kate in her haste to escape from the room. Kate was on the landing just outside the door, and she reached out an arm to steady an obviously flustered Marianna.

"You all right?" she asked with a worried frown.

"Of course!" Marianna hurried to reply. She averted her face from Kate's scrutinizing gaze, saying, "We should be going downstairs now. I'm terribly afraid we shall be late for our performance!" She scurried across the landing and started down the staircase, a thoughtful Kate in her wake.

She was relieved that Kate did not question her immediately about her private conference with Caine. She was also relieved that Caine did not approach her again before she and Kate left the saloon and began strolling back to the hotel following their last performance of the evening. Now, as she walked beside her friend, their heels clicking in unison along the muddy boardwalk, she involuntarily shivered.

"Are you cold?" Kate solicitously asked, turning to the younger woman with a tiny frown.

"A little," Marianna murmured, drawing her fringed shawl even closer about her shoulders. It was not the brisk night air which chilled her, she was tempted to admit, but she was still resolved not to reveal the unpleasant confrontation to Kate.

"I don't suppose you want to tell me what went on between you and Caine," Kate nonchalantly remarked.

"It was nothing really," Marianna murmured. "He merely wanted to speak with me about my performance."

"He thought there was something wrong with it?"

"No, not exactly," she answered uneasily. "He simply offered me a few suggestions." It would be such a release to reveal the true circumstances to her friend, but she could not do that. Perhaps, she told herself hopefully, something would happen so that they could leave the saloon sooner than Kate had estimated.

"What the hell would he know about singing?" Kate irritably snapped, then fell abruptly silent as she glimpsed something from the corner of her eye, something which caused her to quicken their pace along the boardwalk.

"Kate, what is it?" demanded Marianna, detecting the grim look on the other woman's face.

"Just keep on walking!" Kate commanded, her voice dropping to just above a whisper. Marianna glanced sharply at her, but had no time to question further as they were suddenly confronted by four obviously intoxicated men, men who had been following them since they had left the saloon.

"Hey, look what we got here! It's them two fancy pieces from the Golden Nugget!" one of the four thickly exclaimed. They were unkempt and foul smelling, and the two young women attempted to move past them.

"Come on, Annie. They're just drunk," Kate murmured close to Marianna's ear. Their attempt to ignore their assailants failed when the four ruffians merely stepped unsteadily forward, blocking the women's path.

"Where do you think you're going?" another man belligerently demanded. "Ain't we good enough to talk to? You damn sure don't mind stooping to pick up our money when we throw it to you!" He was the largest of the group, a menacing scowl on his heavily bearded face.

Marianna and Kate clasped one another's hand as they swiftly looked about for assistance. They saw that they were virtually alone with the men accosting them, the boardwalks fairly deserted at that time of night. They were also well away from the saloons, though still some distance from the hotel at the far end of town. Kate, deciding that no help would be forthcoming, at least not any time soon, reached into her shirt pocket and pulled out her small silver pistol.

"Now you fellows just move out of the way and let us pass," she commanded with apparent unconcern, waving the pistol briefly. "I don't want to have to use this on any of you, but I think you ought to know that I sure as hell will if you don't move and be on your way." Marianna's widened gaze fastened on the pistol before moving to the faces of the four men. They visibly hesitated, a glimmer of fear in four pairs of bloodshot eyes.

"What good you think that little pea-shooter's gonna do against four of us?" the large man muttered with a derisive snort, his momentary fear apparently vanished.

"Who wants to be the first to see?" Kate mockingly retorted. Marianna saw the large man hesitate again, before unexpectedly lunging forward, his huge hands reaching for Kate. Marianna's scream was cut off by the sound of a loud report. She saw the large man holding his arm, bright red blood streaming from between his coarse fingers, and she gasped as she saw that he had managed to wrest the gun from Kate's grasp. She had no time in which to think about what

229

was happening as she and Kate were suddenly seized by the other men.

Marianna fought wildly against the hands which were trying to grip her arms and legs. She kicked and flailed and screamed repeatedly, while Kate was attempting to scratch at the eyes of her single assailant, her own loud curses and screams prompting the large man watching them to laugh scornfully. There was the unmistakable sound of fabric ripping as the two young women continued to struggle against their assailants, and Marianna's eyes filled with hot tears of helpless frustration as she felt herself being half-dragged, half-carried off the main boardwalk and into a side alleyway. She couldn't see Kate at all, could only focus on the grinning, leering faces of the two men who were clawing at her velvet gown. Please God, she silently, fervently prayed, please let someone hear our screams and come to help us!

She was forced down onto the hard, cold surface of the ground now, her petticoats being pushed up about her waist, her legs continuing to kick at the men who were trying to subdue her. She screamed again, her throat feeling raw, her entire body beginning to ache in weary agony. She heard Kate scream from somewhere near her, then heard the sound of another gunshot shattering the night air.

"Let them go," Lyle Caine ground out in cold fury, his dark eyes narrowed and dangerous.

The bruising hands were removed from Marianna's body, and she immediately scrambled to her feet, her hands clutching at the torn shreds of her velvet bodice.

Kate was suddenly at her side, her own disheveled appearance giving evidence that she had been just as sorely treated. The two of them watched as the four would-be rapists fearfully backed away from Caine's gun, though it appeared they were more afraid of the man himself than the weapon he held.

"We didn't mean no harm, Lyle!" one of them cried in a whining voice.

"No?" Caine quietly remarked, one eyebrow raised.

"This wouldn't have happened if that blond bitch hadn't pulled a gun on us!" the large man defensively added, still holding a dirty hand to his wounded arm. He glared murderously toward Kate, who met his glare with a particularly vengeful one of her own.

"Get out of here. If I ever see you so much as glance at these ladies again, I'll—" Caine calmly threatened, his expression appearing almost savage.

"We're going, we're going," the large man grumbled. He and the others moved slowly at first, their steps becoming hurried a short distance away. Lyle Caine turned back to Marianna and Kate as he replaced the pistol inside his coat pocket, his face registering genuine concern as he asked, "Are you all right?"

"Thank goodness you came along!" Marianna breathed, her voice quaking with emotion. "Kate, are you all right?" she repeated Caine's words, placing an arm about her friend's shoulders.

"Just a little shaken up," Kate replied with a sardonic grin. "We do look a sight, though, don't we?" she remarked, glancing at Marianna and then back at herself. She turned to Caine then. "I don't know how you happened to hear us, but I'm sure as hell glad you did!"

"I usually take a stroll at night," he explained with a brief smile. His eyes returned to Marianna, who now hurried forward to grasp his arm, her eyes shining with warm gratitude.

"I . . . I don't know what we would have done if you had not chanced to come along! Thank you, Mr. Caine." She smiled tremulously up at him, oblivious to the fact that her willing touch on his arm sent up a powerful flare of desire deep within him. His hand moved to cover hers, tightening as he said, "There's no need for thanks, Annie. If those bastards had done you injury—" he murmured, only to be cut off by Marianna's hand moving on his arm.

"I would rather not think of it. Again, Mr. Caine, you have my immense gratitude." Kate moved to take hold of Marianna's arm, saying, "It's time we got ourselves back to the hotel. Thank you, Caine," she spoke solemnly, moving down the boardwalk with Marianna now.

"Surely you don't think I'm going to allow you to walk unescorted after what just happened?" he replied, striding to take Marianna's other arm. Neither of the women protested, although Kate didn't fail to notice the way Lyle Caine's arm moved about Marianna's shoulders before they had traveled far.

Once they had bid goodnight to their rescuer and were safely upstairs in Marianna's room, the two young women collapsed upon the bed, both of them shaken after the terrifying ordeal. They lay there in silence for several moments, before Kate painfully arose from the bed and moved to inspect her appearance in the large oval mirror.

"Damnation, Annie! I'd no idea I looked every bit as bad as you!" she ruefully commented, viewing the pale bruises on her arms and shoulders, the torn and bedraggled gown that was once the finest costume she owned. Her blond hair was tangled and streaming, her face smudged and dirty.

"Oh Kate, why did this have to happen? Everything was going so well. I foolishly believed us safe," Marianna remarked with a heavy sigh. She climbed off the bed and stepped across the floor to stand beside Kate, then gasped softly at her own reflection.

"There's no such thing as a place that's safe, honey," answered Kate, frowning darkly. "Everywhere you go, there's men like that who'll try to take advantage of you, who'll make you feel cheap and dirty. Skagway's no different from any other town, save for the fact there just happens to be more men like that here right now. The rush has brought out the lowest vermin in the world, all of them looking to get rich, to make a fast dollar and then cheat someone else to get more. There's no reason to let what happened tonight scare you away. We just got unlucky," she philosophically concluded with an expressive shrug of her shoulders.

"But then we were fortunate as well, weren't we? Mr. Caine happened along when we needed him most," Marianna pointed out, sighing as she glanced down at her torn and dirty bodice, the ripped lace of her petticoats trailing the ground.

"Yeah, he did," Kate replied, her voice barely audible. She and Marianna decided to continue their conversation at a later time, since they were both in desperate need of a hot, soothing bath. Kate's thoughts became occupied with wondering which costumes would replace those which were now ruined, while Marianna found herself thinking of Alex once more.

He had been right about the dangers, but she had refused to listen. Lyle Caine's insulting proposition had been unsettling enough, she reflected with another sigh, easing her aching body into the large tub of steaming water, but then the attack had occurred as well. It was odd that everything had happened on a single night, she thought, closing her eyes and sinking lower into the healing warmth. But she certainly didn't want to dwell on either unfortunate incident. She didn't want to think about Lyle Caine or those four evil men.

Where was Alex now? she suddenly wondered, her eyelids fluttering open as she took up the cake of soap and began scrubbing at her pink flesh. Would he return in three days, or would it be longer? She knew without a doubt that he would be furious if he learned of Caine's proposition, of the attack on herself and Kate. He would be angry enough over the fact that she had disobeyed him yet again.

Later, as sleep eluded her, she thought of Alex once more. No matter how often she declared she despised him, she realized that his strong, powerful arms seemed a safe haven to her. She couldn't help comparing him to Lyle Caine, and there was little contest in her mind as to which was the more attractive, the one who represented warmth and security. And passion, a tiny voice broke in on her thoughts to add. An irresistible, splendidly rapturous passion that made her forget about all else.

Rolling swiftly to her side, she punched at her unresisting pillow and resolutely closed her eyes. But, as usual, although she was constantly pushing Alex Donovan from her mind and trying valiantly to keep him from touching her heart, he just as persistently invaded her dreams.

The night's frightening event seemed far away when Marianna and Kate came downstairs for breakfast the following morning, a bright and comfortably cool morning that chased away almost all memory of the storms which had come in the night. The startling news which was shortly to be given them was another link in the baffling, varied chain of events occurring to them since they had arrived in Skagway only five days earlier.

"Miss Markova? Miss LaRue?" a man spoke as he rose from his seat on a chair in the spacious hotel lobby. He had seen them coming down the stairs and had hurried over to greet them.

"Yes?" Marianna was the first to answer, gazing in puzzlement at the short, gray-haired man with the grizzled, peppered beard. He looked much like all the other prospectors she and Kate had seen, although he was quite a bit older than the usual.

"I got something to tell you and I aim to make it brief," he announced, loudly clearing his throat before continuing. "Old Tim wanted you to have this." He thrust something at Marianna, offering no further explanation for the moment.

"What is it?" she murmured, hesitating so that Kate reached out and took it from the stranger's hand. The blond woman muttered an appreciative curse as she opened the small leather pouch and viewed its dazzling contents.

"It's gold, Annie!" she happily declared, offering her partner a look. "Why, there must be several hundred dollars' worth in here!"

"Why are you giving this to us?" asked Marianna in confusion. "And who is Old Tim?"

"You mean who *was* Old Tim," the man amended, shaking his head sadly. "He was my friend and partner, the best of either a man could ever have. He passed on last night. He gave me his share of the gold before he died, telling me to see that you two ladies got it. Said he wanted you to have it, 'cause you reminded him of his lost youth. He heard you sing every night, till last night, that is. Said you were the sweetest nightingales he'd ever heard. Leastways, you sure made him happy with your singing."

"But, didn't he have any family he wished to give this to? Or perhaps you, as his partner—" said Marianna.

"You mean to tell me your late partner wanted us to have all this gold simply because he liked our singing?" Kate interrupted in disbelief, still clutching the pouch in her hand.

"Yes, ma'am, that's the right of it. And Tim didn't have any family left," he answered, turning back to Marianna. "We had only each other. We'd been partners for nigh on to twenty years. The two of us made it to the gold fields and back a few months ago, but his health was starting to fail him even then. And, as far as my being his partner, well, he wanted you to have his share of the findings. I'm an honest man, ladies, and I'd never have been able to live with myself if I hadn't done what Tim told me to do just before he breathed his last." He nodded briefly in their direction, turning about as if to leave.

"Wait!" Marianna cried, but Kate grabbed her arm and said, "Let him go. He did what he had to do. There's no call to embarrass him any more."

"But I merely wished to thank him!"

"Any fool would know we're grateful," Kate murmured, her gaze returning to the contents of the pouch as she poured a few sprinkles of the gold dust into the palm of her hand. "Look at this, Annie! There ought to be more than enough here to buy us our own place!"

"Don't you feel the least bit reluctant to take the gold? After all, we didn't even know the man!"

"Why should this be any different than the rest of the money we've been getting? This Old Tim fellow just wanted us to feel appreciated, that's all. And I'm sure as hell not going to lose any sleep over it!"

"All the same," Marianna remarked with a faint sigh as she and Kate began moving toward the front doorway, "I wish we had known who the man was.

Imagine how lonely he must have been, no family, no wife to comfort him. He leaves all his worldly possessions to two strangers who entertained him in a saloon."

"Come on, Annie," said Kate, attempting to hurry her friend along. "We've got to get on out and start looking for our place!"

Marianna gazed heavenward for an instant, inwardly smiling at the other woman's single-mindedness. It was all so incredible, she mused, the way things kept happening to them. But at least this time the occurrence was a pleasant one, she told herself as she and Kate stepped out into the bustling center of the town.

Fifteen

"I say we head on down to the hotel before paying a visit to the Golden Nugget," Alex suggested to the man riding beside him. The two of them reined their mounts toward Skagway's main street, the cold, blowing rain chilling them as they urged the horses onward to seek shelter from the late afternoon storm.

"Sounds good to me, Donovan," replied the grinning giant of a man who accompanied him. "You know, I'm anxious to make the acquaintance of this Caine fellow. From what you've told me about him, there's no doubt the thieving bastard believes himself comfortably secure."

"Why shouldn't he? There's no one to defy him. He controls most of the town, as well as the so-called 'law.' That's why I thought it best if there were two of us working against him, Sean. It might just make things go all that much faster."

"And why is it you're suddenly so concerned with how fast our mission goes?" Sean Cleary asked with a sardonic grin on his ruggedly attractive face. "Could it have something to do with that wife of yours?"

"It could," Alex replied with an answering grin of his own. They reached the hotel, dismounting and leading their weary horses around back to the livery stable. A few minutes later found them inside the hotel lobby.

"There's little hope of any rooms being vacant, but I thought we'd get a bite to eat here at the hotel before settling in somewhere," Alex remarked, he and Sean removing their dripping hats and jackets. He stepped up to the front desk, soon discovering that all the rooms were indeed taken. Then, on sudden impulse, he asked if the young blond woman who had been performing at the Golden Nugget Saloon a couple of weeks before was still staying at the hotel.

"She sure is," the clerk readily acknowledged. "But she and that pretty dark-haired one she sings with aren't at the Golden Nugget any longer. They've got their own place a little ways down the street now," the young man added. He then said with a frown, "We don't allow no men upstairs to bother them." He was a bit taken aback at the fierce look in Alex's golden eyes, mistakenly believing it was his warning which had caused the tall man's sudden, dark displeasure. Alex muttered a savage curse and turned away from the apprehensive young clerk.

"What is it, Alex?" Sean demanded, catching sight of his friend's grim expression.

"Damn it, she's still here!" Alex ground out.

"Who?"

"Marianna!" replied Alex, lowering his voice as the two of them moved out of earshot of the other people in the lobby.

"Your wife?" Sean asked with a slight frown.

"My wife," Alex answered with a curt nod. "She was supposed to be safely back at my grandmother's house in Sitka for the past couple of weeks. How in blazes did she manage to slip off . . ." he angrily muttered to himself, his deep voice trailing away as his eyes narrowed in fury.

"That doesn't matter," Sean remarked. "What's important is that she's still here in Skagway, still where Caine can possibly use her against you!"

"I'm way ahead of you there, Cleary," Alex tightly stated, abruptly replacing his sodden hat atop his head and drawing on his equally drenched jacket.

"Where are you going?"

"To find my wife!" he announced in a dangerous tone. Sean hurried to don his hat and coat as well, following Alex as he strode purposefully from the hotel and back out into the driving rain.

It didn't take long for Alex to locate his errant spouse. He glimpsed the large, hand-painted sign above the doorway of the narrow building near the center of town, the words "Kate and Annie's" leaving little doubt as to the restaurant's proprietorship. Alex paused outside on the boardwalk and peered inside the large window, his gaze narrowing as he caught sight of his wife inside. She was smiling as she took the orders of a group of young men seated at a table near the rear corner of the restaurant, men whose admiring stares only served to make Alex's temper that much closer to exploding.

"I wonder how she and that partner of hers happened to be able to buy this place," Sean spoke beside him, his gaze following Alex's and finding Marianna. "Is that your wife?" he asked in appreciative surprise. When Alex merely nodded curtly, he remarked, "I'd no idea she was every bit as beautiful as you described her, Donovan!" Alex muttered something unintelligible and jerked about, stalking back down toward the hotel. "Aren't you going to go inside and let her know you're back?" Sean questioned in puzzlement, easily keeping pace.

"Not yet. It's imperative that no one know she's my wife, remember? If I went in there in my present state of mind, the secret would most definitely be out!" Alex declared, smiling faintly despite his anger. "We've got some strategy to talk about, Cleary," he commanded, the two of them disappearing inside the hotel once more.

Later that evening, Sean Cleary sauntered inside the restaurant belonging to Marianna and Kate. He smiled at the bright ginghams and calicoes which so cheerfully decorated the interior, the delightfully feminine touches the two young women had given the place. He seated himself at a table near the small stage which had recently been erected along the back wall. He saw no sign of either Marianna or her partner, a young woman who had been described to him by Alex earlier in the day.

He recalled the way Alex had gravely cautioned him against revealing his true occupation to anyone. This was his first visit to Skagway, for he had been stationed

242

up at the summit of the White Pass for the previous several months, along with the other members of his regiment in the North West Mounted Police who strove to keep the peace among the gold-seekers who crossed the border on their way to the Klondike.

He and Alex Donovan had known one another for well over a year, and Sean was proud to have been selected to work with Alex on their present mission. It was not uncommon for the governments of their two countries to work in harmony, he reflected, waiting for someone to take his order, but he and Alex were more than co-workers. They shared a common bond, a deep friendship that made their mission together that much more important.

Alex's asking him to come here tonight wasn't exactly in the usual line of duty, Sean told himself with an inner chuckle. But Marianna was unfortunately already involved, and he would do anything in his power to help protect Alex's wife.

"The show's about to start, so you won't be getting anything to eat till after it's over," a buxom young woman informed Sean as she scurried past, her arms laden with plates of steaming beef stew and freshly baked sourdough bread.

"But I'm starved!" he good-naturedly protested, charming the young woman with a broad, dimpled grin. She hesitated only a moment before impulsively setting one of the plates of food before him, saying, "That'll have to do you." She was rewarded by a playful wink and another grin, and her cheeks blushed rosily as she hurried to deliver the other plates to another table of hungry men, one of her customers complaining loudly when told that his supper would be a few minutes late in arriving.

Sean had just finished off his meal when Kate and Marianna appeared, the two of them dressed in short, tight-fitting satin dresses. Marianna wore a deep blue costume, while Kate's was of an equally rich shade of pink. The predominantly male crowd cheered and applauded loudly as the two young women climbed the few steps up to the stage.

A small, balding man took his place at the upright piano in the corner, and Kate announced with a beaming smile, "Thank you. Now, what'll it be tonight?" Her gaze scanned the faces of the men before her, and she laughed softly as a booming voice called out, "Jeannie with the Light Brown Hair!"

"All right," she agreed with a decisive nod toward the man at the piano. The noisy room quieted as the first strains of music began and the voices of the two young women sweetly filled the air.

Sean Cleary's startlingly blue eyes fastened on Kate the moment she appeared on stage. His gaze suddenly widened, then narrowed, before settling with appreciative single-mindedness on the attractive blonde.

Kate's own gaze was sweeping across the crowd of listeners, until it was abruptly drawn back to the handsome giant of a man seated only a short distance away. He was staring at her in a disturbingly intense manner, only the hint of a smile on his face as he watched her.

Though momentarily, unexplainably flustered, she

continued with the song, but the words "light brown hair" reminded her of the man staring at her, and she found herself gazing at him once more. His hair was thick and sandy colored, a matching moustache on his tanned countenance. Even seated, she mused, he looked to be well over six feet in height, his muscles well displayed by his flannel shirt and fitted trousers. And his eyes, she thought, unable to tear her own away from him for the space of several long moments, his eyes were downright mesmerizing.

Sean suddenly caught Kate's gaze with his, and he smiled. A slow, warm, enchanting smile that caused its recipient to sharply avert her sparkling gray eyes, but not before Sean Cleary had caught a glimpse of an answering glow in their depths. He smiled again, to himself this time, and folded his arms across his broad chest, glancing only briefly at Marianna before fixing Kate with another stare.

Kate valiantly attempted to ignore the strange man as she and Marianna finished their first song and soon began another. It was a lively, flirtatious rendition of "Wait for the Wagon," with Marianna and Kate moving down off the stage to playfully serenade some of the men. Kate was aware of the tall stranger's gaze upon her as she smiled and sang to the men, though she resolutely avoided him.

Once the performance had drawn to a close, Marianna solicitously questioned, "Is something troubling you, Kate?"

"Troubling me? No. Why?" She and Marianna were in the back storage room, the two of them hurriedly changing clothes.

"You seemed a bit preoccupied when we were singing tonight."

"Must have been your imagination," Kate evasively murmured, slipping off her costume. Had it truly been that obvious? she wondered with a sudden frown. Damn! she silently swore. You'd think she was nothing more than an innocent little schoolgirl. She'd seen attractive men before, hundreds of them, so why should that one have seemed so different to her?

The way he had stared at her had made her feel as if he was undressing her, and it troubled her that the sensation was not all that unpleasant. What was there about him that should cause her to go all breathless and soft inside? she chided herself, pulling her petticoat over her head with a vengeance.

"Are you coming back to the hotel with me?" Marianna asked, interrupting Kate's turbulent thoughts. She stood ready and waiting, her own figure now encased in a modest, sedate calico.

"No, you go on ahead," Kate replied, busying herself with the buttons of her own simple dress. "Just be sure and have Andy walk with you. I'm going to stay here and make sure everything's locked up tight and proper. Closing time's not that far off." Marianna peered closely at her friend before remarking she'd see her at the hotel later, then returned to the main room in search of her escort, the quiet little man who accompanied them on the piano each night.

Marianna bid Andy goodnight when they reached the hotel, thanked him for seeing her home, then climbed the staircase to her room. Withdrawing the key from her skirt pocket, she unlocked the door to her room and stepped inside, tossing her things upon the quilt-covered bed. She lit the lamp beside the bed, sinking down onto the mattress as she began drawing off her shoes. She rose to her feet with a loud gasp when she perceived someone sitting in the chair in one corner of the room, a lazy smile on his handsome face as he silently watched her.

"Alex! What are you doing here?" she breathlessly demanded. Without waiting for him to answer, she angrily said, "You have the most abominable habit of sneaking into my room and frightening me half to death!"

"And you, my dearest little vixen, have the most abominable habit of disobeying me at every turn," Alex nonchalantly countered, leaning back in the chair and still watching her, his booted ankles crossed, his thumbs hooked through the belt loops at his waist. There was a faint, mocking grin on his face, but Marianna glimpsed the dull, dangerous gleam in his golden eyes. It occurred to her that she could scream, could summon assistance, but she then reasoned with herself that Alex could hardly be intent upon abducting her and placing her on board his schooner again, since his schooner was now back in Sitka.

"I told you I would not return to Sitka," she defiantly reminded him, lifting her chin a trifle higher as she faced him squarely. Her heart was seized by a wild fluttering as she gazed at him, her pulse racing. She was dismayed to feel her cheeks rosily blushing, for she remembered all too well the last time she had seen him—the tempestuous, deliciously wicked night they had shared!

"Our last night together has been in my mind a lot these past two weeks," Alex quietly remarked, smiling as Marianna raised widened, astonished eyes to his. It was as if he had read her thoughts, and she became convinced he was laughing at her, taunting her.

"Has it? I've managed to put it completely from my thoughts!" she obstinately declared, her eyes flashing as she drew herself proudly erect.

"You're not a very convincing liar, my love," Alex responded with a low chuckle, prompting her to bristle at his amused manner. Before she could speak, he stood up from the chair and crossed the short distance between them with slow, purposeful strides. "How did you do it, Annie? How did you get away from Ivan and the others?" he unexpectedly demanded, the expression on his face growing quite solemn as he towered above her.

"With surprising ease!" she triumphantly answered, refusing to back down from the smoldering anger she saw reflected in his gaze. "I very much doubt if they even realized I was gone until well away from Skagway. But what does that matter? I told you I would not sail, that I would find some way to remain here."

"For two weeks I've believed you safely back in Sitka," Alex muttered, half to himself. His eyes narrowed abruptly, his large hands closing about her upper arms. "I ought to turn you across my knee and give you the spanking you so richly deserve!" His low threat was punctuated with several brisk shakes which caused her thick raven curls, already loosening from their pins, to swirl about her face and shoulders. "Don't you realize what danger you've placed yourself in by so foolishly defying me?"

"Why should I know such a thing when you have never seen fit to reveal the true nature of your business here?" she hotly retorted, her fiery blue-green gaze sending daggers at his head. "You certainly do not appear to be the single-minded gambler you would have me believe!"

"Your point is well taken, my love," he quietly said, striving to keep his temper under control. "You'll simply have to trust me when I tell you that we must continue to conceal the fact of our marriage. No one must even know we are acquainted, do you understand?"

"I should understand much better if you would only tell me why I am supposedly in danger by remaining in Skagway!" she exclaimed, jerking from his grasp and marching indignantly away to stand by the single window. She whirled round to face him again, suddenly yearning for there to be some sort of truce between them. "Kate and I have our own restaurant in town now, and I have every intention of remaining here as her partner," she declared more calmly.

"How the hell did that happen? Did Lyle Caine give you the money?" Alex jealously queried, moving to confront her more closely once again.

"Of course not!" Marianna vehemently denied, glaring up at him. She suddenly recalled the displeasure Caine had revealed when she and Kate had informed him they were leaving his saloon. Marianna had encountered him several times since, but he had been very polite each time, never mentioning his shocking proposition or his anger at her leaving.

"No?" Alex asked in disbelief.

"No! Kate and I were fortunate enough to receive a substantial amount of gold from a prospector, an older man who died a short time ago. He instructed his partner to give the gold to us," she rapidly explained, then broke off, furiously telling herself that she owed him no explanation. "I have nothing further to say to you, Alex Donovan! And I sincerely hope you are not going to make a disagreeable habit of appearing uninvited in my room!"

"That's exactly what I intend to do," he commented with a meaningful gleam in his golden gaze, his hands reaching for her again.

"Do you truly believe I will allow you to keep treating me like—" she seethed, furiously slapping away his hands.

"Like a wife?" Alex sardonically finished, ignoring her futile efforts to discourage him from pulling her into his arms.

"You have the audacity to think you can disappear to only God knows where for two weeks and then expect me to—"

"I'm flattered to know that you've been counting the days," he interrupted again, driving her to distraction with his mocking, amused remarks. She heaved an angry sigh, helplessly pushing against his determined, well-muscled chest as his arms moved to surround her with unhurried intent. "I thought I'd missed you last time," he told her with a soft chuckle, his gaze holding hers as his head lowered, "but that was nothing compared to the agony I've felt without you these past couple of weeks!"

"You think only . . . only of satisfying your lust, don't you?" Marianna raged, just as furious with herself as with him. She could rant and rave at him, quarrel with and defy him, but she could not resist him! She had felt a confusing surge of happiness when she had first seen him sitting there, so maddeningly handsome, in her room. And now, now, she silently berated herself, she was very near to surrendering totally to him yet again. She was both ashamed and breathlessly excited at the thought.

"Not lust, my beautiful firebrand. Love," he told her in a deep voice barely above a whisper. She moaned softly as she melted against him, his lips closing upon hers with their familiar, sensuous persuasion. He kissed her with a tender, unhurried passion, a passion that swiftly grew in intensity until his mouth was hungrily devouring hers. She gasped in surprise as Alex suddenly spun about with her still in his arms and lay backwards upon the softness of the bed, his wife landing full-length atop him.

Marianna gasped again as his hands began raising her skirts and petticoats, his fingers grasping the top edge of her bloomers and pulling them slowly, provocatively downward. He reluctantly drew his warm mouth from hers as he reached to draw her undergarments all the way down and off, his fingers moving to the buttons on the front bodice of her dress. He grew impatient before he had unfastened more than a dozen buttons, but that was enough for him to be able to push the edges of her bodice aside. Then he swiftly untied the ribbons of her lacetrimmed camisole, which enabled him to tug it down so that her firmly rounded breasts were revealed to him.

Alex pulled her gently upward toward the head of the bed so his lips could fasten tenderly about one of her rose-tipped breasts, his hands returning to softly caress and knead her enticingly curved buttocks. She grew faint with the wildly spiraling passions building to a fever pitch deep within her, and she cried out softly as one of his hands moved to the very center of her femininity, his long, supple fingers causing her to gasp, her own fingers entwining in his thick auburn hair and clutching his head closer to her sensitive breasts.

Finally Alex himself could stand no more, and he reached beneath Marianna to swiftly unfasten his trousers, his lips capturing hers with brief, fiery intensity before his hands grasped her about her slender waist and lifted her upward, then eased her down upon his throbbing maleness.

Marianna clung feverishly to him as he moved within her, his hands steadying her, then returning to her finely molded hips, his searching lips drawn back to her quivering breasts. His fingers gently dug into the white flesh of her buttocks as she matched his rhythm and breathlessly rode atop him, the two of them seeking the joyful explosion in perfect unison. When it came, Marianna cried out softly and collapsed against him, left totally drained, with Alex experiencing much the same languor.

Later, after Alex had surprised her by announcing he must soon be off, revealing only that he had business at Lyle Caine's saloon, Marianna became incensed with him again. She was setting her camisole and bodice to rights once more, her eyes searching for her undergarments when Alex suddenly remarked, "You know, my love, being with you like this almost makes me glad you managed to get off that blasted schooner! Of course," he then solemnly added, watching her as he leaned against the wall near the doorway, "you've created a very difficult situation by remaining here in town. I must admit that I'm not entirely certain whether to try to send you back to Sitka again or not."

"What?" she angrily responded, abruptly rising from the bed as she finished with the last of the buttons. "Haven't we quarrelled over that enough as it is? How dare you think you can come in here and . . . and use me, then announce that you're still contemplating packing me off to your grandmother in Sitka!" Her eyes blazed with their splendid blue-green fire, her color high, and Alex mused to himself that she had never appeared lovelier, or more desirable, than she did at that moment. But, lovely and desirable or not, he firmly vowed, he could not allow her to endanger herself with her headstrong, defiant willfulness!

"I did not use you, as you so eloquently put it," he attempted to reason, his golden gaze narrowing down at her. "You are my wife. Sooner or later, you're going to realize that we belong together. But that isn't the point here now. What's important is that you heed what I tell you, Marianna. To begin with," he told her with a brief scowl, "I want you to stay away from Lyle Caine."

"Stay away from him?" she indignantly repeated. "How dare you insinuate that I am seeking him out!"

"I'm not insinuating anything of the kind. I'm just warning you not to have anything to do with him. And furthermore," he commanded, his temper rising again, "I'm not too happy with the way you continue to flaunt yourself before all the men in town."

"I do not flaunt myself before anyone!"

"I saw you tonight. I was watching you from outside that place you and your partner of yours mysteriously managed to buy."

"You were spying on me?" Marianna gasped out, then defensively retorted, "I have done nothing to be ashamed of, Alex Donovan! I shall continue to perform, and I shall remain cordial to Lyle Caine if that is what I wish to do!"

"Are we forever destined to be at odds whenever we're out of bed?" Alex sardonically quipped, smiling faintly down at her. "If so, then I propose we attempt to spend the remainder of our married life together safely between the covers!"

Marianna gasped at his teasing remark, completely failing to see the humor of it. She fixed him with a haughty, scornful look, the expression on her beautiful face one of cold dignity.

"You shall never touch me in that way again, do you

hear me, Alex Donovan? I despise you, I despise your lustful assaults!" She knew she was lying, knew there was not an ounce of truth in her words, but she wanted to hurt him, to repay him for his egotistical, overconfident conquest of her! She was furious with him for trying to run her life again, and she would have said or done anything in that moment to defy him.

Alex's handsome features became suffused with a dull, angry color, his eyes gleaming with a savage light. Her words had not achieved the desired result, but had instead only served to make his usually controlled temper reach a dangerously high level of intensity. He said nothing for several long, tense moments while his wife continued to glare up at him. She was in truth already beginning to experience remorse for what she had said, but she displayed no evidence of it to him.

"As I said before, my dearest bride, you are not a very convincing liar," Alex finally murmured in a low, even tone. Then, before Marianna could possibly have guessed his intent, his hand shot out with remarkable speed and seized her arm, tugging her none too gently along with him toward the chair in one corner of the small room. He took a seat on the chair and yanked a stunned Marianna face-down across his knees, her long black curls trailing the floor as Alex tossed up her skirts and petticoats.

"What do you think you're doing?" she wrathfully demanded, beginning to twist and squirm across his lap. She could see nothing but the shadows on the floor, for her clothing was falling down about her flushed, darkly frowning face.

"I'm doing what someone should have done long before now," Alex ground out, raising his large hand and bringing it down upon her bare bottom with a resounding slap. Marianna was at first too shocked to so much as whimper, but she began to loudly protest and demand that he release her an instant later, her cries of outrage muffled by the folds of the garments covering her head. She gasped again as the palm of his hand found its target again, stinging her wriggling derrière. He spanked her several more times as she threatened and cursed him, then finally ceased the humiliating punishment as he stood to his feet, Marianna spilling unceremoniously to the floor as he stalked to the doorway again. She swiftly extricated herself from the layers of calico and fine white cotton, blushing fierily as her eyes blazed vengefully up at Alex.

"Remember what I said about Lyle Caine," Alex tightly muttered, his own features still giving evidence of his anger. "I'll repeat this little episode the next time I see you if you've not yet learned to obey me," he grimly promised before opening the door cautiously, peering out into the hallway to make certain he was unseen, then leaving Marianna alone in the room. She could only sit and watch as the door closed softly behind him.

She muttered a most unladylike curse as she rose to her feet, yanking her skirts and petticoats back down around her legs. She was so angry she could barely move, but she finally began pacing about the room, her arms tightly crossed against her heaving bosom, her entire body trembling.

No one had ever dared to spank her before! Not even the schoolmistresses had so much as touched her when dispensing discipline. And now, now, she indignantly seethed, Alex Donovan had not only used her body, he had then proceeded to humiliate her! She put a hand to her buttocks, cursing again as her flesh still burned from Alex's punishing hand.

She suddenly burst into tears, whirling about to land face down upon the bed, burying her face in one of the pillows. Sobbing miserably, she could no longer think or reason or plan, could only pour out her unhappiness upon the dampening softness of the pillow.

When Kate came upstairs a short time later, she knocked gently upon Marianna's door, but received no response. Believing her partner to have already fallen asleep, she moved down the hallway to her own room, her turbulent thoughts allowing her no rest as she climbed into bed.

Sean Cleary's smiling face refused to leave her mind. She still did not know what to think of their bewildering encounter.

He had been waiting outside the restaurant when she and one of the waitresses, Lorna, had finished locking up and come outside to pause on the front boardwalk while the two of them donned their woolen cloaks against the damp and chilly night air. Kate was at first unaware of Sean's presence a few steps away from the front door of the building.

"Good evening, Miss LaRue," Sean's pleasant, deep voice rang out, initially alarming both Kate and Lorna. The two young women whirled about to face him,

Lorna, smiling rather saucily, while Kate merely eyed him coolly.

"What do you want?" Kate rudely asked. She was feeling unaccountably flustered as he stared down at her, moving forward to tower above them.

"I'll be walking Miss LaRue home tonight," Sean unexpectedly proclaimed as he turned to Lorna with a beguiling grin. Lorna smiled even more encouragingly up at him, her smile abruptly fading as Kate fixed her with a quelling glance.

"The hell you will," Kate responded in annoyance, presenting her back to him and grabbing Lorna's arm. She wasn't afraid of him, but there was something about him that threw her into uncharacteristic confusion.

"Run along now, Lorna," Sean good-naturedly commanded, taking a gentle but firm grip on Lorna's other arm and propelling her away from Kate and on down the boardwalk. The young woman hesitated a moment, disappointed that the tall, muscular stranger was apparently not interested in her, before she did as he had bid. She ignored her employer as Kate angrily called to her. Sean and Kate were left standing alone in front of the restaurant, the gray clouds in the sky above making the night darker than usual.

"Who the hell do you think you are?" Kate resentfully demanded, rounding on Sean. She was nonplussed when he simply grinned disarmingly down at her from his considerable height, a full head taller than herself.

"The name's Sean Cleary, and I suggest we start

walking toward the hotel if we don't want to catch our death of cold," he cheerfully responded, seizing her arm and drawing it through his. Kate jerked her arm away, gazing up at him with anger in her lovely gray eyes.

"I choose my own escorts, Mr. Cleary!"

"Call me 'Sean,' Kate," he quietly insisted, so much warmth in his smile that she was once again at a loss.

"Why in blue blazes should I want to call you anything?" she irritably snapped, shivering suddenly as a gust of cold wind whipped about them. Sean took her arm again and pulled her easily along with him, heading toward the hotel.

"Because the two of us are going to mean a lot to one another, Kate LaRue." She gasped softly in stunned amazement at his startling words, and she didn't seem to realize that she was calmly strolling along the boardwalk with him in spite of her earlier protests.

"Oh?" she sarcastically countered, a twisted little smile on her attractive face. "And what makes you so damn sure of that?"

"A pretty young woman such as yourself shouldn't go about using such rough language all the time," Sean softly declared, ignoring her question. Kate decided she'd had just about enough of this Sean Cleary's highhandedness, his arrogant assumption that he possessed the power to charm any woman on earth. She uttered a blistering curse and jerked her arm away once more, her eyes blazing.

"Look, I don't know who the hell you are or why you've decided to make me the recipient of your addlebrained, unwanted attentions," she lashed out at him, further infuriated by the way he continued to grin down at her, "but you can damn sure keep away from me!" She glared at him once more before spinning about on her heel and marching off down the boardwalk, unaware that Sean stood and watched her until she had disappeared inside the hotel a short distance away.

Now, as she lay feeling restless upon her bed, she could not get him out of her mind. Wishing she had been able to talk to Marianna, although she was not the sort who usually went around telling anyone else what she was thinking or feeling, she crossed her hands beneath her head and stared unseeingly up at the ceiling. It was a long time before she fell asleep.

Marianna's mind was equally troubled. The unpleasant, explosive confrontation with Alex bothered her a good deal more than she cared to admit. But she too finally drifted off into a dream-filled slumber, her last waking thoughts of Alex.

Sixteen

Marianna and Kate both showed the effects of their less-than-restful nights the following morning. There were faint circles beneath their eyes, and there was a certain preoccupied air about them as they conducted business at their restaurant throughout the day, although neither seemed to notice anything unusual about the other.

Marianna found herself frequently wondering if Alex would perhaps seek her out again that day, or that night, and her eyes strayed more than once toward the doorway as she busily took orders and served meals. Kate's eyes were also drawn to the restaurant's entrance, although she would not admit to herself that Sean Cleary had anything to do with the direction of her thoughtful gaze.

Both women were surprised, as well as disappointed, when neither Alex Donovan nor his friend put in an appearance that evening. Two days passed, and still they had not seen or heard from the men who were so much in their thoughts.

On the third night after Alex's return to Skagway, Marianna was making preparations to leave the restaurant and retire to her room at the hotel when Lyle Caine unexpectedly approached her, sauntering through the front doorway and smiling broadly as he caught sight of the dark-haired young beauty he was so patiently pursuing.

"Looks like you and Kate are doing quite a business," he remarked as Marianna counted out the day's earnings. She raised faintly surprised eyes to his face, momentarily startled by the sound of his voice.

"Yes, Mr. Caine, we are," she coolly answered, finishing her counting and placing the various bills and coins in a small metal box to be transferred to the bank the following morning. Why had he sought her out tonight? Marianna wondered, instinctively glancing about for either Kate or Andy. She hadn't spoken to him in several days. He had been in the restaurant on only three occasions during the past two weeks, and had merely smiled cordially at her before leaving each time. He had yet to mention the shocking proposition he had once made to her, the kiss he had forced upon her. Perhaps, she decided with an inward sigh, smoothing a few wayward curls away from her lovely face, perhaps he had finally come to the conclusion that his hopes of securing her affections were futile. It would be a great relief to her if such were the case, for she had more than enough to worry about as it was, what with Alex Donovan plaguing her thoughts and dreams so relentlessly.

"I'm happy to hear of your success," he replied,

though not too sincerely. "The Golden Nugget hasn't been the same since you left, Annie," he unexpectedly remarked, his tone lowering as he gazed deeply into her troubled eyes. He leaned closer, resting one arm on top of the tall counter situated near the doorway. "It isn't just your singing, it's you." The meaningful expression in his dark eyes increased Marianna's unease.

"I've told you before, Mr. Caine, that Kate and I were naturally quite grateful for the opportunity you offered us, but that it was time for us to leave your saloon." He could be so charming at times, so chilling at others, she told herself. She began to experience an increasing feeling of dread, dread that he was about to renew his offer of a partnership that entailed more than just business, and her eyes once again searched for any sign of her partner and the piano player. She breathed a tiny sigh of relief when Kate and Andy moved out of the storage room and came toward her, Kate's gray eyes narrowing in visible displeasure at Caine's presence.

"Evening, Lyle," Kate casually murmured, handing Marianna her cloak. "Something we can do for you?"

"You can allow me a few moments in private conversation with your partner," Lyle Caine replied just as casually, his eyes moving back to rest upon Marianna's solemn features.

"Sorry, can't do that. Annie and I have a thousand things to talk over tonight," Kate pleasantly refused, tossing her own cloak about her shoulders. She blithely ignored the way Caine's lips compressed into a thin, tight line of anger, and she briefly turned to the silent man beside her, saying, "That's all for tonight. You can go on home now, Andy."

"Are you sure you don't want me to walk the two of you home, Miss Kate?" Andy questioned, sharply eyeing Caine.

"No, thanks. We may have had a run of bad luck once," she dryly commented, flashing a half-smile in Caine's direction, "but I don't think anyone will bother us now." Andy hesitated a few seconds before donning his own hat and coat and moving slowly out of the restaurant, obviously reluctant to leave the two young women alone with Lyle Caine. Once Andy had gone, Caine quietly declared, "I'll be more than happy to escort you to the hotel." His offer was apparently meant to include both Kate and Marianna, but his eyes never wavered from Marianna's face. His next words were just for her. "I'd like to have a few words alone with you."

"I told you," Kate interjected, "that Annie and I have business of our own to discuss." Marianna was dismayed at the way Lyle Caine's eyes narrowed, the expression on his face hardening. She quickly decided to intervene, not wishing to be the cause of any unpleasantness between Kate and the man who suddenly seemed quite intimidating.

"Very well, Mr. Caine. You may escort us to the hotel. The private conversation you desire with me will have to take place in the hotel lobby." That should be safe enough, Marianna told herself, allowing Caine to place her cloak about her shoulders as the three of them started walking out of the restaurant. Kate said nothing further as she moved along the boardwalk beside her partner, Lyle Caine on Marianna's other side. The twilight sky was free of clouds, the long daylight hours just beginning to fade into night.

Caine made small talk with Marianna as they went, but it was obvious he had a great deal more on his mind than the light, amiable conversation he shared with her. He was taking hold of her hand to draw her arm through his when Marianna and Kate both gasped softly as they caught sight of the two men striding along the boardwalk toward them. Lyle Caine muttered a curse beneath his breath, his hand tightening on Marianna's.

"Well, if it isn't the infamous owner of the Golden Nugget and his two former songbirds," Alex Donovan mockingly quipped, a rather scornful grin on his handsome face. There was no hint of the mingled fury and jealousy raging within him as he merely glanced briefly in Marianna's direction, his golden eyes fastening with unmistakable challenge on Lyle Caine's visibly displeased countenance. Marianna could feel her cheeks coloring, and she proudly lifted her head as she refused to look at Alex again.

"What do you want, Donovan?" Caine quietly demanded, his gaze moving for an instant to the taller man beside Alex. "It seems to me like you and your friend here would be anxious to try and win back some of what you've lost in my place the past three nights," he contemptuously remarked, forgetting about Marianna for the moment.

"Does it?" Alex sarcastically retorted, his own gaze

flitting toward the two young women who stood silently by, both of them avidly watching the subtle battle taking place. "You know, Caine, I still admire your taste." He grinned boldly, provoking Marianna to say, "Would you mind allowing us to pass? The night air is cool." She was angered when his golden gaze dismissed her and swiftly returned to Caine. She was further infuriated by her undeniable delight when she had first seen him, although she now felt an overwhelming impulse to slap his arrogant face.

Kate and Sean both seemed detached from the proceedings. Sean's deep blue eyes, twinkling with irrepressible humor, never moved from Kate's face. Kate, on the other hand, appeared to possess a sudden fascination for the buildings across the street, her sparkling gray eyes striving to mask the look of expectation they had first displayed when Sean approached. The expression on her face was one of bored indifference, but Sean Cleary was not so easily fooled.

"You heard the lady," Lyle Caine stated with a deepening frown while Alex merely chuckled.

"'Lady'?" he loudly repeated, then laughed with insulting significance. "Since when is one of your women deserving of that particular term, Caine?" he derisively questioned. Sean's eyes finally moved away from Kate as the expression on his face darkened, his faintly worried gaze moving back and forth between Alex and Caine.

Marianna drew in her breath sharply, and she suddenly wondered what game Alex was playing. A very dangerous one, she told herself, glancing apprehensively up at the darkly menacing man beside her. Why was Alex so determined to provoke a quarrel? Was she herself possibly the reason?

Lyle Caine's hand instinctively moved toward the pistol he kept concealed in his coat pocket, but he apparently thought better of his initial reaction as his eyes met Alex's. He was puzzled as to why Donovan, usually such an imperturbable character, was behaving with such uncharacteristic belligerence. Nevertheless, he decided, now was not the time to press the issue. He smiled with chilling calm as Marianna heaved an inward sigh of relief.

"We'll discuss your lack of manners toward the lady at a later date, Donovan," he smoothly declared, faintly smiling once more as he moved forward with Marianna's hand still clasped firmly in his. It appeared for a tense moment as if Alex would not move aside, but Sean's warning hand on his arm finally prompted him to take a step backward so that Caine and the two women could pass.

"What the hell were you doing, Alex?" Sean muttered in a low voice as Alex stood and watched the trio leave, a fierce scowl on his handsome features. "What would we have done if Caine hadn't decided to back down?" he demanded.

"I'd have put an end to his damned, criminal ways once and for all," Alex ground out, still watching as his wife strolled beside Caine. Sean looked speculatively at his friend, heaving a sigh.

"And you'd have blown the whole investigation

when you killed him. I don't blame you for wanting to slit the bastard's throat, but you'll have to restrain your murderous instincts till the investigation's completed and we have everything wrapped up tight and proper," Sean remarked with a sardonic grin, satisfied when Alex turned to him and smiled ruefully.

"You know, Cleary, there are times I wish you didn't make so much sense, damn you!" Sean chuckled softly in response, and the two of them turned their steps toward the Golden Nugget. Alex remained in a quiet, dangerous mood, though he forced himself to concentrate on his work as he and Sean sauntered inside the crowded saloon and took a seat at one of the card tables.

Marianna and Lyle Caine, meanwhile, stood alone in the hotel lobby. Kate, reluctant to leave her partner alone with Caine, nevertheless excused herself and went up to her room. The only other person in the brightly lit lobby was the desk clerk, and he was safely out of earshot as Caine escorted Marianna over to some chairs in the opposite corner. A welcome heat was emanating from a huge iron stove as Caine seated himself across from Marianna and began.

"I think you already know what I want to talk to you about." There was only the hint of a smile on his darkly attractive face as he stared intently at her.

"If it has anything to do with your offer of a partnership—" Marianna stiffly replied, her thoughts still on Alex and the bewildering way he had behaved. She once again recalled the way Lyle Caine's hand had reached for his gun, and her manner became even more aloof.

"It does," he cut her off, leaning back in his chair. "I told you my patience would eventually run out," he meaningfully reminded her, his gaze looking particularly hawkish now. "I've bided my time, Annie. I've been more patient with you than I've ever been with any other woman. I've waited and watched. But, I think it was a mistake to be so patient with you."

"Mr. Caine, I don't wish to hear—"

"You're going to hear all I have to say," he firmly insisted, cutting off her protests yet again. There was an unfathomable gleam in his dark eyes, a certain determination on his face that frightened her. She was tempted to run, to flee upstairs to the safety of her room, but she remained. "I don't know why I've allowed things to go on this long," he continued, staring across at her. "Maybe I felt you really were different somehow. Different or not, you have no more time. My patience has run out. I want you back at the Golden Nugget tomorrow night, Annie Markova."

"And if I refuse?" Marianna haughtily replied, becoming incensed at the way he apparently believed he could manipulate her. She would not allow her fear of him to make her display cowardice.

"There are many ways I can make you agree," Caine smiled evilly. "But I want you to come to me willingly. That offer of a partnership still stands."

"Don't you really mean that offer to become your mistress?" Marianna furiously countered, rising quickly to her feet as her eyes flashed defiantly down at him. "How dare you! How dare you believe you can threaten me into giving myself to you!" He rose slowly to his feet as well now, looming over her as his eyes raked her trembling body.

"There's something you'd best learn right now. I get what I want in this town, Annie. I'm generally a fairly easygoing man, except when I'm crossed. As long as people do as I tell them, there's no trouble. I take care of those who work for me. As long as you do things my way, you'll have no complaints. I'll see that you have everything you want," he informed her in a deceptively controlled voice.

"I want nothing from you! I don't care if you believe you control everyone in Skagway, Mr. Caine—you do not control me!" she retorted. She whirled about, intent upon ending the disagreeable confrontation, but his hand gripping her arm with bruising force detained her.

"You'll regret it, Annie," he spoke softly, his voice barely above a whisper now as his eyes glowed with a dull light. "You'll regret it if you refuse my generous offer. This is the last time I'll make it. After this, I'll just take what I want. You'll be mine, willingly or not. The choice is yours," he confidently declared. There was a veiled threat of harsh treatment if she chose the latter, and Marianna felt another surge of fear.

"Take your hand away from my arm, Mr. Caine," she disdainfully commanded, fixing him with a bravely defiant glare. She waited breathlessly as he did not respond for several long seconds, a muscle in his left cheek twitching as his dark eyes narrowed in silent rage. Then he released her arm, his punishing fingers leaving bright red marks on her white flesh. He looked capable of violence toward her in that moment, and

Marianna's alarmed gaze flew to the young desk clerk. She glanced back at Lyle Caine with wide, anxious eyes before spinning about and escaping up the stairs.

Kate was waiting for her in the hallway outside her room. She hurried toward Marianna with a worried frown as she glimpsed the look of horror on her partner's lovely young face.

"Annie, what is it? What did he do to you?" Kate demanded. "If he touches you again, I'll—" the blond woman seethed.

"Oh, Kate!" Marianna hoarsely whispered, the two of them rapidly moving inside the room. "I'm afraid I underestimated him. I never realized he was ... was ..." she shakily remarked, breaking off as a powerful shudder tore through her.

"You never realized what a cold, calculating, heartless son of a bitch he was?" Kate finished for her with a bitter smile. She placed a comforting arm about the younger woman's shoulders as they sank down onto the bed. "I didn't know exactly what he was up to, playing the part of a gentlemanly suitor, but I sure as hell knew what he wanted! All that nonsense about a partnership was just his vile way of getting you into his clutches. Once he'd used you and tired of you, you'd have been left with nothing!"

"How did you know about his offer?" asked Marianna in surprise, still feeling the unpleasant effects of her encounter with Caine.

"I listened at the door."

"Why didn't you let me know you knew?"

"Thought it might be better if I pretended ignorance," Kate answered simply. "Look, honey, I'd be a fool not to realize you haven't got the worldly wisdom of a flea! I've been keeping my eye on Caine whenever he's been around you. I knew he'd get tired of waiting sooner or later. Men like that aren't used to having women turn them down." She sighed heavily. "We've made a lot of friends in this town, Annie, but I don't know if any of them would stand up to Caine if it came right down to it. We'll have to think of some way to change his mind about you."

"How do you propose we do that?"

"I don't know. Give me some time to think on it. Are you all right?" she demanded, rising to her feet and opening the door. As Marianna smiled tremulously and nodded, Kate said, "Try not to think about it anymore tonight. We'll come up with something. There's got to be some way to defeat Lyle Caine. But, if worse comes to worst, I guess you could go on back to that family of yours in Sitka . . ."

"No. I have no intention of allowing Lyle Caine or anyone else to force me to leave when I do not wish to do so!" Marianna courageously declared. She and Kate smiled briefly at one another before Kate left her alone in the room.

Later, after she had soothed her tense body in a tub of hot water and was returning to her room, Marianna thought of Lyle Caine and his threats once more. Wondering how she was possibly going to extricate herself from the terrible situation, she clutched her cotton wrapper more closely about her suddenly shivering form.

Perhaps Alex . . . she found herself thinking, then briskly shook her head as if to dispel the notion. No, she mused with a faint sigh escaping her lips, she could not bring herself to ask Alex Donovan for help, not in this situation. It was quite obvious that he detested Lyle Caine, that he was jealous of the man's attentions toward her. Just the same, she reflected, lying upon the bed and gazing pensively toward the window, it would be such a relief to tell Alex. Alex was so strong, so confident. She knew he would do everything in his power to protect her from Caine.

She lay quiet and still on the bed for a long time, her mind wandering until she finally drifted off into a sleep of emotional exhaustion. It was much later, most of the night already gone, when her eyelids fluttered open. She sleepily wondered what had served to awaken her from such a deep slumber, the question in her mind answered as she saw the brass knob on her bedroom door moving counterclockwise in the semidarkness.

Marianna gasped as she abruptly sat upright in the bed, her heart leaping wildly within her breast as the door was eased open and a man's dark form was revealed. She opened her mouth to scream, but no sound was emitted before she recognized the golden eyes staring down at her.

"Alex!" she breathed, closing her eyes for a brief instant. They opened and widened again as she came up on her knees in the bed, her hands on her hips as she wrathfully demanded, "Why in heaven's name do you keep doing that? Couldn't you just once consider knocking on my door like a sane person?"

"I don't want anyone to know I'm here, remember?" he replied with a low chuckle, his appreciative gaze drinking in the sight of her thick tresses streaming about her face and shoulders in wild disarray, her beautiful, curvaceous body well displayed by the thin cotton wrapper she was wearing.

"I distinctly remember locking that door!"

"Locks are of little consequence to a man in love," he teasingly murmured, moving closer now. The smile on his face was replaced by a slight frown as he said, "We haven't got much time, so I'll make this as brief as possible. You and I are leaving for Bennett this morning."

"What?" Marianna responded in bewilderment, sinking back down upon the bed.

"We're traveling up the Pass to Bennett. I've got to leave this morning, and you're coming with me," Alex informed her, taking a seat on the bed beside her. His expression was unusually grim, and Marianna raised questioning eyes to his face.

"Why? Why are you going to Bennett, and why do you believe I'm coming with you?"

"I've got some business to attend to there. That's all I can tell you about my reasons for going. But, as for your coming with me, you don't honestly think I'd consider leaving you here, do you?" he demanded with a faint scowl.

"I fail to see that you have any choice in the matter!" she obstinately decreed, her eyes flashing. "I'm not leaving Skagway, Alex Donovan, and I'm certainly not leaving to travel anywhere with you!"

"Yes you are," he countered in an authoritative tone of voice. "I can't trust you to stay out of trouble while I'm gone, so you'll have to come with me. I hadn't originally considered the idea of taking you with me, but I think it's the best solution now. Especially after finding you with Caine again. Damn it, woman, I told you to stay away from him!"

"I didn't go near him! He came into the restaurant as we were closing and insisted upon escorting us home," she defensively replied.

"Is that all he wanted?" Alex demanded.

"No. I mean yes!" Marianna quickly amended, but not before Alex had detected a telltale note of distress in her voice. He slid closer to her on the bed, one of his large hands warmly covering both of hers. His eyes were gentle, his expression suddenly tender.

"What is it, my love?" Marianna was still reluctant to tell him, though it was difficult for her to hold back in the face of such genuine concern. But she merely shook her head in response, averting her gaze from his. If she told him, she silently reasoned, it would cause a great deal more trouble between Caine and him. And, even though she would not ask herself why, she did not want to see Alex endangered. She now realized how menacing Lyle Caine could be, and she did not want to be the cause of a violent confrontation between the two men.

"Nothing," she finally murmured as Alex continued to stare at her in close scrutiny. "Alex, I do not wish to accompany you to Bennett," she calmly told him.

"Sorry, it's the only way," he said, rising from the

bed and stepping across to the window. "You'll have to get up and get dressed now. I've already got all the provisions we'll need." He turned back to her, a troubled look in his own eyes. "I'm not going to leave you here, Annie, so you may as well accustom yourself to that fact, and quick!"

"But what about Kate? What about the restaurant and our singing and—" Marianna began, only to be interrupted by a particularly stern-faced Alex.

"I think you've had enough of your little adventure! As for your partner, I'll have Sean think of something to tell her to explain away your sudden departure."

"And just who is Sean?" she irritably queried, still not quite believing what she had just heard. Go to Bennett with Alex? Bennett, she knew, was just over the border. She had heard many prospectors remark that the White Pass was treacherous, even in summer. How could Alex expect her to travel all that way with him? It was all happening so fast, her head was spinning.

"A friend. He'll remain here in town while we're gone. I'll tell him to keep an eye on your partner." He moved away from his stance at the window now and grasped Marianna's arm. "Come on, we don't have much time left."

"You must be insane to believe I'll go with you!" Marianna raged, struggling to free her arm. "You're forever attempting to force me to do your bidding, Alex Donovan! Well, I will not do it."

She began to fight him like a wildcat, her struggles abruptly ceasing as he took hold of her other arm and threatened in a low, even tone of voice, "I'll use the same methods as the last time if you prefer. Either you come along with me of your own free will, or I'll gag and tie you again, Marianna!"

"And what if I were to scream for help right now?" she stubbornly replied, blue-green fire meeting golden flame.

"Try it," he muttered with maddening confidence. Marianna hesitated only the space of a second before opening her mouth and yelling at the top of her lungs. Alex uttered a savage curse and clamped a hand across her parted lips, but not before she had managed to be heard by several of the hotel's occupants. It was obvious that Alex hadn't truly believed she'd take him up on his challenge, and his temper was near the boiling point as he snatched up the lamp beside the bed and sent it forcefully crashing through the glass of the single window.

Marianna's eyes widened in stunned astonishment as Alex lifted her bodily and climbed out the window, his hand still clamped across her mouth as she was momentarily too shocked to fight him. He stood along the narrow railing that ran alongside the upper story of the hotel before suddenly dropping to the ground with his wife still securely in his arms, the two of them landing unharmed in the alley below, though Marianna experienced an uncomfortable jolt when they met the ground. Before she quite knew what was happening, Alex had managed to make his way around back to the stables and was meeting a tall man with a moustache, the same man Marianna had seen him with earlier that evening.

"Hurry, Sean," Alex commanded, unceremoniously handing Marianna to the other man while he swiftly mounted one of the waiting horses. Then, before she could say anything at all, the man called Sean lifted her onto the horse in front of Alex, Alex's powerful arms imprisoning her as Sean tossed a woolen blanket over her thinly clad form. Alex's hand silenced any screams that might have been forthcoming as he said to Sean, "Good luck, Cleary. I'd appreciate it if you'd think of something to say to Kate about Marianna's disappearance. Oh, and look after her as well, though I doubt if I need to be telling you that," Alex added with a sudden grin.

"You can count on me," Sean responded with an answering twinkle in his blue eyes. "Good luck to you, Donovan. You have my word that I'll keep an eye on Caine while you're gone." Alex nodded curtly at the man before reining his mount away from the stable, a second horse laden with supplies tied to follow behind, as well as a third animal for Marianna.

Alex held Marianna tightly before him as they rode away from the hotel, soon leaving the town behind. She felt as if she was in some sort of a trance, but was warmed by the heat of Alex's body as she glanced surreptitiously up to see a set look on his handsome face as they moved along the trail.

Seventeen

Marianna, sitting alone inside the tent Alex had erected earlier that day, reflected that she would never be able to forget the grueling journey of the previous few days. The White Pass Trail had proven to be every bit as difficult as she had heard, though not as much for her as for the gold-seekers who were faced with the prospect of hauling the required supplies up to the summit. Still, she told herself with a weary sigh, bending down to remove the muddy, thick-soled leather boots Alex had purchased for her, she could at least hold her head high whenever she recalled the trip she had made with Alex.

After riding away with her from Skagway, Alex had paused briefly in one of the many dense forests outside of town. He dismounted and roughly pulled Marianna down as well, the dawn breaking as the cold morning air cut through Marianna's scant attire.

"Here. Put these on," Alex curtly ordered, thrusting a bundle of clothing into her unsuspecting arms. It was the first time he had spoken to her since so flamboyantly abducting her from the hotel, and she was in no mood to be civil to him.

"Alex Donovan, you are the most arrogant, insensitive, autocratic man I have ever known!" she fumed, quaking with the force of her anger. "And you are sadly mistaken if you believe I will wear these!" she obstinately declared, hurling the clothing to the cold ground with a vengeance, her beautiful face proudly defiant.

"You're the most aggravating female I've ever known, my love," Alex lazily countered, bending down to retrieve the clothing with infuriating calm, "and you'll either put these on right now, or I'll put them on for you," he threatened, the smile on his face in direct contrast to the expression of simmering fury in his golden eyes. Marianna silently challenged him only a brief moment before she reached out and snatched the bundle from his hands, whirling away from him and disappearing behind a cluster of thick bushes a few feet away. She emerged a short time later, more than a bit scandalized at her vastly altered appearance.

The plaid flannel shirt, obviously meant for a boy, was a trifle too fitted across her bosom, the coarse trousers tight about her rounded hips but much too large at her slender waist. She had fastened the leather belt on the last notch, which left several inches dangling absurdly free. She wore red flannel longjohns underneath it all and looked nothing at all like the elegant, fashionable young lady who had been such a smashing success in the best of London's social circles.

"If you dare to say one word . . ." Marianna feelingly

muttered toward Alex, noting the look of suppressed amusement on his handsome face. She marched proudly forward, drawing on the coarse, heavy jacket he had also provided, her movements quite abrupt. "Surely you cannot expect me to remain dressed in this ridiculous attire for the duration of our journey?"

"Why not?" he nonchalantly responded, his arms crossed against his chest.

"Because it's—it's humiliating and improper!"

"Since when are you so concerned with propriety, my love?" Alex quipped with a mocking half-smile, before moving to the horses. He soon returned with a pair of boots and a hat. "That ought to do it," he remarked, handing her the last of the items he had brought for her. "Now, come on. We've wasted enough time as it is."

"Oh! I suppose a few minutes of your precious time weren't worth assuring that I did not freeze to death!" she indignantly declared, jerking on the boots and angrily tugging the hat down over her thick curls.

"That wouldn't have been a problem if you'd only done as I told you and dressed back in your hotel room. Damn it, Marianna!" Alex tightly uttered, striding forward to grasp her shoulders, a fierce scowl on his face. "Why the devil did you scream like that?"

"For the simple reason that I did not wish to be spirited away by you again, Alex Donovan! I told you I did not want to come with you!" she furiously cried, her blue-green gaze meeting his golden one squarely. Alex remained silent for several long seconds. Then he muttered a scalding oath and dragged her along with him to the patiently waiting horses. He tossed Marianna up into one of the saddles before swiftly mounting the second animal, turning back to his wife to order curtly, "Keep that blasted jacket buttoned!"

Marianna's eyes flew downward toward her chest, noting once more how snug and revealing the too-small shirt was. She wanted to fling words of blame at Alex's head, but thought better of it and bit back the sarcastic retort which rose to her lips. She glared resentfully at Alex's back as he grabbed the reins of her mount and nudged his own horse forward, the two of them riding on toward the beckoning mountains ahead.

There had been no more time for conversation, heated or otherwise, between them after that. The days became an unpleasant, painful blur for Marianna as Alex led her along what was often referred to as the Skagway Trail toward the Klondike, the first few miles relatively easy as they traveled along the river. The trouble began as the trail narrowed, large boulders frequently obstructing their path up into the mountains. Although there were still quite a number of people using the trail as a means of reaching the gold fields, they were inconsequential when compared to the vast hordes of men and women who had traveled up through the White Pass during the winter of 1897-98.

The trail was cluttered with abandoned sleds and other goods, and Marianna was horrified to glimpse the remains of horses and other animals as she alternately rode and walked behind Alex. Their pace was slow, the route increasingly arduous as it crossed swamps, forests, an infinite number of streams and creeks, and deep canyons. It was so narrow in certain spots that it was difficult for two riders to pass one another, and the ground was deeply rutted and muddy in many places.

Marianna could focus only on making her way along the trail, oblivious to the other people she saw, finally oblivious even to Alex as she forced herself to concentrate on keeping up behind the horses ahead of her. Though he allowed her several opportunities to rest throughout the journey, she was nonetheless bone weary whenever they camped for the night. It was all she could do to eat the food Alex prepared each night before she fell into an exhausted and dreamless sleep.

When they finally reached the summit and crossed the border into Canada, Alex informed a relieved Marianna that they would spend the remainder of the day camped alongside one of the clear mountain streams, then move on to Bennett the following morning. There were many other travelers who chose to spend a welcome break at the summit. Their numerous tents were erected in what was another of the many camps which had sprung up along the gold-rush trail.

Now, as Marianna removed her boots and lay back upon the pile of blankets she had placed on the ground beneath the cover of the tent, she closed her eyes and sighed. As difficult as the trip had been for her, she realized that it had also provided her with a sense of accomplishment such as she had never before known. Though Alex had never said so, she knew he was proud of her.

But then, she asked herself with a sudden frown, why should she care whether Alex Donovan was proud of her? Why should she care whether he had formed a good opinion of her these past few days?

She sighed again, folding her arms beneath her head as she stared up toward the bleached canvas which offered her protection against the chilling wind. Alex had left her alone for a short time while he fetched water and gathered wood for a fire. It was odd, she mused, moving a hand to twirl a strand of her dark hair between two fingers, but she realized that she shared a certain closeness with Alex, an inexplicable camaraderie she'd never felt before with him. Perhaps it was because of the journey, because of the hardships and dangers which they had faced together. They had not talked much, had not even spared more than a glance for one another since leaving Skagway. They were much too tired to quarrel! She heaved another sigh as she then reflected that Alex had not even touched her these past few days.

Rising to her feet, she glanced down at her travel-worn clothing in dismay. It was no wonder that Alex hadn't touched her! she ruefully decided, wrinkling her nose in distaste at her dusty attire. Not only had she been unable to wash her clothes, she had also been forced to bathe herself as best she could in a pan of hot water each morning, sponging at her shivering body with necessary haste. I must look a fright, she sadly told herself, sinking back down onto the blankets.

"Annie, love, I've got a surprise for you!" Alex's deep voice cheerfully announced. His hand held back the tent flap as he ducked his head inside. "I borrowed this from the woman who set up that makeshift hotel across the creek," he explained, his other hand dragging a metal hip-bath through the opening. Marianna's eyes widened in obvious pleasure as she hurried forward to lovingly touch the old tub.

"Oh, Alex! How did you know a real bath was what I so desperately wanted?" she exclaimed, her eyes shining and a bright smile on her lovely young face.

"Isn't a husband supposed to be able to read his wife's thoughts?" Alex teasingly replied, rewarded for his efforts by the warmth in her gaze as she looked up at him. "It will be a while before I have enough water heated, but I've got the fire blazing now. In the meantime, you can get out of those clothes and wrap yourself in a blanket. The woman who runs the hotel has a girl who does laundry. I suspect they're making more money than most of the poor souls who are killing themselves to get to the Klondike!" he remarked with a quiet chuckle.

"Thank you," Marianna murmured in simple gratitude, favoring him with another smile. He stared impassively down into her beautiful face, his heart thumping wildly in his chest, before he exited the tent and left his wife to her privacy.

She hummed softly to herself as she gladly drew off the trousers, shirt, and longjohns, wrapping herself in a blanket as Alex had suggested. She smiled to herself, reflecting how important such a usually simple pleasure had become as she waited for Alex to bring the water inside and fill the tub. It took him several trips, but she was at last afforded the opportunity to slip her aching body into the soothing warmth of the steaming liquid. Alex announced his intentions to bathe as soon as she had finished, then took himself off to deliver her discarded clothing to the laundress.

Marianna vigorously scrubbed her white flesh until it was pink and glowing, too enchanted with her bath to take much notice of the coarse lye soap she was using. The air inside the tent was extremely cool, but it didn't bother her as she splashed water on herself to rinse away the soap, then bent her head downward toward her knees to rinse her flowing black tresses. When she finally forced herself to emerge from the tub, she peered about for something to wear, settling for the heavy woolen blanket once more. The faint smile on her face was suddenly replaced by a look of consternation as she realized that she would have no clothing until her things had been washed and dried. And that, she told herself with a sigh of annoyance, would take hours!

"It's a good thing the weather's decided to hold up here," Alex amiably commented as he reappeared a short time later. Marianna was sitting on the ground, the blanket wrapped securely about her body as her damp locks curled in almost comical disarray about her face and shoulders. "You shouldn't have tried to wash your hair, Annie, my love. You might have taken a chill," he good-naturedly proclaimed, tossing his hat onto the ground beside her as he began removing his own clothing.

"I am most profoundly grateful for your concern!"

she sarcastically retorted, frowning darkly. "Do you have any idea as to when my clothes will be ready?"

"She said it would be late this afternoon." Another twinkle of amusement sparkled in his golden eyes as he remarked with a soft chuckle, "You look like a drowned kitten." He finished unbuttoning his shirt and drew it off, his fingers moving to unfasten his trousers now.

"You're . . . you're not planning to take a bath now, are you?" Marianna suddenly demanded, her eyes widening as he began slipping his trousers downward. Her cheeks blushed crimson as he merely grinned mockingly down at her, and she sharply averted her gaze.

"Why so shocked, my love?" he laughingly questioned, standing totally naked now, his lithe, muscular leanness exposed to the chilling air. "We've both been in this state of undress many times before."

"Yes, but not so . . . so . . ." she faltered, breaking off in confusion. There was something about the intimacy of the situation that threw her emotions into chaos. Her eyes flew swiftly back to Alex as he loudly grumbled, "Damnation! That water's like ice!" She stifled a giggle at the look of dismay on his handsome face, then was unable to tear her fascinated gaze away from his splendid masculine form. She blushed rosily once more as he caught her watching him, the slow smile on his countenance making her feel all tingly inside.

Marianna did not look at him again as he quickly soaped and rinsed his body, the sounds of his bathing seeming quite loud to her ears. Once he had dressed again, he effortlessly dragged the tub back outside into the gray light of the cloudy summer day. Marianna was surprised when he returned inside the tent, and she felt herself grow increasingly breathless as she viewed the unmistakable look of desire in his golden gaze.

"This is the first time in all too many days that we've had the chance to really talk," he remarked, taking a seat on the ground beside her and moving a hand to lightly caress her blanket-wrapped shoulder.

"There are still people all about us," she reminded him, glancing down toward the blankets spread beneath them.

"Yes, but we can try and pretend we're all alone," he replied with a faint smile. "I think it's time I told you how well you've done, Marianna. There aren't many women with the pampered upbringing you had who could have held up so admirably these past few days."

"Is that supposed to be a compliment?" Marianna indignantly demanded, jerking her shoulder away from his hand, her eyes flashing as they so often did in his presence.

"You must admit you *were* spoiled and pampered," Alex pointed out with a disarming grin, ignoring her visible displeasure as his fingers returned to her shoulder.

"I admit no such thing! While it's true that I received a very good education, that I attended the best schools in England, I was never pampered! I can assure you that quite the contrary was true!"

"Are you saying that even your dear old papa didn't

spoil you?" Alex taunted, his golden eyes full of merry humor. He was a bit perplexed at the abrupt change in her mood at the mention of her father.

"My father may have been wealthy, but he was far from being the doting parent you seem to imply," she bitterly recalled. "I would have traded each and every one of my elegant frocks, all of my luxurious surroundings, for one kind word from him!" she lashed out, her eyes brimming with hot tears.

"My poor little love," Alex murmured in a deep, sincere voice. He ignored Marianna's protests as he drew her against his broad chest, his arms wrapping securely about her trembling softness. "I wish I were able to erase all the unhappiness in your past, Marianna," he tenderly declared, his fingers now gently stroking her damp curls as he cradled her head upon his strong shoulder. "But I realize that even I do not have the power to do so. If you'll allow me, though, I can do my best to make your future full of love and laughter."

"How? By behaving like a second father to me?" she responded with biting sarcasm. "By trying to take his place?"

"The last thing I want is to be a father to you, my love," Alex stated in a low tone, his arms tightening about her. "I love you in a most decidedly unparental fashion! And, if you'll only admit that you care for me as much as I for you, we can set about building that bright future together. We can give our children a legacy of deep, abiding love such as you've never known before," he concluded, his voice dropping to just above a whisper. He gently clasped Marianna's face between his hands, gazing so intensely into her widened eyes that it seemed he would see into her very soul. A powerful current passed between them in that moment, and Alex groaned quietly as his arms surrounded her once more, his warm lips claiming hers in a searing kiss.

Time stood still for them as they spent the next hour safely ensconced in their own private world, unmindful that neither of them had eaten anything since much earlier that morning, uncaring that the raging fire Alex had so carefully nurtured just outside the tent was burning down into nothing more than a pile of smoldering ashes. There was a fire within them, a fire that blazed fiercely enough to keep them warm, to ward off the chill of the brisk mountain air that smelled so fresh and sweet.

Eighteen

"You wait here while I have a word with one of the men," instructed Alex, leaving Marianna to take a seat on a large, smooth rock. She raised her face toward the warmth of the morning sun, breathing deeply of the wood smoke-scented air as she curiously watched the proceedings before her.

They had arrived at Log Cabin, British Columbia, a short time earlier. The Canadian customs were located here, the spot where the Mounties carefully checked to make certain each gold stampeder was bringing in the required amount of supplies, a regulation intended to prevent, as far as possible, loss of lives. There were still more than five hundred miles to be traversed before the gold fields, so Marianna was glad that Alex was not interested in prospecting.

There were crowds of men and a few women there at the check point just over the summit, and she wondered what sort of life various people had led before surrendering to the temptation to follow the lure of gold. The day had dawned crisp and clear, and there was a pleasant aroma of boiling beans and salt pork mingling with the smell of smoke. Dogs barked at nothing in particular, men laughed and swore, and several prospectors argued with the red-coated Canadian authorities who sought to do their duty. There were a number of tents and ramshackle wooden buildings scattered across the magnificent landscape, and Marianna smiled to herself as she mused that Skagway seemed a modern metropolis compared to the bustling camp before her.

"Come on. We're cleared to move on," Alex said, returning to her side and taking the reins from her hands.

"You've never yet explained to me why it is so imperative for you to travel to Bennett," Marianna told him, allowing him to assist her in mounting her horse. "And why is it that we're allowed to pass through when everyone else must bring in a certain amount of supplies?"

"Didn't anyone ever caution you against asking too many questions, my love?" Alex quipped, evading her inquiries as he led the way onward toward Bennett.

"You might at least enlighten me as to why I was forced to accompany you!"

"What? And put an end to the pleasure afforded you by speculating about it?"

"Why can't you ever be serious when I'm trying to discuss something with you?" she fumed, her beautiful face stormy beneath her wide-brimmed hat.

"In this particular instance," replied Alex, a shadow of grimness crossing his features, "it's simply because I can't provide you with all the answers you're seeking. But, I will tell you that there is a highly important poker game set up to take place in Bennett tonight. And I have every intention of becoming one of the participants." He threw her a brief glance before gazing ahead toward the trail again, affording Marianna a glimpse of the determined light in his golden eyes. She couldn't comprehend why Alex should have dragged her along on such a strenuous journey for the sake of taking part in a mere poker game, she mused as she urged her horse to keep pace with his.

They reached Bennett later that same day. Alex had told Marianna that it had once been the largest tent city in the world. More than ten thousand people had camped there the past winter. The stampeders had impatiently waited for the ice to break up to enable them to sail on down the Yukon River to Dawson, the Klondike boomtown that was the northern terminus of both the White Pass and Chilkoot Trails. As Marianna rode in silence beside Alex, she viewed the evidence of the gold-seekers' boatbuilding efforts, for there were many scraps strewn about the mountainous country-side, the vibrant blue of the huge lake in the distance.

Marianna continued to be amazed at the number of people involved in their various tasks as she helped Alex erect the now-familiar tent. There were still but a few women about, although she did catch sight of one young woman scurrying along in her gathered skirts, her knitted shawl clutched tightly about her body. She was obviously with child, and Marianna gave silent thanks that she herself had not been forced to travel in such a delicate condition.

By the time the sky began to darken for the brief hours of the summer night, Marianna was again feeling close to exhaustion. She resented the fact that she was expected to remain alone in the tent while her husband took himself off for an evening of gambling.

"I still cannot believe we have traveled all this way because of some ridiculous card game!" she said to Alex as he drew on his jacket and prepared to leave. "Perhaps you truly are nothing more than a greedy adventurer, Alex Donovan! If so, then I fail to see why you have seen fit to involve me in your disgusting schemes!"

"I've told you why I couldn't leave you behind in Skagway," Alex calmly responded. Her eyes widened as he suddenly withdrew a small, gleaming pistol from his coat pocket. "Here. I don't think you'll have any trouble, but just in case, I'll leave you this." He took up her hand and placed the gun into her palm. "Can I rely on you to know how to use it?" he asked with a sudden grin.

"I'm quite certain I can manage if the need arises," she proudly replied. Then, as he smiled and turned toward the tent flap, Marianna unexpectedly said, "Alex, please be careful." Her cheeks flushed as he turned back to her with an expression of mingled surprise and pleasure on his handsome face.

"I give you my word I'll return to you in one piece. In the meantime, you stay here inside the tent, understand?" he solemnly cautioned, his hands grasping hers for a moment. "I'm only going to be a few hundred yards away."

"Wouldn't it be better if I were to come along with you?" she suggested, plagued by a feeling of uneasiness, a feeling that had been growing deep inside her all day.

"Definitely not. These men aren't the sort before whom I'd want to flaunt my beautiful, desirable young wife! No, it's best if you remain here and out of sight," he concluded, leaning down to bestow a gentle, searching kiss upon her lips. "I should be back before dawn," he added, and left her alone in the tent.

Marianna's mind was in turmoil as she sat in the darkening interior of the canvas tent. Her thoughts turned to Kate, and she wondered how well her friend was managing without her assistance. Probably quite nicely, she decided with a faint smile. Kate was most certainly capable of overcoming any problems which might arise. Still, thought Marianna as a soft sigh escaped her lips, she wished she had not been forced to leave her responsibilities in Skagway.

But then, a tiny voice at the back of her mind reminded her, she wouldn't be here with Alex now. And wasn't she just the slightest bit pleased to be sharing this adventure with him? Wasn't she actually just a little delighted he had brought her along?

She rose abruptly to her feet, her trousers making a quiet, rustling sound as she paced restlessly inside the tent. A vivid recollection of the intimacy she had shared with Alex the day before came forward in the midst of her turbulent thoughts, but she sought to ignore the disturbingly delectable memory. The past few weeks, weeks she had spent as the wife of Alex

Donovan, had brought about an irreversible change in her. What would she do with her life once the gold rush had ended? Would she perhaps remain in Skagway? Would she choose to return to London?

No, she quickly answered herself, she could never return to her life in London, never return to the society she had once embraced. She had always felt a yearning, deep inside her, for excitement and adventure, hadn't she? she mused, pulling aside the tent flap to gaze outside into the dusky, star-studded sky.

And what about Alex? Why did the thought of leaving him cause her pain instead of pleasure?

"I tell you, we got to do it tonight!" Marianna suddenly heard a man hoarsely whisper from a spot just outside the tent. Although she couldn't explain why, she felt herself become frightened. She stood quiet and motionless as she allowed the tent flap to drop slowly back into place, her eyes widening as she listened.

"Are you sure he's the one?" another man demanded in a low voice.

"He's Donovan all right. The description I got of him leaves no doubt in my mind!" the first man insisted.

Donovan? Marianna repeated to herself. Why, they were talking about Alex!

"But we ain't received any orders about just how to do it. Could be that it'll just bring us a whole hell of a lot of trouble!" the second man pointed out, an unmistakable note of fear creeping into his rasping voice.

"Damn it, Murdock, don't you go all lily-livered on me! The boss said to get rid of him, and that's just what we got to do! If we don't take care of the bastard right away, we'll sure as hell be in a lot of trouble!"

Marianna was afraid to so much as breathe as she listened, her heart pounding in her chest. She instinctively reached for the pistol she had left lying on the blankets, her fingers tightening almost painfully about the cold metal.

"You got any idea why we're supposed to get rid of him?" the more timid of the two questioned.

"It's got something to do with a woman. That's all I know!" the bold one impatiently answered. "Come on. This here's his tent."

"What are we gonna do?"

"I seen him down at Barkley's a while back. Thought we'd ransack his tent and make it look like someone was out to rob him," the first man answered with a soft, evil chuckle.

Marianna felt perilously close to panic, the color draining from her face as she heard them moving around to the front of the tent. She had no time to ponder the dangers of the situation as she flew to the rear of the tent and rapidly scrambled underneath the canvas, heedless of the way the hard, rocky ground scratched one side of her pale face as she frantically sought to escape. Once outside, she did not pause, whirling about to hurriedly search for Alex.

She was oblivious to the curious stares she attracted as she ran, her steps slowing as she felt tears of frustration springing to her eyes. Which tent housed the poker game Alex had mentioned? she frenetically wondered, turning this way and that as her eyes swept hastily across the tent-dotted surroundings.

She finally approached a kindly older man who stared out at her from his stance just inside the canvas of his own tent, and she urgently asked, "Do you know which tent belongs to a man named Barkley?" She was certain that was the name one of the two conspirators had spoken. "Please, do you have any idea where I might find it?" she breathlessly demanded.

"Barkley? Oh yeah," the man answered after a thoughtful moment's hesitation. "He's one of them bigwigs always trying to run things. You'll find his tent just ahead there," he directed, his finger pointing the way, "the large one there that's set apart from the others just a mite." He watched impassively as Marianna muttered a barely audible "thank you" and scurried off, casting more than one surreptitious glance over her shoulder as if expecting to see someone following her.

Alex was leaning negligently back in his chair and holding the winning hand in the latest round of play when his wife came bursting in through the opening to the tent. He leapt to his feet when he saw her, his features tightening as he viewed the scratches on her lovely face, the look of panic in her blue-green eyes.

"Annie!" he exclaimed, forgetting all about the important poker game for the moment, forgetting about the four other men who raised annoyed faces toward the unwelcome intrusion.

"Oh, Alex! I had to come!" Marianna gasped out, ignorant of how truly disheveled and distressed she appeared. Alex's hands on her shoulders steadied her, his eyes gazing deeply into hers as he quietly demanded, "What is it? What's happened?"

"I heard them talking just outside the tent! They were talking about you, and they said something about—" she started to explain, her entire body trembling. She was shocked when Alex abruptly cut her off.

"You can tell me all about it later, my love," he loudly announced with an amused chuckle, turning back to the other men with a rueful grin. "You know how these things are. The slightest noise sets them off sometimes!" he mockingly commented, facing Marianne again with a certain gleam in his eyes. She stared up at him in stunned amazement, looking at him as if he had suddenly gone insane.

"Alex, didn't you hear me? I was trying to tell you, to warn you about—"

"And I said you can tell me all about it later, sweetheart," he interrupted, smiling once more at the grim-faced men. He briefly glanced back at his wife, the expression in his eyes silently warning her to keep quiet as he jovially asked his fellow players, "You fellows don't mind if the little lady stays a while, do you? I assure you she won't make a sound." He was already leading a totally bewildered Marianna to an extra chair situated in a darkened corner of the large tent.

"You know we don't allow no women," a tall, slender man a few years older than Alex grumbled. He glared at Marianna, his pockmarked face appearing almost hostile in the lamplight.

"I don't see that it matters as long as she sits there

and keeps her mouth shut," another man begrudgingly remarked. "What do you say, Barkley?" he asked, turning to a heavyset, middle-aged man with thinning brown hair.

"Fine with me," the man known as Barkley lazily drawled, his small gray eyes moving insolently over Marianna before returning to Alex's face. "Just as long as the two of you haven't planned this little scene as an opportunity to cheat."

"If I were a more sensitive man, Barkley," Alex responded with another low chuckle, pushing a speechless Marianna down onto the chair, "I might just take offense at that remark. But, I understand your concern, and I assure you the lady knows nothing whatsoever about poker!"

"Just make sure her eyes don't stray too much," Barkley smoothly cautioned. Alex stared down into Marianna's questioning gaze, but he merely shook his head slightly, his solemn expression throwing her into further confusion. She could only sit and watch as he resumed his seat at the table.

"I still say she should go!" the slender man irritably muttered as Alex retrieved his cards. "This ain't no place for a man to be playing nursemaid to some skittish little—"

"Are you planning to call or pass?" Alex nonchalantly broke in, a deceptive grin on his handsome face. The man muttered something unintelligible and the game continued.

Marianna sat in the corner, the absurdity of the whole situation causing a surge of hysterical laughter to well up within her. She suppressed the temptation to scream at the five of them, to demand to know why a game of poker was more important than a man's life. She realized that Alex must have his own mysterious reasons for behaving so strangely, but, whatever his reasons, they did not alter the fact that there were two men plotting to kill him!

She put a hand to her cheek, wincing a bit as she tenderly fingered the raw scratches on her skin. Her hand moved to the pocket of the trousers she wore to withdraw a handkerchief, and she gasped faintly as she felt the pistol therein, causing Alex's golden eyes to fasten on her for an instant as he concentrated on the game.

The night proved to be one of the longest Marianna had ever endured, the game lasting into the wee hours of the next morning. Finally, Alex slowly rose to his feet and announced he'd lost enough for one night, then moved to awaken his sleeping wife. She had fallen asleep less than an hour earlier, so weary she could no longer force herself to remain awake. Alex was well aware that the other men watched him as he firmly shook Marianna's shoulder.

"It's time we were leaving, dear," he murmured in a low tone of voice, his back turned toward the men who stared at them. There was an almost savage light in his golden eyes as he glanced at the scratches on her face once more, but he quickly schooled his features to remain inscrutable as he grabbed her arm and pulled her gently to her feet.

"Alex?" Marianna sleepily spoke, her eyelids fluttering open as she felt herself being led along, his powerful arms supporting her about her waist as they moved.

"You'll have to sit in on a game again sometime, Donovan," Barkley remarked with a deep rumble of laughter, replacing the fat cigar in his mouth as he greedily raked up the last of his winnings.

"You wouldn't want me to deprive you of another opportunity to clean me out, eh?" Alex sardonically quipped, nodding curtly at the group of men as he and Marianna left the smoke-filled tent. The cold air hit Marianna full force as Alex hurried her away, the silence of the tent city providing an almost eerie setting.

"Where are we going?" Marianna asked, shivering as she drew the edges of the jacket more closely about her body. Gone were the last vestiges of sleepiness as she recalled the treacherous scheme which had sent her in search of Alex the night before. "Alex! Those two men were plotting to kill you!" she repeated in renewed horror, halting abruptly.

"Did you get a look at their faces?" Alex muttered, taking a firm grip on her arm once more and propelling her along beside him. She held back again.

"No, I did not! I was too busy trying to get out of the tent before they came inside! I was too concerned with finding you to warn you!" she bitterly informed him. "Why did you not allow me to explain what had happened? And why was I forced to spend the night sitting rigidly in that chair?"

"Why don't we start with your telling me exactly what you thought you heard," Alex calmly suggested, now leading her away from the surrounding tents and over toward a nearby stream. There were few sounds to interrupt the stillness of the night, and the two of them kept their voices low as they talked.

"I know what I heard! I heard two men talking about you. They mentioned you by name! They said that their boss, whoever he is, ordered them to get rid of you!"

"Did they happen to say why their 'boss' wanted me dead?" Alex casually inquired.

"I did hear them say that it had something to do with a woman," she told him, her face turning ashen again as sudden realization dawned on her. "Oh, Alex, you don't think . . . you don't think it was—" she murmured in horror.

"Caine?" Alex provided the name. "I must admit he seems like the probable candidate. But, tell me, did those two men see you?"

"I don't think so. They were coming inside the tent, planning to make it appear as if someone had tried to rob you, when I managed to slip underneath the back of the tent and come to warn you," she finished.

"Were you followed?"

"I don't think so. I kept glancing back, but I don't think they ever suspected I was inside the tent listening. They mentioned something about having seen you down at Barkley's tent, which is why I knew where to find you."

"And now the others are certain to suspect—" Alex muttered in obvious displeasure, clipping off the remark as if he'd already said too much.

"Pray, Mr. Donovan, forgive me for thinking only of saving your life!" Marianna sarcastically countered.

"We'll have to move on out before dawn," Alex said, ignoring her last retort. His face became pensive, his eyes moving to rapidly scan the area. "I don't think we're being watched, but it's impossible to know for sure."

"But why didn't they try something when we left Barkley's tent just now?" Marianna whispered in puzzlement, her own widened gaze sweeping about.

"Who knows?" he responded simply. "Perhaps they didn't want to make any moves with you around." He paused for a moment, then turned to gaze down into her upturned face. "Do you still have the gun I gave you?" At her brief nod, he smiled faintly and said, "You stay here. I'm going back to the tent to salvage what I can in the way of supplies."

"What about the horses?"

"If we're lucky, they'll still be where I left them," he muttered, his golden eyes glowing dully. "Horses won't do us much good on the Chilkoot, but we can take them as far as the summit. We'll head on down to Dyea and lay low there for a few days."

"Alex, I think I should go back to the tent with you!" Marianna insisted, her eyes full of mingled fear and concern.

"No. You just stay here like I told you!" he commanded, pushing her firmly down onto the ground behind a large rock. "Don't worry. They'd be the world's biggest fools to try and tangle with you!" he flippantly remarked, flashing her a quick grin before turning about and striding away, his tall form soon disappearing in the midst of the pale tents.

Marianna hesitated only a fraction of a second before getting up from behind the rock and scurrying after Alex. She moved stealthily nearer their tent a few moments later, nearly gasping aloud as she perceived the lone man stepping just as furtively toward the opening, his face hidden by the hat pulled low upon his head. She instinctively opened her mouth to scream a warning to Alex, whom she believed to be inside the tent.

"Shhh!" she heard someone whisper behind her, prompting her to jerk about in heart-stopping alarm. It was Alex who scowled so menacingly down at her, whose tall, muscular form towered above her in the semidarkness. "What the hell are you doing here? I told you to stay put!" he ground out, his voice low and furious. He dragged her behind a cluster of small boulders several yards away from their tent, but Marianna's eyes flitted back to where she had seen the man.

"He went inside the tent!" she informed him, nodding briskly in the tent's direction.

"I know it, damn it!" he furiously muttered.

"What are we going to do now?"

"We? 'I' am going to go in there and have a little 'talk' with our 'friend' while you do as I tell you this time and stay here!" he ground out. "Damnation, woman, things are in enough mess as it is without you gallivanting about! Now stay here!" he furiously commanded before spinning about on his booted heel and moving slowly back toward the tent.

Marianna's eyes momentarily flashed at his rude treatment of her, but she forgot about any annoyance she felt toward him as she breathlessly watched him disappear inside the tent, his hand reaching to withdraw from his coat pocket a small pistol identical to the one he had earlier given his wife. She waited for what seemed like an eternity, but she neither saw nor heard anything. Growing increasingly alarmed, she disobeyed Alex yet again and began stepping cautiously toward the tent, putting aside any fear for herself as she sought to discover what had become of Alex.

She gasped loudly as she was suddenly seized from behind, a rough, calloused hand moving to still her cries as a voice rasped threateningly in her ear, "You must be the little gal I heard tell so much about!" Murdock's partner chuckled quietly, and Marianna gasped again as she felt the gun he pressed firmly against her side. "Now, let's you and me get ourselves inside that there tent and see what's been going on!" He held her clasped tightly in front of him like a shield as he moved forward, Marianna's feet dangling helplessly above the cold ground. She tried to scream against the man's bruising hand, tried to warn Alex.

"Hold it right there, Donovan!" Marianna's captor quietly commanded as he thrust aside the tent flap and burst inside with Marianna still held securely before him. "Drop the gun or I'll put a hole clean through her!"

306

Marianna nearly fainted with relief when she glimpsed Alex standing victorious over an unconscious Murdock, but her initial relief gave way to renewed terror when she realized what the remaining assailant intended. Alex's fingers tightened on the pistol for only an instant, his handsome features contorted with rage when he saw the gun pressed against his wife. His golden eyes gleamed with cold fury as he reluctantly lowered his pistol, and Marianna sagged in defeat against her captor.

"Let her go," Alex tightly demanded, his savage gaze never straying from the man's black-bearded features.

"After I kill you, I think I'll just see that the little lady gets on back down to Skagway," the burly fellow declared with an evil snort of laughter.

"I'm the one you want. She's got nothing to do with this!"

Marianna's mind was frantically searching for an avenue of escape as Alex and the man talked. Her eyes widened even further as her fingers suddenly came into contact with the pistol still concealed in her pocket. She was uncertain if Alex caught the speaking glance she sent his way, her hand carefully moving to grasp the pistol as her captor seemed completely unaware of her presence, the gun in his own hand pointing directly toward Alex now.

"Alex!" Marianna suddenly shrieked, tossing the pistol in her husband's direction as she violently twisted against the man. She flailed at him with her arms and legs, succeeding in knocking his arm momentarily

307

upward so that Alex was afforded the opportunity to snatch up the gun she threw his way. He moved with lightning speed, his finger pulling the trigger before the man could bring his own gun down again. The bearded man crumpled lifelessly to the ground, a bullet lodged in his skull, leaving Marianna to slide wordlessly to her knees as her legs buckled beneath her.

"Marianna!" Alex lunged to catch her as she swayed. "Are you all right?" he demanded, his powerful arms wrapping about her trembling body.

"I think so! Oh, Alex, is he dead?" she breathed, her horrified gaze drawn to where the man lay sprawled mere inches away.

"Quite," Alex assured her. He hugged her against him for only a second longer, before unexpectedly rising to his feet and pulling her up with him. "Come on, we've got to get out of here!"

"Get out of here? But why? Now that they're both dead, they can't—"

"The other one's still alive, not that it matters. What matters is that I can't stand here and wait for the possibility of some blasted do-gooders taking it upon themselves to conduct an inquiry into all this!"

"But why not? You killed the man in self-defense, didn't you?" she pointed out in confusion.

"I don't have time to calmly explain all my reasons at this particular moment, but suffice it to say that I don't need the attention! Now, come on!" He grabbed her hand and pulled her swiftly along with him as he paused to snatch up a bundle of supplies and then hurried from the tent.

Alex was vastly relieved to find their horses still standing where he had tied them earlier, and he tossed a numb Marianna unceremoniously up into the saddle before swinging up onto his own mount. The two of them soon left Bennett—and the two would-be murderers—behind as they urged the animals back down along the moonlit trail.

Nineteen

The long daylight hours stretched into a cool, cloudless evening as Marianna slid wearily from the saddle. She and Alex had finally drawn their horses to a halt in a quiet, densely wooded area well off the trail. Putting a hand to the aching muscles of her lower back, she dragged the hat from her head and ran slender fingers through the tangled raven tresses which now fell in splendid disarray about her face and shoulders.

"We may as well make camp here for the night," Alex decisively stated as he dismounted and began untying the saddlebags.

"Alex Donovan, when are you going to explain to me why it was necessary for us to flee Bennett with such bewildering haste?" Marianna inquired, following her husband as he started off toward the rushing stream nearby, pausing briefly to grasp the reins of both animals and lead them along. "You've barely spoken to me throughout this entire day. Don't you think you owe me some sort of explanation?" She watched as he turned to unsaddle the horses with slow, unhurried movements, prompting her to declare in exasperation, "It is time you saw fit to trust me!" He did not immediately reply, continuing with his task of leading the weary animals to drink from the cold mountain stream. Marianna eyed him resentfully, the events of the previous night having already strained her emotions to the limit.

She blinked in amazement, initially uncertain she had heard Alex correctly when he turned back to her to reply, "You're right." He smiled faintly at the surprise on her face as he looped the reins about a low-lying branch, the animals bending down to graze at the thick, aromatic grass which lined the stream. The spot in which Alex had chosen to make camp was still and secluded; only the tranquil sounds of the water rushing over the smooth rocks and the leaves softly rustling in the gentle breeze broke the quiet solitude surrounding them.

"Then you really do intend to tell me the truth?" Marianna asked, following Alex's example as he took a seat on the ground, his eyes gazing toward the water.

"I now have little choice in the matter," he dryly retorted, removing his own hat and flinging it negligently aside in the grass. He leaned backward, turning upon his side to face Marianna as he supported himself on one elbow. "I've wanted to trust you, my love, wanted to be able to tell you the truth long before now, but I believed it to be too dangerous for you to know."

"What you really mean is that you didn't trust me enough!"

311

"You must admit," he pointed out with a rueful grin, "that you certainly didn't offer me any encouragement to consider you trustworthy. You have forever defied me, continually done the exact opposite of what I commanded!" He smiled again as her eyes flashed and she bristled, but he spoke again before she could offer him a scathing reply. His handsome features grew solemn as he said, "I suppose I should begin with my reasons for being in Skagway."

"I have always suspected that it was for another reason than merely to gamble," she interjected, folding her legs beneath her as she braced her back against the rough bark of the tree behind her.

"I needed to project that image to others. It was agreed upon that I should appear to be nothing more than an adventurous young man with a penchant for games of chance."

"Agreed upon?"

"Agreed upon by myself and my superiors," he explained, then paused a moment, his golden eyes full of an unfathomable light as a shadow of remembrance crossed his tanned face. "It all began with a friend of mine named Drew Stromberg. Drew and I grew up together in Sitka. We were more like brothers than friends. He was a bit of a daredevil, a truly adventurous sort who delighted in excitement such as the gold rush seemed to offer. He tried to persuade me to travel to the Klondike with him, but my responsibilities at home forced me to return. I never saw him again. He was found murdered outside one of the saloons in Skagway shortly after his arrival, his throat neatly sliced from ear to ear."

Marianna shuddered at his gruesome words. She did not protest when Alex slowly moved to her side, placing his arms about her and drawing her against his soothing warmth.

"I wouldn't have even known about his death if it hadn't been for that letter from Skagway. I'm still puzzled as to who might have sent it, or why I was chosen as its recipient. It spoke of Drew's death, and it mentioned the possibility that a man called Caine might have had something to do with his murder."

"Caine?" she softly gasped, another shiver running the length of her spine. Her widened gaze met Alex's almost savage one, and memories of his repeated cautions regarding Caine came flooding back.

"The unknown informant offered no absolute proof, but the letter planted enough seeds of suspicion in my mind to prompt me to journey to Skagway myself. When I was unable to get any answers of my own, I contacted an old friend of mine and requested an invitation. The friend, it so happened, was a high-ranking member of the Mounties. It wasn't long before he had recruited me to take an active role in the investigation, a joint mission between our two countries. That was several months ago."

"I don't understand," Marianna murmured in puzzlement, drawing away from him a bit so that she could peer speculatively up into his face. "You have been involved in investigating your friend's death all this time? If Caine is indeed guilty, why have you not arrested him?"

"Drew's murder was never solved," Alex quietly remarked. "But I still believe Caine was responsible. The reason the investigation has continued for so long is because we discovered a powerful and far-reaching network of crime operating up here, from Skagway all the way to Dawson. It was much larger, much more organized than we had originally believed. Our efforts to break it apart have been very time consuming, requiring a great deal of patience and painstaking gathering of information."

"But," she demanded, more than a trifle stunned by what she was hearing, "is Caine involved in the criminal activities taking place?"

"We have substantial evidence that Lyle Caine actually controls the entire operation," he grimly told her, drawing her back against him. "I'm not talking about a simple matter such as cheating at cards, Annie. The crimes are varied and differing in magnitude— rolling and robbing unsuspecting men outside saloons, fake telegraph offices set up in order to ascertain how much gold a man might have on him, kidnapping, murder, and so on."

"So that's why you disappeared for those two weeks," she murmured, half to herself, her beautiful face pensive. "But why was it necessary for you to participate in the poker game at Bennett? And why did we have to leave so hurriedly after what happened?"

"Barkley made it known he was willing to sell some information regarding Caine and several others who hold positions of power in the organization. And, since Barkley insisted on meeting with someone in Bennett, I was ordered up there under the pretense of joining in that high-stakes game. As for our haste in leaving, it was imperative that I not be publicly questioned about those two men who were supposed to kill me. I didn't want to risk blowing my cover, and I didn't want to be connected with any of Caine's men."

"If they were indeed his men," she murmured, her mind spinning. Alex working for the government as a secret investigator? And Lyle Caine the ringleader in a powerful criminal organization? It was a bit much to digest at once, and her head ached with the turbulence of her thoughts.

Her expression grew puzzled again as Alex suddenly grasped her shoulders and almost roughly set her away from him, giving her a sharp, searching look as he firmly demanded, "Has something been going on between you and Caine?"

"Of course not!" she hotly denied.

"I believe there's something you haven't told me, isn't there? Caine wouldn't order me killed because the two of you indulged in a harmless little flirtation!"

"But you don't know that it was because of me—" she vigorously protested, her face flushed with fiery color. She remembered all too well her confrontation with Caine in the hotel lobby a few days ago, recalled his unnerving threats. But how could Alex possibly suspect what had happened?

"You yourself related the fact that those two up in Bennett mentioned it had something to do with a woman!" he ground out, his golden eyes narrowing as his fingers tightened on the soft flesh of her shoulders

315

beneath her jacket and flannel shirt. "Now, suppose you tell me exactly what's been going on with Caine!"

"I have never encouraged him!" she insisted.

"Perhaps not, but Caine's not the sort of man to let that stop him from getting what he wants. Now, tell me, Annie," he harshly commanded, beginning to lose patience at her obvious reluctance to talk to him about Caine, "has he ever touched you? Has he ever come right out and announced his intentions toward you?" He shook her slightly for emphasis, and Marianna gasped softly, her eyes wide and full of trepidation.

"Yes," she finally answered, her voice barely above a whisper as she swiftly averted her gaze. The expression on his face became one of cold fury, his eyes narrowing as he valiantly sought to retain control over his boiling temper.

"And how long ago was that?" he calmly demanded, though his brows drew together in a fierce scowl.

"It was that same night when he escorted Kate and myself home, the night we encountered you and Sean," she hesitantly told him. "But he did offer me a partnership in his saloon one night shortly after Kate and I began singing in the Golden Nugget," she went on to admit. "And he . . . he made it known that he expected me to become his . . . his mistress," she finished, then gasped again as Alex muttered a savage oath, visibly battling with his increasing rage before forcefully muttering between clenched teeth, "Did he force you—"

"No!" Marianna hurriedly assured him, his meaning quite clear. She briskly shook her head in denial, breathlessly proclaiming, "He did nothing more than kiss me! But, I resisted him; I refused his offer of a partnership. Then, that night he escorted us back to the hotel, he told me that if I did not come to him willingly, he would force me to his bed! He boasted of controlling the town, Alex, of possessing the power to take whatever he wanted. And he threatened to use whatever means he deemed necessary to bend me to his will."

"So that's why he wanted me dead and out of the way," Alex remarked in a deceptively composed tone. "I've long believed him to be suspicious of me, of my activities, and I always expected him to make a move sooner or later. I just didn't think it would be because of you."

"But how did he know of our relationship? Even Kate was ignorant as to our marriage!"

"I don't think he knows we are husband and wife, my love," replied Alex with a faint, mocking grin. "I think he became enraged with jealousy when it was reported that you and I were seen together on the trail. And, you must admit, it must have appeared undeniably suspicious when you disappeared, after setting up that howl, from your hotel room and I disappeared from town at the same time."

"Then everyone will be aware that you and I—"

"And the need to keep our marriage a secret will no longer exist," Alex interrupted. He finally released her, rising to his feet and leaning an arm against the tree. "I don't think it will have any undesirable effect on my work," he thoughtfully remarked, still fighting against

317

the simmering fury within him. "And whether I like it or not, you're already deeply involved. I've been afraid someone would seek to use you against me, against the investigation. Now, I can only do my best to protect you."

"If you had only trusted me, perhaps I could have been of some assistance to you!" Marianna asserted, scrambling up to confront him, her eyes flashing brightly.

"If you had only listened to me and stayed far away from Lyle Caine, we might not be in this mess!" he angrily countered. "And if you had only told me the truth about his damned, lustful attentions toward you, I migh not have faced the possibility of being killed back in Bennett!"

"You know that is not true! Would it have mattered if I had indeed told you before now? I think not, Alex Donovan! You would still have insisted upon my accompanying you, wouldn't you? You would still have offered me little choice in the matter!" she exclaimed, refusing to back down in the face of his smoldering fury. "It is through no fault of mine that Lyle Caine desires me!"

"Isn't it?" Alex clenched his hands into tight fists now. "If you had obeyed me in the very beginning, if you had returned to Sitka as I told you to do, then you never would have met Caine, he never would have been afforded the opportunity to feast his blasted eyes on your well-displayed charms!"

"It is totally absurd, the way you keep harping about my returning to Sitka!" Marianna stormed, her eyes blazing militantly up at him.

"Absurd or not, you wouldn't be involved now if you had only done as I commanded!"

"Commanded?" she repeated, then gave a short, humorless laugh. "That is precisely the reason the two of us should never have entered into this mockery of a marriage! You treat me as if I had not a brain in my head, as if I were not capable of making any of my own decisions! I am a grown woman, and I certainly do not require someone such as you to tell me how to live my life!"

"Ah, but then you're forgetting one relatively minor detail, aren't you?" he countered with biting sarcasm, still refraining from laying hands on her. "I am your husband, my dearest little wildcat, and I am the one person in this world who is entitled to tell you how to live your life!"

"As soon as we return to civilization, I shall file for divorce!" she carelessly pronounced, her anger driving her beyond reason.

Alex's features hardened, concealing the sharp pain her words inflicted upon him. It was difficult at times for him to continue to cherish the hope that she would one day love him as he loved her, that she would put aside all her fierce pride and admit that the two of them belonged together. He might have lost all hope then, if he did not firmly believe her to care deeply for him. It was quite apparent that her feelings for him were intense, and he was convinced that it was love, not hate, which burned deep within her.

"You don't know what you're saying," he finally

responded, his voice low as he stared down at her, his face inscrutable.

"I know perfectly well what I am saying! I will not remain your wife! I will not allow you to control my life any longer!" she raged, suddenly raising one hand to bring it forcefully against his sun-bronzed cheek. She was startled by what she had done, and she raised eyes full of consternation to his immobile features, a moment of charged silence hanging uncomfortably between them. Then Marianna astonished both Alex and herself as she unexpectedly burst into tears.

The dangerous look on Alex's face was replaced by an expression of warm tenderness and understanding as he reached for her, drawing her unresisting, weeping form into his comforting embrace. He held her tightly against his muscular chest for a moment, then sank to the ground and cradled her on his lap, his arms wrapped securely about her as she wept. Her sobs were violent and heartbreaking, all the hardships and dangers of the past several days feeding her tears as she allowed Alex to hold her.

Finally, when it appeared the storm of tears was abating, Alex pressed a gentle kiss to the top of her head, murmuring quietly to her as she sniffed against his shirt, her beautiful face flushed and streaked with the evidence of her weeping, the trembling of her body beginning to still.

"My poor darling," Alex softly remarked, his hand smoothing the hair from her face, "it's small wonder you broke under the strain. You've held up with remarkable, admirable fortitude. I could not have asked for a better traveling companion than you have proven yourself to be," he added with a brief smile.

"I have never been able to abide weepy females!" Marianna shakily declared, dashing away the last of her tears and sniffing again. She was grateful for the handkerchief Alex pressed into her hand, and she blew her nose and dabbed at her moist eyes before collapsing back against him.

"I've never minded them in the least, not when they're as beautiful as you," Alex teased. A heavy sigh escaped his lips as he regretfully said, "Much as I would love to sit here and hold you like this forever, the night is growing cold and it's time I set about building a fire." But when she would have removed herself from his lap, he held her fast, causing her to glance at him in confusion. He had apparently changed his mind, for in the next instant he was kissing her with a hunger she soon matched, and he muttered, "To hell with the fire!" before claiming her lips once more, tightening his hold upon her as she sighed inwardly, her arms winding about his neck as the kiss they shared grew even more inflamed.

It was not long before Marianna's clothing was removed, Alex placing his naked form atop her welcoming softness, the two of them lying between the blankets Alex impatiently snatched up and tossed upon the grassy earth beside the stream. The horses continued to graze peacefully a short distance away, seemingly oblivious to the two humans making passionate love in their presence.

Their lovemaking was indeed quite fervent, heightened by their raw emotions and sense of danger. Marianna moaned low in her throat as Alex's hands ran insistently over her rounded curves, his lips searing her satiny flesh. As always, their words of anger and their never-ending clash of wills were all forgotten as they surrendered themselves to the consuming rapture.

Alex's mouth gently suckled at her breast, his long fingers tenderly stroking all the secret places of her womanly form, her soft cries urging him provocatively onward. She gasped when his warm tongue teased at the pink nipple of her full breast, his hand lifting the quivering roundness even higher for his moist caress. The gleaming whiteness of her slender thighs opened to his knowing touch as his mouth sought her other breast, and her hands clutched almost feverishly at his head, her fingers entwining in his thick auburn hair. The midnight black of her own tresses cascaded about her face and shoulders with glorious abandon as her head moved restlessly from side to side upon the woolen blanket, her beautiful eyes clouded with a soft glow of desire.

"Marianna, my wild Russian bride," Alex now murmured against the silken column of her graceful neck, his low, husky voice holding only a touch of loving amusement. His lips returned to press against Marianna's, and he gasped into her parted lips a moment later when she grew emboldened, her fingers trailing downward to the hardness which sprang from the cluster of auburn curls between his lithe, muscular thighs. His golden gaze blazed fire into her blue-green one in silent understanding as he finally plunged within her, thrusting tenderly and slowly at first, until driven to move with increased urgency as Marianna delighted him by wrapping her finely molded legs about his waist.

Oh Alex! Alex! her mind silently cried as her emotions whirled round and round with almost terrifying speed. This was Alex, her Alex, and he could make her feel so apart from herself that it disturbed her, frightened her, made her forget all else in the world save him. The indescribable, overwhelmingly powerful sensations built to a fever pitch as she held him breathlessly against her, matching his rhythm with an increasing fire of her own.

Finally, she lay stunned by the sheer force of their mutual fulfillment, Alex striving to regain his breath as well. He softly brushed her flushed cheek with his lips before rolling to his back upon the blanket, pulling his wife close beside him, her soft curves nestled against the hard planes of his masculine body in a perfect fit.

"We're damned near going to freeze to death if I don't eventually get up and build that fire!" he declared with a quiet chuckle, his words in direct contrast to his actions as he hugged her tightly.

"Alex?" she said, her breathing just now returning to normalcy.

"Yes, my love?"

"If Lyle Caine truly seeks to have you killed, won't it be terribly dangerous for us to return to Skagway?"

"Now that's a hell of a thing to discuss immediately after making love!" he muttered in mock exasperation. He heaved a sigh before speaking again. "I don't believe he'll be so careless again, not after what happened in Bennett. To tell the truth, I'm not certain what his next move will be. Things are starting to fit together pretty quickly in the investigation now. That's why Sean was assigned to work with me in Skagway. As a Mountie, he doesn't really hold any authority there, but his part will come in after all this finally comes together, after we've gathered enough concrete evidence against Caine and his men."

"But I fear he will not allow that one unsuccessful attempt on your life to prevent him from trying again," she admitted, an expression of renewed apprehension on her lovely countenance.

She was surprised when Alex merely laughed and spoke in a voice brimming with humor, "I'm flattered to learn you are concerned for my safety!" He laughed again when he glanced down to view the stormy effect of his teasing remark, a sudden frown of annoyance on Marianna's face. "Is it so humiliating to admit that you care about my welfare, my love? Would it really be so terrible to give totally of yourself to me?"

"I have no desire to lose myself in any man, Alex Donovan!" Marianna snapped, bemused at the irrational anger she was displaying.

"There's no danger of that," replied Alex with a broad grin, still holding her securely within his powerful embrace. "Your considerable spirit is one of the many things I love about you. That's what first attracted me to you. But, sooner or later, something will happen to make you realize that you return my love full force, that you have been denying yourself the pleasure of loving me without restraint. That barrier of yours will topple one day, dearest Annie, and you'll finally be freed from all the pain and bitterness of the past. You'll come to me with the full realization of the love I believe you to hold deep within your heart."

He felt her stiffen within his arms, glimpsed the defensive look which now crossed her countenance. He hugged her once more before rising to his feet and silently drawing on his clothing, leaving Marianna to lie impassively alone. She watched as he set about building the fire to ward off the increasing chill of the night.

His words had perplexed and affected her far more than he realized. She could not deny the fear she had experienced on his behalf back in Bennett, the way she had sought to warn him against danger. And she certainly could not deny the fear she now felt at the prospect of their return to Skagway. Indeed, she told herself with an inward sigh, she cared a great deal more than she cared to admit. Alex Donovan had become an important part of her life, whether she liked it or not. She could not bear the thought of his being killed, or even harmed, by Caine or anyone else. But, love? Love was still a mystery to her, something she knew nothing about.

Her subconscious told her that it would be heaven to give totally of herself when the two of them were making love. But still she held back, refused to surrender a tiny part of herself buried deep inside. She could give fully of herself in the physical sense, she reflected as she lay gazing thoughtfully up toward the darkening sky, but there was still something, something inexplicable, that she had yet to surrender to him.

Silently berating herself for her introspection, she left the warmth of the blankets and hurriedly dressed, glancing surreptitiously at Alex, who seemed to be concentrating only on the fire he had now started, his own handsome features unusually pensive as he placed more branches in the midst of the rapidly growing flames. The horses whinnied softly as she approached them, her hand reaching out to smooth the shaggy mane of one as he raised his head from the grass. The wind had died down into a faint, whispery breeze, and Marianna mentally shook herself as she turned back to help Alex with the preparation of their supper, their first meal since a hurried breakfast much earlier in the day.

After eating they settled down for the remainder of the night. Marianna allowed Alex to hold her in his arms once more, and she snuggled up against his warmth, soon drifting off into a peaceful sleep. Alex, however, remained awake, his golden eyes shifting frequently to the slumbering form of the beautiful, headstrong young woman beside him.

Twenty

The unusually mild and pleasant weather which had held for several days disappeared the following morning, replaced by low-lying gray clouds and a drizzling rain, ending the earth's brief respite from chilling moisture. Alex and Marianna rose early and were well on their way by midmorning, the two of them seeking to shield themselves from the wetness by donning heavy canvas coats.

Their progress was slow, the trail leading mostly uphill back toward the summit. Once there, they were forced to leave the horses behind and proceed on foot, but they encountered no difficulty in disposing of the animals. Two men traveling together on their way to the gold fields were more than happy to purchase the horses from Alex, leaving him and Marianna to trudge carefully down the steep, muddy trail.

It was four miles down the Chilkoot to the next camp, a settlement of two frame buildings, one log cabin, and a profusion of tents. By the time Alex and Marianna reached the large camp much later that day, they were covered with mud and very much in need of food and rest. The "hotel," occupying one of the weathered frame buildings, offered a place to sleep and a plate of hot food, so Alex turned his steps in that direction as Marianna followed wearily behind. Her legs were sore and aching from all the hiking, her back and shoulders equally pained from carrying one of the saddlebags throughout the long hours of the journey. She was wet and tired and in no mood for Alex's teasing as they stepped inside the shelter of the hotel and he remarked, "You look like something the cat dragged in." He grinned, his amused gaze sweeping up and down her muddy, bedraggled form, his eyes pausing to linger on the rounded curve of her breasts revealed beneath her damp flannel shirt as she hastily drew off the drenched coat.

"If my appearance is so unappealing, then pray, do not force yourself to look upon me!" she sarcastically countered, her eyes flashing as she moved indignantly past him and toward the rough-hewn, unpainted front desk where a plump, matronly woman stood, her attention focused on the money she was counting.

"We should like accommodation, if you please," Marianna politely announced. The older woman glanced up, astonished to view the beautiful, obviously cultured young woman before her.

"Accommodation?" the woman repeated with a slight frown, then gave a boisterous hoot of laughter. "Honey, if you're saying you want a place to spend the night, then this here is it!" she loudly declared, one hand gesturing in a broad sweep to include the large room in which Marianna and Alex stood. Marianna turned to peer at the dimly lit confines of the building, and her gaze widened as she finally took notice of the numerous men who were sleeping on the bare wooden floor, their bedrolls unfurled side by side.

"But don't you have any rooms?" inquired Marianna in puzzlement.

"We got a few upstairs, but they're just as full up as down here," the woman answered, then smiled broadly as she suddenly caught sight of Alex. "Donovan! Well, I sure didn't expect to see you back this way for another while!"

"How are you doing, Rose?" He smiled in response, sauntering forward to stand beside Marianna, who glanced back and forth between the two in mild surprise. Rose patted unconsciously at her silver-streaked blond hair, her plump face wreathed in more smiles as she left her position at the desk and bustled around to embrace Alex with an enthusiastic hug.

"Mighty glad to see you again, you young scoundrel! What brings you back so soon?"

"The irresistible call of adventure," Alex quipped, turning to seize Marianna's hand and tug her forward. "Rose, this is Marianna, my wife," he proclaimed with another disarming grin. Rose gasped softly, her eyes narrowing as she now stared critically in Marianna's direction.

"Didn't know you'd gone and gotten yourself a wife, Donovan," she murmured with an unmistakable touch of displeasure at the news. "I don't mind telling you that Mercy had sort of been hoping . . ." she began, her

329

voice trailing away as Marianna met her gaze coolly. "Oh well, I'm glad to meet you, Mrs. Donovan." She extended her hand toward Marianna, who took it and grasped it with a tentative smile. Rose responded by nodding briskly at the younger woman, then turned back to Alex. "We ain't got a room for you two, I'm sorry to say. But, if your wife doesn't mind, she's welcome to bunk in with me and Mercy while you do the best you can out here." She started to move away, pausing to murmur, "I expect you two are near to starving. Come on out to the kitchen and I'll rustle you up something to eat."

"That's very generous of you," Alex replied with another brief smile. Rose left the two of them alone for the moment, her voice ringing out as she loudly called for her daughter, uncaring of the fact that she might possibly disturb the slumbering prospectors. Alex glanced at Marianna, glimpsing the look of uncertainty in her eyes. "It's all right. I've known Rose and her daughter for quite a few months now. You'll be perfectly safe with them."

"She certainly didn't offer you any felicitations on your marriage, did she?" Marianna mockingly observed. "I received the distinct impression that I am not entirely welcome."

"You just took her by surprise," he casually replied, taking her by the arm and leading her through a doorway toward the kitchen. Marianna soon no longer cared whether she was welcome or not, for the day's efforts had provided her with a voracious appetite, and she gratefully partook of the steaming plate of stew and

330

cornbread Rose placed before her. Once she and Alex had eaten their fill, she was led up the creaking stairs by Rose, the older woman showing her the bathroom.

"I expect you'll be wanting to wash the mud from your body. There's clean towels and a cake of soap there by the tub," she said, nodding to indicate the items. "I don't know where Mercy's gotten off to, but she'll be mighty upset if she misses seeing Al—your husband," she hastily amended, spinning about on her heel and scurrying off down the hallway.

Marianna took great pleasure in her bath, the first she'd had since the one at the summit of the White Pass several days ago. When she had scrubbed and soaked to her heart's content, she wrapped herself in the voluminous robe Rose had thoughtfully left upon a hook beside the tub. She wrinkled her nose in distaste at her soiled clothing on the floor, then wondered if she might perhaps be able to borrow something from Rose's daughter.

Opening the door, she stepped outside into the darkened hallway, now wondering which room she would be occupying that night. Rose was nowhere in sight, and Marianna decided to venture back downstairs, though reluctant to do so while wearing only a robe, her wet hair streaming wildly down her back. Nevertheless, she stealthily crept down the staircase, peering outward over the snoring, restlessly tossing men scattered about the main room.

She reached the foot of the stairs and began tiptoeing back toward the kitchen, halting abruptly when she heard a familiar masculine voice on the other side of the door. The woman's giggling entreaties she heard did not belong to Rose, she furiously realized.

"Come on, Alex," the apple-cheeked, buxom young woman seductively pleaded. "Just because you're married now doesn't mean we can't still be friends!" She laughed throatily again, her hands clutching at Alex's bronzed arms as she sought to bring his muscular chest up against the full breasts thrusting provocatively from beneath the thin cotton of her bodice.

"Be a good girl and go away and leave me to my bath, you little vixen!" Alex good-naturedly resisted. He had been preparing to ease into the steaming tub of water Rose had filled for him a short time earlier, before taking herself off to settle a highly vocal dispute between two guests upstairs. Mercy had slipped in just as Alex had drawn off the last of his muddied clothing, her unexpected appearance prompting him to snatch up a towel to cover his nakedness. The towel was now wrapped securely about the lower half of his lithely muscled body.

"If I go away now, will you promise to come up to my room later? Ma doesn't come up till almost dawn. We can lock the door and have ourselves a really good time!" she purred, still advancing persistently upon Alex.

"And what do you think my wife would say to that?" Alex responded in a deep voice brimming with amusement, his golden eyes twinkling down at the pretty blond-haired girl.

"Your wife? What's she got to do with it?" Mercy

demanded, standing still now.

"Everything!" Marianna exclaimed, dramatically swinging open the door to confront the room's occupants. Her color was very high, her eyes blazing their brilliant blue-green fire, and she was nearly shaking with the force of her emotions. Her gaze fastened on the young woman before her, then moved to where Alex was standing near the stove. Her eyes, initially widening when she perceived his shocking state of undress, rapidly narrowing in outrage.

"Who the hell are you?" Mercy angrily cried, more than a trifle annoyed at the intrusion.

"This, Mercy," supplied a broadly grinning Alex, "is my wife." He was obviously enjoying Marianna's display of jealousy.

"Your wife?" repeated Mercy for the second time in the last few moments. Her mother had already revealed the startling, displeasing fact of Alex Donovan's marriage. She had mistakenly believed Alex's wife to have already retired for the night somewhere upstairs. At least that is what she thought her mother had said.

"I am indeed his wife," Marianna frostily declared, her gaze haughtily searing Mercy's countenance, "and I would appreciate it if you would henceforth refrain from attempting to seduce my husband in your mother's kitchen, or anywhere else!" Alex suppressed a chuckle as the two women glared venomously at one another for the space of several long seconds, his wife obviously emerging the victor as Mercy abruptly wheeled about and flounced away, slamming the door behind her.

"And you! You, Alex Donovan," Marianna now seethed, whirling on him with a vengeance, "how dare you indulge in such a deplorable, clandestine meeting under the same roof as your own wife! And wearing nothing but a towel!"

"Did anyone ever tell you how beautiful you are when overcome by jealousy, my love?" Alex quipped, strolling unconcernedly forward to stand peering down at her, an unabashed smile on his handsome face.

"Jealousy?" Marianna breathed, her wrath visibly increasing. "Oh! Your arrogance, your egotism never ceases to amaze me!"

"And it never ceases to amaze me how my desire for you seems to increase threefold whenever I see you like this," he unwisely retorted, reaching for her now. The smile on his face quickly gave way to an expression of open-mouthed surprise as Marianna muttered an oath she had often heard issuing forth from her husband's lips, pushing against him with all her might. She caught him off-guard, and he lost his balance, stumbling backwards to land in the middle of the bathtub directly behind him. There was an accompanying splash, water flying everywhere as Marianna spun about on her bare heel and marched out of the kitchen.

Alex lay stunned in the few inches of water remaining, then suddenly threw back his head and laughed aloud. He tugged the sopping towel from his body, wringing it out before tossing it heedlessly to the puddled floor of the kitchen.

Marianna flew up the stairs, encountering Rose in the hallway. The older woman's features were kindly as

334

she demanded to know if something was wrong. Marianna violently shook her head, her beautiful face still flushed.

"Would you please tell me in which room I am to sleep tonight?" she asked in a low, tremulous voice.

"The last one on the left down yonder," Rose informed her, frowning in bewilderment as she watched Marianna treading swiftly down the narrow hallway and disappearing inside the room indicated.

The incident was still unpleasantly fresh in Marianna's mind the following morning when she once again descended the staircase, clad in a shirt and pair of trousers Rose had "borrowed" from a begrudging Mercy. She had slept little, faint circles beneath her eyes and a pale, drawn look on her beautiful features as she met Alex's cheerful greeting with rigid aloofness. He was waiting for her at the foot of the stairs, smiling up at her in such a way as to make her want to slap him.

"What? No fond 'good morning' from my dear wife? No tender kiss after a night spent apart?" he mockingly asked, his smile swiftly fading as he demanded with genuine concern, "Are you unwell, Annie? You look a bit pale."

"I'm quite well, thank you," she coolly responded, her eyes level with his as she stood upon the next to the last step with Alex directly in her path. He gave her one last searching look, then took her firmly by the arm and escorted her into the area which served as the dining room. It was already overflowing with people, every seat on the rough benches beside the long tables occupied by hungry men who were preparing to make the most difficult part of their journey to the Klondike.

Marianna was aware of the many eyes staring curiously in her direction as she and Alex moved through the room and into the kitchen beyond. Rose was busily frying eggs in a cast-iron skillet, the oven full of half a dozen loaves of baking bread. The various aromas mingled in palatable satisfaction, but Marianna barely noticed.

"Morning, Rose," Alex good-naturedly announced. The woman turned to greet him with a beaming grin.

"Morning, you handsome rascal! You and your wife sit down at the table there and I'll get your breakfast just as soon as Mercy gets back with some more firewood." She turned back to her cooking, sparing only a passing glance in Marianna's direction.

Alex gallantly held the chair for Marianna as she silently took a seat at a small oak table situated in a corner of the room. He seated himself next to her, reaching across to touch her hand with his when the back door swung open and Mercy swept inside, her arms laden with wood. Being the gentleman he was, Alex immediately rose and helped the girl deposit the wood beside the stove, oblivious to the way his wife was glaring at his back.

Marianna was dismayed at the renewed fury blazing up inside of her as she watched Alex with Mercy, his actions undeniably innocent. But she could not view the two of them together without recalling the unfortunate little scene of the night before, and she was astounded at the force of her jealousy.

Jealousy? her mind repeated in bewilderment. She had refused to examine the true motives for her vengeful behavior, had refused to so much as glance in Mercy's direction when the girl had finally crept inside the room where Marianna lay on the floor, pretending to sleep. She had attempted to convince herself, though she had failed miserably, that the reasons for her temperamental outburst were righteous, that even if she did not wish to consider herself Alex's wife, there was no excuse for his flaunting his lustful associations with other women!

She spoke not a word as Alex returned to the chair beside her, and she remained silent throughout breakfast. Alex, on the other hand, conversed quite amiably with both Mercy and Rose. And, when it finally came time for Marianna and Alex to leave and be on their way toward Dyea, Mercy boldly embraced the handsome, golden-eyed man and kissed him soundly on the lips. Marianna's own lips compressed into a thin line of renewed anger, but she managed to murmur a polite word of gratitude to Rose before whirling about and stalking down the trail, leaving Alex to catch up to her in a few long strides, the darkness of the morning clouds matching her mood.

"What a pity you could not have tarried longer with your winsome little paramour!" Marianna bitterly remarked, the first time she had spoken since the two of them had left the hotel nearly half an hour earlier. It was just beginning to rain again, their steps forced to grow slower upon the muddy, rutted ground they carefully traversed.

"Who?" Alex innocently questioned, smiling inwardly as he led the way through a tangle of spruce, hemlock, and cottonwood trees. The terrain had grown rougher since they had left the camp, and Marianna vaguely reflected that Alex had been right about horses being of little use on the trail. But horses were not foremost in her mind at the present.

"You know perfectly well!"

"If you're talking about Mercy," he replied, halting unexpectedly and nearly causing Marianna to collide with him, "she was never my 'paramour,' as you so charmingly put it."

"No? Then try and explain away the reference she made to the suggestion that the two of you remain 'friends'!"

"I've made quite a number of visits to Rose's place. And I honestly can't deny that her daughter has made no secret of her 'admiration' for me," he admitted with a disarming grin, gazing down at Marianna as the rain splashed across them, "but there was never anything between us. However," he added, a mischievous sparkle in his eyes, "I cannot deny that I didn't exactly lead the life of a monk before setting eyes on the woman who finally managed to ensnare me!"

"Ensnare you?" gasped Marianna, ignoring the rivulets of water coursing down her flushed cheeks as she raised her face to his. "Alex Donovan—" she furiously began, only to be quickly interrupted.

"There's no need to flare up at me, my love," he laughingly admonished, his hands moving to her shoulders as he towered above her. "I'm immeasurably delighted to learn that you care enough about me to have been jealous of Mercy. I know I've teased you mercilessly, but you must believe me when I tell you you've no reason to be jealous of any woman. My affections, my undying love, have already been captured by a beautiful, headstrong firebrand of a woman who even causes me to forget that I'm standing in the pouring rain with several miles still to travel before this night."

Marianna stared speechlessly up at him, thrown into confusion by his remarks. On the one hand, she wanted to tell him, in no uncertain terms, precisely what she thought of his smug self-confidence, while on the other hand, she felt all vexation with him rapidly melting away. Her emotions were most definitely in a quandary, her perplexity mirrored in her shining gaze.

A faint smile tugged at Alex's lips, and he surprised her by suddenly lowering his head and brushing her lips with a tender kiss. He turned without another word and started down the trail again, leaving Marianna to stare at his retreating back for several seconds before shaking herself out of the puzzling daze and taking off after him.

The two of them were relieved to view the buildings of Dyea in the nearing distance shortly before nightfall. The rain had ceased by midmorning, though the moisture it had deposited on the already saturated trail made for another long day of wearying, slippery travel.

"As you'll soon see," Alex remarked as they trudged toward the beckoning town, "Dyea's quite different from Skagway. The town sprang up on the marshes and tidal flats when the rush began. It's nothing more than a jumble of some log and frame buildings and tents, and its streets are always muddy. Quite a few stampeders have passed through here, but the harbor's too shallow, which is the reason Skagway became the main port."

Marianna gazed ahead as they moved closer, her eyes widening at the spectacular setting of the town— the vivid blue of the harbor between the low, forest-clad mountains, the snow-covered peaks in the distance. Musing that the town itself did not appear terribly impressive, she reminded herself that it nonetheless represented a welcome return to civilization and an opportunity to rest.

There were still quite a few people in Dyea, although their numbers were certainly nothing to compare with the mass of humanity in the neighboring town of Skagway. Alex and Marianna were able to get a room at one of the hotels, which proved to be comfortable and tastefully decorated.

"Why don't we get something to eat?" Alex suggested, closing the door to their room and dumping the saddlebags on the polished wooden floor. He watched as Marianna glanced unhappily down toward her muddied clothing.

"I should like to take a bath first," she murmured, frowning as she examined her appearance. The only mirror in the room, she quickly noted, was a small oval one hanging high above the washstand in the corner.

"I'd say they're accustomed to the mud here. But," he

ruefully agreed, "I think a bath would indeed take precedence over hunger at this point. You go ahead. To tell the truth, I've got some business to attend to."

"Business?" Marianna repeated, her gaze moving sharply to his face. "Does it have anything to do with your work as—"

"Now that we've returned to civilization, my love," he briskly interrupted, "you've got to be careful. Though it's safe to discuss it whenever we're alone and can be certain we're not being overheard you mustn't ever mention it to anyone else, understand?" he grimly cautioned, removing his damp coat and tossing it on the floor beside the saddlebags.

"I understand," Marianna somberly replied. "But can't you tell me who it is you're going to see, and why?"

"Not at this point."

"Then you still don't trust me!" she snapped, her eyes blazing.

"Let's just say it's safer if you don't know anything about it right now," he quietly stated, moving toward the door. "I'll probably be back before you've finished with your bath. And I'll see about finding you something else to wear," he told her with a brief half-smile, closing the door behind him as he left.

Marianna stared after him, displeased that he had not seen fit to take her into his confidence. Her curiosity was aroused and she determined that she would persuade him to tell her the truth of the matter when he returned. After all, she reasoned with herself as she bent down and searched through the saddlebags for the robe Rose had generously given her, she already knew so much about Alex's work that one more minute detail wouldn't matter.

She was soon relaxing back against the oversized bathtub in the small bathroom down the hall, the steam curling upward from the water. Her flesh was glowing from the scrubbing she had given it, her hair clean and flowing damply about her slightly pink shoulders as she lay with her eyes closed.

Suddenly, she detected the sounds of the doorknob being rattled. Certain that she had remembered to lock it, she raised startled, increasingly alarmed eyes toward the door. A feeling of panic descended upon her as the knob slowly turned, and she vaguely recalled that she had already been in the midst of such a scene once before. She hastily rose to her feet in the tub, snatching up a towel and clutching it to her bosom, then gasped as the door was eased open and a familiar head appeared.

"I grew impatient," he blithely remarked, his handsome face wearing only a faint grin. Before she could reply, he entered the room and closed the door softly behind him.

"Alex Donovan," Marianna seethed, "why must you always do that? May I remind you that I locked the door to ensure myself some privacy? Now get out this instant!" she imperiously commanded, her beautiful face stormy.

"Not until I've had my bath."

"What?" she cried, then immediately lowered her voice to a fierce whisper. "What do you think you're doing? I am not yet finished with my bath!" She watched, her eyes growing very round, as he began removing his shirt.

"That's the whole idea," he told her with a soft chuckle, a wicked light in his golden eyes as they swept boldly up and down her dripping form, the thin towel providing little protection from his searing gaze. He tossed the shirt to the floor, then took a seat in the chair beside the tub to draw off his boots.

"You must be insane to believe I would allow you to . . . to . . ." she said indignantly, her voice trailing away as she searched for words.

"It's only fair that you share your bath with me, seeing as how mine was so rudely interrupted last night." The boots were also tossed aside as he stood and began divesting himself of his trousers.

"Rudely interrupted by whom? Mercy or me?" she sarcastically countered. "You may dispense with this ridiculous notion of yours at once, do you hear me? I have no intention of sharing my bath with you!" Her face blushed as the trousers were discarded, his fingers moving to his long underwear. He inched them down and off, finally standing totally naked before her. "Alex," she now pleaded, her hand feebly moving outward as if to ward him off, "please!"

"Please what?" he retorted, one eyebrow raised mockingly in her direction. Before she could hope to stop him, he had stepped into the tub and was standing in front of her, looming above her a moment before nonchalantly sinking down into the water. Marianna gazed down at him in disbelief, then gasped aloud as the towel was suddenly yanked from her body and she was pulled unceremoniously down into the tub as well, her soft curves landing atop him as water splashed heedlessly to the floor.

"Alex!" she gasped. She pushed against him, but to no avail. His arms went about her squirming form, his lips capturing hers. She was very much aware of the way she was pressed so intimately against him in the water, the way her full breasts made contact with the curling hair on his muscular chest. His hands moved to clasp her firmly rounded buttocks as he tugged her upward into his embrace, the pulsing hardness of his manhood pressing demandingly against the silken flesh of her thighs.

"I recall facing a veritable tigress the last time I was near a bathtub," Alex lovingly teased, momentarily drawing his lips from hers, his handsome face now flushed from the warmth of the water as well, his eyes gleaming with the promise of passion.

"Alex," Marianna shakily murmured, attempting to escape him one last time, "surely you must see that this—this is impossible!" she finished with another fiery blush, her skin warm and tingling, her raven tresses floating like a dark curtain about them.

"My grandmother always said the word 'impossible' should never be part of my vocabulary!" he quipped, then took her lips with his once more, his hands gently caressing her trembling curves. She surrendered herself to the flare of overwhelming desire she experienced at his touch, returning his increasingly urgent kisses with fervor.

344

The water swirled about them as they kissed, as Alex's mouth trailed a fiery path downward to Marianna's breasts, his gentle fingers pushing one rose-tipped peak upward so that his warm lips could close upon the delicate, highly sensitive nipple, his tongue wreaking havoc upon Marianna's senses as it sensuously encircled, provocatively teased. She closed her eyes against the flames of her passion, gasping anew as Alex moved to do the same to her other breast, its pale, rounded perfection gleaming with the veil of moisture which coated it.

"Alex!" breathed Marianna as his mouth returned to her parted, gasping lips, his fingers searching out the moist, secret place between her thighs.

"It's a good thing this tub is so large, isn't it?" he murmured, his lips moving to the delectable hollow at the curve of her shoulder.

"Oh Alex, we can't—" she feebly protested, almost beyond all reason.

"We can and will," he huskily asserted, a faint smile curving his lips. He surprised her by suddenly seizing her about the waist and lifting her up and back, seating her in his lap and drawing her legs forward so that they were straddling his lean hips, his own legs stretched out in the tub as he slowly raised himself into a sitting position. Marianna gasped anew as his hard manhood pressed demandingly against the rounded cheeks of her bottom and his fingers returned to their delightful torment, his lips almost bruising hers with their intensity as she leaned forward into his powerful, wonderfully potent kiss. Another gasp ended in a faint cry as Alex clasped her buttocks in his large hands and lifted her slightly, his throbbing member sheathing within her and seeming to touch her to the very core.

He began a slow rotation of his hips, driving her nearly mindless with the intensely erotic sensations he was arousing within her. She clung to him as if she were drowning, her desire heightened to such a level that it was almost more than she could bear as she moved with him, his mouth returning to her breasts as he tugged her insistently forward, his hands still tightly clasping her buttocks. They soon lost themselves in their mutual, wildly abandoned passion, the tempo of their movements increasing until they both violently shuddered with the shattering fulfillment that could not be denied them.

It was a very flushed, and slightly wrinkled Marianna who emerged from the bathroom a short time later, leaving her husband within to finally proceed with his bath. She was still feeling slightly appalled at the shocking intimacy they had just shared, and her cheeks flamed again as she scurried to their room, painfully embarrassed when she glimpsed the man and woman who directed highly curious stares toward her before she disappeared from view.

Twenty-One

Though Alex had originally intended for them to remain in Dyea for the space of two or three days, he changed his mind, offering Marianna only an evasive explanation when he announced that they would be sailing back to Skagway the very next day. The two of them enjoyed a restful night in the hotel, arising much refreshed by the night's sleep.

Marianna was pleasantly surprised to discover the pretty, only slightly oversized dress Alex had purchased for her, and she was vastly relieved to be able to discard the shirt and trousers which had been her costume during the previous days. She was mildly astonished to find that Alex had remembered to supply her with all the necessary underthings, her cheeks faintly blushing at the thought of his choosing the intimate garments for her.

They arrived at Skagway shortly before noon, the late summer day a relatively warm and sunny one. Alex escorted Marianna down the gangplank of the small steamer and across the wharves, leaning closer as he said, "I've got to make contact with Sean right away. But since I have no intention of letting you out of my sight just yet," he added with one of his disarming grins, "you'll have to come along."

"But don't you think it might be dangerous?" asked Marianna with a deep frown, grasping at the folds of her skirt to prevent the hemline from trailing in the mud as they neared the end of the crowded wharves.

"What? To make contact with Sean, or to take you along?" he countered, his golden eyes twinkling irrepressibly in spite of the very real danger he knew to exist. Marianna, however, refused to be put off.

"Won't Lyle Caine, or some of his men, be watching for you?"

"Probably. But it would look terribly suspicious if I behaved as if I expected trouble. I'll just have to take my chances."

"Do you know where to find Sean?"

"He'll more than likely be having his meal about now. That Cleary can put away more food than anyone I've ever known before!" he remarked with a soft chuckle, endeavoring to hide the actual preoccupation of his thoughts.

"Alex," spoke Marianna with a thoughtful expression on her face, "could we begin our search at the restaurant? I'm quite anxious to see Kate and let her know I'm safe."

"Of course. That's as good a place as any to start. But," he sternly cautioned, his voice dropping as they stepped up onto the boardwalk at the edge of town, "you're not to tell Kate, you're not to reveal anything

348

about my work, understand?"

"I'm absolutely certain that Kate can be trusted!" Marianna defensively replied.

"Obey me in this, Annie," Alex insisted, his voice low and even. "A great deal may depend upon it." He offered no other remarks on the subject as they finally reached the restaurant and stepped inside.

Kate was taking an order near the doorway when she glanced up to find Marianna smiling across at her. The pretty blond woman forgot all about her hungry customers as she immediately flew to embrace her partner, obviously delighted at the younger woman's return.

"Annie! Oh honey, it's good to see you again! I was starting to get a mite worried about you." Marianna hugged her fondly in response, inwardly perplexed as she suddenly realized she had no idea what Sean had told Kate about her abrupt departure.

"I . . . I'm sorry I was forced to leave without first telling you," Marianna faltered, touched by her friend's display of affection. "I shall be happy to explain things to you now that I have returned." This last was spoken with a hasty glance in Alex's direction. He appeared not to hear her, however, as his gaze suddenly found Sean. Kate turned to watch with Marianna as Sean stood up from the table a few feet away and greeted Alex as he strode forward. There were so many men and so much noise during the restaurant's busiest time that no one seemed the least bit interested in the reunions taking place.

"Is Donovan the one you went away with?" Kate

unexpectedly asked, nodding toward Alex as he and Sean began moving toward the women.

"Yes," Marianna truthfully answered. There was no time for further talk between them at the moment as the two tall, handsome men came to stand before them.

"Annie, my love, it seems I've been quite remiss in never offering a proper introduction between you and my friend here," Alex declared, faintly smiling as he took Marianna's arm in a decidedly possessive grip and pulled her forward to face Sean. He was so much taller than her that she was forced to raise her face by several degrees to look squarely into her eyes, the most startlingly blue eyes she had ever seen.

"I'm glad to see you back, Mrs. Donovan," Sean seriously proclaimed, though there was a telltale glimmer of amusement in his unwavering gaze. Marianna recalled the last time they had seen one another, the night Alex had spirited her away from town. She was dismayed to feel the hot color rising to her face, and she composed herself quite admirably before saying, "Thank you, Mr. Cleary." She glanced back at Kate, who stood surveying the scene with a solemn look on her face, betraying none of the surprise she had felt when Sean had addressed her partner as "Mrs. Donovan."

"I hate to leave you so soon, but you should be safe here," Alex remarked to his wife, smiling briefly toward an impassive Kate. "Sean and I will return this evening to make certain you get back to the hotel."

"Where are you going?" demanded Marianna, then could have bitten her tongue for it. Alex merely grinned unconcernedly and left with Sean, but not before Marianna saw the meaningful look which passed between the attractive giant of a man and Kate, a look which Kate hastily attempted to ignore.

"Come on, Annie. Let's go on in the back room and talk," suggested Kate, leading the way as she and Marianna moved through the noisy, crowded room. Several men called out to Marianna as she went, expressing pleasure that she had finally returned. She smiled warmly at them as she followed Kate.

"I once told you I wouldn't pry into your past. What you do, or what you've done, is no business of mine. I just wanted you to know it's good to have you back. The customers have missed you, and I've missed you," said Kate, taking a seat on a wooden crate in the dimly lit storage room. "I've never taken such a shine to one of my partners before. And, well, I don't mind telling you that I was worried about you."

"What has Sean told you?" She seated herself beside her friend, discomfited by the fact that she still couldn't tell Kate the entire truth.

"Only that you left town with some family member and would return in about a week. I didn't question him about it, even though it sounded pretty strange. I figured you had your reasons for leaving so suddenly."

"I've wanted to reveal the truth of my marriage for some time now, but . . . but we had agreed to keep it a secret for a while."

"I had a feeling there was something between you and Donovan the first time I saw the two of you together at the Golden Nugget," commented Kate with a quiet little laugh.

"I'm sorry I couldn't tell you," Marianna murmured sincerely. "It would have been such a relief to share it with you. And, as for my absence these past several days—"

"You don't owe me any explanations," Kate broke in with a slight shake of her blond head. Her friend smiled in silent gratitude, the subject abruptly changing as Marianna mentioned Sean again.

"Has Mr. Cleary been a frequent customer?"

"Yes," Kate answered following an instant's hesitation, then muttered beneath her breath, "damn him!"

"What did you say?"

"Nothing." She stood to her feet then, dusting off the back of her gathered cotton skirts. "It's time I was getting back to work."

"I'm sorry you were left to run the place by yourself while I was gone," stated Marianna, rising as well, "but I intend to make up for every bit of extra work my absence caused you!"

"Just do your best," Kate uttered practically as they took themselves off to deal with the hungry, impatient crowd in the other room.

Alex and Sean, meanwhile, were engaged in a discussion of their own.

"Did Barkley come through?" Sean asked once he and Alex had retired to the privacy of a small log building at the far end of town.

"He passed the information all right, but I still don't trust him," Alex replied, his handsome face wearing a grim look. "And, because of that trouble with those two Caine sent up there to kill me, I wasn't able to meet with Barkley again."

"But you don't know for sure that Caine was the one who arranged that attempt on your life, do you?"

"No, but from what Marianna told me she overheard, there's very little doubt left in my mind."

"So Caine really is after your wife," Sean muttered thoughtfully. "I'm sorry she's involved, Alex."

"Not half as sorry as I am!" Alex retorted with an expressive grimace. He sighed heavily. "I'd put her on another ship bound for Sitka, but I know she'd only manage to make her way back here somehow!"

"Things are going to be a bit touchy with Caine now, aren't they?" remarked Sean.

"They may get even touchier when I pay him a visit in a short while. By the way, has anything out of the ordinary been going on while I've been gone?"

"Just what you heard over in Dyea about that young fellow. He complained loudly about being cheated at the Golden Nugget, was forced out by some of Caine's men, then was found dead the next morning. As usual, we've no solid evidence that points to Caine himself, but things are heating up. Things are heating up fast."

"I know. I'll be glad when all this is over with and Marianna's safe at home," he murmured half to himself. Striding across to fling open the door, he and Sean left the cabin and headed toward Lyle Caine's saloon.

True to his word, Alex arrived with Sean at the

restaurant just prior to closing time that night. As the four of them left the restaurant and strolled down the boardwalk toward the hotel, Marianna and Alex paired off ahead.

"Have you seen Caine?" she immediately demanded.

"I paid a visit to him earlier," Alex casually answered.

"How did he behave? Did he say anything about your reappearance here in town?"

"He seemed a bit annoyed to see me," recalled Alex, his mouth curving into just the hint of a smile, "and he was even more annoyed when I warned him to stay away from my wife."

"Oh Alex, you didn't! Why, he'll be even more determined to do you harm if you persist in provoking him!"

"I'd say he was provoked enough when I announced the news of our marriage," Alex told her with a low chuckle. "But, seriously, my love," he added with a sudden frown, "I don't want you so much as talking to him. There's no need for me to remind you how dangerous he can be."

"No. This is one time when I shall be only too happy to heed your warning," she responded with a troubled expression in her beautiful eyes.

Behind them, Kate and Sean were involved in a strained conversation of their own. They spoke in low, hushed tones, although Kate seemed to want no part of the discussion.

"What's the matter, Kate? I wouldn't have taken you for the sort of woman who's afraid of anyone. Why are you so afraid of me?" questioned Sean, inclining his head so that he was afforded a better view of the attractive blonde's face. He had attempted to take her arm, but she had abruptly snatched it away.

"What the hell makes you think I'm afraid of you?" Kate furiously whispered, refusing to so much as glance up at him as she gazed straight ahead.

"You're afraid to face up to your feelings. There's no way you can honestly deny what's between us, but you're too frightened to admit it."

"Why don't you just leave me alone?" Kate hissed, her eyes blazing up at him for one brief moment.

"Now how can you expect me to do that after what's happened between us, after I've told you how I feel?" he responded, his voice low and vibrant with emotion.

"Nothing has happened between us!"

"You would call the kiss we shared nothing?" he remarked with a touch of laughter. "I could feel it right down to my toes! And I've a sneaking suspicion it affected you much the same."

"That blasted kiss was a mistake! And just why, after one ridiculous kiss, are you so all-fired convinced that there could ever be anything more between us?" she contemptuously demanded. "There's no way on God's green earth I'm going to let myself get roped into a no-win situation with you, Sean Cleary, kiss or no kiss!" she declared, her cheeks flushed with hot color. "Now leave me alone, damn you!"

Sean was about to respond when they arrived at the hotel. Kate abruptly murmured something to Marianna, shot the big, sandy-haired Mountie one last scathing glance, then fled up the stairs to the sanctuary of her room. Marianna and Alex exchanged puzzled looks at Kate's odd behavior, while Sean merely bid them goodnight and strode swiftly out of the hotel.

Marianna had been pleased to discover that Kate had made arrangements with the hotel to hold her room until she returned. At least she would still have the privacy of her own room, she mused as she and Alex paused inside the hotel lobby. It then occurred to her that it was highly probable Alex would invade that privacy yet again.

"You go on up. Stay in your room and lock the door," Alex commanded.

"Suppose someone else possesses your reprehensible talent for picking locks?" she couldn't refrain from taunting, her eyes shining challengingly up into his. She quickly sobered, asking, "Are you going back to the Golden Nugget tonight?"

"Of course. Don't worry, though. I've arranged for someone to watch the hotel and make certain no one comes near your room. No one save myself, that is," he informed her, giving her a quick kiss as he turned to leave. "Don't wait up for me, my love!" he threw over his shoulder.

Marianna indeed prepared to offer him a fitting retort, but she thought better of it and watched him go, a slow smile appearing on her beautiful countenance. Gathering up her skirts, she quickly ascended the stairs to go in search of Kate.

"Kate? Kate? May I speak with you a moment?" she asked quietly, tapping on the door of her partner's room. It was opened a few moments later, revealing an uncharacteristically red-eyed Kate, who hastily attempted to conceal the evidence of her weeping. "What's wrong?" Marianna breathlessly demanded, swiftly entering the room as Kate closed the door behind her.

"Nothing," lied Kate, averting her flushed face as she whirled about and moved to stand at the curtained window.

"Kate," Marianna solemnly remarked, staring at the other young woman, "I know we agreed not to pry into one another's lives. You yourself repeated as much just today. However, if there is something troubling you, something causing you grave distress . . ." she said, her voice trailing away into an expectant silence. It was nearly a full minute before Kate spoke.

"You know, I don't mind telling you that it isn't easy for me to open up with anyone, especially another female," she said, a faint, bitter smile on her face as she turned back to Marianna. She suddenly appeared much younger, much more vulnerable, prompting the younger woman to smile sympathetically as she sank down upon the softness of the bed. Kate took a seat on the opposite side, poised just on the edge. "I suppose it's best if I just come right out and tell you. You just might be able to understand, at least a little," she concluded with a heavy, rather desperate sigh.

"I shall certainly try," Marianna assured her with another soft smile of encouragement.

"First, my name isn't really Kate LaRue. It's Kirsten Johannson. My folks were Norwegians who came to this country before I was born. They owned a farm back in Kentucky. Not that it was much of a farm, mind you. But, I've got a hell of a lot of good memories of the years I spent on that old farm," she murmured with a faraway look in her eyes.

"Do your parents still live there?"

"No. Mama and Papa died during an outbreak of influenza a few years back. I was only twelve at the time. Me and my younger brothers and sisters were divided between several aunts and uncles and cousins. I was the unlucky one. I had to live with my Uncle Olaf and his wife, a sour-faced woman who turned out to be the meanest bitch that ever lived! Never a kind word, never anything but criticism and punishment from that woman. Uncle Olaf wasn't much better. Anyway, I endured three years with them until finally getting a bellyful and getting myself the hell out of there!" Her lovely features took on an expression of tormented remembrance now. "I ran off with a traveling salesman, of all things. He took me to Kansas City with him, promising to marry me. He never kept his promise, of course, and I finally got wise and left him."

"But you were only fifteen!" Marianna uttered in disbelief.

"I might have been only fifteen on the outside, but I was a hell of a lot older on the inside!" Kate cynically remarked. "There'd never been anyone before him. I was disillusioned, as they say. I finally made my way to New Orleans, which is where I first started singing. I stayed there for a year or two, then headed west. San Francisco was where I ended up. I spent a few years there." She paused, rising to her feet and moving restlessly back to the window. "I haven't led a very saintly life, Annie. Not that I've ever worked as a whore or anything, but, just the same, what I am now is a far cry from the scared, naive little fifteen-year-old gal who left with that smooth-talking salesman seven years ago."

"I had surmised that you had led a rather . . . well, a rather colorful life," Marianna told her with another brief smile. "But, what has all this got to do with your present, obvious distress?"

"Everything!" Kate cried, jerking away from the window and plopping down onto the bed again. "I don't want to get hurt anymore, Annie. Oh, I know I act like I'm tough as nails, but I've got feelings just like anyone else! And I don't want to go through the anguish that falling in love, or what I foolishly thought was love, has always brought me!"

"Falling in love?"

"Why the hell did Sean Cleary ever have to come into my life? Why the hell did he ever—" she quietly raged, breaking off abruptly.

"Sean Cleary is the man you've fallen in love with?" queried Marianna in surprise.

"Who said I was in love with him?" Kate wrathfully demanded.

"I thought that's what you meant when—"

"I don't know, damn it!" wailed the other young woman, her face stormy and her eyes narrowed. "I don't want to love him. He's the type of man who'll expect a lot from me, Annie. And I don't know how I'd handle it when he found out I hadn't lived up to his expectations!"

"Has he told you what his expectations are?"

"No. But I'd be blind not to realize where things are heading," she answered miserably.

"How can you possibly know how things would turn out with him? Are you upset because you fear a broken heart, Kate, or because you subconsciously believe yourself beneath him, because you don't feel you are good enough for him?"

"I'm as good as anyone else!" she retorted, but her voice lacked conviction.

"Exactly," Marianna agreed in satisfaction. "Which is why you cannot allow your past to spoil any chance for future happiness." Hadn't Alex said that to her before? she suddenly reflected.

"I don't suppose I should expect you to be able to understand," Kate wearily answered, glancing pointedly toward her partner now. "After all, you're married to a man you love, a man who loves you, aren't you?" She was mildly puzzled when Marianna's face colored.

"Yes. But, that doesn't mean you should discount what I am saying!" Did she love Alex? The answer continued to elude her, mainly because she knew she was not ready to accept it.

"Maybe you're right," Kate finally allowed, lying back upon her bed and placing an arm across her eyes. She said nothing else, though Marianna waited for the space of several long moments. She decided to leave her friend alone with her disturbing confusion, returning to her own room with her own equally troubled thoughts.

She was awakened with a slow, tantalizing kiss much later that night, a kiss that seemed to draw all her emotions from deep within. In her dreamy state of mind, she allowed the kiss to continue for several long moments before finally opening her eyes and coming fully awake.

"Alex! I didn't hear you come in," she breathlessly murmured, her eyelids fluttering closed again as his lips lingered at her silken throat now. "Alex!" she squealed softly in protest, pushing firmly against him. "What happened tonight?" she demanded.

He reluctantly raised his head, heaving a sigh when he perceived he would have to give her the answers she wanted before he could hope to continue with his seduction.

"Nothing much. But Caine's beginning to get more and more careless, Annie. And there's talk that folks here in Skagway are starting to get fed up with his control of the town."

"Did he say anything to you tonight?"

"Only that he noticed I was enjoying a remarkable run of good luck," recalled Alex with a broad grin.

"Are you truly such a competent gambler, then?" inquired Marianna with a slight frown, sitting up in the bed and drawing the covers farther up against her nightgown-clad bosom.

"Yes, as a matter of fact. Something I inherited, no doubt," he remarked with another grin. "I don't think we'll have to stay up here that much longer," he added in a more serious vein, bending down to remove his boots. "If things keep progressing the way I believe they will, we'll be able to wrap things up within the next few weeks."

"You mean we shall be leaving Skagway then?" Marianna asked, her beautiful face pensive.

"Precisely." He stood to remove his shirt and trousers now, the pale moonlight streaming in through the window, illuminating his splendid masculine form.

"Alex," she said, attempting to draw her attention away from his actions, "I think you should be aware that there appears to be trouble brewing between Kate and your friend Sean."

"Kate and Sean?" he repeated, clad only in his underwear now. "Well," he philosophically remarked, "if there is any trouble, Sean Cleary's perfectly capable of dealing with it."

"Perhaps. But I seriously doubt if he's ever encountered anyone quite like Kate before. And I don't think she's encountered anyone like him before, either."

"Then they'll have to work things out the best they can, won't they? We've got a rocky romance of our own to deal with, remember?" he quietly chuckled. Marianna's eyes widened as he climbed into the bed beside her, his naked flesh making contact with her own as he lost no time in removing the barrier of her nightgown. Soon, they were once again transported to the special world inhabited only by the two of them, though Alex did make one last teasing remark. "It's a pleasure to make love in a bed again, isn't it, my love?" After that, all talk, all coherent thought was set aside for quite some time.

Twenty-Two

"I really think it suits you well, Kate. That shade of blue is quite becoming with your hair and eyes," opined Marianna with a decisive little nod. She and the other young woman were taking a much-needed break from their duties at the restaurant, treating themselves to a visit to one of the well-stocked general stores in town.

"I don't know," murmured Kate, holding the soft wool dress before her and eyeing it critically. "It does look like it'd be about the right size."

"Then you should buy it," insisted Marianna, reflecting that this was the first time Kate had displayed any interest in her appearance, other than her concern over the costumes they wore for their performances. She wondered if it had anything to do with Sean, but deemed it wisest to refrain from mentioning the man at all. Kate's revelations of the previous night were still fresh in her mind.

Wandering past the various crates and barrels stacked in nearly every inch of floor space, she gazed curiously at the odd assortment of goods for sale. A few other customers came and went, but she paid them little heed as she strolled leisurely about the store, leaving Kate to the difficult task of choosing between the dresses she was still surveying. Her gaze, however, was caught and held when a young, boyishly attractive man strode inside. He halted abruptly when he caught sight of Marianna, then beamed with obvious delight.

"Marianna!"

"Andrei?" she gasped, unable to believe her eyes. There was no mistaking that face, that voice, she mused, astonished at seeing him there. When he swiftly crossed the short distance between them and enveloped her in an enthusiastic hug, she asked, "What are you doing here?"

"I never expected to find you here in Skagway, dear cousin!" he said with a pleasant rumble of laughter. "I had hoped to be able to locate Alex, but I honestly didn't know if you'd still be with him!"

"You've yet to tell me what you are doing here. What did your parents have to say about your coming?" she questioned, keeping her voice low. She glanced toward Kate, ascertaining that the blonde was still totally occupied in trying to make her selection.

"About what you'd expect them to say! Mama threatened, Papa lectured. But I had to come, Marianna. I was tired of existing in the same little world there in Sitka, tired of watching life pass me by. Like any other young man my age, I wanted to experience some adventure!"

"So you're here to experience adventure," replied Marianna with an indulgent half-smile.

"I haven't yet decided when I'll head on up to Dawson. I thought I'd hang around here in Skagway for a while first. Where is Alex?" he then asked.

"At the present, I've no idea. However," she reluctantly told him, the unwelcome image of Lyle Caine suddenly flashing into her mind, "you will most likely be able to find him at the Golden Nugget Saloon this evening. I'm sure he will be glad to see you, Andrei, though I don't think he'll be pleased that you've come to the one place where you face the best possibility of getting into some sort of mischief!"

"Well I like that!" he indignantly countered, appearing much offended. "We're much the same age, remember? And you're here, aren't you? Besides, you're only a woman! If this place isn't too dangerous for you, then it certainly shouldn't be too dangerous for me!" For a moment he seemed to Marianna to be even more immature than she remembered. She watched as he curtly nodded his head at her, then spun about and stalked from the store.

If Kate had noticed the incident, she concealed her knowledge as she and Marianna soon returned to their restaurant, the rays of the late afternoon sun filtering through the thickening cover of clouds. The town was alive with men and women bustling about, horses and wagons moving down the rutted streets, and the ever-present lure of gold. Marianna's thoughts, however, were briefly centered on her young cousin and the very real danger he might possibly be facing as a result of his association with her and Alex. She sighed inwardly, musing that Alex would probably know how best to handle Andrei.

She had not even seen Lyle Caine since returning from Bennett. Kate revealed that he had only come into the restaurant once during Marianna's absence, that he had remained for a very brief time and then exited without a word. Marianna experienced the sudden chill she felt whenever thinking of him, and she resolutely forced her thoughts away from the villainous Caine as she and Kate set about getting ready for the evening crowd.

They were in the middle of their last performance when Caine appeared. Dark and menacing, he moved among the audience with his hawk's gaze fastened unblinkingly upon Marianna. He paused to lean negligently against the wall a few feet away from the stage, a ruthless look on his face as he watched his prey.

Kate saw him first, and she gently nudged her partner. When Marianna's gaze fell on him, she felt an almost paralyzing tremor of fear, but she managed to regain her composure and finish the song, vividly aware of Caine's eyes on her. She had known she would see him again sooner or later, realized some sort of encounter with him was inevitable, but she was still nonplussed now that it had finally happened. He moved not a muscle as he stared at her, and she was feeling almost faint by the time she and Kate bowed to the appreciative applause and left the stage.

"He's trying to intimidate you, Annie," offered Kate. They stood alone in the back room, Marianna's beautiful face wearing a distracted expression. "I don't think he'll bother you again, not with Alex and Sean around to keep an eye on you," she added, placing a comforting arm about the younger woman's faintly trembling shoulders.

"You don't know what he's truly like! He's more evil, more treacherous, than even you suspected!"

"How do you know that?" Kate sharply queried.

"I—" Marianna faltered, catching herself before she made the mistake of mentioning the incident up at Bennett, "I just know! And I'm afraid he'll stop at nothing to get what he wants. Alex and Sean will be in danger if they try to defy him," she distractedly remarked, cautiously peering through the doorway again to see if Caine was still there. She heaved a sigh of relief when she saw he was not.

"You mean if they try to keep him away from you? Or are you maybe referring to something else?" Kate suspiciously inquired, her perceptive gaze missing none of Marianna's visible concern.

"I think I shall step outside for a bit of fresh air," she announced, evading the question altogether. She hurried to the rear door which led into the alleyway, swiftly opened and closed it, then leaned back against its rough, hard surface. Breathing deeply of the cool night air, she remained outside for several minutes, still perplexed about Kate's probing questions. When she decided to return inside, her hand moving down to grasp the doorknob, another, larger hand closed over hers.

Marianna gasped in heart-stopping alarm, her widened gaze flying upward to rest upon the coldly smiling face of Lyle Caine. She stood as if rooted to the spot, his eyes peering into hers with mesmerizing, almost hypnotic force.

"Don't make a sound, my dearest Annie. You'll not tell anyone about our little meeting, or I'll make certain your devoted husband is found dead by morning," he uttered in a low voice, his hand tightening painfully on hers. It was an unusually dark and cloudy night, and the semidarkness served only to make him appear even more sinister as he loomed above her, the two of them completely alone behind the row of buildings.

"Haven't you already tried that, Mr. Caine?" she bravely retorted, her eyes flashing with unquenchable spirit. She jerked her hand from beneath his and turned to face him squarely. He appeared somewhat taken aback by her remark for an instant, but quickly recovered his chilling poise.

"Perhaps," he said with another malevolent smile. "But I assure you I would not fail this time."

"What do you want?" she calmly demanded, though she was inwardly aching with fear. She was tempted to call out for help, to alert Kate to Caine's presence, but she resisted the temptation and instead decided it best to hear him out.

"You know what I want. I warned you that my patience had run out, remember? There's still time to change your mind, still time for you to prevent any further unpleasantness. You can come to me now."

"And what of my husband, Mr. Caine? Or have you conveniently forgotten that I am married now?"

"I've forgotten nothing," he spoke through clenched teeth, his features tightening, his eyes narrowing. "As I told you before, I could have taken you by force. That's undoubtedly what I should have done. But you've bcome a strange obsession with me, Annie. I can't explain why, but I wanted things to be different between us. I wanted you to come willingly, to ease this damnable yearning I've felt for you since first laying eyes on you. You should be flattered that I allowed you the privilege of making me wait!"

"Once again, I must refuse your 'generous' offer to grace your bed, Mr. Caine! Since you are so accustomed to taking whatever you want, then you should encounter no difficulty whatsoever in finding another woman, one who would appreciate the 'honor' you do her by wanting her as your mistress!" Her hand clasped the doorknob again, and she was surprised when he did not attempt to stop her. She paused momentarily, turning back to him to say, "And it would make no difference if I were not married. My answer would still be the same!" She flung open the door and disappeared inside, leaving Caine to glare savagely after her.

Alex was playing poker inside the Golden Nugget at the same time Caine was confronting Marianna, but he was happily ignorant of his wife's predicament. Andrei had finally located his old friend, his boyish face flushed with excitement as he watched the game.

"Four pretty ladies, gentlemen," drawled Alex, presenting his winning hand as the other participants grumbled in defeat. He raked the chips across the table, turning to an admiring Andrei with a sardonic grin. "There's no sense in playing if you can't play to win, my friend." Inwardly, he was cursing the fact that Andrei had made such a public point of his friendship. He would have liked to have kept the foolhardy young man uninvolved, but it was too late now.

"You may have taught me how to play poker, Alex, but it wasn't anything like this," Andrei ruefully observed, fascinated by all the raucous activity inside the large saloon. "There isn't anything to compare with this back home!" he added, gazing wide eyed about the place.

"Deal me out," Alex lazily instructed, rising leisurely to his feet and clapping Andrei on the back. "Come on, young Markova. I'll buy you a drink." The two of them made their way through the crowd to the bar. After procuring two glasses of whiskey, Alex leaned closer to the younger man, saying, "I wouldn't want you to do anything rash while you're in town, my friend. You were right when you said there's nothing like this back home. Skagway is a world apart from Sitka." He raised the glass to his lips and downed the amber liquid in a single swallow. Andrei attempted to follow suit, but the fiery stuff burned in his throat and he proceeded to cough loudly as he sought to regain his breath.

"I guess I'm not used to such hard liquor," he rasped out, his eyes filling with tears. Alex suppressed a laugh.

"You sure could have fooled me," he quipped with good-natured sarcasm.

"Why is it you and Marianna seem to think this place is so dangerous for me?" he demanded, finally able to breathe normally once more. "Damn it, Alex, I can't just sit at home with my parents for the rest of my life!"

he added with a reproachful look.

"I understand you better than you think I do," replied his older friend, smiling faintly. "And I know how you feel. All I'm saying is that you'll have to grow up fast if you don't want to get into any trouble here."

"Since when have you become such an old sober-sides?" Andrei frowned. Alex merely smiled again, the smile freezing on his handsome face as he caught sight of the dark-clad man who had just entered the saloon.

Lyle Caine's eyes searched the room, narrowing imperceptibly as they lit upon Alex. He began stepping, with deadly composure, toward Alex, ignoring the greetings of a handful of other men as he kept moving straight toward his adversary, his features set and grim.

"You know, Donovan, I thought you might be interested in knowing I just had the pleasure of your wife's company," he blatantly revealed, trying obviously to engage Alex in some sort of confrontation. Alex's own golden gaze filled with silent fury, his face tightening at Caine's taunting statement. Andrei watched with avid curiosity, his eyes flitting back and forth between the two obvious foes.

The music in the background swelled to a crescendo just then, and Alex waited until it died back down before replying, "I thought I told you to stay away from her." His voice was cold and hard, his eyes glowing with barely concealed rage. It took all his strength of will to refrain from violence, to keep from smashing his fist into Caine's detestable, smirking countenance. "Damn it, if you've so much as touched her I'll—" he threatened, the sudden image of Caine's hands on Marianna driving him almost beyond reason.

"You'll what?" Caine challenged mockingly, removing a cigar from his coat pocket and bringing it up to his lips with apparent unconcern. His dark eyes, however, met Alex's with unspoken meaning.

Alex was about to respond when Sean appeared at his shoulder. He glanced at his friend from the corner of his eye, fully aware of the reason for Sean's sudden appearance. He'd have to keep from losing his temper, Alex reluctantly told himself. Things were getting too near the end for him to risk ruining their chances for total success with his personal vendetta against Caine. He sensed that Marianna was safe, that Caine was merely trying to goad him into losing control. The thing now, he decided, was to pay a visit to Marianna and make certain she was unharmed. His violent tendencies toward Caine would have to wait.

"The time's coming, Caine," Alex finally countered, his handsome face wearing the ghost of a smile, "and I'm looking forward to it." He grinned unabashedly at the other man, then sauntered casually away and out of the saloon, a relieved Sean and a bewildered Andrei in his wake.

"Alex? Alex, why'd you back down so easily?" Andrei questioned as the three of them marched along the boardwalk, heading for the restaurant now.

"Hush, boy," Sean sternly admonished. "This is something that doesn't concern you, something you wouldn't understand."

"But you've never backed down like that before, not

as long as I can remember!" Andrei protested, ignoring Sean's warning as he turned back to Alex.

"Run along now, Andrei. Maybe I'll be able to explain it to you someday. But not just yet," Alex spoke in a low tone. He relented enough to halt for a moment, placing a hand on the young man's shoulder as he said, "You go on back to the bunkhouse. We'll talk later." He smiled briefly, then spun about on his booted heel and continued on his way. Andrei was left to stand staring after the two tall men, a perplexed frown on his immature features.

Marianna and Kate were bidding goodnight to the last of their customers when Alex and Sean walked in. Alex immediately strode forward to grasp his wife's arm, inwardly much relieved that she was apparently all right.

"Sean, why don't you and Kate wait outside? I've got to speak to Annie alone," he proclaimed. Kate did not protest when Sean took her arm and strolled out of the building with her, the two of them waiting out on the boardwalk in front of the restaurant.

Marianna glanced up at her husband in puzzlement, then swiftly averted her gaze as she glimpsed the searching look he gave her. She was dismayed to feel her face coloring, silently berating herself for making it so transparently obvious that something had happened.

"I understand Lyle Caine paid a visit to you tonight."

"How do you know that?" she gasped, swiftly raising her eyes to his face again.

"I heard it from Caine himself," Alex disclosed, his

expression still grim. He took hold of her other arm, gazing deeply into her beautiful eyes. "What did he say, Annie? Did he threaten you? If he dared to touch you—"

"He wanted to offer me one last chance to come to him willingly," she hastily interrupted.

"Is that all he said?"

"No," she reluctantly admitted, glancing downward again. Her voice was barely audible as she murmured, "He warned me not to reveal the incident to anyone or you would be found dead by morning." An involuntary shiver ran the length of her spine as she recalled his calm, murderous words.

"Well then, it appears the devious Mr. Caine is indeed beginning to lose his grip!" remarked Alex with a quiet chuckle. He grew solemn again as he demanded, "What did you tell him?"

"Exactly what I told him before! I told him I would never come to him, that it would make no difference even if I were not married to you!"

"And that's all that happened?"

"Yes. I was honestly surprised that he didn't attempt anything, that he allowed me to go so easily. And I haven't told anyone else about it, Alex. I think it's quite odd that he mentioned it to you himself!"

"It may be odd, but it's following a pattern. I told you he's been getting more and more careless, remember?" He released her arms and moved away, frowning thoughtfully as he paused to stand near the stage.

"Something else happened today," she suddenly

remembered. "Andrei is here in Skagway."

"I know. He was at the Golden Nugget tonight."

"Oh Alex, I'm worried about him! I'm afraid Caine may seek to use him against us, just as you were afraid I would be used." She crossed the short distance separating them, an anxious expression in her blue-green eyes as she gazed up at him. "What are we going to do now?"

"The same as we have been doing. We bide our time. I don't have any intention of allowing you to go anywhere without being watched by myself or one of my men. As a matter of fact, I'm curious to know how Caine managed to get close to you tonight."

"I stepped through the rear door for a few minutes, after I had earlier observed Caine watching me during our last performance. I cannot comprehend how he could possibly have known I would be outside!"

"You're not to go anywhere else alone, do you understand?" Alex sternly decreed, his hands moving back to her shoulders, his gaze holding hers.

"What about you? Aren't you in a great deal of danger? Who is going to look after you?" she demanded, more frightened for him than she cared to admit.

"Don't worry about me, my love," he answered with one of his endearing, boyish grins. "I've managed to get this far without anything happening to me."

"But something would have happened to you up in Bennett if I had not chanced to overhear those two men!" she pointed out, her face flushed beneath his lovingly amused gaze.

"Then I suppose I should consider you to be my guardian angel. A beautiful, headstrong, temperamental angel at that!" he added, startling her by planting a loud, highly enthusiastic kiss upon her parted lips.

Kate and Sean, still waiting together on the boardwalk outside, happened to glance inside just then, witnessing the two lovers' kiss. Sean chuckled quietly.

He turned back to Kate, whom he had been attempting to engage in conversation the past several minutes, and observed, "From the way I see it, those two will never lead a very tranquil life!"

"Maybe they don't want one," murmured Kate, feeling decidedly restless and impatient, wishing Alex and Marianna would hurry so she would no longer be left alone with Sean. She was much too aware of his proximity.

"Do you?" he then asked, his eyes never wavering from her attractive young face.

"Do I what?" she irritably demanded, glancing back inside and frowning as she perceived Marianna still thoroughly occupied. She resolutely endeavored to ignore the way Sean so pointedly stared down at her, conscious of his gaze in spite of the unusual darkness of the night. She tugged her cloak more closely about her body and pulled her hat farther down upon her head as protection against the increasing wind.

"Do you want a tranquil life, Kate LaRue?" he quietly repeated, repositioning his own hat as well.

"What difference does it make what kind of life I want? We don't always get what we want in this world!"

she countered, an unmistakable note of bitterness creeping into her voice.

"I'm going to get what I want," Sean confidently declared. "You may as well know now that I'm not the sort of man to waste precious time. I suppose you've already guessed that, given the way I grabbed you and kissed you the other night," he commented with an unabashed grin.

"Yeah, and you're damned lucky you're still in one piece!" she retorted with unconvincing bravado.

"I think I've already fallen in love with you, Kate," he astonished her by casually stating.

"Hell, the least you could have done was come up with a line I haven't heard a hundred times before!" she sarcastically responded.

"Allow me to rephrase that," he insisted with another brief smile. "I know I've already fallen in love with you!"

"You're not going to get anywhere with me, Cleary," Kate asserted, facing him now with a stormy light in her eyes, "so there's no use in wasting any more of your precious time!" She couldn't allow him to see how much his declaration, albeit a rather clumsy one, had affected her.

"Then prove it by kissing me again."

"I damned sure will not!"

"What's the matter? If you're so convinced we'll never mean anything to one another, then why not prove it to both yourself and to me by the most sure-fire way I know how? If neither of us is affected by it, then I'll be more than happy to drop the whole thing."

"You're out of your mind!" she cried, actually quite flustered by his amazing challenge. Deciding that she'd had just about enough of the disturbing little scene being enacted between them, she whirled about and began marching away from the restaurant.

"Kate! Kate, come back here!" Sean called after her, smiling broadly to himself as he moved to give chase. His long strides brought him close behind her within seconds. He reached out and took hold of her arm, pulling her to an abrupt halt and then forcing her about to face him. She stood, eyes blazing fierily up at him, while he opened his mouth to speak.

The words never came. A shot rang out, its loud rapport shattering the cool night air. Kate watched in paralyzing horror as Sean clutched at his chest, a grimace of immense pain on his handsome face. Before she knew what was happening, he had knocked her to the boardwalk and placed his body atop hers, shielding her from any remaining danger.

Although the sound of gunshots was quite common- place in Skagway at that time, a handful of concerned citizens came running toward the spot where Sean lay wounded on the muddy boardwalk, Kate pinned securely beneath him. Alex and Marianna were the first to arrive, having heard the shot just as they were leaving the restaurant.

"Damn," Alex ground out, his face a mask of fury as he glimpsed the bleeding form of his partner and friend. Marianna immediately flew to Kate, assisting the other woman in extricating herself from beneath the wounded man.

"Are you all right?" Marianna anxiously inquired, helping Kate to her feet.

"Is . . . is he dead?" Kate quietly asked, her features pale and deceptively impassive as she glanced down toward Sean. She was oblivious to her own bruised, disheveled appearance. The other men gathered around Alex as he knelt beside the tall Mountie, one of the curious onlookers shaking his head at this latest act of violence in what had become an increasingly lawless town.

"Not yet," Alex muttered, leaning closer in an attempt to examine the wound. "Somebody help me get him over to the hotel," he commanded. He and three other men proceeded to lift an unconscious Sean, the four of them moving carefully toward the hotel. "And one of you other men send for the doctor!" Alex threw over his shoulder. As a young, strapping fellow left to do Alex's bidding, Marianna and Kate began following after the somber procession.

"Kate, are you sure you're all right?" The blond woman had not spoken again, and Marianna placed a supportive arm about her waist.

"Why would anyone want to kill him? Sean Cleary wasn't the type to give enough offense to warrant something like this. Why the hell would anyone want to do him harm?" Kate murmured dazedly.

"I don't know. But I'm sure Alex intends to find out."

"We never had any warning, never saw anyone. He was gunned down in cold blood, just like an animal. And you know what really bothers me, Annie?" she asked, her mouth twisting into a smile of bitter irony, her eyes shimmering with the gathering tears, "His first thought was for me. His first instinct was to protect me, damn him!"

Marianna glanced sharply at her friend in surprise, but judged it best not to offer any comment just then. She and Kate hurried to catch up to Alex and the others as they neared the hotel entrance.

"You can take him up to my room," Kate spoke as she regained some measure of composure. She moved past them and started up the stairs to lead the way. Soon Sean was lying pale upon the bed, his breathing ragged. Kate and Marianna scurried about to fetch water and bandages to staunch the flow of blood, while Alex took a seat on the bed beside his friend.

"What happened, Kate?" he quietly demanded, continuing to press a kerchief against the wound. He took the clothes Marianna gave him, his expression growing even more solemn as the light of the lamp afforded a better glimpse of the gaping wound.

"I was heading away from the restaurant and Sean came after me," Kate dully recalled. "He had just caught up with me when I heard the shot. He grabbed at his chest, knocked me to the ground, then fell on top of me, obviously trying to protect me." She gazed down at the unconscious man, her heart turning over in her breast.

"Did you see anyone suspicious around before then, anyone who might have been watching you?"

"I don't remember anyone else about. But it was a bit dark, so I can't be certain if someone was watching us or not," she told him, pausing briefly before asking, "Do you have any idea who might have done it, Alex?"

"I've got an idea, but I'm not ready to divulge it just yet. Damn it, where is that doctor?" he exclaimed, tossing aside the blood-soaked cloths and replacing them with the clean ones Kate pressed into his hand. Marianna watched as her partner sank down onto the bed behind Alex.

"Perhaps you should lie down, Kate," she solicitously suggested.

"I'm fine," Kate murmured, then remarked in a voice barely audible, "for a moment there, right after it happened, I thought the big ox was dead. I thought he was dead, damn it!"

The doctor finally arrived. Kate and Marianna watched in worried silence as he examined Sean's wound. He straightened and tersely announced that the bullet would have to be removed at once. Though it had fortunately missed any vital organs, he added, it would nonetheless have to be dug out of Sean's chest without further delay. Alex insisted that the two women leave the room, but they both defied him by obstinately declaring they would remain.

Less than an hour later, Sean lay resting upon the bed, his wound cleansed and bandaged. The doctor assured them that the patient should recover if infection did not set in, but cautioned that he would require constant attention for the next several days.

"You two go on to bed. I'll stay up and watch him tonight," Kate announced, motioning Alex and Marianna toward the doorway.

"You already look worn out," Alex responded with the ghost of a smile. "I'll stay with him."

"There's no sense in us standing here arguing about it all night! It's my room, and I'm staying with him!" Kate stubbornly insisted, a determined look on her face. Alex, sensing there was no way he could possibly hope to dissuade the determined blonde, took Marianna's arm and led her from the room. Marianna paused briefly to hug her friend before leaving, saying, "Please don't hesitate to let us know if Sean takes a turn for the worse, or if you need help." Kate smiled softly in gratitude, then turned back to the unconscious man on the bed.

"Oh Alex, do you really think he'll be all right?" asked Marianna as they entered her room and Alex quietly closed the door behind them.

"Sean's strong. He'll pull through." In spite of such apparent confidence, he appeared troubled about something as he took a seat in the chair and began pulling off his boots.

"What is it?" she perceptively queried, moving to stand before him, a slight frown marring her own beautiful features.

"Remember when Kate asked me if I had any idea who might have tried to kill Sean?" At her nod, he continued. "I didn't want to say anything in front of Kate, but I think I know why Sean was shot."

"Why?" she breathlessly questioned.

"Caine, of course. I think he arranged this latest little incident. Only I don't believe Sean was supposed to be the target."

"What do you mean?"

"It was pretty dark tonight, wasn't it? Just dark enough to make it difficult for someone standing some distance away to be able to see clearly the faces of a man and a woman who leave your restaurant and start walking back to the hotel. I think Caine's hired gunman made a simple mistake, a mistake that nearly cost Sean his life. I think I was supposed to be the one shot tonight, not Sean."

"But," she replied in confusion, "why? Caine has certainly been afforded ample opportunities to do something such as this before now. Why tonight?"

"Because, just as I told you earlier, he's beginning to get careless. I think what happened tonight was brought on by his obsession with you, my love."

"Oh Alex!" she gasped out in horror. "You mean he tried to have you killed because of what I said to him earlier, because I—"

"Not because of what you said to him," he assured her, rising to his feet and drawing her into his comforting embrace, "but rather because of his jealousy, his hatred for me."

"If what you are saying is the truth, then perhaps you should consider relinquishing your role in the investigation. Perhaps we should leave Skagway at once!" she emotionally suggested, burying her face against his shoulder as a sudden tremor shook her.

"I've accomplished too much, come too far to pull out now, my love. But I think it would be best if you left town. I've been torn between the desire to have you here with me and the desire to see you safely away. I'd have sent you away long before now, only I didn't believe you'd stay away. Now, however, I think you understand what we're up against."

"Which is exactly why I will not leave!" she defiantly proclaimed, drawing away a bit in order to raise shining eyes to his unsmiling countenance. "We're in this together, Alex Donovan! And I give you fair warning that I would indeed manage to return again if you sought to send me away!"

"Annie, you don't know what—" he firmly began, only to fall silent as her fingers pressed against his lips.

"There's no use in quarrelling about it, for you know I shall have my way in this!" she told him, smiling triumphantly up into his handsome, faintly scowling face. He muttered a curse, heaved a sigh of resignation, then seized her hand and placed it about his neck, his warm lips claiming hers before she had guessed his intent.

Outside, the heavens opened up and a pouring rain began to drench the earth. Inside, Alex and Marianna were engaged in equally tumultuous pursuits, the two of them soon joining together in the ultimate, rapturous embrace.

In a room down the hall, Kate was leaning over Sean Cleary, brushing his shadowed cheek with her soft lips. She knelt beside the bed, tightly closing her eyes as she began praying in silence, praying for the "big, handsome ox of a man" to make it safely through the night.

Twenty-Three

The rains continued, virtually without cease, throughout the following two days. Sean remained feverish, slipping in and out of consciousness. Kate rarely left his side, often so weary she would drift off into a restless sleep in the chair beside the bed. Marianna insisted upon relieving her for at least a brief spell each evening, but Kate would not stay away long before returning and firmly ejecting Marianna, and sometimes Alex, from the room.

Marianna reluctantly complied with her husband's instructions to close the restaurant each day before nightfall, though she was allowed to oversee its operation for the duration of the long daylight hours. Each night, however, found her safely inside the hotel, either in Kate's room or her own.

Although there were no further attempts on Alex's life during those two days, Marianna was nonetheless vastly relieved when he returned to her room late each night. He would hold her warm and secure within his strong arms, his love for her casting out all fear for a brief time. She frequently pleaded with him to remain watchful and wary of Lyle Caine, for she knew Alex continued to spend part of each night gambling at the Golden Nugget.

Sean regained total consciousness on the third day after the shooting. His eyes opened, blinked rapidly, then focused on the brightly papered wall opposite from where he lay. He turned his head slightly upon the pillow, his gaze softening as it fell upon the slumbering form of Kate in the chair beside him. Slowly moving to prop himself up on one elbow, he instead collapsed weakly back against the mattress, his head spinning.

"Sean?" murmured Kate, awakening with a start when the bedsprings bounced noisily beneath her patient. "Sean, can you hear me?" she anxiously questioned, rising from the chair and bending over him with a worried frown. Her long blond hair cascaded about her face and shoulders, her dress sadly wrinkled as a result of her fitful dozing in the chair. To Sean, however, she appeared a vision of loveliness.

"Of course I can hear you. I recall being hit in the chest, not in the ear!" he responded with a soft chuckle, his blue eyes twinkling irrepressively, then abruptly clouding with pain as he clutched at his bandaged chest.

"Just what did you think you were doing, trying to move like that?" she sternly chastised, drawing the covers up to his bare shoulders once more.

"How long have I been here?" he demanded, wincing as another sharp pain shot through his chest.

"More than two days now," she quietly answered,

resuming her seat in the chair. "The doctor said you were to stay quiet and still. He said you could have some broth once your fever finally broke." She felt as if she were babbling like an idiot, so she lapsed into uncomfortable silence as Sean's gaze cleared again and he asked, "Have you been here the whole time?"

"What difference does that make?" Kate evasively replied. "The important thing is, your fever's broken and that's a good sign. I expect you're feeling a powerful hunger about now." She rose to her feet and stepped across to the washstand, where Marianna had earlier placed a covered kettle of beef broth.

"Where's Alex? I've got to talk to him," Sean said, his voice slightly hoarse.

"I haven't the vaguest notion where he is, but it wouldn't make any difference if I did. You don't need to be visiting with anybody till you've gotten some of this broth into that empty stomach of yours," she firmly decreed, her hands carefully holding a bowl of the still-warm mixture as she returned to his side.

"You mean to tell me that's all I get to eat?" he remarked, eyeing the bowl's contents scornfully. He slowly raised himself a bit higher against the pillow, his movements slow and cautious as he experienced another twinge of pain.

"It's what the doctor ordered." She smiled in spite of herself, amused at his woeful attitude as she began feeding him the broth.

"Where are my clothes?" he suddenly demanded, frowning darkly as he swallowed another spoonful.

"Why?"

"So I can get dressed!"

"Get dressed?" repeated Kate in disbelief. "Sean Cleary, you won't be stirring from that bed for at least the remainder of the week!"

"And just who was it decided that?"

"It didn't take any deciding! You lost an awful lot of blood and you'll be weak for a time. You can't risk moving too much for fear of starting that hole in your chest bleeding again," she responded with exaggerated patience. "But if you feel like you want to blame someone for your predicament, then go ahead and blame me!"

"Blame you? Why should I blame you for anything?" He gazed at her in bewilderment, his clear blue eyes fastening upon her suddenly flushed countenance.

She set aside the bowl of broth, her hands tightly clasped together in her lap as she replied flatly, "It was because of me that you took that bullet, remember? Because I was acting like a silly schoolgirl instead of a grown woman. Though I still can't figure out who would have wanted you dead, I can't help but feel somewhat responsible for helping to make you such a ready target!" she concluded, her voice displaying more emotion now.

"What peculiar kind of reasoning is that?" he demanded with an ironic grin.

"It isn't peculiar at all, damn it!"

"Lord, save us from the strange logic of a woman's mind!" he sardonically quipped, rolling his eyes heavenward. She bristled beneath his amused gaze, but he merely took her stormy face between his two large hands, staring deep into her flashing eyes as he said, "It was through no fault of yours that someone shot me, Kate LaRue. They'd have found an opportunity to take aim sooner or later if they were so inclined. So you stop all this nonsense about my present situation being your fault, do you hear?" he gently but firmly commanded. He was just pulling her closer for a kiss when the door opened to reveal Marianna.

"Well, I'm glad to see you're obviously feeling much better!" she declared, coloring a trifle as she realized she had interrupted what appeared to be an intimate scene.

"I'd feel a whole lot better if someone saw fit to feed me some solid food!" Sean muttered with mock ferocity. Kate had abruptly resumed her seat in the chair when she saw Marianna, and she sat there with eyes momentarily downcast as her partner told the good-natured Mountie, "Now you must do everything Kate tells you! After all, she has almost single-handedly nursed you these past few days. Why, we were unable to persuade her to leave your side for more than a few moments at a time." She was puzzled by the sharp, quelling glance Kate suddenly shot her.

"Is that so?" Sean murmured, his own gaze moving back to the young blond woman.

"What are you here for, Annie?" demanded Kate, avoiding Sean's studying gaze.

"I decided to close the restaurant a bit earlier today. Two of the waitresses are down with bad colds, and this interminable rain seems to have dampened my spirits as well," she quietly answered.

"Are you feeling unwell?" Kate now asked with genuine concern, rising to her feet and moving to the younger woman's side. She put a hand to Marianna's forehead. "You might just have a bit of a fever."

"I'm fine. Just a bit tired, that's all," Marianna insisted. She smiled down at Sean again. "I can't tell you how relieved I am to find you conscious again. Alex will be so pleased. He was every bit as worried as the rest of us, though I doubt if he will admit as much to you!"

"Thank you for your concern, Mrs. Donovan," Sean warmly replied.

"I should think we had progressed far beyond such formality by now!" she laughingly told him before leaving.

She returned to her own room and lay down upon the bed, a sudden dizziness making her head spin. The dizziness was accompanied by an uncertainty in her stomach, and she vaguely wondered if she had perhaps contracted an illness. She eventually drifted off into a dreamless sleep, awakening again several hours later when Alex slipped inside her room.

"Did anything happen tonight?" she immediately queried, shaking off her drowsiness as she sat upright in the bed, still fully clothed.

"I don't know if it's merely my imagination or not," Alex remarked, sitting on the bed beside her, "but I could swear Caine knows something." His face grew thoughtful, his golden eyes staring off into space.

"What makes you believe that?" Anxiety gripped her at the thought of such a possibility.

"Nothing I can put into words. Just something in his behavior," he replied, his voice low and even. He glanced back at Marianna. "What are you doing still dressed?"

"I wasn't feeling very well. I didn't intend to fall asleep," she hastily explained, feeling unaccountably irritable all of a sudden.

"What's the matter?" he asked with a concerned frown, leaning closer to peer into her pale face.

"I don't know!" she answered a bit snappishly.

"Perhaps I should fetch the doctor."

"No!" she loudly disagreed, prompting Alex to stare at her in growing puzzlement. She lowered her voice and added more calmly, "I'm certain it's nothing serious. Probably simply low spirits. If only this rain would let up . . ." Her voice trailed away as she gazed toward the gray light filtering through the curtains.

"Would you like for me to stay with you a while longer?" Alex generously offered, having intended to remain for a short time, then return to his work. He was baffled when his words only seemed to annoy her.

"Why? So you can ease your selfish desires?" she sarcastically retorted.

"You know that's not what I meant," he tightly responded, his eyes now glowing dully.

"Do I? Sometimes I feel as if I am nothing more than a . . . a whore for you, a creature existing only for your lustful pleasure! You sneak in and out of my room like a thief in the night, don't you?" She was inwardly perplexed at her irrational anger toward him, but she could not seem to control it.

"I won't even dignify that blasted nonsense with a reply," he said, rising abruptly to his feet and moving to the doorway. "Though I know you're in no frame of mind to believe me, I happen to love you with all my heart, and I can only hope this strange mood of yours will pass by the time I see you again!" He paused to stare silently into her beautiful, stormy face, then left.

Marianna watched him go with an odd pain twisting at her heart. She miserably collapsed back against the pillow, hot tears filling her eyes. Experiencing a sharp pang of remorse for the way she had spoken to Alex, she resolved to make amends when he returned. She closed her eyes, placing an arm across her forehead as the tears spilled over from her lashes to form a glistening path down her cheeks.

Alex, after checking on Sean and finding his friend to be much improved, couldn't erase the memory of his wife's cruel words as he strode back to the Golden Nugget. Her words had stung him, stung him to the core, though he chided himself for making so much of them. He would speak to her again in the morning, believing, for no definable reason, that his work this night would not end for some time yet.

Two hours later found Alex involved in a highly competitive game of poker at Caine's saloon. The stakes, as well as the tempers of the participants, were high, and Caine himself was one of the players. A large crowd had gathered about the table, but no one dared speak a word as they watched with avid interest.

Alex was aware of Caine's hawkish gaze on him at several points throughout the game, but he chose to ignore it. His fury toward the man was already such that he knew it would take little provocation to make him abandon the rigid control he sought to maintain over his own strained temper.

The latest round ended with Alex the winner, and he was in the process of casually raking the chips across the felt-covered surface of the table when the man seated to Caine's left suddenly leapt to his feet and cried, "You cheatin' son of a bitch! There weren't no way you could've drawn those aces!"

Andrei, standing directly behind Alex, and several of the other onlookers gasped at the charges the man levelled at the golden-eyed gambler, while Caine merely leaned negligently back in his chair, chewing on his cigar as his dark eyes narrowed speculatively toward Alex. An expectant hush fell over the entire room, the bright lights of the lamps above glaring down upon the charged atmosphere.

"I think you'd better withdraw those words, mister," Alex quietly declared as he remained seated, his handsome face wearing an inscrutable look. He gazed levelly at his accuser, a thin, wiry fellow with greasy blond hair and bloodshot eyes.

"I ain't gonna withdraw what I know to be the truth!" he gruffly responded. His red-rimmed eyes flitted down toward Caine and then back to Alex. "No man's gonna get away with cheatin' me out of my gold!" There were several murmurs of support for his brave statement, and some of the men began mumbling something about justice needing to be done. Caine slowly removed the cigar from his mouth and drawled lazily, his eyes never leaving Alex's face, "You know, Donovan, I've often wondered how you could manage to win so often without having some kind of trick up your sleeve. Seems to me like you just finally got caught."

"Alex Donovan would never cheat!" Andrei interjected, his gaze hastily sweeping across the crowd.

"Come to think of it, I've had a sneaking suspicion for a while now that Donovan's just too damned lucky!" another one of the players piped up, his eyes glancing toward Caine just as the accuser's had done. There was an increasing roar of agreement amongst the crowd, many of whom were at least half drunk. Their expressions grew quite ugly when Caine slowly stood to his feet and said, "Gentlemen, I think what we have here is a clear-cut case of dishonesty at cards. Now, what do you think we should do about it?" Alex's face wore a strange half smile as he met Caine's seemingly triumphant gaze. When his hand moved slowly toward his gun, his arm was immediately pinned to his side by some of the surrounding men, the pistol removed from his reach. As the crowd in the saloon, incited by Caine's subtle mastery of the situation, began loudly discussing what they should do by way of punishment for one they were nearly all now agreeing was guilty, Andrei slipped unnoticed out of the place, his frenzied steps taking him in the direction of the hotel.

"I say we tar and feather him!" one man near Alex shouted.

"I say we tie him to a post and flail the skin off his back!" another clamored.

"Why don't we just string him up?" This cold-blooded suggestion met with the most enthusiastic approval, but Caine unexpectedly intervened at this point. He stared smugly down at a still and silent Alex.

"We've got to make this legal and proper," he smoothly asserted, chuckling softly as Alex glared defiantly up into his face. "And, seeing as how there's more than enough of us here, I say we elect a judge and jury and try him now."

"It don't make no difference, since we're just gonna hang him in the end anyway!" a man gleefully remarked, others joining in the boisterous laughter.

"Just the same," Caine decreed, smiling again, "it will all be legal and proper."

Alex finally arose, the crowd falling silent. His golden gaze moved slowly about the room, falling on the malevolent faces of the bloodthirsty mob, before returning to Caine.

"How convenient for you," he remarked with a brief, ironic smile. "You always get others to do your dirty work, don't you, Caine?" His gaze returned to the men surrounding him. "Whether you believe me guilty or not, what you're planning is a mockery of justice. I'm entitled to a fair trial just like anyone else. Why don't you ask yourselves why Lyle Caine is so anxious to preserve the semblance of legality? He's never bothered with appearances before now, has he? Ask yourselves how many men have lived to question his authority. It just so happens that I am innocent of the charge, but that isn't what's important here. What matters is that you don't allow him to goad you into doing something you'll only live to regret, that—"

"That's enough talk from you, Donovan!" Alex's original accuser loudly interrupted. The others began grumbling again, and Caine ordered some of his men to take the accused and lock him in a back room till after the trial, evidently not even planning to allow Alex to speak in his own defense.

Alex fought against the hands which roughly dragged him across the saloon and into the small, darkened room to the rear of the building. A couple of men were posted outside the door inside the saloon, an equal number outside the exterior entrance to the saloon.

The "trial" was in full progress within minutes. Alex paced inside the room, remaining undaunted as he coolly tried to think of something, some way to prevent what appeared to be the inevitable. Still not certain whether Caine's clever plan was the result of the man's obsession with Marianna, or a possible discovery of Alex's true occupation, he wondered how he could manage to get word to Sean. It wasn't just saving his own neck he was thinking of, he mused, but his role in the investigation as well, his knowledge of certain people and events that he knew to be invaluable to the undertaking's success.

The mock trial was rapidly drawing to a close when Alex thought he heard a noise outside. He waited in mounting anticipation, suddenly remembering Andrei. Of course! he told himself, feeling a measure of hope returning. Andrei might have been able to get word to Sean after all! He watched the door which led out to the wooded area behind the saloon, certain he had detected the sounds of a struggle. Praying that his mind wasn't merely playing tricks on him, he was greatly relieved when the door suddenly eased quietly open to reveal a slightly swaying, but grinning, Sean. Andrei and another man were waiting outside.

"Damnation, man, don't you think we've got enough troubles without you going and getting yourself hanged?" the tall Mountie whispered.

"What the hell took you so long?" Alex retorted in a hushed voice. He and Sean hurried out of the room, they and the two others making their way quickly through the wooded area to a clearing nearby. Alex was shocked to see Marianna there, her beautiful face barely visible beneath the wide-brimmed hat she wore as protection against the chilling rain.

"Alex!" she breathed out, nearly fainting with relief as he came striding toward her. She was clad in a man's shirt, trousers, and canvas coat which she had hastily thought to borrow from Andrei, and her hand was grasping the reins of an impatiently snorting horse.

"What is she doing here?" he demanded, rounding on Sean.

"It was none of my doing," the other man replied with a touch of amusement. "After she and Andrei came to me, there was no power on earth to keep her from coming!" He put a hand to his chest, his wound beginning to pain him again. He had been forced to lock Kate inside her room in order to come, and he certainly didn't relish the prospect of facing her when he returned to the hotel.

"Oh, Alex, I had to come!" Marianna proclaimed. "I certainly wasn't going to remain behind while you go off for who knows how long, leaving me to wait without knowing—"

"I suppose I damn sure don't have any choice, do I?" he curtly broke in. He turned back to Sean. "We'll head back to Dyea for a spell. I'll get word to you." He almost roughly lifted Marianna up into the saddle, then mounted the horse beside hers. It was then that he noticed Andrei mounting yet another horse. "Where do you think you're going?" he demanded with a fierce scowl.

"With you," Andrei stated simply. "After all, I was the one responsible for keeping your neck from being stretched tonight!" he added with a boyish grin.

"Fine. The more the merrier!" Alex sarcastically muttered. He glanced toward the fourth man, a solemn fellow near his own age. "Thanks, Swenson. I'd appreciate it if you'd help Cleary keep an eye on things while I'm gone." The man nodded in silent response. "Take care of yourself," Alex then said to Sean.

"You do the same." He watched as Alex, along with Marianna and Andrei, reined about and galloped swiftly away into the rainy night. Then he and the man called Swenson slipped down a side street and made their way back to the hotel, the two of them chuckling together at the thought of Caine's displeasure when he discovered Alex Donovan had escaped his treachery yet again.

*　　　*　　　*

Kate LaRue. however, was in anything but a chuckling mood by the time Sean returned to unlock the door. She was infuriated by his treatment of her, resentful as she once again reflected that he would never have succeeded in doing such a thing if she hadn't been too blasted fearful of hurting him to react with the strength of which she was entirely capable!

Her eyes narrowed wrathfully as she heard the key turning in the outer lock. She stood with head proudly erect and hands on her hips, ready to confront Sean when he eased open the door and stepped unhesitantly inside.

"I'm sorry I had to lock you in, Kate, but you were just so all-fired determined to keep me from going!" he uttered by way of mingled apology and defense for his actions. His lips twitched beneath the blond moustache as he attempted to suppress the smile tugging at the corners of his mouth. He closed the door behind him, then waited patiently for the outburst he fully expected to be forthcoming.

"And just why do you think that was?" she snapped, her gray eyes blazing into his. "I haven't spent all my time nursing you back to health these past few days to stand by and watch you risk a relapse by going traipsing off into the night!" Her rising temper was fueled by the involuntary flinch of pain which crossed his features, his face paling beneath its golden tan. "You're hurting, aren't you?" she spoke accusingly, her brisk and angry manner masking the deep concern she felt on his behalf.

"It's nothing. Just a little twinge," Sean insisted,

smiling unabashedly down at her again.

"You're soaking wet, to boot!" she irritably declared.

"You know why I had to go," he now stated, his expression growing solemn.

"There were others to see to it!" she countered, realizing how irrational she must sound. Inwardly, she knew that he had indeed been the only one to take charge of Alex Donovan's rescue, and yet she was nevertheless fuming that the mission had necessitated his being placed in danger himself. Her reaction didn't make any sense, not even to herself, she thought with a frown, so how could she possibly expect to explain it to him? "I guess there's no need to ask whether or not your little plan was successful, since I can well see you're anything but unhappy over its outcome!"

"He got away," Sean replied with a brief nod, moving away from the door and toward the center of the room where she still stood. "Marianna and Andrei went with him."

"I figured Annie'd have her way in that!" Kate sardonically remarked. Now that Sean Cleary was back and safe, she was beginning to feel increasingly foolish for the way she had behaved about his going. Giving silent thanks that her partner had not witnessed her confrontation with Sean, for she was certain Annie would have misinterpreted the whole thing and taken it to mean that she didn't want Alex rescued from a lynching, she turned about and presented her back to Sean. She was greatly disturbed by the fact that she suddenly experienced an overwhelming urge to cry. What the hell was the matter with her?

400

"Kate, don't you think it's time we talked?" He was there behind her, his large hands closing on the softness of her shoulders as he firmly but gently forced her about to face him.

"I think it's time you got back into that bed," she asserted, feeling quite flustered by his nearness. "We sure as hell don't want you to catch pneumonia on top of being laid up with a bullethole in you!" She attempted to pull away, but he would not release her. Finally, she raised her eyes to his again, her breath catching as she viewed all his love for her shining forth from his vivid blue gaze.

"You're not fooling me, Kate LaRue. I know why you didn't want me to go tonight. It's nothing to be ashamed of, sweetheart."

"I'm not your sweetheart!" she childishly retorted.

"You're right," he unexpectedly agreed, but then added, "you're much more than that. You're my own true, beautiful, strong, courageous love. I love you. And I think you feel the same way about me." He was smiling softly down at her, his hands beginning to pull her close.

"You don't even know me!" she protested, her own hands pushing against his muscular arms. "I'm not the type of woman men fall in love with, Sean Cleary!" she exclaimed, dismayed to feel the hot tears springing to her eyes.

"You're the type of woman I fell in love with," he tenderly reminded her. "And I know enough about you to know that I want to spend the rest of my life with you. I want to marry you."

"No you don't!" she contradicted, jerking away from him now. "You're too fine a man to get mixed up with the likes of me," she murmured, her voice falling to just above a whisper. "Damn you! I tried to discourage you! I've tried to keep from allowing anything like this to happen!"

"Don't you think it's about time you told me what it is that's got you so terrified of loving me, of my loving you? I can promise you that nothing's going to make any difference about the way I feel about you!"

"I've known a lot of men, more than I care to remember," she tightly revealed, refusing to face him as she stood near the large chest of drawers in one corner of the dimly lit room. "None of them were like you, Sean. But still, I thought I loved them. I was always hurt, always the loser. And I finally decided I'd had enough of love and all the trouble it brings!"

"I knew your life hadn't been an easy one, my dear," responded Sean, crossing the space between them in a few long strides. He stood gazing intensely down at her bright head, one of his hands moving to gently touch her silken hair. "As for the men you might have known before me, they were all fools. And you're as big a fool as them if you keep denying yourself love, true love, because of the past!"

"But, I—" she began, whirling about to face him, only to have him cut her off.

"I love you, Kate. Do you love me?" he softly demanded.

"I . . . I didn't want to fall in love with you!" she replied in an accusatory tone.

"May I take that to mean you do?" he mockingly quipped, refusing to delay any longer as his arms wrapped about her and he pulled her close, oblivious to the aching wound in his chest. His head lowered, his lips taking hers in a tender kiss that rapidly became more demanding, more urgent, until both of them were left lightheaded.

"By the way," Sean remarked a short time later, sitting on the edge of the bed with Kate cradled lovingly on his lap, "what is your real name?"

"What makes you so sure the one I've been using isn't the same one I was born with?" she countered saucily, delighting in the way his arms tightened about her once more.

"Just a hunch, I suppose," he retorted with a broad grin, his eyes glowing with the certainty of her love.

"It's Kirsten. Kirsten Johansson."

"Kirsten," he repeated thoughtfully. "I think I'll call you Kate," he teasingly proclaimed, laughing at her look of mock outrage. She was not afforded the opportunity to bristle for long, since his warm, passionate lips claimed hers for yet another searing kiss, all else, including the issue of names, momentarily forgotten. Kate's heart swelled with love, a love she realized she had never known before, and she returned Sean's impassioned embrace with an answering fire. All her emotions were freed at last, and she was no longer afraid.

Twenty=Four

Under normal circumstances, Alex and his two companions would have made camp for the night just outside of Skagway, but since circumstances were anything but normal, they traveled under cover of the darkness, pausing to rest only briefly a few times on their way to Dyea. It would have been much faster to travel via the Lynn Canal, as Alex and Marianna had done once before, but necessity forced them to travel overland throughout the night.

They reached the mud-bogged town just after dawn the following morning. There had been scant opportunity for conversation throughout the hard journey, but Marianna now ventured to ask a question.

"Won't they search for you here?" She and the men drew their mounts to a halt before the same hotel where she and Alex had previously stayed. The rain had by this time mercifully slowed to a drizzle, the skies momentarily lightening by several degrees as they swung down from their saddles to stand ankle deep in the thick brown mud.

"Not likely," Alex replied, instructing Andrei to lead the horses around back to the stables. "Those men won't see things quite the same way in the cold light of day as they did in that frenzy Caine whipped them into last night. Caine will be the only one to give it more than a passing thought." He took her arm and led her up the steps into the welcoming shelter of the building.

"You don't believe Caine will attempt to find you, then?"

"Our friend Caine's going to have more than enough to occupy his time and energy in the very near future without bothering about me," Alex mysteriously answered. It was obvious to Marianna that he was in no mood for further discussion on the subject, so she fell obligingly silent as they moved across the hotel lobby.

The three of them were upstairs in one of the rooms a short time later when Alex surprised the other two by announcing, "I've got some business to take care of. Andrei, you stay here with Marianna." Without allowing for any discussion whatsoever, he stepped toward the doorway.

"Business?" repeated Andrei.

"Don't you think I should accompany you on this matter?" suggested Marianna, casting her husband a sharp, meaningful glance.

"It's best if I go alone. Meanwhile, you two could sure use a bath," he remarked with a crooked grin, ignoring the avid curiosity on Andrei's boyish face, as well as the frown of displeasure on his wife's beautiful countenance.

Once Alex had gone, Andrei turned to his cousin and declared, "You know, I'm finding a lot more adventure than I ever bargained for!" He chuckled quietly. He hesitated a moment before asking, "Marianna, what's Alex up to?"

"What do you mean?" she innocently responded, inwardly dreading his questions. It would have to be Alex's decision to tell him the truth, she reminded herself. But, Andrei had already proven himself a worthy, quite helpful ally, she then reflected.

"I mean that I'm not quite as dense as the two of you seem to believe! I can no longer believe Alex Donovan is up here merely for the gambling and adventure and escape from responsibilities back home it offers him. Take what happened last night, for instance."

"Lyle Caine and Alex have apparently been enemies since he first came to Skagway," she offered, hoping that would satisfy him. It did not.

"From what I heard between Caine and Alex that night someone tried to kill Sean, I'd say you appear to be at the center of their shared animosity." When Marianna did not reply, he added, "But, I don't think that's all there is to it. I think there's something else going on, and I think you ought to let me in on it!"

"I suggest you put these questions to Alex when he returns," his cousin murmured, gathering up some things from one of the saddlebags and heading for the door. "I, for one, intend to refrain from contemplating all this until after I've had my bath and something to eat!" she replied flippantly, flashing him a bright smile before exiting the room.

Given all that had happened in the short time since Andrei had made contact with them, it was only natural that the young man should be so curious, she reflected, removing her muddied clothing as she prepared to climb into her bath. Andrei would not be put off for long, she thought as a heavy sigh escaped her lips.

As for Alex, she realized he had undoubtedly gone to speak with his secret associate in Dyea. She could only pray that the danger to him would end soon, that the investigation would draw to a close and he would no longer have to contend with Lyle Caine's dastardly schemes. It was immensely disturbing to think of all Caine had done, even more frightening if she allowed herself to dwell on what he might attempt the next time.

She closed her eyes as she lay back against the tub, a rosy blush rising to her face as she suddenly recalled the last time she had bathed there. How could a man be so exasperating and yet so devastatingly irresistible at the same time?

Alex returned much later that morning, only to face a barrage of questions from an impatiently waiting Andrei. Marianna couldn't help but admire her husband's skillful diplomacy with the younger man. He revealed nothing of his true occupation, yet supplied Andrei with enough reasonable-sounding, albeit completely useless, answers to satisfy him. Andrei finally took himself off to examine the town, leaving Marianna alone with her husband at last.

"Are you perhaps planning to keep me ignorant of

what you discovered as well?" she demanded, sinking down onto the bed. She glanced toward the window, dismayed to see the rain beginning once more.

"Ever curious, aren't you, my love?" he quipped, sauntering across to take a watchful stance at the window. "It seems that last night's little incident was indeed prompted by more than your beauty." He smiled faintly, turning back to her as his eyes narrowed slightly, his face becoming grim. "Caine received some very pertinent information about me, just as I expected. Its source was someone within our organization, someone who was apparently no longer immune to the powerful, highly persuasive resources Caine and his men possess."

"He knows?" she whispered in growing fear.

"Not everything, but enough. And even that won't make any difference a short time from now."

"Why not?" she anxiously queried.

"It's finally happened, Annie," he told her in a low, resonant voice, suddenly striding forward and lifting her from the bed, his arms drawing her close. He wore a look of deep satisfaction, a look of tired but triumphant pleasure. "Barkley's information checked out. And others followed suit, providing vital names and details. All these months have finally paid off. I just got the word that we've finally got enough evidence to blow apart Caine's entire operation."

"You mean that you . . . you don't have to remain here any longer?" she asked in disbelief, stunned by what she had just heard. Was it truly all over with?

"My part isn't finished just yet," he said, shaking his

head. "Of course, we hadn't counted on my having to leave Skagway," he admitted with a frown, releasing her and pacing a bit restlessly about the room, his expression increasingly pensive. "It's going to make things a bit more difficult."

"Make what things more difficult? What more can you do?"

"I'm awaiting further orders now. But no matter what they are, I've certainly no intention of going home until I've finished things with Lyle Caine!"

"Oh Alex, why should you place yourself in danger again because of him? If there is truly enough evidence to arrest him, then you should leave him to the proper authorities!" she reasoned, unable to face the prospect of Alex courting such danger when it was not even necessary for him to do so.

"You expect me to forget about what he's tried to do to you, what he's tried to do to me? And what about Sean? Oh no, my love," Alex feelingly countered, "I'm going to reserve the honor of dealing with Lyle Caine for myself!" His golden eyes blazed, his lips compressing into a thin line.

"But that's . . . that's absurd!" she declared just as emotionally, rising to her feet and moving to take hold of his arm, forcing him to cease his movements and face her. "I certainly cannot blame you for hating the man, for wanting to see him pay for his crimes. I want that every bit as much as you! But, it isn't worth your risking your life for the sake of male pride!" Her eyes flashed up at him, her beautiful face flushed with the force of her emotion.

"You don't understand," he ground out.

"Of course not! I'm only a woman, after all!" she vehemently retorted. "A woman who has been deeply involved in this as well, a woman who has had to contend with days and nights of awful uncertainty, of wondering what terrible thing might happen next! I tell you, Alex Donovan, I will not stand by and watch you throw your life away for the sake of foolish revenge!"

"Why not?" Alex quietly parried, startling her with the question.

"What?" she responded in bewilderment.

"Why should it matter to you whether I am alive or dead?"

"Because . . . because I naturally do not . . . because . . ." she faltered, her beautiful face shadowed by visible confusion.

"Because you love me?" He quietly supplied the words, staring deeply into her widening gaze as it flew to his handsome, solemn features.

She opened her mouth to speak, but the words would not come. The silence hung heavy and deep, the atmosphere charged with fateful expectation. Alex's mesmerizing gaze held Marianna's almost frightened one, the look on his face softening as his hands moved tenderly to her faintly trembling shoulders, his lips curving into a smile so full of warmth that she could scarcely breathe.

"Alex! Alex!" exclaimed Andrei, bursting through the door without bothering to knock. His face was alight with excitement, his words accelerating so rapidly that it took a great deal of concentration to decipher them. "There's been a slide up on the trail! Tons and tons of mud and boulders burying only God knows how many men! They're organizing a rescue party right now! Come on, Alex! We've got to get going!" he finished breathlessly, impatient to be off.

Alex and Marianna both stared at him, their faces registering mutual shock. Alex calmly turned back to his wife and quietly said, "Much as I hate to leave you, I'll have to go and help. Did you bring your pistol?" He smiled briefly at her silent nod. "I don't know when we'll return. Stay in this room. You'll be safe here." He wrapped his powerful arms about her and clasped her tightly against him for a moment, then was gone, he and Andrei soon striding out of the hotel to join the other men gathering in the muddy street.

Marianna felt numb as she sank down onto the bed. It had all happened so quickly. She hadn't even kissed him goodbye, hadn't even told him to have a care, to return to her safely. And now he was gone, gone to place himself in yet another perilous situation.

Sighing despondently, she stood and crossed slowly to the window, the rain forming tiny rivers as it coursed down the glass. She thought of the men who had fallen victim to the slide. She prayed that those still alive would be rescued before it was too late, then added a prayer for the safety of the search party.

Her thoughts returned to the scene Andrei had so unexpectedly interrupted. What, she now asked herself, her expression becoming thoughtful, would she have said to Alex if Andrei had not intruded? What would she have done?

411

"Oh Alex, Alex," she murmured aloud, her hand distractedly clutching at the lace-trimmed curtains. Why was she so afraid to face the truth?

The truth? her mind repeated. It hit her like a lightning bolt. Her eyes widened and shone with the answer, a look of absolute wonderment on her face. She loved him! She loved Alex Donovan, the man she had been so emotionally, so violently clashing with since the first moment the two of them had met. He had found the way to her heart in spite of all the barriers she had erected, in spite of her determination to despise him.

When had it happened? she now wondered, still in a state of shock at admitting to herself the one thing she had vowed never to feel. She realized she could not name a specific day, a specific occurrence. But, she knew she had been falling in love with him from the very beginning. It had simply taken her all this time to be able to face it. Her love had finally grown to such a degree that she could no longer deny it.

Alex had known, she reflected with a slow smile, moving away from the window to wander leisurely about the room. She was still so amazed, her mind spinning with such a whirlwind of tumultuous thoughts, that she was unaware of her movements. He had tried to help her see it so many times. And he had always remained patient and loving, no matter how defiant or obstinate, or even hateful, she had been toward him.

She paused in front of the large oval mirror hanging on the wall next to the door, examining her reflection, certain she must appear vastly different from the confused young woman who had entered the room such an unbelievably short time earlier. There was no physical indication of the change in her, but it was there just the same. She had changed in that one brief instant when her love for Alex had so startlingly, so dramatically made itself known!

Whirling away from the mirror, she laughed softly, hugging the knowledge to herself. It was so clear to her now—her concern for Alex, their shared, tempestuous passion, her unwillingness to leave him these past few weeks when Lyle Caine had made things so increasingly dangerous. Why, she then mused, it had been obvious to everyone but herself!

She must tell Alex at once! she thought with another jubilant smile. They had already shared so much together, she now experienced an overwhelming compulsion to delay no longer, to go to him and declare her love, her regret for her unwillingness to face the truth sooner.

The smile on her beautiful countenance was abruptly replaced by a crestfallen look as she realized Alex would probably not return for quite some time. And, once again recalling the danger he would undoubtedly face as he assisted the others in attempting a rescue up on the treacherously saturated trail, she whispered another heartfelt prayer.

Twenty-Five

Marianna was blissfully unaware of how very much her prayers would be needed.

The rescue party's task was an exhausting and gruesome one. The rains continued relentlessly throughout the long day as they dug out the bodies of the men who had been crushed by the mud and rock which had swept down upon them without warning. The slide had covered a wide portion of the steep trail, halfway between town and the camp where Alex and Marianna had once stayed. Alex and the others sensed that there would be few survivors found, but they nonetheless refused to give up hope as they banded together in their grim task.

The hours wore on but all sense of time had been lost. By midafternoon, the heavens, as if to atone for the destruction wrought by the endless days of drenching moisture, suddenly cleared, the golden rays of the late summer sun warming the heads of the large numbers of men who continued to dig in the oozing mud.

Andrei worked uncomplainingly alongside his mentor, his initial excitement swiftly fading as he viewed the mangled bodies of the victims, their faces frozen horrendously in death. A group of men and women traveled down from the camp at the summit, thoughtfully providing drink and nourishment for the searchers.

"Why don't we take a break for a spell?" Andrei suggested, breathing hard from his exertions. He, like all the others, was coated from head to foot with a mixture of sweat and mud. He raised his face gratefully toward the sun as he set aside his shovel.

"You go ahead," Alex replied. "I'm going to move farther up on the trail. There might just be some men trapped in those rocks," he remarked, pointing toward an area covered with more boulders than mud.

"But surely someone would have heard them calling for help by now."

"Not necessarily." Andrei watched him trudge across the mud, his face set in determination. Neither of them had had any sleep for more than twenty-four hours, and Andrei was close to exhaustion. He wondered how Alex could keep going, his eyes flitting back up the trail to see his friend making his way across the rocks now.

It happened a split second later. First, there was an alarming rumble, followed by a shout of warning from someone. Andrei's boyish features wore a look of puzzlement which turned to horror as he gazed up toward the mass of earth hurtling downward, trapping a handful of men, including Alex, in its deadly path.

"Alex!" whispered Andrei, then yelled as loudly as

he could, "Alex! Alex, watch out!" But it was too late.

It seemed to Marianna as if she had been waiting an eternity. The day's vigil was nerve-wracking as she prayed and hoped for some word of what was happening up on the trail. She grew more anxious with each passing hour, her worst fears soon to be realized.

The afternoon was drifting into the early hours of the evening when there was a knock at her door. It was a soft, seemingly hesitant knock, as if the person standing just outside her door was reluctant to disturb her. Nevertheless, she snatched up the pistol from where she had placed it on a table beside the bed, her hand tightly grasping it within the pocket of her skirt. She opened the door a mere fraction at first, her eyes widening in joyful surprise.

"Andrei! Oh Andrei, I'm so glad to see you back safely!" Her eyes moved swiftly up and down his mud-caked form, returning to his equally grimy face as she smiled and asked, "Where's Alex?" He did not immediately answer, prompting her to ask again. "Where is Alex? Isn't he with you?" A sudden terror clutched at her heart as she viewed the look of misery on his boyish countenance, the expression of deep sadness in his red-rimmed eyes.

"There . . . there was another slide," he choked out. "I didn't want to come back, but . . . but they said I wouldn't be of any use like this, that I'd only . . . only be in the way . . ." His voice trailed away as he suddenly swayed alarmingly, his knees buckling beneath him as his body and his emotions finally reached the breaking point. He collapsed onto the floor, Marianna catching him beneath the arms as she fell to her knees with him.

"Andrei! What is it? Andrei, what are you talking about? Where is Alex?" she demanded, helping him to take a seat on the floor, his back propped against the doorway. "Where is he?"

"I'm afraid he—he may be dead, Marianna."

She gazed at him in shock. Dead? Alex dead? No! No, it could not be true!

"What do you mean?" she questioned with outward composure. "What do you mean by 'he may be dead'?" Dear God, no! Please, Lord, please don't let it be true! her heart beseeched.

"The second slide. Alex was there. He couldn't get out of the way in time. They were still searching for him and for the others when I left," Andrei murmured, his voice barely audible. He closed his eyes against the onslaught of tears which threatened to erupt again.

"Then they don't know for sure if Alex was killed?" she probed, a glimmer of hope flaming deep within her. She knew he wasn't dead! Alex was such an integral part of herself, she would know if he were dead, would feel it within her very soul.

"No. But," he said, averting his eyes from hers, "I don't think there's much hope of finding him alive. I saw it happen, Marianna. And I'm ashamed of the way I went all to pieces. I should have taken hold of myself and remained to search for him. I shouldn't have let them talk me into coming back without finding him!"

"They were right in sending you back," she quietly declared. "You've withstood all you can for the moment, dearest Andrei." She smiled tenderly across at him, then rose to her feet, a certain light in her blue-green gaze. She hurried across the room to snatch up the pair of trousers she had earlier discarded, pulling them on underneath her skirts and petticoats.

"What are you doing?" asked her cousin, scarcely able to keep his eyes open as he remained slumped against the doorway.

"I want you to get some rest," was all she would say. She quickly drew off her dress and petticoats, donning the shirt she'd borrowed from Andrei and buttoning it on over her camisole. She then took a seat in the chair at the foot of the bed and began pulling on her boots.

"Where are you going?" Andrei queried. Stunned disbelief crossed his muddied features as a sudden thought occurred to him. "Surely you're not thinking of going up—"

"Of going up to find out for myself if my husband is alive or dead?" she finished. "That is precisely what I am going to do! I know, deep in my heart, that Alex is alive, Andrei. And I want to be there, waiting for him, waiting to tell him how much I love and need him, when they find him!"

"But you can't go up there! You don't know what it's like. There's mud and rock everywhere, bodies being dug out of the muck and laid aside beneath the trees in a makeshift morgue—"

"I don't care what it's like!" she firmly interrupted, tugging the hat down over her dark curls. "Alex may be injured, may need my care. I cannot sit here and wait to discover just how badly he's hurt! And I have to make certain he's found before it's too late," she spoke with a slight catch in her voice.

"What makes you think you can do that?" he demanded, his own voice growing weaker as complete exhaustion began to overtake him.

"I can do anything to save the man I love," Marianna solemnly replied, and then was gone.

She was able to join another group of men, and a few women as well, traveling up the trail to offer assistance, several of them having sailed over from Skagway when news of the slide reached the neighboring town. It briefly occurred to Marianna that some of the men might possibly be the same ones who were planning to lynch Alex Donovan only the night before, men who would now be attempting to rescue him.

The journey was fortunately an uneventful one. Marianna's eyes widened in shock when they beheld the slide area, and a terrible dread caught her in its grip. There was so much destruction, so much mud and rock covering the trail, that it was impossible to see how anyone could have survived. She had earlier glimpsed the half-dozen bodies lying beneath a row of trees back down the trail toward town and torn her horror-stricken gaze from the terrible sight. She recalled it now, however, as she watched the growing numbers of men searching for other victims.

"Please," she pleaded with a grim-faced man momentarily resting from his exhausting efforts, "can you tell me if any of the men caught in the second slide have been found yet? My husband, Alex Donovan—" she explained.

"We ain't found no one alive since noon, ma'am," he regretfully told her, shaking his head slowly. Like Andrei, he appeared about ready to drop as he leaned on his shovel.

"But, have you . . . have you then found any victims of the second slide . . . have you found any bodies?" she breathlessly demanded. A heavy sigh of relief escaped her lips when he answered, "Not any that I know of. You might go on up yonder and ask someone up there," he suggested, gesturing farther up the trail. "But, I wouldn't advise it, ma'am. There's liable to be more slides." He nodded curtly in her direction, then took himself off to resume his work.

Heedless of his warning, Marianna began making her way slowly across the sea of earth and rock, her boots sometimes sinking several inches into the thick mud as she climbed. There were people everywhere, men digging alone, others forming groups to move boulders, women doing their part by serving much-needed sustenance.

Marianna could not help but become increasingly fearful as she received a negative response to all her inquiries concerning Alex as she waited for more victims to be uncovered. She kept herself occupied, joining in the work with the other women, but her thoughts were never far from Alex. Several hours passed, and still no word.

The long daylight hours began to draw to a close, the darkening skies becoming alight with thousands of right, twinkling stars. Marianna had finally grown too weary to trudge about in the mud any longer, and she sank down upon a flat-surfaced rock jutting up from the moist earth, her eyes moving unseeingly upward to the splendid panorama above. A growing sense of panic welled up deep within her.

Alex had been missing since early that afternoon, she told herself, her eyes filling with the tears she had stoically held back for so long. Even if he had survived the mudslide, could it truly be possible he was still alive? Could she trust her instincts any longer? What if he *were* dead and had been all this time? she frantically wondered, choking back a sob.

She realized then how very much she loved him, even more than she had at first believed. Had it really been earlier that same day when her love for Alex revealed itself to her? And had love come to her at last, only to be so cruelly destroyed?

Alex had never even heard her say the words he had waited so long to hear, she then thought, finally starting to give in to overwhelming despair. All hope was rapidly diminishing now. Even the searchers were beginning to give up, she despondently noted, increasing numbers of them leaving. Marianna sternly ordered herself not to surrender to hopelessness, not to abandon visions of Alex still alive, but a dull ache was spreading throughout her entire body now.

She suddenly recalled Alex's fateful words to her, spoken the night they had camped beside the stream after fleeing Bennett. He had told her that something would happen someday, something to make her realize

how much he meant to her, how much she loved him.
The tears began coursing silently down her beautiful
face as she thought of Alex's insight and his unwavering
ing love for her.

Memories of Alex crowded together in her mind.
Memories of their first meeting, memories of their
honeymoon and Alex's persuasive lovemaking.
Memories of their tempestuous relationship and the
dangers they had faced together. Most of all, however,
she thought of his love. He had loved her, more than
anyone else ever had or ever would, she now realized.

"Come on, honey. You come on back down with us,"
a kindly older woman suggested as she appeared beside
Marianna.

"I cannot leave. Not yet," Marianna insisted, her
voice hoarse and low. The other woman shook her
head, her own eyes filling with tears as she viewed the
look of utter heartbreak on Marianna's face, the
deepening pain in her blue-green eyes. She did not
speak again, simply turning and slowly walking away
into the dusky night.

It was quiet and still now, and Marianna was soon
almost completely alone. A few men remained behind
to spend the rest of the night at the camp that had
earlier been set up. But everyone else was gone, certain
there was nothing else to be done.

Marianna did not think of any possible danger to
herself. She no longer knew what to think or believe. A
terrible numbness descended upon her, and she buried
her face in her hands. She could no longer pray, and she
did not even seem aware of the fact that she was sitting

ut in the chilling night air on a mountain trail, with no
ne but a handful of strangers within miles. Nothing
nattered anymore, she dully reflected, nothing would
ver matter to her again with Alex dead.

The numbness quickly gave way to a searing pain in
er chest, and deep, quiet sobs began wracking her
weary body. She grieved for the man she had come to
ove too late, the man whose body would perhaps never
e found. She wept for what might have been, for all
he time she had wasted by hardening her heart against
im, for her continued defiance of him. She wept for a
part of herself that would die with him, for the fact that
he could not bear the thought of life without Alex
Donovan there beside her.

Suddenly there were strong arms wrapping about
er, holding and comforting her as she sobbed so
wretchedly. Gentle, soothing kisses rained across her
ace as her hands were clasped between two larger,
mud-streaked ones, a deep voice murmuring softly to
er. It seemed like something out of a dream, and she
was at first so emotionally drained she did not realize
hat what was happening was quite real.

Marianna finally opened her tear-filled eyes, raising
er dirty, streaked face toward the one who sought to
give her comfort. She gasped aloud, her gaze widening,
er eyelids then fluttering closed as she abruptly grew
aint. She lapsed into unconsciousness for only an
nstant, awakening to joyfully find that the beloved
 face swimming before her shining eyes had not
disappeared.

"Alex! Oh Alex, you really are here!" she whispered,

throwing her arms about him and hugging him as if she would never let him go.

"Yes, my love," he murmured, holding her so tightly she found it difficult to breathe.

"Dear God, I—I thought you were dead!" She began sobbing again, but the tears now spilling from her eyes were caused by a profound relief, a profound happiness such as she had never known before.

"Hush now, sweet Annie," he soothingly murmured, holding her close while she wept. He sank down upon the rock, clasping her in his strong arms as if she were a mere babe, rocking her gently until her tears were finally spent.

"But how?" she asked, raising her face to his again. "They searched for you for hours! We thought you had been killed in the second mudslide!"

"I was trapped in a sizeable crevice in the rock up there," he explained, nodding in the direction of the steep incline which led toward the summit. "I tried calling for help for a time, but then decided I'd best not use up the limited supply of air I had." His handsome face was scratched and bruised, traces of blood in the dried mud which caked his skin.

"You've been up there all this time?"

"Until a short time ago. And, I must say, I was beginning to get pretty worried!" he ruefully admitted, his teeth very white against the grime on his face as he flashed her a quick grin. "But never let it be said a Donovan gives up so easily. It took me all this time to dig myself out." His golden gaze grew clouded now. "What are you doing up here, anyway?"

"Waiting for them to find you," she stated simply, burying her face against his broad chest, uncaring of the extra grime which now coated her hair and face. "I had given up hope," she tearfully declared, her arms tightening about his waist.

"Do you really care that much then?" he quietly demanded, his hand moving to gently lift her chin so that he could stare deeply into her expressive eyes.

"Yes Alex, I do," she replied without hesitation, smiling up at him with such tenderness, such love, that it made his heart sing. "I love you, Alex Donovan. I love you with all my heart."

"Hearing you say that makes everything that's happened worthwhile, my love," he huskily responded, his lips closing upon hers as he lifted her up into his embrace. They remained like that for several long moments, until one of the men who had stayed behind approached them, his thin features wearing an almost comical expression of astonishment.

"Say, ain't you Alex Donovan?" he asked. At Alex's brisk nod, he said, "We heard you was buried in that second slide!"

"I was, in a manner of speaking," Alex replied, still holding Marianna close.

"Wait till everybody gets wind of this! We'd just about given you up for dead. And there you be, coming out of the whole thing with hardly a scratch!" the man commented with a chuckle, shaking his head in amazement as he left them alone again.

"It really is a miracle, isn't it, darling?" Marianna remarked with a sigh of contentment. "To think you were there all this time, that someone might have been able to help you if they had only known. Oh Alex, what you must have gone through all these hours!" she realized with a faint shudder.

"No more than what you have apparently endured, my love," he replied, his lips against her hair. "But, it's over with now. And we'd best be getting some rest before trying to head back to town," he concluded, reluctant to let her go. There was so much still to be said between them, so much he wanted to share, so much he wanted to know in return. But there would be time for that later.

"Poor Andrei will be so relieved. He was quite devastated when he believed you to be dead," she recalled, drawing away from him at last, noticing for the first time the fatigue that lined his beloved face. Both of them were so exhausted they could go no farther, Alex decreed, placing a supporting arm about her slender waist as they stood and began trudging the short distance up to the camp.

After a few, all-too-brief hours of sleep, Marianna and Alex journeyed back down the trail to Dyea, smiling at one another as they glimpsed the welcoming sight of the hotel. Several men turned to stare in astonishment at them as they made their way down the main street. Alex was well known to many of Dyea's inhabitants, and it was not long before news of his mysterious, totally unexpected reappearance spread throughout the town.

Andrei was soundly sleeping in the room where Marianna had left him, still clad in his mud-caked

426

boots and clothing as he lay peacefully upon the bed. Marianna felt the tears starting to her eyes once more as she watched the way Alex awakened his friend, Andrei at first groggily acknowledging the older man's presence, then crying out in exuberance when he realized Alex had safely, miraculously returned.

A short time later found Marianna alone in the room. She gratefully peeled off her shirt and trousers, then wearily tugged off the heavy boots. Andrei had tagged along with Alex to clean up, but Marianna discovered she was, for the first time in her life, too tired to care about the bedraggled, muddy state of her appearance. She climbed upon the bed, drawing the quilt, already soiled from where Andrei had slept, up over her aching body as she closed her eyes.

Alex smiled tenderly down at the slumbering form of his wife when he entered the room shortly thereafter. Deciding not to disturb her, as if such a thing were possible, he quietly closed the door on his way out. He left the hotel to pay a visit to his contact, anxious to discover if any orders had come through during his unplanned absence.

Marianna awoke feeling much refreshed, though she became apprehensive when she saw that Alex was not in the room. Because of all that had happened, she was reluctant to be parted from him, even for a brief time, fearful lest something else occur to endanger him once more. She was therefore quite pleased, not to mention relieved, when the door suddenly opened to reveal her devilishly handsome husband.

"Where were you?" she asked, sitting upright in the

bed, her sleep-tossed curls streaming wildly about her pale shoulders. "And have you managed to get any sleep?" she worriedly added, spying the faint circles beneath his golden eyes. Her heart turned over in her breast when she was also afforded a clear view of the numerous bruises and scratches on his beloved face.

"Andrei and I were just down the hallway. And to answer your last question—yes, a little," he responded with a faint smile, moving to take a seat on the bed beside her. The bright sunlight filtering through the curtains at the window touched the room with a soft golden glow, and Marianna was puzzled by the sudden, inexplicable shyness she was now experiencing. "You look much improved!" Alex remarked with a teasing, loving grin, his gaze moving intimately over her.

"How gallant of you to utter such a falsehood!" she mockingly retorted, a rosy blush rising to her cheeks as she glanced downward, then frowned expressively at the very visible evidences of her ordeal. "I'm really quite ashamed that I have not bathed before now."

"I'm well aware of your admirable inclinations toward bathing!" he playfully quipped, amused as she blushed again. "In truth, however, you have never appeared more beautiful."

"Nevertheless, I shall seek to remedy my despicable state without further delay!" she staunchly declared, flinging back the covers as she bounced off the bed, her bare feet padding across the wooden floor as she scurried about to prepare for her bath. She wore nothing but her thin undergarments, and Alex felt his desire for her rising to an alarming intensity.

"Couldn't your bath wait? There's still so much for us to talk about," he remarked in a low, resonant voice, rising from the bed and moving purposefully toward her. It was obvious to her that he had a great deal more than "talk" on his mind.

"No, Alex," she firmly replied, then added by way of explanation, her uncharacteristic shyness quite apparent to him now, "I want to look my best for you." He smiled down at her in understanding, wanting her so badly that it hurt, and yet wanting everything to be perfect between them. No barriers, no restraints.

"Very well. But don't be long!" he commanded with mock ferocity. Marianna laughed softly as she left the room, pausing briefly to smile at him, her shining eyes full of an unspoken promise.

Alex was growing increasingly impatient by the time his wife returned. He had already removed his clothing and lay waiting for her on the bed, and he glanced rapidly away from the window to face her as the door swung open. His eyes widened, then narrowed in appreciation of her glowing loveliness. She was wearing a simple cotton wrapper, her damp curls framing her softly smiling face. There was a certain something in that smile, and in those sparkling blue-green eyes of hers, that told him this time would be different.

Marianna approached the bed with slow, purposeful steps, halting on the opposite side from where Alex was raising up on his elbows. She stood perfectly still and quiet for several long moments, causing him to gaze up at her in puzzlement, a questioning smile on his handsome countenance.

"Is something wrong, my love?" he asked, thrown into further confusion when she only smiled rather mysteriously in response. His confusion soon vanished, only to be replaced by growing delight as his wife reached downward to begin untying the fabric belt at her slender waist, then drew the edges aside with tantalizing slowness. There was a flare of returning desire in his golden gaze as the wrapper was discarded, floating heedlessly to the wooden floor, and he saw that Marianna was wearing nothing more than that mysterious smile which so captivated him.

She stood proud and unashamed before him, her splendid, curvaceous beauty displayed in all its glory as the sunlight filled the room and touched her with its revealing radiance. Alex's gleaming eyes traveled up and down the length of her exquisite, womanly form with intimate, appreciative leisure, until returning to linger on her face, the expression in her own eyes leaving very little doubt as to her intentions. She was offering herself to him completely, offering willingly, fully of herself for the first time, wanting to show him in the most demonstrative way she knew how that she loved him with all her heart, mind, and spirit.

"Come to me, Marianna," Alex whispered, his strong arms lifting upward, his eyes full of golden fire. Marianna did not hesitate. She slid beneath the covers and into his warmly inviting embrace, their sensitive, naked skin making delectable contact.

"Oh Alex, I never believed I could love anyone the way I love you!" she tremulously declared, pressing her soft, silken curves even closer against his lean, muscular hardness.

"My dear firebrand," he responded with a low, adoring chuckle, "I had at times despaired of ever hearing you utter words such as that!" His fingers trailed gently, enticingly up and down her spine now, his lips brushing her forehead with a tender kiss, then following a sensuous path to her mouth as she raised her face toward his. The kiss was so charged with fervent passion that both Alex and Marianna felt as if they were being carried away on a raging tide of ecstasy, an ecstasy such as they had never known before, and his hands began increasing their subtle, skillful methods of amorous persuasion.

He frowned when she unexpectedly drew away. She smiled at his sharp intake of breath an instant later as their roles were reversed and she became the sweet tormentor, her own lips teasing provocatively as they moved from his mouth to the pulse beating so rapidly at his throat, then lower to his broad, muscular chest. Her tongue swirled playfully across his sun-bronzed flesh, graceful fingers inching downward to lightly clasp his powerful, throbbing manhood.

Alex gasped loudly as her loving, gentle touch stirred his blood. His hands clenched into tight fists at his sides as she boldly, fearlessly aroused him. And when her warm lips returned to his softly gasping mouth, he rolled so that she was beneath him, murmuring hoarsely against her ear, "Enough, my love, else you will drive me to madness before it is time!" He gazed deeply into her eyes, and she smiled again.

"I only sought to give you the pleasure you have given me," she laughingly replied, her voice barely above a whisper.

"Impudent wench! I can see that it's time you were reminded who's master here!' he proclaimed, chuckling at her obvious enjoyment of the situation, her new sense of power. His eyes were gleaming with a fiercely impassioned light as his lips captured hers once more. A fire, burning hotter and more intense than ever before, coursed through Marianna's veins as she met his flaming desire with all the love in her heart.

She was soon to recall Alex's words regarding who was master as he set about to concentrate totally on her pleasure. His lips and tongue teased at the soft flesh of her throat, then at her full, rounded breasts as she strained upward, her fingers clutching almost convulsively as they entwined in his thick auburn hair. His warm, moist tongue flicked across the rose-tipped peaks as his lips gently suckled, his hands now moving downward to part her trembling thighs, his fingers searching for the pink softness hidden there.

Marianna moaned quietly, her head tossing restlessly to and fro, her raven tresses fanning in wild disarray across the softness of the pillow. She was driven nearly mindless as he kissed every smooth, silken inch of her quivering body, and she gasped repeatedly, the sensations assailing her more intense, more overwhelmingly potent than she had ever before experienced. In that small part of her mind which was still capable of thought, she realized that it was her love for Alex which made all the difference in the world, that it was their mutual love which so powerfully heightened this wondrous intimacy only the two of them could share.

Finally, just when Marianna believed she would faint with the sheer force of her passion, Alex lifted her buttocks in his two strong hands, positioning himself above her as his lips claimed hers once again. She moaned deep in her throat as he plunged into her, his manhood sheathing perfectly within her inviting warmth. The last remnant of coherent thought left her in that moment, and she moved instinctively beneath him as the tempo swiftly increased to a frenzied, almost violent crescendo. It was not long before they were both crying softly aloud, soaring heavenward in the most complete, rapturous fulfillment they had ever known.

"I never realized it could be like this!" Marianna remarked in wonderment, awed and somewhat shaken by what had occurred a few moments earlier. She lay nestled against her husband in the bed, his arm holding her close as he smiled tenderly down at her.

"A mere promise of things to come!" he whispered lovingly, though he himself was quite pleasantly amazed that it had been so good between them. He, too, realized that it was Marianna's love for him, coupled for the first time with his abundant love for her, that had made it so special.

"If only it had not taken me all this time, if only—" she spoke, her eyes filling with tears of regret for all the time she had wasted.

"There's no sense in agonizing over what's already

passed," he interrupted, his finger pressing gently against her parted lips. "But just the same," he added, his golden eyes twinkling down at her, "perhaps I should have arranged to get myself trapped in a mudslide before now."

"How can you possibly make light of it?" protested Marianna with a deep frown. "I shall never be able to forget the emptiness, the absolute desolation I felt in that moment when I lost hope. I didn't want to go on living without you, Alex," she finished with a heavy sigh.

"There's no danger of that," he confidently responded, pressing a tender kiss on the tip of her nose. "Haven't you yet realized that I'm indestructible?"

"When are you going to realize that you're not?" she countered, her eyes growing a trifle stormy. "Why must you always be in the midst of these dangerous situations? It is as if you actually enjoy being in constant peril!"

"I am a man who seems to thrive on adventure," he admitted with a soft chuckle, "but you must believe me when I say I'm looking forward to a less eventful, even peaceful, life with you, my love."

"Do you truly believe we will ever have such a life?"

"No," he replied, laughing aloud now at the sudden look of consternation on her beautiful face. "We're both too strong willed, too obstinate and hot tempered to ever live in total harmony. It would be unrealistic to expect that. But, I do believe most of our life together will be happy, and most definitely satisfying," he concluded with a wicked grin in her direction. She opened her mouth to offer him a suitably mocking retort, but there was suddenly an insistent knock sounding at the door.

"That cousin of yours has a great deal to learn about timing!" Alex sardonically declared, flinging back the covers and hastily donning his trousers. Marianna was about to rise as well, but he shook his head and said, "You stay there. This won't take long!" He marched over to the door and flung it open, his handsome face wearing a faint scowl of displeasure. Marianna burrowed deeper beneath the covers.

"Sorry to disturb you, Donovan, but this won't wait," she heard an unfamiliar masculine voice say. She watched in puzzlement as Alex glanced hastily in her direction, then back at the man who stood hidden from her view in the narrow hallway.

"What are you doing here?" Alex demanded in a hushed tone of voice.

"It's no longer imperative for us to keep our association such a closely guarded secret," the man replied, then asserted, "but it still wouldn't do for anyone to overhear what I've come to tell you." He started to move past Alex and into the room, but Alex momentarily barred his way.

He turned back to Marianna and remarked, "You'd best put something on, my love." He grinned at her obvious embarrassment, but she ignored him as she scurried to don the wrapper she had so audaciously discarded a short time earlier. She was seated in a high-backed wooden chair beside the window when Alex finally ushered the man inside, a faint blush remaining on her lovely features.

"Please forgive my intrusion, Mrs. Donovan," the tall, slender man earnestly apologized when he caught sight of her. "Your orders have come through," he now spoke to Alex as the two of them stood together just inside the doorway. He lowered his voice in an apparent attempt to keep Marianna from overhearing, but Alex hurried to assure him that she was already well aware of the situation.

"Whatever you've got to say can safely be said in my wife's presence," he pronounced, favoring Marianna with a brief smile before returning his attention to the man who had served as his contact for so many months.

"Very well. I guess I know how well I can trust your judgment by now, don't I?" the man responded with only the ghost of a smile. "You've gotten your wish at last, Alex. You and Cleary have been put in charge of rounding up Caine and all his men. There's a whole shipload of reinforcements, specially deputized men, on their way up to Dyea from Juneau right now. They'll be arriving here at any time now. You're then to proceed to Skagway at once."

"Why the hell didn't I know anything about this before now?" demanded Alex.

"I think they figured they'd keep it quiet until the last moment," the other man answered with a shrug of his shoulders. "I have to admit that it seems to me they've cut things a bit close. But, those are your orders, delivered by a courier less than a quarter of an hour ago."

"Thanks, Jim." Alex clasped the man's hand in a firm handshake for an instant. "I'll be sure and let it be known what a good job you've done."

"I'll just be glad when it's all over with. Maybe then I can get back to that little gal of mine back home. Matrimony sure has done wonders for you!" he remarked with a broad grin. He tipped his hat at Marianna and bid them both farewell, then left them alone again.

"But, how are we going to return to Skagway with Caine waiting to have you hanged?" Marianna questioned, rising to her feet and hurrying across to Alex's side.

"That won't matter now. He's going to be much too concerned with other problems to worry about having me lynched," Alex thoughtfully answered, his own thoughts preoccupied with other details. He moved past her and over to the window, his handsome face wearing a pensive frown. "What's that you said about 'we'?" he suddenly demanded, turning back to face her. "Don't tell me you've gotten it into that beautiful head of yours that you're coming with me?"

"Andrei and I will both be accompanying you!" she insisted. "And surely you haven't gotten it into that obstinate head of yours that we'd allow you to go without us?" she added mockingly, but with determination.

"All right," he unexpectedly acquiesced, fully realizing that there was no way he could prevent the inevitable, "but you'll have to stay out of sight at the hotel, is that understood?" He crossed the few feet of space which separated them, his eyes staring commandingly down into hers. "The last thing I need at this crucial stage is to have to worry about the sort of trouble you're so entirely capable of getting yourself into!"

"May I remind you that it was not I who was nearly murdered in Bennett, who was close to being lynched by a mob the other night, who was buried in a mudslide—"

"You've made your point, you little termagant!" He cut her off with a rueful chuckle. He paused to take her in his arms and press one last, searing kiss upon her lips, then released her and quickly set about getting dressed.

She was soon left alone with her own preparations as he hurried down the hallway to alert Andrei to their plans. A sense of excitement, of anticipation, tempered with an equal fearfulness, was growing within her as she thought about what was to come. And she took a brief moment to offer up another prayer, a prayer that Alex would once again be kept safe, that he, Sean, and the others would meet with success. Lyle Caine would finally be made to pay for his crimes, she reflected, and she and Alex would at last be free of his evil interference in their lives. It was a comforting thought, and one that rose to her mind several times in the hours that followed.

Twenty-Six

They were on their way to Skagway within a few
short hours. Alex had decided that speed, no matter
what the risk, was of the essence, so he, Marianna,
Andrei, and the two dozen men under his command
traveled on one of the small steamships which sailed
frequently between the two neighboring towns. Alex
had already formulated a plan, and he briefed the
special deputies on what was expected of them. Now he
was increasingly anxious to speak to Sean, but
precisely how he was going to contact the Mountie
without Caine immediately suspecting anything had
not yet been determined.

"I'll have to keep my presence unobserved by Caine
or any of his men until after things get rolling," Alex
spoke beside Marianna as they neared Skagway. He
gazed at the cloudless sky overhead, reflecting that they
would soon have the cover of darkness to aid in their
activities. If all went as he hoped it would, Caine's
criminal empire would be destroyed that very night.

"Then Andrei and I will take Sean the message. After

439

all, since you've already decided that we must remain a
the hotel, we'll be able to get word to him to meet wit
you," she suggested, wanting to get involved in at leas
a small way.

"I don't want you in the middle of all this, Annie," h
declared with a frown. "If Sean isn't at the hotel, the
Andrei will have to be the one to find him. No matte
what happens, you're to stay there."

"But—"

"That's my final word on the matter," Alex sternly
decreed, then muttered just under his breath, "I should
have obeyed my initial instincts and left you in Dyea!"
He abruptly reached out and pulled her close, his
powerful arms holding her tightly against him for the
space of several long seconds. Marianna fell silent
sensing her husband's concern. The cool evening
breeze swept off the glistening blue waters of the canal
chilling them slightly as the ship approached the
wharves of Skagway. The crew made ready to drop
anchor.

The men who had been assigned to Alex were
sequestered in the hold, and Alex soon joined them.
Marianna and Andrei were left alone on the deck, both
of them feeling mingled trepidation and excitement at
what was to happen that night. They felt a growing
impatience as the ship finally docked, and Marianna
pulled the hood of her cloak more closely about her
face as she whispered to Andrei, "I think we should
make our way to the hotel as quickly as possible, and
without revealing our identities to anyone."

"No one's going to notice us if we just proceed calmly

440

and in an inconspicuous manner," Andrei reasonably pointed out. "Just as Alex said, Caine won't be expecting us."

"Perhaps. But I'm so afraid something will go awry. And if anything did go wrong, then Alex would be in jeopardy," she murmured with an inward shudder. Tonight's maneuver would be the culmination of all the months of Alex's hard work, but it would also possibly be the most dangerous assignment of all, she realized, closing her eyes against the thought of anything happening to him.

"Come on. Let's get going!" Andrei quietly commanded, taking hold of her arm and leading her nonchalantly down the lowered gangplank. Marianna's heart was pounding rapidly within her breast, but she forced herself to walk slowly and unconcernedly beside Andrei as they now trod along the wharves. They had reached the main street of town within minutes, satisfied that they had apparently attracted no attention among the numerous other men and women traversing the boardwalks. Nevertheless, Marianna was vastly relieved when they stepped inside the hotel and began climbing the stairs to the second floor, and she whispered a quick prayer that Sean would be in Kate's room.

"Annie!" Kate cried in joyful surprise as she flung wide the door. She immediately enveloped Marianna in an embrace of genuine affection.

"Where is Sean?" asked Andrei, peering hastily inside the dimly lit room and glimpsing no sign of the tall Mountie.

"What is it?" Kate demanded, perceiving the grim expressions on the faces of the two cousins. "What do you want with Sean?" Her blue eyes narrowed as she glanced back at Marianna.

"Oh Kate, I'll explain everything to you just as soon as you tell us where to find Sean!" There was such urgency on Marianna's face now that Kate did not hesitate another second.

"He's over at the Golden Nugget. He said he needed to be there tonight, but he didn't say why. He's only been up and about one day, and even that was against my better—" She broke off as Andrei abruptly spun about and hurried back down the narrow hallway to the staircase.

"Let's get inside the room," proposed Marianna, linking her arm through her bemused partner's and leading her through the doorway. "I shall attempt to explain everything to your satisfaction while we await Andrei's return," she added with a faint smile, closing and locking the door behind them.

Andrei, meanwhile, lost no time in getting over to the Golden Nugget to find Sean. It occurred to him that it was a touch ironic, his walking freely into the saloon which belonged to the very man he was attempting to help defeat. He thought no more about it, however, as his searching gaze found Sean. The tall blond man was engaged in a game of dice at the moment, raising a glass of whiskey to his lips as he played the part to perfection. He gave no indication that he had seen Andrei when the younger man approached, but he quickly declared to the surrounding, boisterous crowd that he'd had enough of being thwarted by Lady Luck for one night and was going to take himself off to other, more interesting pursuits. Andrei took the cue and said not a word as he waited a brief moment, then followed Sean out of the saloon and into the gathering twilight.

"What is it? Where's Alex?" whispered Sean as he turned back to Andrei. The two of them were well away from the saloon by this time, and Andrei looked as if he would burst with impatience.

"He's down at the wharves, waiting for you! On the ship we took from Dyea. He said you were to get down there and meet with him right away!"

"What's the name of the ship?" demanded Sean, a pensive frown on his sun-bronzed face.

"The *Mary Ellen*. Her captain's in on this, too."

"Thanks, Markova," the older man paused to say, then turned his steps in the direction of the waterfront. Andrei watched him go, sorely disappointed that he could take no part in the night's activities alongside Sean and Alex and the others. But he recalled Alex's orders, so he heaved a sigh and started reluctantly back to the hotel, still cursing the fact that he would miss out on all the excitement, and instead be holed up in a hotel room with two women. It seemed to him in that moment that life was extremely unfair.

"Sean Cleary is a Mountie?" Kate LaRue was repeating in stunned amazement when Andrei knocked lightly upon the door. Marianna cautioned her friend to silence, then called out, "Who's there?"

"It's me. Andrei. Open up!" came the rather irritable reply. Marianna quickly unlocked the door to admit him.

"Did you find Sean?" she anxiously queried.

"Yes. He started heading down to the docks as soon as I gave him the message." Andrei flung himself into a chair near the window, staring moodily out into the evening's semidarkness.

"What's all this about?" Kate impatiently demanded, jumping off the bed to confront the other young woman. "So far, all you've told me is that Sean Cleary and Alex Donovan are partners, that they're working together against Lyle Caine and his organization. Who is it they're working for? And what the hell is this about Sean being a blasted Mountie?" she finished, her voice rising as she folded her arms tightly against her bosom.

"Sean and Alex are working together under an arrangement between the two governments. Sean is a member of the Northwest Mounted Police, and Alex is simply a special agent of sorts," Marianna explained.

"Why didn't Sean tell me the truth? Why didn't you tell me?" Kate accusingly questioned, her eyes sparkling with immense and quite visible displeasure at having been kept so uninformed.

"I wasn't even supposed to know myself. But because of Caine's . . . advances toward me, I was soon very much involved. I wanted to tell you, but Alex assured me that it was safer for everyone if you did not know. As for Sean, please don't blame him, Kate. I'm quite certain he was also forbidden to reveal any of this to you."

"What the devil's going on tonight?" Kate now calmly asked, sinking back down onto the edge of the bed beside Marianna. Her mind was whirling with all she had heard, but her foremost thought was of Sean and the danger he might be facing.

"Alex was ordered to bring in special deputies and round up Caine and all his men. I don't know what his exact plans are for accomplishing that, but I'm confident he will succeed," she declared, hoping her voice carried more conviction than she actually felt. There was a nagging uneasiness in the pit of her stomach, much the same as she had experienced when Alex had gone to assist in the rescue of the mudslide victims. Her blue-green eyes became faintly clouded with worry, and Kate's own perceptive gaze did not fail to glimpse it.

"Then what the hell are we doing sitting here?" the spirited blonde loudly remarked, bouncing off the bed again. "I say we get off our backsides and go see if we can help!"

"Alex said we were all to say here," Andrei interjected, drawing his attention away from the window.

"You mean to tell me we're expected just to sit here and wait to find out whether our men are dead or alive?" Kate responded in disbelief.

"I understand how you feel," Marianna spoke with a sigh, "for I certainly don't relish the prospect of remaining here in total ignorance of what is transpiring. But there is nothing we can do."

"Damnation!" muttered her friend, pacing restlessly

about the room, her full skirts swirling each time she turned. "Don't tell me I've finally found the right man, and a blasted Mountie at that, only to lose him?"

"It would be unwise to allow ourselves even to consider such a possibility at this point," Marianna replied, moving to Kate's side and placing a comforting arm across the other woman's shoulders. "It may be quite some time before we hear anything."

"Damn that Sean Cleary! I'll wring his neck if he lets anything happen to himself!" She and Marianna gazed at one another in silence for an instant, then both laughed softly at the incongruity of Kate's statement. Andrei merely shook his head at what he perceived to be the absurd reasoning of women, wishing that something, anything would happen so that he could get involved.

At that same moment, however, Alex and Sean had completed their discussion of strategy, and Sean was on his way to begin contacting Alex's men in Skagway to inform them of the plan. They were to assist the deputies by identifying Caine's men. Alex had made it quite clear to everyone that Caine was to be saved until the last, that confronting the leader of the villainous organization was to be his sole, pleasurable responsibility. He was looking forward to the final encounter with great anticipation.

The Canadian authorities had already been alerted to the mission, and they would be watching the borders in case any of Caine's men managed to escape. Two of Alex's men were stationed at the wharves to make certain that no ships set sail until after the maneuver was completed. Any of Caine's men already across the border would be rounded up by the Mounties within the next few days. Alex smiled to himself in satisfaction, although he was still wise enough to realize that things might not go as smoothly as planned. There was always a chance for at least a minor miscalculation, but he would do his best to ensure victory. It had taken a long time, but his efforts were finally going to pay off.

He thought of Marianna then, and he suddenly frowned. He knew she was safely in her room at the hotel, but he was nevertheless uneasy about her being in town. Muttering a silent curse, he glanced up from his vantage point aboard the ship to see Sean returning, a half-dozen other men in his wake. It was time.

"All right. This is it," Alex said, his voice low and even. "You all know what you're supposed to do." His gaze swept across the numerous faces of the men before him on the deck of the ship, then he nodded curtly toward Sean to indicate for him to lead everyone into town. Alex would soon follow, but he would be heading straight for Caine's saloon.

Andrei shifted restlessly in the chair as he pushed aside the curtains at the window for the hundredth time. Still observing nothing of any particular interest, he allowed the curtains to fall back into place as he rose to his feet and stepped over to the washstand to pour himself another glass of water. Marianna and Kate gazed at one another in silent understanding as the minutes ticked by with agonizing slowness.

447

"Well, at least we haven't heard any gunshots yet," Kate remarked with a twisted grin. She reached over to the small carved table beside the bed and turned up the lamp. "There's no use in keeping it so dark in here, is there? After all, isn't there an old saying or something about keeping your lamp burning brightly in the window till your true love comes home?" Her halfhearted attempt at levity failed dismally. Marianna only managed the merest hint of a smile, while Andrei positively glowered in her direction. Kate settled back upon the bed and fell silent once more.

The three of them were startled a few seconds later when a noise was heard. It sounded like the doorknob was being rattled, as if someone was trying the lock. Marianna and Kate jumped to their feet in alarm, and Andrei hurried over to the door, obviously intending to open it.

"No, Andrei!" Marianna vehemently whispered. "It might not be Alex or Sean!"

"Who else would it be?" he countered. "No one else knows we're here." He nonetheless decided to placate her, and he paused close to the door as he called out, "Who is it?" Kate and Marianna glanced at one another in growing puzzlement when there was no response. Andrei became concerned enough to seize Marianna's pistol from atop the large chest of drawers as he tersely repeated, "Who is it?"

His question was met with silence once more. The two women clung to one another as Andrei raised the pistol, pointing it directly toward the doorway. Still, no sound came from the other side of the door. It seemed like they waited for an eternity. When they were all becoming convinced that it had been nothing more than an inconsequential mistake, the door was unexpectedly kicked open, slamming back against the wall with violent, resounding force.

Marianna stifled a scream as Andrei pulled the trigger, the bullet whizzing harmlessly past one of the tall, burly intruders who loomed so menacingly before them. The two men lunged inside, one of them grappling with a valiantly struggling Andrei, the other attempting to seize Marianna. Kate fought like a wildcat as she launched herself upon the man's back, kicking and flailing at him, her nails digging into the weathered flesh of his bearded face. Marianna twisted and squirmed against the arm clamped like a band of steel about her waist, and she opened her mouth to shriek at the top of her lungs.

Andrei suffered defeat in a humiliatingly short amount of time, and he now lay unconscious upon the floor, his boyish face bruised and battered, one of his arms nearly snapped in two by the assailant's powerful hands. The man hurried forward to help his partner subdue the violently struggling women, and Marianna felt panic overtaking her as it appeared no help was forthcoming. Kate was snatched off the man who held her friend, and she transferred her wild battling to the other assailant, who merely laughed at her efforts. It was not long before the two young women were dispatched into unconsciousness by a single, skillful blow from each of the dark-bearded intruders. The men wrapped Kate and Marianna in the covers they

449

roughly yanked off the bed, then swiftly carried their limp captives from the room and toward the back staircase of the building.

It was some time before Andrei regained consciousness. He winced at the sharp, searing pain in his arm, but he resolutely staggered to his feet, shaking his head as if to clear it. It was only an instant until he remembered what had happened before he had been knocked aside, and he staunchly held on to his injured arm as he walked unsteadily from the room, telling himself that he must find Alex. He swayed dizzily more than once, but he remained determined, his steps leading him down the stairs and out of the hotel.

Alex was still down at the waterfront, taking charge of the men who had already been rounded up. They were guarded by a handful of deputies armed with guns, and Alex was pleased at the way things were progressing. His plan to begin at the bottom of Caine's organization in Skagway and work patiently up to the top appeared to be entirely successful. He was further satisfied to hear that several of the townspeople, those who were apparently fed up with Lyle Caine's tyranny, had joined in to offer assistance to the deputies. The number of others who dared to interfere were relatively few, and the last report he had been given, less than five minutes earlier, led him to believe that even more townspeople would lend their support as the night wore on.

He was preparing to head toward Caine's saloon when he caught sight of Andrei and Sean. Sean appeared to be supporting most of the younger man's weight as they made their way toward Alex, the moonlight casting a silvery glow over Andrei's pale and Sean's solemn features.

"What is it? Where's Marianna?" Alex curtly demanded, rushing forward to help Sean with the younger man. They lowered him to a large wooden crate on the dock, and Andrei leaned back against another stack of crates.

He breathessly replied, "Two men. I . . . I think they were Caine's men. I've seen them at the Golden Nugget before. They must have taken the women." His head was spinning, but he forced himself to remain conscious.

"He tried to protect them, Alex, but it was no use. He said Kate and Marianna were both gone when he came to," Sean ground out, his blue eyes gleaming with a murderous light. Alex's gaze became equally savage, and he cursed himself for foolishly believing Caine wouldn't try anything at that late stage of the game.

"Let's get going, Cleary," he tersely commanded, a terrible pain clutching at his heart. Dear God, keep her safe!

"What are you planning to do?" Sean asked, his own heart aching at the thought of Kate in danger.

"I'm the one Caine will want to see. He'll no doubt be wanting to try and strike a deal. I'll have to pay a visit to him, alone."

"What do you want me to do?" asked the grim-faced Mountie.

"I want you to lay low out back. In case I don't come out alive, you'll have to handle things." Alex glanced down at a barely conscious Andrei, and he muttered another curse. He would never forgive himself for underestimating Lyle Caine. If anything happened to Marianna . . . no, he sternly commanded himself as he and Sean set off, he had to keep his wits about him if he expected to be of any use to her at all.

Still, a voice at the back of his mind persisted, he knew that he couldn't live without her. And he'd kill Lyle Caine with his bare hands if she had suffered any harm.

His golden eyes were narrowed and glowing with coldblooded fury and determination as he strode purposefully toward the bright lights and raucous laughter of the Golden Nugget Saloon.

Twenty-Seven

Marianna's eyelids fluttered open. She had been dreaming, floating languidly on a soft cloud, drifting higher and higher toward the sun, its bright rays touching her body with soothing warmth. Regaining total consciousness now, she became aware that what she had perceived to be the sun was in actuality nothing more than a number of glowing lamps, the flames beneath the smoke-tinged glass dancing and flickering with irregularity. She stared up at the light, vaguely noting the shadows which traveled across the smooth surface of the painted ceiling.

"Dear God!" she suddenly whispered, sitting bolt upright on the red-velvet-covered settee as her head spun. The realization of what had happened before she lost consciousness returned to hit her full force. Her widened, anxious gaze swept frantically across her surroundings, and she was struck by their familiarity. It was Lyle Caine's office, his private room above the saloon. She was alone in the room, but she knew with certainty that Caine would not be far away.

Rising dizzily to her feet, she pressed a hand to her bruised and aching jaw, then flew hurriedly toward the door, only to discover that it was locked. Her frenzied steps took her to one of the velvet-draped windows, and she began trying to open it, possessed of no clear idea of what she would do if her efforts succeeded, knowing only that she could not merely sit idly by and await Caine's return.

"Did you really believe me so foolish as to allow you to escape me now?" a voice brimming with amusement spoke from a short distance behind her. Marianna whirled about to face him, dismayed because she had not heard him enter. She had been too involved in her desperate attempt to escape, and now silently cursed her ill fortune. She forced herself to remain calm and maintain a semblance of outward composure. "It wouldn't have done you any good, you know," Caine lazily remarked, nodding to indicate the window. "My men have the building surrounded."

"Where is Kate? What have you done with her?" she imperiously demanded, her eyes flashing with unquenchable spirit. She cautioned herself to refrain from displaying the terror welling up inside of her, wisely realizing that her only chance lay in rational, dauntless behavior.

"Your charming partner is being held in a safe place elsewhere for the moment, but you'd do best to concentrate on yourself," he replied with a soft, decidedly evil laugh. His dark, hawkish eyes moved boldly and insolently over her as he closed the door behind him and began slowly crossing the distance between them. He still appeared the suave, smoothly controlled, darkly attractive man she had first believed him to be, but there was something different about him now, something in that piercing gaze of his that bespoke a terrible violence just below his polished surface. She had been afforded a faint glimpse of that violence twice before, and fear clutched at her heart as she instinctively began backing away from him.

Lyle Caine laughed again, unexpectedly pausing at the large rolltop desk. Marianna gazed at him in bewilderment as he started gathering up some papers and placed them in a small, black leather pouch. He appeared to have forgotten her presence for the moment, and did not so much as spare her a glance.

"It's rather ironic when you think about it. Your husband's little scheme has afforded me the perfect opportunity, as well as the means, to leave Skagway."

"What do you mean?" She could move no farther as her back made contact with the sumptuously flocked paper on the opposite wall of the spacious room. Her eyes darted furtively to the doorway, then back to Caine.

"I told you that you would be mine sooner or later, didn't I, dearest Annie? Now, you'll be my ticket to freedom as well." He finished with his task and turned his attention to his beautiful captive once more. His eyes fastened greedily on Marianna's flushed face, before drifting lower to the curve of her full young breasts. She glanced hastily downward, a look of consternation on her face when she perceived the torn bodice of her simple cotton dress and how the fabric had been ripped away during her earlier struggles with her abductor.

"Alex—Alex will never allow you to get away!" she declared with admirable bravado as her hands moved to draw the tattered edges of her bodice together. Her glorious raven hair was streaming wildly about her face and shoulders, trailing down her back in gleaming disarray.

"Won't he?" He chuckled softly, his eyes narrowing as they glowed with an intense light. Marianna gasped inwardly as he began stalking her again, and she desperately attempted to stall for time, praying that Alex would find her soon.

"I don't know why you believe having me brought here in such a cowardly fashion will help you in any way whatsoever! Your men will all be arrested soon and there will be no place for you to hide!"

"I won't need to hide, my dear." He seemed to be enjoying himself immensely, still treading leisurely forward as Marianna sought to elude him.

"Alex will be coming for me!" she cried, making her way toward the door as his steps relentlessly continued to bring him closer.

"I'm well aware of that fact. I have no doubt that we may expect your dear husband within the next several minutes. Indeed, that is part of my plan."

"What are you going to do when he comes?" Marianna fearfully questioned, forgetting her own danger for the moment.

"Though it would give me the greatest pleasure, aside from the pleasure you shall give me, to kill him, it

456

will set your mind at ease to learn that such is not my intention. No, I need Alex Donovan alive. He's going to arrange for the two of us to leave Skagway together."

"No! Alex will never allow you to escape!" She was mere inches from the door now, and her hand began reaching stealthily for the brass knob. She was more than ever determined to get away, for she did not trust Caine and did not believe him when he proclaimed that he would not try to kill her husband. She would have to prevent such a confrontation—escape and warn him!

"He'll allow anything when it comes to saving the life of his beautiful young wife. But enough talk of what is to come. Since Donovan should be here very shortly, I propose that we not waste any more time on useless discussion." He lunged forward just as Marianna wrenched open the door, her scream cut off as Caine's arm clamped about her waist like a vise. He yanked her roughly backward and into his arms, his booted heel kicking the door closed once more.

"I'll never be yours, no matter what you do, no matter what you plan!" she gasped, struggling valiantly against him. Her hands beat against his chest, her legs kicking and flailing as he held her with unsuspected, sinewy strength.

"You'll change your mind," he confidently asserted, his smile becoming a contemptuous sneer. He stared into the fiery depths of her blue-green eyes, and laughed again as he twisted both her arms behind her back and pulled her up tightly against his leanly muscled form while her feet dangled helplessly above the carpeted floor. "I'm a very wealthy man, Annie, my love. A very rich and powerful man. I've never met a woman who wasn't at least a little seduced by those two attributes. But aside from that, there are other ways I know of to coax you into willingness," he stated with a slow, sensual grin, a look of pure lust shining forth from his dark eyes.

"I hate you, Lyle Caine! I will never come to you willingly! I will never belong to you!' Marianna vehemently countered, hot tears of pain starting to her eyes as her arms were cruelly pulled tighter behind her back. His action also served to cause her barely covered breasts to thrust higher, and she cried out as his head lowered and his lips feasted hungrily, almost savagely on the softness of her curved flesh. She kicked and squirmed against him with all her might, but to no avail. Her mouth opened as she tried to scream, but her throat was suddenly dry and she felt increasingly faint when his lips captured hers. He kissed her with his practiced, worldly sensuality, and she nearly gagged with the nausea which rose in her stomach.

Something snapped within her at that moment. She would not be his victim! She would not allow him to do this to her! She could not allow what was beautiful and precious between herself and Alex to be dishonored by the likes of this evil, disgusting man!

She suddenly overcame her faintness and nausea and began to fight him again, with much more determination and vigor than ever before. It took him by surprise when she launched this new attack, and he relaxed his hold upon her. Marianna took advantage of his surprise, bringing both her knees up to forcefully connect with his unguarded manhood. He groaned and muttered a blistering curse, abruptly releasing her as he doubled over with the excruciating pain she had managed to inflict.

Now was her chance! she triumphantly thought, flying to the door again. But, just as she reached it, a loud, insistent knock sounded on the other side. Momentarily closing her eyes in stunned disbelief, telling herself that fate could not be so cruel, she spun about and searched frantically for another avenue of escape, but it was too late.

"Mr. Caine?" a deep voice rumbled from outside the room, knocking twice more.

Lyle Caine staggered to his feet, straightening with visible difficulty as he made his way over to the door and flung it open. He said nothing to Marianna, but his gaze met hers for a brief instant, the dangerous gleam in his eyes causing a tremor of fear to run the length of her spine. She stood near the settee, her hands crossed protectively against her bosom, her sensitive flesh feeling as if it had been scalded by his revolting touch.

"Well, well, if it isn't the outraged husband himself," Caine derisively smirked. Marianna's widened gaze flew to the doorway, and she bit back the anguished cry which rose to her lips when she caught sight of Alex.

"He said you wanted to talk to him," Caine's man, the same one who had abducted Marianna from the hotel, gruffly announced. He held a gun pointed directly at Alex's broad back.

"Come in, Donovan. Your charming wife and I have

been getting better acquainted while awaiting your arrival," taunted Caine, recovered enough to move nonchalantly aside as Alex and the man with the gun stepped inside the room. Alex's gaze flew sharply to Marianna, and it was with a great strength of will that he controlled the violent tendencies which threatened to overpower him when he viewed her torn dress, the purplish bruise on her jaw, and the look of rising panic mirrored in her tear-filled eyes. If there had ever been any doubt in his mind that he would end up killing Lyle Caine, such doubt was now forever vanquished.

"Are you all right?" Alex quietly murmured, his lips compressing into a thin line of fury. Marianna could manage only a nod, not trusting herself to speak as she stifled a sob. Seeing his handsome, beloved face was almost more than she could bear as she realized with a terrible feeling of dread that the two of them were in more danger than ever before.

"How very touching," their dark-eyed adversary sarcastically remarked. "But I suggest you dispense with such tender concern and give all your attention to what I have to say."

"What is it you want?" demanded Alex, moving as close to Marianna as he dared and sending her a bolstering look that told her to have courage.

"Safe passage out of Skagway." He sauntered closer to Marianna himself now, the rage boiling inside of Alex as he watched the way Caine's arm possessively draped across Marianna's shoulders. "A ship. Provisions. Some of my men to serve as the crew," he coolly enumerated.

"And what about Marianna?" Alex questioned in a

low, even tone that belied the murderous fury in his heart.

"She comes with me. You see, I don't trust you, Donovan," stated Caine with a soft chuckle. "If you keep your word and meet all my demands, then I'll consider releasing her at a later time," he easily lied.

"Surely you don't really expect me to agree to that?"

"You have no choice. Your wife is my prisoner. If you or any of your men try to interfere, you'll face the risk of endangering her life. Of course, there's always the remote possibility that someone will merely shoot me in the back as I am attempting to leave town," Caine observed with a faint, mocking smile. "So, I've also taken a certain little precaution in case you decide to break your word."

"And what the hell is that?" Alex ground out.

"Kate LaRue," replied the other man with another triumphant sneer. "It just so happens that your wife's partner is at this moment being held somewhere near town. She's safe for the time being, but my men have orders to kill her if they don't receive instructions to the contrary from me within the hour."

"Kate!" Marianna whispered in horror, her eyes flying to her husband's face as a shadow of renewed panic sparkled within their blue-green depths. She stiffened beneath Caine's arm once more, sickened by his nearness, but knowing that she should not dare to antagonize him any further. Alex's scowling features swam before her as she fought back the rising tide of desperate tears. How could they possibly hope to defeat Caine now?

"So it's come to this," Alex scornfully responded,

emitting a short laugh of utter contempt. "The wily, clever Lyle Caine, master of every kind of criminal on earth, leader of a highly successful organization devoted to villainy, now reduced to using defenseless women. Hiding behind their skirts won't save you, Caine. Sooner or later, you're going to pay for what you've done."

"Your philosophical rambling won't change matters any, Donovan. Either you agree to my demands, or Kate LeRue will be dead within the hour."

"How do I know you'll keep your part of the bargain? How do I know Kate isn't already dead? And how do I know you'll release my wife once you're safely away?"

"You'll simply have to trust me, won't you?" Caine replied nonchalantly. Alex looked to his wife, his heart twisting at the sight of her face, now drained of color. The expression of utter agony in her eyes nearly drove him to lose control, but he regained his composure as he contemplated all that Caine had said.

Marianna watched as her husband's face grew stony and impassive. Alex, Alex! her mind silently cried. What are we to do?

"All right," he suddenly capitulated, his golden eyes shimmering with an unfathomable light. "You send word to your men to release Kate unharmed, and I'll see to it that you're given the freedom to sail. As for Marianna, I want to know exactly when you plan to release her."

"If all goes as planned, and I encounter no interference, then I'll consider putting her ashore at Juneau." His gaze challenged Alex's, and he knew the other man did not believe him. But he also knew that it did not matter. Donovan had no choice, he mused in satisfaction.

"Very well. You win." Alex spared one last glance toward Marianna before he turned to leave. All the love in his heart, all the courage he sought to give her, was in that glance, but Marianna couldn't refrain from calling out in heart-rending despair, "Alex!" She wanted to tell him how much she loved him, how much she wanted to believe they would emerge victorious from what she knew would be the last battle with Caine, but the words would not come. And Caine's arm tightened about her, prompting her to fall silent once more.

Alex did not look back. The man holding a gun on him pressed the barrel of the shotgun menacingly against the tall, golden-eyed man's back as he urged him out of the room.

"Shall we make ready to leave, my dear Mrs. Donovan?" Lyle Caine caustically suggested, laughing as she finally obeyed the overwhelming impulse to jerk away from him.

"You'll never get away with this!" she feelingly declared, her eyes blazing defiantly up at him.

"It's time you started practicing more civil behavior toward me," he retorted, drawing on the jacket he had retrieved from the back of his desk chair. "After all, it won't be long before the two of us are completely alone together. And that's when I intend to begin giving you a taste of what it's going to be like between us."

"Aren't you the least bit concerned about your men, about all those who are being arrested at this very moment? Your despicable little empire is crumbling at last!" she exclaimed, stalling once more. Perhaps, if Alex and Sean were given enough time, something would develop, something to prevent—

"I care nothing about anything or anyone, save myself and you, my defiant little beauty," he quietly declared, interrupting her thoughts as he stepped toward her again. He smiled as she backed away, but he moved past her and opened the doors of a huge, mirrored wardrobe in the far corner of the room. He reached inside and withdrew a hooded cloak of fur-trimmed, dark blue wool, then tossed it at a warily puzzled Marianna. "Here, put that on. We can't have you walking beside me half-naked, can we?"

Marianna, still endeavoring to delay their departure, slowly donned the cloak, drawing it gratefully across her trembling shoulders and bosom. She was painfully aware of Caine's hawkish gaze upon her as she moved to make a pretense of adjusting the cloak before the mirror hanging near the window. Seconds later, he was there behind her, seizing her arm and propelling her out of the room with him, the two of them descending a rear staircase which led behind the stage and down toward the back door of the building. Marianna could hear the laughter and music from the crowded saloon, and she began praying that someone would realize what was happening, that something would occur, and soon, to stop Caine before it was too late.

At that same time, Sean Cleary and a number of other men were already beginning a frenzied search of the town in an effort to find where Kate was being held. Alex had told Sean all that had passed between himself and Caine, and neither of them was foolish enough to trust him. Sean was, like Alex, tempted to kill the devious Caine without further delay, but the most important thing was to rescue Kate, and thereby prevent Caine from sailing away from Skagway with Marianna as hostage. But Alex did not reveal to his friend that he would never, no matter what the cost, actually allow Caine to set sail with his beloved wife. Nothing mattered to him as much as Marianna, and he could only hope and pray that he would not be forced to make the decision to sacrifice Kate LaRue. Not only was she an innocent pawn, she was also the woman his friend loved.

As the minutes ticked past and more and more men joined in the desperate search, Sean became like a man possessed. There was a savage light in the Mountie's eyes, a steely gleam that boded ill for the men who had dared to involve his woman in such danger. When he found them, he grimly vowed, never allowing himself to contemplate defeat, he would choke the life from the bastards with his bare hands!

Kate LaRue sat quiet and still in the tiny, airless cabin, watching with feigned disinterest as the two men facing one another in mutual belligerence across the small, rough-hewn table raised their voices in yet another heated argument. The only light in the room came from a single lamp on the table, its dull glow casting long, distorted shadows upon the muddied wooden floor.

"And I'm tellin' you, you lily-livered son of a bitch,

CATHERINE CREEL

we ain't gonna make it out of here unless we make a run for it now!" the larger of the two angrily contended. He was the one who had brought Kate to the cabin on the edge of town, but he was also the same one who had once taken a bullet in the arm from Kate's pistol, the same man who, along with three others, had attacked the two women that night Lyle Caine came so heroically to their rescue.

"You callin' me a coward?" the other man wrathfully responded. He was considerably smaller, but appeared equally dangerous, his eyes full of an almost insane light. "Who is it's wantin' to light out of here before hearin' from the boss? You know what our orders are. We're to stay here with the woman till we get word from Caine!"

"And I'm tellin' you that he don't give a damn what happens to us! He'll be long gone before we get word! That's why I say we take the woman and get goin' now!" the coarse, burly giant roaringly decreed.

"No one's leavin' here!" They glared at one another for several long moments. Kate merely sat and calmly surveyed the explosive scene, her mind spinning and preoccupied with other thoughts. If she could just make it to the door while the two of them were arguing . . .

She jumped in shocked alarm when the larger man suddenly pulled a gun and shot his accomplice, the loud report echoing about the stifling confines of the one-room cabin as the dead man crumpled to the floor. Her eyes widened in further alarm when the victor turned his fierce gaze upon her, advancing upon her now with visibly malicious intent.

"You might as well get it through that thick skull of yours right now—I'm not going with you!" Kate bravely maintained, rising to her feet and facing him with outward calm, although she trembled inside. Surely someone had heard that shot, she told herself, battling the impulse to scream in rising terror. Just a few more seconds, she decided, then she'd start screeching like a banshee.

"You ain't gonna have no say about it, you stupid little bitch!" He was reaching for her, but she managed to elude him as she ducked and scurried over to the door, actually succeeding in opening it a tiny bit as she began screaming at the top of her lungs. Her scream turned into a cry of pain as her long blond tresses were suddenly caught and cruelly yanked, her head snapping backward as the door was slammed shut by her obviously enraged captor.

"That wasn't too smart of you! All you've done now is make certain I either kill you, or gag and tie you and take you with me!" he snarled, then laughed sadistically as her struggles made it necessary for him to wrench her arm behind her back to subdue her. "You got enough fire in you to warm any man, don't you, Yellow-hair? It'd be a real shame, yes sir, a real shame to have to kill you without first havin' me some of that there fire!"

"Let go of me, you damned, cowardly bastard!" she uttered through a cloud of pain. An image of Sean rose before her, and she bit back an anguished sob. "You sure as hell won't get far before they catch up with you!"

"They ain't gonna try anything with you along," he

muttered, thinking aloud. He chuckled as he said, "Guess I'll just have to give you another little 'lovetap' to keep you quiet for a while." Kate twisted futilely in his grasp as he raised his fist, but before he could bring it into forceful contact with her already bruised and swollen jaw, the door burst open to reveal Sean Cleary. There were two other men behind him, but Kate had eyes only for the tall, flinty-eyed Mountie.

"Sean!" she breathed, then gasped loudly as she was abruptly thrust aside by her captor. She landed in a tumble of skirts and petticoats on the hard floor, shaking the tangled mass of bright hair from her face as she glanced back at Sean. "Watch out, he's got a gun!" she choked out in warning.

Sean, however, had already glimpsed the other man's weapon, and he hurled himself forward before Kate's captor could take aim, his large hands closing about the burly villain's throat. Kate watched in stunned horror as the man she loved grappled with Caine's man, the two of them well matched in both size and strength. Sean, however, possessed a skill and cunning his opponent lacked, and he was also driven by a fierce desire for revenge for what the man had done to Kate. In the end, the two men who had accompanied Sean to the cabin were forced to seize the Mountie and pull him off the half-dead man, for it appeared that Sean meant to kill him. Their orders were to take everyone alive, at least as far as possible. They dragged the man, along with the body of his accomplice, outside, leaving the two lovers alone.

Kate flew to the Mountie's side, nearly sobbing with

relief as his powerful arms closed about her. He simply stood and held her for several long moments, softly murmuring her name.

"How did you find me?" she finally asked, raising her bruised and swollen face to his. He scowled darkly when he saw the marks of her ordeal.

"Someone told us they thought they'd seen Caine's men coming this way. We weren't sure if the information would turn out to be worth anything, until we heard a shot. And we were closing in when I heard you scream," he said in a voice full of emotion. His arms tightened about her briefly, before unexpectedly releasing her, his hands closing upon her shoulders as he gazed solemnly down into her glistening eyes. "We've got to get down to the waterfront. Caine was using you to force Alex into letting him leave town, and he's still got Marianna. We've got to let Alex know you're safe before Caine gets away!" He suddenly reached down and lifted her effortlessly in his strong arms, striding quickly through the doorway and out of the cabin.

"I can still walk," she protested feebly.

"It'll be faster this way," he replied, then smiled tenderly down at her as he added, "Besides, I don't intend to ever let go of you again." Kate returned his smile, her hands locking behind his neck as he hurried along through the moonlit streets. Her smile faded as she thought of Marianna, and she shuddered at the image of her friend in the grasp of the fiendish Lyle Caine.

Twenty-Eight

Alex Donovan paced tensely beneath the late summer moon, the soles of his leather boots connecting almost noiselessly with the gray, weathered planks of the wharf. Dear God, he inwardly muttered, were they going to receive word from Sean or not? If they didn't hear anything within the next few minutes, he'd be forced to risk ending the life of an innocent woman. But he'd have to do it. Because, he reflected with a deepening frown, it was impossible even to consider the alternative. He could not allow Lyle Caine to escape, but, more than that, he could not allow his wife to be taken away as a hostage.

He worriedly glanced toward town, then back at the small steamship, the same one he and his men had used to travel from Dyea to Skagway. His features tightened as he thought of Marianna and Caine, the two of them waiting below. Alex had never intended for things to get this far, never intended for his wife to be taken aboard the ship. But Caine had left them little choice, what with the way he had approached the wharves with Marianna held securely before him, the point of a knife pressed threateningly to the slender curve of her throat. If they had attempted to move against him, they would have endangered her life.

He could still feel her eyes burning into his and the terror she had transmitted to him through the expression on her pale, beautiful face. Alex told himself that he would never forget that look.

His narrowed, savagely glowing gaze traveled a short distance away to sweep across the faces of the half dozen men, Caine's men, who were scattered about the deck of the ship, making ready to sail. Their impassive, shadowed features seemed to reflect a certain smug triumph, and Alex knew that he would have to make his move within minutes.

It was his job to concentrate on apprehending Caine and the other criminals, but he could still think only of Marianna. The rage within him blazed to an almost deafening roar in his ears as he realized she was at this moment alone with Caine in one of the cabins below.

"There's someone coming!" one of the deputies announced, nodding briskly toward the town. Alex had ordered the area cleared, although several townspeople lined the boardwalks and watched the proceedings from a safe distance away. The outlaws who had already been rounded up were now safely incarcerated in one of the buildings on the opposite edge of town, but the maneuver had for the most part been set aside in order to deal with the dangerous predicament at hand.

Let it be Sean! Alex silently pleaded, a surge of

profound relief filling his heart when he glimpsed his tall friend making his way along the narrow wharf, a visibly shaken but safe Kate still clasped in the Mountie's arms. Alex did not hesitate any longer.

"All right. Let's close in!" he commanded the men about him. He and the others stormed toward the ship now, swiftly drawing their guns as they prepared to board and capture the crew. They were aided by the element of surprise, but Caine's men were also armed, and a fierce battle ensued as the deputies streamed onto the deck to be met with anticipated resistance.

Alex, seemingly oblivious to the danger he faced, rushed aboard the ship and headed below, his only thought to save Marianna. He was driven by this sole purpose as he made his way through the darkened passageway toward the captain's cabin, grim determination on his tight-lipped features. His steps led him instinctively to the largest cabin on the ship, the sound of gunshots echoing downward as he paused before the closed door.

Pressing close to the door, he frowned when he failed to perceive voices within. But he hesitated no longer, hurtling his powerful, muscular body against the door, crashing into the cabin with his pistol clasped defensively in one hand.

"Alex!" cried a startled Marianna. His golden gaze swept hastily across her pale face before rapidly scanning the dimly lit confines of the room.

"Where's Caine?" he urgently demanded as she flew to the safety of his arms.

"I don't know! He left only seconds before you came!" she tremulously revealed, raising her tear-

472

streaked countenance to his apprehensive one. "As soon as he heard the gunfire, he bolted from the room without a word!"

"Come on. He couldn't have gone far, and I've got to get you out of here before he decides to try something else!" He quickly set her away from him, his large hand firmly gripping her smaller one as he turned back to the doorway. Marianna gasped, her eyes widening in renewed horror as they rested on the sinister, malevolently smiling face of Lyle Caine.

Alex protectively thrust his wife behind him, raising his gun. But, it was too late. Caine stood in the doorway with a gleaming, pearl-handled pistol aimed directly at the taller man's heart.

"Drop it, Donovan." When Alex did not immediately respond, Caine chuckled softly and said, "You can try it, but there's always the possibility that your sweet wife will get hurt." He moved all the way inside the cabin now, quietly closing the door and turning the lock, his hand never wavering, his eyes never leaving Alex's face.

Marianna watched in horrible, numbing shock as Alex finally lowered his arm, his own pistol slipping to the floor to land with a muffled thud on the carpeted cabin floor.

"That was very wise of you," Caine remarked with another faint smile.

"It's too late now, Caine. You're finished," Alex declared in a low, steady voice.

"Not entirely," the other man smoothly countered. "I may be facing a momentary defeat, but I'll find a way out of this. I always do," he confidently asserted.

"There's no way out of it this time. Your organiza tion has been busted wide open, your men arrested We've got enough evidence to hang you," Ale responded with a brief, mocking grin. His eyes wer glowing with a dull light, his mind spinning as h contemplated his next move.

"Oh, I might be arrested. But they'll never hang me You see, there's always someone willing to allow gree to overcome principles. Even the law," Caine sar donically uttered. "But, to the business at hand, th business of how I'm going to kill you, Donovan."

"No!" cried Marianna. She attempted to step from behind Alex, but his hand closed firmly upon her arm and held her fast. "You can't do that!" she tearfully protested, peering at Caine as she leaned around Alex' broad shoulder.

"Why can't I?" Caine asked in a voice brimming with fiendish amusement.

"You . . . you have said that you wish for me to com to you willingly. I give you my word that I shall do so i you spare his life," she answered, then gasped softly a Alex's hand tightened painfully on her arm.

"The hell you will!" he ground out, his handsom face a mask of white-hot anger.

"You needn't concern yourself about it any further Donovan, for your wife's generous offer to sacrifice herself won't save you. It's too late for that now," Cain muttered, his dark eyes narrowing as he stretched ou his arm a bit farther, the pistol still clasped menacingly in his hand. "I should have killed you a long time ago."

"You tried. Remember?" Alex disdainfully taunted his muscles tensing imperceptibly as he prepared to strike. He'd have only one chance. One chance to save both himself and Marianna.

"Let's just say I made an error in judgment when choosing the men," Caine replied with a short, derisive laugh. "But, there'll be no errors this time, Donovan. If I'm to be charged with the multitude of crimes you and your cohorts have apparent intentions to charge me with, then why not add another murder to the list?"

"Please, no!" Marianna pleaded, desperately twisting in Alex's grasp now. She grew dizzy with rising panic, her thoughts a tumultuous jumble as she sought to think of some way to save Alex.

"At least allow her to go free," Alex calmly demanded with a brief nod in Marianna's direction. He watched Caine's eyes closely, knowing that he'd be able to receive some indication therein of when the man was going to pull the trigger.

"No. I want her to watch you die." His fingers twitched upon the upraised gun, and Alex suddenly relaxed his hold on Marianna. Without pausing to consider the wisdom of her actions, she broke away from her husband and impulsively launched herself toward Caine.

The brief instant in which Caine was distracted enough to lower his guard was all the time Alex needed. He lunged forward and seized Caine's arm, twisting it until the man was forced to release the pistol. Marianna, who had not reached Caine before Alex moved, now backed against the door as she gazed wide eyed at the fierce struggle between the two men.

Alex grappled with Caine, his handsome face almost savage as he wrestled his opponent to the floor, his fist smashing into Caine's face with brutal force. A stream of bright red blood poured forth from Caine's shattered nose, but he swiftly countered with a blow to Alex's midsection. Alex grunted with the pain, momentarily backing away.

Marianna choked back a scream when Caine staggered to his feet, his hand reaching inside his boot to withdraw a long, bone-handled knife. There was no fear on Alex's face when he saw the knife; instead, an expression of such cold, murderous fury that it actually caused his adversary to experience a small glimmer of alarm. The feeling only served to further enrage him, and he rushed at Alex with the knife. Alex managed to dodge the weapon's gleaming sharpness, but the man came at him again and again, his dark features twisted into a malignant sneer.

Marianna told herself she should run, should try to summon help, but it seemed as if she was frozen to the spot. Her frantic gaze suddenly lit upon Caine's pistol. It was lying unnoticed on the floor, mere inches away from where she stood.

"I should never have trusted anyone but myself to kill you, Donovan! To think that I almost denied myself the pleasure of cutting your heart out!" Caine spoke with an evil chuckle, the blood spilling from his nose to drip heedlessly to the floor below. He brandished the knife as if to boast of his intentions, while Alex merely stared at him in watchful silence, trying to anticipate Caine's next line of attack. When it came, he was ready, and he grabbed Caine's arm and forced him backward, the two of them stumbling against the captain's desk and chair, then crashing to the floor once again.

They twisted and rolled, the knife still in Caine's hand as he poised above Alex. Its deadly point moved slowly, relentlessly toward Alex's chest as his hawk-eyed enemy suddenly appeared to possess an almost superhuman strength. Alex clenched his teeth as he battled to prevent the knife from being imbedded in his vulnerable flesh, his hand closed about the other man's wrist. The struggle continued with excruciating uncertainty, until the loud, unexpected retort of a single gunshot rang out, shattering the charged silence of the ship's cabin.

Alex watched in stunned astonishment as Caine jerked his head back, then closed his eyes, faintly moaning. He went limp, and Alex swiftly diverted the knife as Caine collapsed atop him, the life slipping from his body. Alex pushed the dead man aside. His golden eyes flew toward the doorway, where Marianna stood as if transfixed, her hands clutching Caine's gun.

She spoke not a word, her horror-stricken gaze moving from Alex to Caine's body, then back. He was there to catch her as her legs suddenly gave way beneath her, the pistol slipping to the floor again as Alex lifted her in his powerful arms.

"I thought he would kill you. I had to do something," she brokenly faltered, burying her pale face against Alex's shoulder.

"It's all right, my love," Alex murmured soothingly, hugging her so tightly she thought her ribs would break. But she didn't care. All that mattered to her was that Alex was alive. Lyle Caine couldn't attempt to hurt him any longer.

Someone began pounding upon the door at that point. Alex recognized Sean's voice, and he slowly moved to unlock and open the door, Marianna still clasped securely in his embrace.

"We got down here as fast as we could," Sean breathlessly exclaimed, visibly relieved to see them. "Where's Caine?" His gaze followed Alex's to the lifeless body inside the cabin. "He's dead?" the Mountie quietly asked, already certain of the answer. At Alex's curt nod, he said, "His men put up quite a fight, but it's all over now."

"How many of our men lost or injured?" Alex solemnly demanded. Marianna felt drained of all energy as she rested in his warm, secure embrace, but she raised her head to anxiously query, "Did you find Kate? Is she all right?"

"Yes," Sean answered her first, flashing her a tender smile. "None lost," he then stated, glancing back at Alex. "Three injured, one of them pretty seriously, but I think he'll pull through. Two of Caine's men were killed, the rest suffering a few injuries." He paused a moment, a faint sigh escaping his lips as he and Alex gazed at one another in silent understanding. "It's finished at long last."

"Now that Caine's dead," Alex murmured, moving past Sean and the handful of other men. His lips gently brushed Marianna's forehead as he strode back down the passageway and up to the deck with her, the moon casting a silvery glow upon them both as he held her close to his heart.

Twenty-Nine

"I can't believe this is happening to me, Annie. Me, Kate LaRue—"

"Or rather, Kirsten Johansson," Marianna amended, smiling warmly at her blond friend. "You and Sean are perfect for one another. And you deserve this, Kate," she added with heartfelt sincerity, "you deserve to be loved as Sean will love you." She stepped back to scrutinize the results of her efforts as the late morning sunlight filled the room where the two of them stood alone for the last time.

Kate was resplendent in dove gray satin. Her blue eyes sparkled with happiness, her cheeks becomingly flushed. Her attractive, lightly freckled face was free of powder and rouge, her shining curls arranged in a simple yet flattering style. Marianna smiled again in satisfaction at the bride-to-be.

"Shall we go?" Marianna quietly suggested.

"There's something I'd like to say first." Kate's eyes suddenly filled with tears, and she muttered a fainthearted curse as she impulsively hugged the other

479

young woman. "You've become a friend to me, Annie. I'll never forget all we shared, the good times and the bad. And I'll never forget your kindness." She drew abruptly away, dashing impatiently at the few tears which spilled from her lashes in spite of her firm resolve not to weep.

"I wish you all the best, dear Kate," Marianna spoke in a tremulous voice, her own eyes glistening. "And I shall most assuredly never forget your own kindness, your patience and generosity, and your willingness to aid a spoiled young woman who desperately needed your assistance in learning about life."

"You're a hell of a woman, Annie," murmured her friend, laughing softly through her tears. She grabbed Marianna's hand and tugged her along as she swept from the room.

The wedding of Sean Cleary and Kate LaRue took place outside, beneath the clear, vibrantly blue skies, as the nearby river filled the cool mountain air with the pleasant sounds of water hastening to meet with the welcoming canal. A large number of witnesses had assembled, and even Andrei had managed to leave his bed to attend. Alex stood beside Sean, while Marianna was positioned close to her uncharacteristically nervous friend.

Had it really been only three days ago that the terrible events had occurred? In some ways, it seemed to be nothing more than a dream, an awful nightmare that she hoped would fade as others did.

She thought again of how Alex and his men had found it necessary to protect Caine's men from a mob of vigilantes, how he and the deputies had escorted the criminals to the wharves under heavy guard the next morning. They were placed on a ship bound for Seattle, there to be interrogated by Alex's superiors. Alex had declined to accompany his men there, instead relegating authority to Swenson, who had proven to be a loyal associate throughout the long months of the investigation.

Swenson was also charged with explaining Caine's death to the high-ranking government officials awaiting the ship in Seattle. Alex had sent word that Caine's death had been a simple case of self-defense, assuring Marianna that he anticipated no difficulty as a result of her actions.

Lyle Caine. The mere sound of the name in her mind caused her to shudder involuntarily. She would never be able to forget that she had killed a man, never forget the terrible, reverberating noise as she pulled the trigger and the way Caine's body had jerked. But she knew without a doubt that she would do the same thing again in order to save her husband. She would give her very life for Alex Donovan.

She glanced up and across at him, feeling her heart turn over when he caught her bright gaze and flashed her a disarming grin. There was such a multitude of love and tenderness in those eyes of burnished gold that she found it difficult to concentrate on the vows Kate and Sean were now repeating. She sent him a slow, innocently seductive smile in return, causing his pulse to quicken. Neither of them would be able to recall a great deal of the ceremony afterwards, for they were preoccupied with recollections of their own wedding, an arranged marriage that had joyously become a union of everlasting love.

Two journeys would begin the following morning. Andrei, Marianna, and Alex would sail home to Sitka, while Sean and his new bride were to leave for Dawson. The tall, handsome Mountie had received orders to rejoin his old regiment, now stationed in the Klondike region.

Long before darkness fell, he and Kate lay together in the bed, beginning their wedding night a trifle early—by mutual consent. A faint breeze wafted gently through the upraised window, and it seemed as if the two of them were entirely alone in the world, the other hotel occupants nonexistent as the newlyweds celebrated their love.

"Tell me then, Mrs. Cleary," Sean teasingly inquired, his hands lingering to her smoothly rounded hips, "how do you think you're going to take to life as the wife of a Mountie?" His vibrantly blue eyes were soft and glowing, his thick, sandy hair slightly damp and tousled.

"Well, Mr. Cleary," she seriously answered, though her own eyes were dancing with merry amusement, "I think I'll manage well enough, though I can't be entirely certain just yet." An impish smile tugged at the corners of her kiss-reddened mouth.

"Oh? And what will it take for you to be sure?"

"I'd say about fifty years. A good fifty-five, at least." Sean chuckled softly and hungrily claimed her lips again. When he finally raised his head once more, his handsome face wore a sudden frown as he said with mock sternness, "Mind you, there'll be no more of your singing in public places, no more flirting with other men."

"I give you my word that I'll sing only for my husband. But, as for flirting," she saucily remarked, "I never saw the harm in just—"

"You do, and I'll lock you up again," he threatened, cutting her off with a dark scowl.

"You wouldn't have been able to do it the first and only time if I hadn't been so blasted afraid of hurting you!"

"Is that so? Did it never occur to you, Mrs. Cleary, that someone, myself in this particular instance, might have been able to get the best of you?" As she opened her mouth to offer him a suitably outraged retort, he masterfully silenced her with yet another kiss, a teasing kiss that rapidly grew more demanding, fanning the already smoldering flames of their passion. Soon it mattered little which of them had the last word.

Marianna valiantly fought back her tears as she stood upon the deck of her husband's schooner. Alex's arm tightened about her as they watched Skagway fading into the distance.

"I feel as if I'm leaving part of myself behind," she sighed, the salty wind gently tugging at her flowing black tresses, her soft woolen skirts whipping about her slender, booted ankles.

"Well, I suppose you are, in a way. Annie Markova

enchanted an entire town, but Annie Donovan belongs only to me," Alex replied with a low chuckle.

"Did you mean what you said about giving me a position in your shipping business?" Andrei suddenly questioned, moving to the rail beside them. His injured arm was cradled in a cotton sling, the dark bruises on his boyish face already beginning to pale.

"Of course. I can well see there'll be no returning to your former uneventful life after all you've recently experienced," replied Alex. "And I can promise you a suitable amount of excitement and adventure in my employ, though nothing to compare with the events of these past several days," he added with an engaging wink at Marianna.

Andrei appeared satisfied with his older friend's response, and he soon wandered away to speak with the members of the crew. Ivan had been delighted to finally receive Alex's instructions to return to Skagway, for he had been impatiently awaiting word in Sitka. He had been vastly relieved to discover that his employer bore no ill will toward him for having allowed Marianna to escape those many weeks before, and he had been doubly pleased to view the way the two lovers had apparently managed to work out all their difficulties at long last.

Later, as the schooner glided along through the frigid, brilliantly blue waters of the canal beneath the midday sun, Alex and Marianna retired below to the welcome privacy of their cabin. Marianna laughed softly, her beautiful face warming with a rosy blush as Alex's nimble fingers lost no time in moving to the delicate buttons of her fitted, lace-trimmed woolen gown.

"Alex Donovan, must you always be so—so—"

"So desirous of you, my love?" he supplied, grinning down at her, his golden gaze full of love.

"Do you suppose it will always be this way between us?" she asked, her voice whisper soft as she entwined her arms about his neck.

"This way, and better," he quietly declared, his hands momentarily abandoning their purposeful task now to move about her willing, exquisitely curved body. "I love you. Nothing will ever be able to change that."

"I love you more than you will ever know," she murmured, closing her eyes as she snuggled against his broad chest, reveling in the feel of his strong arms about her. She sighed contentedly before remarking, "Someday we shall be telling our grandchildren about this summer, won't we?"

"I'm sure we will. But, they'll most likely never believe it to be anything more than the fanciful storytelling of two old dreamers!"

"Perhaps." She was quiet for a moment, her voice low and brimming with secret happiness when she spoke again. "How many grandchildren do you perceive the future to hold for us?"

"At least two dozen!" he retorted with a brief laugh, his deep, resonant voice ringing out pleasantly in the confines of the spacious cabin. "However, don't you believe it wisest to concentrate instead on the children who will eventually reward us with children of their own?"

"I quite agree." Raising her face to his, Marianna smiled broadly, her blue-green eyes sparkling with joyous amusement. "As a matter of fact, my dearest husband, it so happens that we have apparently 'concentrated' on the matter quite sufficiently."

"What do you mean?" His handsome brow was creased with a puzzled frown as he peered down at her.

"It seems we've already made progress toward those two dozen grandchildren," she teasingly responded. "I'm going to have a baby." Her hands moved instinctively to the smooth, flat planes of her abdomen as she made the announcement, her gaze traveling upward to meet with his again as she awaited his reaction. Mere seconds had passed when Alex gave a shout of joy and exuberantly swung her around, his arms abruptly releasing her as he anxiously queried, "How long will it be? And why didn't you tell me before now?"

"I wasn't entirely certain until speaking to Kate about it yesterday. A physician will still be required to give us the final verdict, but I haven't the slightest doubt. If all proceeds as I believe it shall, then our child will be born in the late winter or early spring, depending upon how you view it." She took his arms and boldly placed them about her once more, smiling at the rather stunned, but undeniably pleased look on Alex's handsome countenance.

"A child," he murmured in amazement. "Probably conceived on our honeymoon," he then remarked, his eyes gleaming with irrepressible humor. "A honeymoon neither of us will ever forget!" His arms tightened about her of their own volition now, his lips curving into a potently sensuous smile. "I give you fair warning, Mrs. Donovan—this voyage will be even more deliciously taxing than the first we made together!"

"Heed the words of a boastful man!" she quipped with loving sarcasm.

"Heed them well," he huskily replied, chuckling softly as he lifted her upward into a searingly passionate kiss, the hard evidence of his arousal pressing intimately against her softness. Marianna's senses were reeling as the kiss deepened, and it wasn't long before she was being impatiently carried toward the bed, her long, shining hair tumbling riotously onto the pillow as Alex lowered her to the covers. He stood to hastily divest himself of his clothing, then turned his attention to rendering his wife equally naked. Soon, with Marianna's willing assistance, the last barriers were removed, and she strained upward against him as his flesh met hers.

"There's been a considerable alteration in the beautiful young wildcat who once fought me tooth and nail when I joined her in this bed," Alex laughingly noted, his fingers trailing lightly, provocatively across the silken smoothness of her skin.

"Am I no longer beautiful in your eyes, or no longer a wildcat?" she playfully demanded, her own hands following a delectably tormenting path down the bronzed muscles of his back to his lean hips.

"You shall always be both, my love. My own beautiful, headstrong, courageous little firebrand," he murmured, his lips claiming hers in another kiss, a tenderly inflamed kiss that foretold of all the future pleasures they would share.

The outside world receded, leaving Alex and Marianna alone in their time-suspended enchantment. Their hearts beat as one, their very souls joining together in a breathtaking ecstasy that only the truest of loves could kindle and nourish.

Thirty

The moon hung low in the cloudless sky of the late winter's evening, the crisp, woodsmoke-scented air chilling the inhabitants of Sitka who braved the frosty wind to venture outside. Marianna, however, was warm and snug within the walls of the partially decorated house near the outskirts of town, her hands clutching a bolt of pastel fabric as she frowned thoughtfully toward a large bay window.

"Aunt Sonja was quite adamant about this particular shade of blue," she remarked with a heavy sigh. "In truth, that makes it all the more disagreeable to me!" she admitted to the older lady beside her, the two of them sharing a companionable smile.

"You must not allow these details to worry you, my dear," the Countess Borofsky mildly admonished with a gloved hand gesturing gracefully to include the entire house. "My great-grandchild must not be plagued with such inconsequential matters while still in the womb!"

She laughed softly, strolling closer to the window in order to gaze out upon the snow-covered landscape. "I still wish you and Alex had consented to live with me."

"Come now, you know perfectly well that Maria and her new husband are taking exceptionally good care of us! And we shall continue to visit you frequently," Marianna assured her, moving forward to place an affectionate arm about the silver-haired woman's shoulders. "Indeed, once the baby is born, I can promise that you'll see a great deal of all three of us." She put a hand to her enormously rounded stomach, delighting in the slightest movement of the child within her.

"Or six of us, judging by the size of your adorable profile," Alex sardonically commented, stepping through the doorway and moving immediately to his wife's side. "Don't you think you've been on your feet enough for now? If I'd had any notion of how much time you would spend on this blasted house, I might have had second thoughts about building it for you!" He punctuated his words with a mock scowl, then leaned down to press a resounding kiss upon Marianna's parted lips. His grandmother smiled benignly at the two of them, her heart soaring at the knowledge that her beloved grandson had found the sort of love so few people experienced. She and her Nicholai had shared such a love, she reflected with a faint sigh of remembrance.

"Alex!" Marianna feebly protested when he had

490

finally allowed her to speak again.

"I have something for you," he announced with a disarming grin, withdrawing something from his coat pocket. "It's a letter from Kate, delivered by Andrei the minute he stepped off the ship." Marianna impatiently took it from him, tearing it open and then rapidly scanning its contents as Alex and his grandmother both smiled indulgently.

"She writes that she and Sean are expecting a child of their own in the late summer! It sounds as if they are well and happy," she summarized a moment later, the tears which were never far from the surface these days now rising to her blue-green eyes. She folded the letter and placed it in the pocket of her starched white apron, promising herself the time to give it more attention later that evening.

"I must be going," the Countess suddenly proclaimed, pausing to embrace Marianna before leaving the room. "I have a dinner engagement. A tedious one, to be sure, but an obligation to be met." She turned to Alex, pointing a finger at him as she imperiously commanded, "Take good care of her, Alexander. I shall hold you fully responsible for her well-being."

"I should say I'm already responsible for it," he retorted with a wicked gleam in his golden eyes, tugging his wife close.

"Rapscallion!" his grandmother responded with an answering light in her own adoring gaze. "You are so very much like your grandfather," she observed, then hastily took her leave.

"Alex," said Marianna a short time later, "I have been thinking of my father of late. Do you believe I should send him word when our child is born?" She leaned her head against her husband's strong, capable shoulder, the two of them reclining upon a velvet chaise, one of the few pieces of furniture in the newly finished drawing room. A blazing fire burned in the stone hearth, filling the downstairs portion of the large yet simply designed house with a comforting, undeniably homey aroma.

"The decision is yours to make, of course, but I think you'll in all likelihood be troubled about it if you do not," he answered, holding her close as he stared toward the dancing flames. The firelight played across his gently smiling, tanned features, and Marianna found herself musing that he had grown even more handsome in the months they had been home, months filled with both love and laughter.

"I suppose you're right." She sighed faintly, her beautiful face wearing a particularly thoughtful expression. "I must admit, however, that the letter I received from him via Uncle Frederick was not exactly encouraging. I was congratulated for doing what was expected of me, for not disgracing the exalted name of Markova! And yet, I must also admit that I hope our child will touch some part of him, a tenderness locked away these many years since my mother died."

"I wouldn't be in the least surprised if he journeyed all the way to Sitka to pay a visit to his first grandchild," Alex remarked with a brief grin.

"Perhaps, though I won't hold out much hope for that," she responded with another sigh. Then, she brightened, glancing up into his face as she said, "But, I need only you, my darling, only you to make my life complete."

"And what about the other Donovan soon to make his, or her, appearance?"

"There is ample room in my heart for her."

"Her? What makes you so certain it will be a girl?"

"Instinct. A feeling deep within, dear husband," she confidently asserted.

"Is the father not allowed any such instinct? For I have the unmistakable feeling that it will be a boy," Alex masterfully pronounced.

"A father's instinct cannot compare with a mother's. After all, I am the one carrying the babe, remember?" she countered.

"While I cannot deny that obvious fact, I know that I am not mistaken in this."

"Is that so? Well, Alex Donovan, this will then undoubtedly be one of those rare occasions when you are wrong!" Marianna declared, her voice developing an irritated edge to it now. She was not feeling particularly agreeable at the moment, a strangely disturbing sensation assailing her as she sat upright on the chaise, her face appearing almost stormy.

Sensing that the matter possessed the necessary ingredients to develop into a full-blown argument, Alex chose the wisest course of action. He pulled his astonished wife close against him once more and pressed a heart-meltingly amorous kiss to her lips, both of them soon forgetting all save one another.

Michael Sean Donovan and his sister, Alexandria Kate Donovan, made their heartily insistent entrance into the world shortly after dawn the following morning.

GET A *FREE* BOOK!

Just answer the following questions and Zebra will send you one of the four books listed on the back—*absolutely free!*

1. Where do you buy paperback books? (*Circle one or more*)
   Supermarket   Convenience Store   Newsstand
   Drugstore   Bookstore   Other

2. How many paperback books do you buy a month? _____
   a year? _____

3. What magazines do you buy? _____

   _____

4. Where do you buy magazines? (*Circle one or more*)
   Supermarket   Convenience Store   Newsstand
   Drugstore   Bookstore   Subscription   Other

5. What newspapers do you buy? _____

   _____

6. Where do you buy newspapers? (*Circle one or more*)
   Supermarket   Convenience Store   Newsstand
   Drugstore   Bookstore   Home Delivery   Other

7. Do you buy paperback books in the same place you buy
   your magazines and newspapers? _____ yes _____ no

8. Where do you buy Zebra books? (*Circle one or more*)
   Supermarket   Convenience Store   Newsstand
   Drugstore   Bookstore   Other

9. If you circled Bookstore in #8, is this because you couldn't
   find Zebra books at your supermarket, drugstore, newsstand, etc.? _____ yes _____ no

10. Would you spend $6.95 for a large format historical ro-
    mance? _____ yes _____ no

11. What is the title of your favorite Zebra cover?

    _____

(continues on the reverse side)

GET A *FREE* BOOK!
(*see reverse side*)

12. What is the title of your favorite cover on any paperback?
    _____

13. Who is your favorite Zebra author?
    _____

14. Who is your favorite author?
    _____

15. What radio or TV shows do you listen to or watch?
    _____

16. Do you work outside your home? _____ yes _____ no

Send me the following book—*absolutely free!* (Check only one)

_____ PASSION'S DREAM by Casey Stuart

_____ STORM TIDE by Patricia Rae

_____ PASSION'S PLEASURE by Valerie Giscard

_____ SAVAGE EMBRACE by Alexis Boyard

Mail my book to—

name: _____

address: _____

_____

_____

Tear out and mail questionnaire to Zebra Books, 475 Park Avenue South, New York, New York 10016. Allow 4-6 weeks for delivery. Offer expires July 1, 1985. Offer limited to one per customer.